The Savior

By

Jesse V Coffey

© *Jesse V Coffey 2013*

Edin Road Press
1508 Continental Square
Lexington KY 40505

edinroadpress@twc.com

Reprint edition: February 2013

Cover art and layout design by Lorrieann Russell

Published in the United States

Also by Jesse V Coffey

An Opportunity for Resentment
Salt of the Earth
A Wager of Blood

Written as J. W. Coffey

Illusions & Reality

Dedication

This book is dedicated to my late friend, Toby Woodyard – a sweet soul who was too good for this earth. I made him a promise before he died, that when I wrote this book, I would make him a character in it. And I kept my promise.

I miss you, Theroin. Blessed be.

Foreword

Religion fascinates me in so many ways. The different belief systems, the pantheons of Gods and in some religions – Goddesses, have always piqued my interest in why and how we believe the way we do. For the purposes of this book, I researched three religions in particular – Judaism, Celtic Paganism, and Tibetan Buddhism – because I needed to take my hero on a journey through these locations. And, of course, these belief systems play a part in that journey.

But while I expected the differences, I didn't expect the sameness. I didn't expect to find that we may be saying it differently but, in effect, we're saying the same thing when it comes to the soul and how we practice our faith. And I didn't expect to have my own beliefs so thoroughly turned upside down that I would re-invent myself from top to bottom. I didn't expect to re-examine my own faith as deeply as I did. And I didn't expect to take what I learned so deeply to heart that I became more than what I was.

As you read this book, you'll be reading about a fictional hero who meets and befriends at least one historical person. While none of these events happened, their journey is my journey. What they learn, I learned. What they believe, I believe. You see, I sent Toby out in the great big world to find his faith. I didn't care which one until I realized that it didn't matter. *Find your faith* means to find that capacity to *have* faith in the path that chooses you to walk upon it.

There's a saying that I'd like to leave with you as you read this book – *There are many paths up that mountain, but there's only one summit.*

We're all climbing that mountain in the best way we know how. Can you imagine the surprise when we get to the top and find out that we were together all the time and didn't know it?

Enjoy the climb. And enjoy the book. I bid you peace.

The
Savior

Table of Contents

Prologue

. . . breathing . . . .
. . . focusing only on the breathing . . . .
. . . at rest, at peace . . . .
. . . the breathing is all . . . .

Do you have it now?

The man sat on a rattan mat, every part of him at peace. He had learned this deep meditation on his travels, taught to him by an elderly Bodhisattva. The old one had exactly three teeth left in his head, his skin as leathery as the hide of the Brahman bulls that had wandered the streets. But his aged eyes had been sharply focused, his mind as sharp as when he had been a young man. They had engaged in many long conversations. The old one had shared willingly the knowledge and the man had learned eagerly. Well, maybe not as eagerly at the time as he should have been but the man had learned it nonetheless.

An observer would see only the outside: his tall athletic body, perfectly reposed, seated in a lotus position. His legs were crossed, back straight, and his hands were poised in his lap. A shock of dark blonde hair threatened to spill onto his forehead; it was the only movement on the body. An observer would see only the man in meditation.

But inside was the miracle. His heart had slowed down to a mere three beats per minute, barely enough to keep his body alive. His breathing had slowed to one inhale to each three breaths. His mind, that seat of his being and knowledge, was quiet, processing nothing. He thought nothing. He felt nothing. The body did not exist. Only the breathing, only the soul that was his core being. Only the knowing and the visions being given to him.

The room was dark, removing all of the distractions that would have kept him from entering this tranquil state. The curtains were drawn, a tiny sliver of light creeping around the hem of the material to show that it was really daylight outside. There were pillows lying on the floor to sit on, but no sofa or chairs. He had no television, no pictures on the wall, and he kept no books or magazines. His only entertainment was a CD player and his collection of Buddhist chants, and Native American and Celtic music. He kept a small altar in a corner, but it too was kept essentially bare; it contained only a statue and some incense blocks. In his bedroom, there was only a mat on the floor. His apartment was almost as Spartan as the day he had moved in.

He sat, lost in meditation, his consciousness off exploring other realms, other solutions. In front of him was a small brass censor and the smoke was of sweet grass and cedar. The reddish glowing embers didn't light beyond the inside of the container. The smoke rose up in delicate curls until it stretched out, becoming one with the air. A CD of a tribal drumming ritual played softly and it alone marked the passing of time.

It's time.

The man began to awaken from his deep trance. His breathing slowly grew deeper and more frequent, allowing oxygen to penetrate his lungs and into his blood. As the air filled him, his heart accepted the red blood and began to pump it faster through the arteries, taking back the oxygen-starved blood from the veins. The rhythm increased, getting stronger and stronger. His green eyes danced behind the delicate lids, the face becoming a bit more animated now. There were small twitches in his legs as the tissues drank it in and reminded the man that he had let them go for far too long. A smile played at the corners of his mouth, and he extended his legs out, gingerly, to avoid knocking the coals of the incense on the carpet. He stretched all of his muscles, let the pins-and-needles feeling work through, then he stood up. He walked in circles to relieve the electrical sensations in his extremities, bending over periodically to massage an ankle or a calf.

His walking took him by the window. He opened the curtains to let the light in and the panes to release his prayer on the drifts of smoke. Giggles and shouts captured his attention. He looked down on a group of children playing tag in the courtyard that all the apartments shared. One tow-headed boy stood out among the rest. This child played with reckless abandon, running with all his might only to watch his prey skip through his fingers. But the little boy giggled merrily with the rest when he missed, starting the headlong rush at his next intended victim. The man stood at the window, watching as the boy chased a little girl around the yard, then turned away as the prey successfully eluded the grubby fist.

He walked over to the tiny kitchen and started the flame under the kettle. After measuring the rosehips and hibiscus flowers into the infuser, he set it into the mug, added a little wild honey, and went in the bathroom to shower.

He stood without moving, letting the water run over him, caressing and massaging each muscle. He had always been proud of his body, keeping it fit and trim was his past time. He'd found his own techniques to stay in shape, and those he had practiced like a religion. But at some point he'd turned inward, towards his soul, and the inner workings of belief. "Find your faith," his mother had once said. So he did. But the body never changed. Nothing changed over the course of time.

Listening to the water splashing off the tiles, his mind clicked over what he would say and how he would say it. He needed to be smooth and cool. His words had to flow like the water; gently and persuasively. He had to tell it right the first time, because there would be no second chances. He was setting up a confrontation to save a life.

He turned off the water, stepped from the shower stall and toweled his body dry. He slipped into his jeans, socks, and shoes. While trying to decide between the chambray shirt and the light sweater, the kettle started its high-pitched whistle. Screw it, he thought, I'll have to wear a jacket anyway, and grabbed the sweater. He put it on while making his way to the kitchen.

He drank his tea before easing the Army jacket over his shoulders. Before he disappeared, he made sure to turn off the lights.

"Do you have it now?"

The sky was as bright and brilliant a blue as he had seen in a very long time. The last few years for John had been a crawl through a tunnel of hell, but he was finally finding his way back out again. The combined traumas of two divorces, separation from his beloved children, and his ever dwindling career had started to wear in his face. He had found relief in the bottle, just like his father had done, and paid the price for it in two drunk driving arrests. He had searched every religion, every avenue of therapy, and, at this point in his life, was actually able to say he was comfortable with what he had become. He still had his days when he felt ancient, not his fifty-three years; those days were the stone.

But this day was a diamond. Today, he felt calm and at peace with the world and himself. The sky was so blue that the color was as pure as the turquoise he wore around his neck. Standing on the golf course, the green grass was a beautiful accompaniment to the sky. He was comfortable in the slacks and polo shirt that he'd put on that morning. His contact lenses bothered him a little. But, they weren't annoying; he could ignore the discomfort. Right now, he was doing his second favorite thing and after this round, he'd be doing his favorite.

In John's eyes, there was only one thing better than golf, and that was flying. He had his pilot's license and that was his ticket to paradise. He had purchased a new plane – taking possession yesterday – and he was going to try out his new toy later. His pulse quickened slightly at the prospect and he hooked the shot off into the sand trap. His partners made a few smart remarks, but John laughed them off. He made short work on the bad shot and it only cost him a stroke off the lead. He wasn't that upset. It was going to be a good day after all.

He ended a little behind the lead player, a stroke or two off par. The other three men wanted to go back to the clubhouse and have a few drinks, and possibly play another round. John was not to be deterred; he was going flying. He had no real desire for sticking around to watch the others drink since he had finally acknowledged his drinking problem. He wanted to fly. So, he bade the others good luck and took off in his Porsche. He left on that high of good feelings, not knowing that he was hours away from dying.

He arrived at the private airport and changed into a faded pair of coveralls. He paused long enough to chat with the field mechanic, before striding off to his newest acquisition. He loved planes and he loved new toys. He had bought the experimental aircraft on a whim, knowing it would take him some time to get used to the controls, but then, he thought he had all the time in the world. The most he wanted to worry about right now was whether or not the modifications had been done; if not, how he could work around them as he buzzed the golf course.

John came out of the hangar and started to cross the tarmac. He saw another man standing near his plane and hesitated for a moment. He didn't recognize the man, but he was accustomed to being approached by strangers. John was good with people. He was insecure, but made up for it with an outgoing nature and a homespun charm. It was part of the job. John just assumed it was another fan and made a quick look over his shoulder to make sure the mechanic was there if he needed the help. After all, this guy could be one of the crazies.

He was a few steps away before the man seemed to sense his presence and turn toward him. John smiled warmly and the man returned the smile. He opened his mouth to speak but was interrupted.

"Hi. I was wondering if I could have a few moments of your time. I know you're kinda going somewhere, but this is very important. Please?"

He felt odd for a moment, as if he had been here before, done this before; as if it all had been played out before. He dismissed this idea and turned his attention back to the man in front of him. John, being naturally curious, decided to give this stranger the time. It would change his life forever.

Chapter One

The desert stars were diamonds sewn into the fabric of the night sky, shimmering against the black. They were ancient jewels to be treasured, rather than actual pinpoints of forgotten suns, long since dead for millions of years. Tonight, they looked ageless and timeless, as if they had always been there and always would be. The moon was full, a silver coin in the night sky. He could actually see the features of a beautiful woman imprinted on that coin, her eyes closed in the song her full lips articulated. Coyotes provided the descant to the lunar serenade, howling in almost perfect harmony.

Toby stood, thumbs hooked in the belt loops of his jeans, just staring at the sky. He liked this desert above all of those he had been in before. California deserts were a bit different. The others had been fine sand, drifting and moving with the dry wind. The ground here was hard and coarse. Some of the cactus plants were tall and thin; others were short and barrel shaped. He had an undisturbed view here; all he could see were the stars against the night.

Toby's hand moved from his belt to rake fingers through the shock of hair that had fallen over his forehead and brush it from his green eyes before returning to the loop. His dark blonde hair – never thick to start with – had started to thin around his temples. He didn't let that stop him from wearing his hair to his shoulders, although a certain machismo prevented any further length. In his 'wild and wicked youth,' his hair had been his statement, that he was *the man*, so cocky and so sure of himself.

Toby stayed where he was, letting his mind drift back over the last time he had looked at a desert sky this true. That one had been filled with the smells of sweat and salt, of sulfur and brimstone. The nights had been filled with darkness so pure that a cloud dare not touch it. He could be alone with his thoughts, watching the sparkles of the stars and anti-aircraft missiles, and wondering if this was going to be the night.

He heard a snort behind him turned towards the sleeping form. Lying by the fire, wrapped in a blanket, was the reason he was out here tonight. The older man was wrapped in the blanket so that all that could be seen was his angelic face. He was softly snoring in his blissful state, and Toby watched him for a minute. He had a lot to say and little time to say it in.

Toby looked down at this watch and saw that it was already 10:00 p.m. He walked over to the ring of stones around the dying fire, and tossed another log on it. Sparks jumped up like desert fireflies and danced in the air before burning out. He bent down to put a pot of coffee on a makeshift grill and then swung it over the rising flames. Within five minutes, the telltale signs of percolating coffee were dancing against the glass dome of the old pot. He waited until the brew was finished before walking to his sleeping companion to shake him awake.

"Hey, sleepy head. Time to rise and shine. Come on, man. Wake up."

Toby pulled two ceramic mugs out of his backpack. He poured the steaming brew into both and looked to his companion. There had been a small amount of movement, as if the other man had started to stir, but had only pulled the blanket tighter around him. Toby called again, and still no movement. He left the coffee mug sitting within easy reach. He reached down, and this time, with a little less of a gentle hand, grabbed a shoulder and shook it harder.

"John! Come on, *wake up.* It's time."

John's brown eyes opened slowly. He yawned deeply, then struggled to a sitting position, the blanket still clutched tightly around him. He kept blinking, gingerly rubbing his eyes, while patting himself down, checking his pockets.

Toby chuckled under his breath. *Of course,* Toby thought, *he's looking for the contact lens solution.*

John was exhausted from the long walk and he hadn't brought the extra case for his lenses. And why should he have; since he had planned to take them out at home. This whole night had been weird from the moment he'd arrived at the airport. The last thing he wanted to do was take them out; he'd lose them. If only he had his glasses. With a start, he remembered his spare pair in his jacket pocket. Hell, he could get another pair of contact lenses if he had to. Seeing was more important.

He struggled to remember where the hell he'd put the case. He started patting down his pockets, willing his fuddled brain to get its shit together and help him out here. He'd run his hands over his outer pockets several times before he finally remembered that they were in the inner pocket. He pulled out the case, carefully removed his contact lenses one at a time, tossed them into the fire, then put on his glasses. The world came into focus, as much as the dark desert around him possibly could. But just that much felt normal again and he was better, more focused – in more ways than one.

John sat for a moment, trying to understand how he'd gotten here. This man had approached him. Ok, so far, so good. Then, this guy was telling John he needed to come along and it was a matter of life and death. That was where it started getting tricky. John had been around enough of the crazies to know you didn't just jump in a car with someone you just met. But this guy didn't seem crazy. In fact, this guy seemed *familiar*, as if John should know him. Something chimed within him, some small voice inside his head told him that this guy was no crazy and it would be okay.

That made no sense, because John was also pretty damned paranoid. After the Germany incident, he never traveled anywhere without a bodyguard or without some way to protect himself. But that voice again, reassuring and comforting. This man – *Toby,* he reminded himself, the man said his name was *Toby* – was real good with persuasion, because here John was, sitting in the middle of nowhere and willingly. Yeah, so far everything was okay, but still….

Toby motioned to the cup of coffee lying on the ground. John accepted it gratefully and started to sip the brew. Toby leaned back against a rock on his side of the fire and started to drink from his own cup. He watched his companion for a few moments before reaching into his breast pocket and pulling out a pack of Marlboro cigarettes. He reached down, got a splinter from one of the logs, and held it to the fire until it glowed. He held the burning end to the cigarette and inhaled. When the cigarette was smoldering, he tossed the splinter into the fire and exhaled the smoke into the air. Both men watched it rise to the darkness and disappear.

"You know, the People say that smoke is sacred; that it carries our prayers to the spirit world. It was always used when men gathered to talk; to ask for guidance and clearness of thought and spoken word."

John looked across the fire. "And you need this guidance now?"

Toby took another draw off the cigarette before answering. "Oh, yeah. I do."

John nodded, as if in agreement. "Good coffee," was all he said.

Toby smiled and said, "Thanks. I can't do much. But I *can* make coffee. You awake?"

"About as awake as I can be. So. What's all this about? Why am I here?"

Toby took another draw off the cigarette and tossed it into the fire. "I wanted to be alone with you, no distractions or interruptions. And then, when I'm done, I'm going to leave you with the legacy."

John raised an eyebrow. "Legacy?"

"A few years ago, I was given a gift," The corner of his mouth rose in a shy smile as he lost himself in the fire, remembering. "Oh, I suppose some would call it a curse, but you know the old saying – be careful what you ask for, you just may get it. And I sure asked for this. But, it *was* a gift. And the time has come to pass it on."

"And, why me?"

Toby looked across at the older man. "Well, that's where we start getting into the 'hard-to–believe' part of our program. You see, I was *told* to give the gift to you."

John paused, mid-sip, and stared over the rim of the cup at his companion. "And *who* told you to give this to me?"

Toby leaned back against the boulder he was sitting in front of and held the cup in his hands. "Well . . . *you* did," he answered ruefully.

"*I* did?"

"Yes, *you* did. So many hundreds of years ago, in another lifetime."

"Excuse me? *Lifetime?*"

Toby heard the doubt in voice. This wasn't coming out right, damn it. "Ok, call it other directed, if you'd like. I was sent to you by the Goddess."

John set the cup down. He felt a sweat pop out on his forehead. A fear was starting to well up in his stomach and was threatening to race up to his heart.

Great, he really is *one of the crazies,* he thought, *and I'm out here in the middle of nowhere with him.*

He began to look out over the darkness, trying to find some semblance of a way out. It would be a long distance to run, but if he had to, he had to. His heart was beating so fast, and the shine on his face turned into a river running from his body.

What to do, what to do . . . .

Toby could understand the reaction. It was, to say the least, an insane thing to say.

"John, relax. I know how this sounds."

"No, I don't think you do.

"Yeah. I do. Believe me. I've seen more and heard more than you can possibly imagine, and I know how that sounded. But, I assure you, I'm not crazy."

John's started to squirm, looking around about himself, trying to find something.

That's ok, Toby thought, *he'll figure it out. He's heard that before. He just doesn't remember where or when.*

"John, listen to me. *Please.* I am just as sane as you are. I know you have no cause to believe me, but I really am sane."

"No. I don't think so." John seemed to think better of the statement. He waved his hand, a placating gesture. "You know what? I take that back; I'm *sure* you are. I, uh, I think I need to go. I thank you for the walk and exercise, but I really don't think this is a good idea."

Toby set his own cup down now. "John, please, just relax. I'm gonna tell you my story and you'll understand. This is important."

"And *why* is this important?"

"Because, when I have told you my story and passed on this legacy, I'm going to go and pass beyond the Veil."

John cocked his head. "Excuse me?"

Toby sighed. "I'm going to die."

John was even more alarmed. "Look, friend, I don't know how you got me here, but you did. I wish you a lot of luck and I hope you find someone to listen to your story, but I don't think it's gonna be me. Now, if you'll point me towards civilization, I'm gonna take my leave."

"I can't do that."

"Sure, you can. I can make it back on my own. Just point the way."

Toby shook his head. "No, I can't. There *is* no one else. You see, I've followed your work for a long time. You might say, I'm a fan. But, it's more than that. *You* are the one I need to tell this to."

John started to rise. "I'm flattered, but this is not the—"

"Sit down, damn it!"

John fell back hard enough to make his jaw clamp down with an audible click. He had the look of a caged tiger, ready to leap off at the slightest provocation He pushed back from the fire, put some distance between them.

Toby took a very deep breath, letting it out slowly. It helped pull everything back into focus. He relaxed his posture again, willing every muscle to stand down from the alert.

"I'm sorry. I didn't mean to yell. That's not helping my cause, I know, but I can't let you leave." He inhaled slowly again, once more. "Look, you trusted me enough to come out here. I need you to trust me enough to listen to my story. You're safe. I'm not here to hurt you. I'm not even going to leave this spot. Promise."

John sat tensed, then reached behind him. When his hand appeared again, he had a fist-sized rock in it. He laid it on the ground in front of him and picked up his coffee cup again.

Toby saw this, and smiled again. "Is that for me?"

"You could say it's insurance. Just in case."

Toby nodded. "Fair enough."

John picked up the cup and poured more coffee into it. He held out the pot for Toby, who nodded his thanks. When the coffee was poured, both men settled back. Toby was silent for a moment. He watched Toby warily, the rock never far from his grasp. After a few moments, he finally broke the silence.

"So? Spill it. Tell me this story."

Toby took a sip of his coffee and began, "Well, it's all about a man who finally found himself. He was an empty man, although he didn't know it yet. It all began in 1991, when he was sent to Saudi for what became Desert Storm...."

Chapter Two

"Man, this place is a trip and a half, ain't it? Do you know where the hell we are?"

Toby pulled out a grid map, and started checking it out. The problem was the landscape was the same in any one direction: sand, sand, *and more sand.* This stuff was fine, like talcum powder. It was soft and mildly abrasive, always managing to filter into his clothes, his boots and socks, even into his skivvies. He had decided that he might as well be dressed in extra fine sandpaper as try to wear clothes. It amounted to the same irritation. Showering every morning only put more misery on top of it. A good ice cold shower woke a soldier up and put him right back into the kiln of Saudi Arabia, adding a fresh layer of sand to the newly sweat soaked skin. Toby discovered that being a frosted layer cake wasn't all it was cracked up to be.

"Look, bro, that map ain't gonna change. Let's shit or git."

Toby looked up from the map, gave his partner a less than bemused grimace, and dropped his eyes back to the paper. Toby was riding shotgun in this particular little two-man group. The man to his left was Private Bion Roberts, a tall African-American from Chicago, Illinois, and Toby's assigned partner. The Army, in its infinite wisdom, had deemed that two men groups were a better use of resources and they could cover more ground. It was the desert, they said, what could happen? Toby's opinion was "plenty."

He was the squad leader. It was their job to patrol certain sectors while escorting the MASH unit to their next destination to attend to wounded. So, he would divide his group of nineteen into two man groups and take one of the men as *his* partner. If he could only have one man to go with him, he'd pick Bion any day of the week and twice on Sundays. And he did, every time. Bion was as close to a best friend as he was going to have here.

"C'mon, Captain."

Toby looked up from the map again, even more irritated than before. The sand reflected the glare of the sun and the smothering heat made anything more exerting than a slow walk into a new exercise in torture. Toby occasionally had trouble breathing sometimes and heat exhaustion was a common occurrence among the men. The shimmer of the desert floor was so thick that trying to see through it was next to impossible. Toby had on his Army issue blue-blocker sunglasses but they did little to cut the heat-induced effects. It was hopeless and all he wanted to do was go back to base, take off everything but his shorts, and kick back with a book and a beer. It was looking all the more impossible with every passing second.

"*Captain*," Bion said, his own voice sounding frustrated as well.

He rolled his eyes, grunting in exasperation. "Son, if you know where we are or have the least idea, I'm open to suggestion. I don't feel like going off half-cocked, if you don't mind."

Bion opened his door and stepped out on the running board with one foot, leaving the other balanced on the floor in front of the seat. He looked in all directions until Toby thought he wasn't going to fare any better than he had. As he watched his partner, he had to stifle a laugh as Bion actually started sniffing the air. With a quick nod, Bion settled back in the seat, threw the truck into gear, and they were off again.

Toby stared at him, a grin on his face. It took a few seconds before Bion's focus switched from the direction he was taking to the other man in the cab.

"What?" he snapped.

Toby folded his arms against his chest. "You *smelled* camp?" he teased.

Bion's white teeth stood out in contrast against his dark skin as he smiled. "Maybe. But I got me a feeling, bro, and when I gets me a feeling, we are shinin' on."

"Amen, brother, amen!" Toby shook his head, laughing, as he folded the map and replaced it back in the glove compartment. He settled the sunglasses back on his nose, and rested his knee against the armrest on the door. With one arm resting on the open window, he watched the terrain as it passed by and let the driver have his way. There was a radio sitting on the dashboard of the truck and if they really needed it, they could get directions in to the next encampment. Toby had a feeling they weren't going to need them. He was glad to have Bion's company for a lot of reasons; one being that Bion *knew* things. He'd trust Bion's instincts faster than he'd trust anyone else's.

Toby had now been in the Arabian desert for a little under six months. Uncle George had sent the Guard and the "weekend warriors" because no one thought it would go this far or last this long. They found out very quickly that they were dealing with a megalomaniac in Saddam Hussein and *Desert Shield* was upgraded to *Desert Storm*. Uncle George sent in the big guns, the ships, the aircraft, and the artillery, but left the serious soldiers at home. Uncle George *still* didn't think it would go that far. Toby could have told him differently, living it on a daily basis. The nutcase in Iraq wasn't going to give up until they'd bombed his ass to hell and beyond.

They hadn't seen any action, though, so the "mobile" only meant moving for the sake of the ground troupe assigned. They were all about reconnaissance and protection of the hospital staff. They had the morning meeting, got assignments, and were off doing recon of the grid they were assigned to. He wasn't sure which was more thrilling: watching the same scenery, day in and day out, or the endless stream of surrendering Iraqi soldiers that they picked up. In the last week, alone, Toby and Bion had come across fifty men, throwing up hands and giving up weapons. Either way, recon was recon. And, mobile was mobile. It could have been worse, but Toby wasn't sure how.

"You been reading any of that crap passin' as news lately?"

"Yeah," Toby answered. "I been readin' it."

Bion plucked a toothpick out of one of his pockets and stuck it in the corner of his mouth, chewing methodically. "You hear about that soldier got killed?"

"Yeah, I heard about that."

Letters and newspapers were a rare commodity, so anything remotely resembling news spread like a wildfire. The entire unit had heard about the first American soldier killed in combat. The men had analyzed it, discussed it, and had formulated opinions around it. It was the talk of the unit. To the men, it was a brother fallen in battle. To those in charge, it was a morale problem. But, it was *the* hot topic of conversation and a man couldn't go five feet without hearing someone else talking about it.

"I knew that guy," Bion said, simply and with little inflection.

Toby turned his attention to the driver, and leaned against the door, shifting so that his back was now against the armrest. "You knew – no way!"

"Yeah. We was in boot together. He was a good man. Did you know he had a wife and kids? Did you know that?"

"No, I didn't. I take it, you guys were close."

"Shit, when you're in boot, you gotta stick together," Bion snorted out. "You know that. You gotta take the brother's back, 'cause ain't nobody else gonna do it."

"Ok, so you were *buddies*."

"Yeah. We was buddies. His woman used to send shit, like cookies and shit. He showed me pictures of his kids. He had some cute kids." Bion got quiet for a moment before the rest came bursting out in one breath. "His woman was pregnant again. Didja hear that? She was. Didn't mention *that* in the news, did they?"

"No. They didn't."

"The shitheads never do." Bion went back to his silence, watching his side of the gritty terrain.

Toby waited, wondering if Bion was going to add anything else but there was nothing more. So, he went back to watching his side of the desert. The rest of the ride was silent, and Toby got lost in his own thinking about the incident. He hadn't known the soldier, but he was affected by it. He tried to picture the family being told about the death. It had to be hard for them, a wife without a husband and children without a father. He had no frame of reference for losing a child or a spouse, but he knew how he'd feel if he lost *his* dad like that.

Toby was not that close to his father, and hadn't been for a long time. Once upon a time, that hadn't been so, but time could change a man. He'd grown up with a father that was too tough, too strict. The rancor of a raging liberal meeting a diehard conservative made for explosive dinners followed by silent weekends. Toby knew it was a stupid way to be, but taking the automatic opposite of whatever his father said was a habit, like smoking. The only one he ever felt sorry for was his mother. She was caught in the middle every time and it was his only regret. His father had been tight lipped, tight assed, and, in general, a dad. He didn't dislike his father, he just couldn't relate to the man.

A familiar sight suddenly loomed up ahead, and Toby pulled himself out of his reverie, staring ahead in a combination of amusement and amazement. "Son of a bitch, you did it. How the fuck did you do that?" He shook his head again and turned back to

Bion. "You son of a bitch...."

Bion tossed off a laugh and answered, "Yeah, well, I keep tellin' ya – I got the shine. I know things, man." He winked, still grinning. "I ain't hearin' no thank you, man."

Toby retorted, laughing as well, "Tell ya what, bro, I'll buy your dinner."

Bion shook his head and rolled his eyes. "You gotta be kiddin'. Shit's free. You can buy me dinner next leave."

"You're on, bro. C'mon, it's after 5:00 pm and I'm starving. I wanna see what the mailman brung me."

Bion pulled the huge vehicle up to a clearing and brought it to a full stop in front of the first of two huge tents. One served as the command post while the other was the mess hall. There was a steady stream of men going in and out of one entrance, which was the only way to know the difference between the two.

Bion turned his head to address his partner. "Fine, you check your mail, bro. I'll take 'Big Bertha' to the motor pool and meet you in the mess tent."

Toby raised one thumb and nodded. "You are on, bad ass. You are on." He suddenly held his index finger up. "You are one minute late and I'm comin' after your skinny black ass. You hear what I'm saying?"

"Get outa my truck," Bion answered back, teasing in return. "I will be there, brother man. Have my seat reserved."

Toby slapped the side panel of the door, and stepped back, as Bion stepped down on the gas pedal and drove off. The truck was unbearably loud when standing outside of it, and the engine's roar was slow to fade. It was a moment or two after the truck had gone that he realized that there was a great roar coming from inside the huge tent. It sounded like a riot going on inside, with muffled voices shouting unknown words. Toby took a deep breath and sprinted through the door of the command center.

He barely got through the door before he ran into the back of another soldier, a private. The surly man wheeled around, and stopped his fist, barely in time. Toby shot him a warning glance and the lower rank stepped back. The air was filled with curses and shouts of "kick his ass, Dino," and "man, that had to hurt." Toby started wading through the sea of angry soldiers, pushing and pulling his way through the bodies that were tightly packed around whatever was happening. He grabbed one shoulder and ducked as the corresponding fist flew at his face. He had barely made it to the halfway point when he heard a very commanding voice shout, "ten-HUT!" It was enough to grab *everyone's* attention, and twenty men moved as one unit, all snapping to a rigid formation.

Major Frank Wieczhalek was the commanding officer of this particular MASH and a royal hard ass. Whoever had started this was stupid enough to do it where it could be heard. Someone was in for an ass chewing and Toby didn't want to be noticed. The major would be looking for a rank to bust if he thought that rank lost control of the situation. Toby slowly and quietly stepped back the way he had come until he had faded back into the group. So camouflaged, he watched with the rest of them.

The Major strode into the middle of the thicket and gestured with his finger at two men. They were both bearing the beginnings of some serious black eyes and bruises about the face and shoulders. They both took a step forward, stood at attention as Major Wieczhalek nodded coolly. A third man was being helped up by the Major's aide, the clerk who passed out the mail.

"Well, gentlemen," Major Wieczhalek said, his voice equally cool. "Who will be the first to tell me what happened?"

There was no answer.

"I see. Like that, is it?" He leaned forward to one of the men's chests and read a name there. "Collins, it says. Is that you, soldier?"

"Sir, yes, sir."

"Good, we're getting somewhere," Wieczhalek said with a certain amount of satisfaction. "Perhaps you'll tell me what I wish to know. And Private Collins, that is *not* a request, is it."

"Sir, no, sir."

"Then, enlighten me, Collins," the major ordered, his hands now clasped behind his back.

"Rappaport, sir. He just hit me."

The Major's gaze shifted to the other man in the brawl. "And Corporal Rappaport, there was reason for this? You have justification for striking the private?" Wieczhalek met with an uneasy silence from the second man. "Perhaps the Corporal didn't hear me?"

Rappaport took a deep breath before answering with a less than military flair. "Sir, I heard you. I haven't been getting my mail, sir.

Collins has gotten mail every day, been getting newspapers, sir. I just – I wanted *something*, sir." He looked pained as he added, "I'm going crazy over here."

Toby watched the major's reaction and was surprised to see the man's face soften up. Major Wieczhalek was the only career man in the camp. He was in his early 50's, and he had served in Vietnam and Grenada. Toby hoped the man would be fair, that he would know what it was like this far from home.

"Gentlemen." Wieczhalek exhaled, chewing on his lower lip for a moment or two before he nodded and continued. "I cannot have my men using each other as punching bags," he advised in a stern, no nonsense manner. "It simply is not acceptable. I understand frustration and I understand loneliness, but I also understand that if you do not have mutual respect, you are dead. Combat situations make for strange bedfellows, but you are all you have." Wieczhalek cleared his throat. "Collins, I could order you to share the papers with your fellow soldiers, but I would like you to consider one thing. The man you give aid to will be the man who will protect you in the field." He turned to the other man and said, "Rappaport, you are a ranking individual here. I understand what you feel, son, but you are here to set an example. This behavior will not be condoned." Addressing both again, he added, "Gentlemen, you are on report and confined to quarters for the evening. I'll give you a break this time. Another incident such as this and I'll see both of you in the stockade; am I understood?"

Both men snapped out a terse "yes, sir" and a sharp salute before going quiet again.

Wieczhalek nodded and returned the salutes. "Dismissed, gentlemen. Sergeant, show these men to their quarters. I'll trust them enough to not leave a guard on them. These are good soldiers and it was a mistake." To the rest of the group, he said, "Mail call for non-ranking personnel is in the mess tent. I suggest that if you are not officers, you be *there*."

The room cleared fast, a clutter of shuffling feet and mutters of "don't push, you putz." In a matter of seconds, the room was empty, except for Toby, Wieczhalek, his aide, and the rumpled mail clerk. No sooner had the room cleared than the major immediately turned his focus on on Toby.

"Captain Riordan, as I live and breathe. And how much of this little party were you witness to?"

Toby felt a sinking feeling in the pit of his stomach but still yanked his shoulders back in attention. "I arrived a moment before you did, sir."

Wieczhalek waved his hand in Toby's direction. "At ease, Captain. You were not part of this?"

Toby relaxed his posture immediately. "No, sir. I came in to check to see if I had mail and ran into the crowd. I was making my way to the center when you came in, sir."

Wieczhalek nodded at Toby and turned back to the shaken clerk. Toby breathed a sigh of relief, he was off the hook.

"Tompkins, are you well enough to complete your duties?"

The clerk was still a bit shaken but managed to answer in the affirmative with a bit of strength.

Wieczhalek nodded. "Then, be at them. Get the good Captain his mail, first, and then, take care of the men." The Major turned to go, hands still clasped behind his back.

Toby stopped him by asking, "Sir, may I speak freely, sir?"

Major Wieczhalek turned back to him and lifted his chin in question.

"Sir, I was wondering why you didn't put those men in the stockade this time, sir."

Wieczhalek cocked his head, one eyebrow raised. "You question my decision?"

"No, sir," Toby blurted out. "I just— Well, you seem to be a 'by the book' man, sir."

The major nodded again, running his tongue in his cheek. He ducked his head and came over to stand in front of Toby, his back still ramrod straight. "Captain, if you'll indulge an old man, I'd like to tell you a short story." When Toby nodded, he went on. "I was already a career man when Vietnam started. I didn't get sent over there right away. I was stationed stateside. But I surely did want to go there to do my duty. The day my unit got called, I had a telegram telling me that my daddy had just had a massive stroke; they thought he was terminal. I had no choice; I got on the plane with my fellow officers and soldiers."

Toby caught his breath. It was disturbing him and yet Major Wieczhalek was telling the story as matter-of-factly as if he were relaying an order to go recon a new sector. He was now convinced that the major's veins held ice water instead of warm blood. He nodded his understanding and listened as the man went on.

"We were shipped to Danang. From there, my unit was sent to a remote part of the forest. I spent my first three weeks of my first tour of duty up to my armpits in mud and dirty river water, trying to keep from getting eaten alive by mosquitoes as big as aircraft carriers and picking leeches off my dick. I also spent my first three weeks scared shitless that my daddy was dying or dead. I came as close to going crazy as you can get because I had no mail and no word." He unclasped his hands finally, pointing to the exit that the men had taken to leave. "I know what that man is going through. I can't fault a soldier for that. *That* is why they got what they got."

"You wanted to show them that you understood but didn't sanction the fighting?"

"Exactly right and no more."

Wieczhalek turned once more to leave but Toby stopped him again.

"Sir?"

Wieczhalek didn't even turn around the second time. "We secured that area of the jungle and the mail found us again. My mother wrote to tell me that my father had made it through with minor brain damage and with a little physical therapy, he was going to be just fine. Thank you for asking, Captain. Now, as you were."

Major Wieczhalek walked out of the makeshift office, his aide two steps to the left and behind, and that left the clerk and Toby.

Toby thought about what he'd just heard. He wondered how he would have reacted if it had been *his* father. Maybe he didn't always like his old man, but he was still his father's son. Maybe there was love after all. And maybe the Major wasn't such a hard ass after all.

He waited until the clerk had straightened the mail cart again before he was rewarded with a large parcel. He thanked the private and took the brown wrapped box back to the small tent he shared with another of the ranking officers and sat down on the bunk to open it.

His mom was a fantastic baker and she'd filled a large tin with about two dozen assorted cookies; her famous butterscotch oatmeal, along with his favorite chocolate chip and peanut butter. Toby took one at random, closed the lid and started rummaging through the rest of the box. His father had included a Swiss army knife since Toby had lost his on a recon mission a month or more previously. It had all the bells and whistles, even the plastic toothpick. His mother had also included six books, all by his favorite authors. He had made the request for his dog eared copy of *Stranger in a Strange Land* because it had always been the best of his library and his favorite. So, instead of meeting Bion in the mess tent, he sat back on his bunk and opened the tin of cookies again and started to read from the book. He'd read for five hours and half the tin of cookies before realizing that it was after dark. It was his time of night. He had an enlarged paperclip that he used for a bookmark, and attached that to the page. He grabbed his jacket, and put it on as he crossed out of the tent.

Toby stood for a moment, zipping up the front of his jacket. The sky was black and smooth as silk, the stars were the diamonds. This far out from civilization, he felt that he could reach up and touch them. Each constellation was clear and vivid, so close as to be within easy grasp, as if he could simply pluck them into his nimble fingers. A full moon shone down and her beauty was not lost on him. Toby watched until he could swear that he saw the woman's face. She was singing a torch song, her eyes closed and her lips full and ripe. The air was crisp, cool, and peaceful, and the beautiful woman was singing to him. What more could he ask?

A barrage of lights flashed against the darkness to the north. He walked further out, to the edge of the encampment, and saw the anti-aircraft missiles flaring green and gold over Tehran. In the desert, you could quite literally see and hear for miles in any direction. Not that there was anything to see but scrub and sand, but when the missiles were firing, as they were now, it looked like a fireworks display. In a morbid way, it was truly spectacular and quite lovely. He could hear the air raid sirens from the distance. This would go on for quite some time. Toby stuck his hands in his pockets to preserve what little warmth he could and stood watching the light show.

It was a few minutes before he realized that someone was standing next to him, he was that caught up in the sight. When he finally felt the presence, he dragged his gaze from the spectacle. Bion was also watching the light show, silently mimicking Toby's posture. They stood silently for a time, just watching.

Not taking his eyes off the show, he didn't want to disturb the peace. He muttered, "Out enjoying some air, Private?"

Bion's answer was just as quiet. "Can't sleep. Sir."

Toby chuckled. "Same here, bro."

"I figured you'd be out here."

"Yeah."

"You stood me up, brother man."

Shit! "Sorry, man." Toby ducked his head, not that Bion would see it. "Package from home and I got distracted."

"Yeah, home."

Both stood and watched the light show far away, lost in thought. When they spoke, both men spoke together.

"Listen—"

"So, what—"

Only Toby laughed at the incident. "Bion, come on. That was pretty funny."

"Sorry. I – I—"

"Something wrong?"

Bion's voice was heavy, guarded. "Look, Toby, you been a good friend; someone I talk to when I'm buggin'. I need to talk, my friend."

Toby felt the hairs on the back of his neck suddenly stand up. He tried to convince himself that it was just the chilly air of the desert. But an inner sense tried to let him know that was *not* the case here. He felt the urgency in the other man's voice and debated whether he really wanted to hear what Bion had to say. But Bion needed to say it.

He did a quick look around to make sure they were alone. When he was satisfied, he told Bion, "So, talk. What's got you spooked?"

Bion snorted, exhaling before he spoke. "Been thinking 'bout things."

"What things, Bion?"

"*You know*," he snapped.

Toby balled a fist inside his pocket. He knew it was just tension that caused the outburst. He knew he could wait until Bion came to the problem. *He'll get there...let him work it out.*

Bion got control again. "Sorry, man." He sighed. "I always thought 'bout what it was like to live forever. Must be boring as hell, man."

Toby nodded in the darkness. Knowing that his friend couldn't see his grin, he made light of things. "Oh, I don't know, not if you do it right. All the time in the world to read books, learn about the world, and play racquetball. I could get used to it."

"Yeah, maybe." He was still staring up at the barrage. "Shit, just living *one* lifetime is a bitch, you know?"

Toby sneaked a glance out of the corner of his eye. "Yeah. But too many don't even get that chance."

"Like DJ."

Ah...now we come to it. "Yeah...like him." Toby pulled a pack of cigarettes out of his pocket. He held out the pack to Bion, who refused, and then took one out. He lit it from the book of matches in his other pocket. He replaced pack and matches before speaking again. "But, Bion, this is a war. It does happen. It sucks canal water through a straw, but it's part of the job."

Bion made a swift and violent wave at the air with his hand. "Oh, man, you don't get it. I know that! It just...it...just...."

"Makes you think about your own life, doesn't it?" Toby finished for him.

Bion nodded, the sudden burst of anger deflated again. But his words were still animated, he was still confused. "Yeah...*yeah*. I mean, I hurt inside for the brother's family, but, somethin' like this? I mean dyin' like that. It's bullshit, man. I do *not* want to die, not for some fuckin' black shit comin' out the ground. Toby, what the fuck are we doing here?"

Toby stood silent for a moment, watching the light show before them. He was trying to weigh his words carefully. "Good question. I guess there's no easy answer to that one."

"Yeah, well I ain't asking for no easy answer. Just one that makes sense. Because, right now, I'm looking for anything going stateside."

The soldier snapped to the forefront, even though he knew it was going to be wrong. But that sense of duty was still uppermost in him. He squared off his shoulders and faced his friend. "Unauthorized leave? Do I hear you right, soldier? Do you realize what you're saying? And who you are saying it to?"

Bion cursed under his breath, kicking the sand beneath one foot. He cleared his throat and glared at Toby. "Yes, Captain Riordan, I know who I am talking to." He took a deep breath and in a calmer voice, added, "I am talking to my friend, not my fuckin' commander. You dig what I'm layin' down here?"

He felt like a total ass right now, so Toby swallowed the duty bound prick. "Come on, man, that ain't the answer and you know that."

Bion was terse; something else had to be churning inside of him. "No. I don't. Right now, UA looks pretty damn good to me."

"You dumbass, it's a *very* bad idea." Toby barked out, and threw his cigarette on the ground. "You signed up for this gig, Bion. There's no walking away from that. Having an attack of conscience or fear now is not cool. You want to spend the rest of your life running from the law?" He got in Bion's face, inches from being nose to nose, and said, "*Do* ya? Because that's what you'll be doing, you know. Always looking over your shoulder, waiting for the MPs to come take you away for desertion."

"They gotta find me first, man," Bion objected, doing a better job that Toby at keeping his voice down. "They gotta find me first and I know plenty o' places to hide. Ain't none of the brothers gonna rat me out. Won't happen."

"They'll find you. You know that. Besides, who said anything about dying?" Toby wasn't backing down, physically or emotionally. Surely Bion had to know that he was about to screw up the rest of his life. Toby felt very protective of his men and Bion, in particular. He wasn't going to let his friend make biggest mistake of his life. "Tell me, where did you get the idea about dying? Why are you thinking that, bro?"

"I been thinking alot about it. 'Cause of DJ."

Toby relaxed. The problem was named, now it was time to do the reassurances. He put his hand on Bion's shoulder, squeezing affectionately to try and reassure his friend. "Listen to me; this is a big decision, even if it's a wrong one. I can't say the right words to make you understand that. You need to find those for yourself. But, what I *can* tell you is this; I'm here. I haven't lost a man yet, not on my watch. I'm not gonna let it happen now. Look at me and tell me that I'm lying to you"

Bion met his eyes. The moonlight reflecting off of his skin added a soft glow to his features, but made his eyes luminescent. Toby waited while Bion was silent, making that decision.

Then Bion relaxed as well. "No. You ain't. And that helps. A little. But, I am *scared*, bro."

"I know. Me, too," Toby answered, using the same soothing voice his father used to use on him. "And because we're scared, we're careful. I'm watching your back, bro, and I know you're watching mine." He clapped his friend on the shoulder, making light of things. "Hey, we're a team. What can happen to us? Besides, if you do leave, who's gonna watch my back? Some new recruit that can't wipe his own ass? Get serious."

That got a small smile. "Yeah, yeah. Can't have that now, can we?"

Toby chuckled softly. Bion was smiling and had calmed a bit. Not a lot, but it was a start. He smiled back. "Come on, son, let's go get some sleep."

The moment it came out of his mouth, Toby knew it was the wrong thing to say. Bion tightened up again and cursed under his breath.

Thoroughly confused, Toby quickly asked, "What? What?"

Bion practically choked out the words, close to tears. He was tense again. "I been havin' have this weird ass dream. Man, I don't wanna go to sleep."

"What dream, man?"

"Oh, man. Three days now, I been having this nightmare and then, when DJ got killed, it got worse. It's creepin' my shit out."

It was the way he said it that would haunt Toby's sleep that night. Something in the man's voice made the hairs stand up again and Toby was shivering despite the heavy duty jacket he wore. When Bion began to speak, Toby wanted to stop him, but couldn't. He wanted to hear, but he didn't. "Tell me," was all he could say and he lit another cigarette.

"I keep dreaming about you and me on recon." Bion turned back towards the lights in the night sky. His voice took on a hushed and emotionless tone, the words rushing out of him as fast as he can say them. "We're bookin' down this road and this hole opens up in front of us. I keep tellin' your ass it's wrong and you keep telling me we gotta check it out. Next thing I know, see you standing in front of the truck, walking to that hole. I'm tryin' to stop you, but I can't. I try to tell you, 'brother man, don't go in there,' but I can't talk. I open my mouth, ain't nuthin' comin' out."

Toby glanced at Bion, and saw that the man's eyes had become vacant and staring in a trancelike state. Bion was there and somehow not there, telling a tale that was making Toby more and more anxious.

"And then, I'm like shoutin' your name. You keep lookin' at me, but, it's like this light comes out of that damn hole and you're covered in it. You callin' me and next thing I know, I'm out the truck and walkin' to you. And I keep screamin' at you to stop, but you ain't listenin' to me. I know it's wrong, but I gotta follow you in. And, man, I get in that hole and I'm drownin' in sand. Swimmin' in it. I can't find the way out or up and I'm dyin' in it. That's when I wake up."

Toby inhaled deeply and let it out again in long and drawn out rush. Bion slowly lost the blank look on his face, animating again. He reached out to give comfort but Bion just pushed his hand aside.

Toby nodded once, pulling his own shit together. "But, it's just a dream, man. Anxiety dream that was made worse because of what you heard about DJ. Nothing more."

He held out the pack of smokes and the matches and this time, Bion took one. He pulled one out for himself and lit both cigarettes.

Blowing out the first puff of smoke, he went on. "Hell, I remember reading a book about dreams. Guy said that if you have a recurring nightmare like that, you should take control. It won't happen the first time or two but eventually, you're able to control the dream. First, you admit that you're dreaming and then you take control. That's all you have to do."

Bion shook his head, sucking smoke and emphasizing his words with the cigarette waving in the air. "And you buy that shit? You're dumber than you look. I'm tellin' ya. This is real. I know. *I know*."

"Look, Bion, I told you. You're on my team and I'm not gonna let anything happen to you. I'm watching your back. It won't happen. It's just an anxiety dream. Trust me."

Bion swallowed, tossing his butt to one side. He licked his lips nervously. "You sure?"

Toby felt the change, the tension easing out of his friend. "Of course, I'm sure. *Trust me*. Accept that you're dreaming and control the dream. That simple. You'll see. As soon as you get control of that dream, you won't have it anymore. That easy."

"And you read this in a book."

"Sure did."

"And you've tried this?"

"Of course," Toby lied. "Works every time."

Bion nodded, again at ease. "Ok. I'll try it. If you say so. I don't know."

"Hey!" Toby plastered a teasing grin on his face. "Would I lie to you?"

Bion snorted and shook his head, smiling in return. "Yeah, and you're worse than my old man."

Toby punched him lightly in the arm. "Yeah, and you're the son I never wanted. Come on, man, I'm pooped and 0430 gets here too damn early for me."

"Sure. Sure. See you at 0430." With a mock salute, Bion added, "Sir."

Toby turned for another look at the light show. The air seemed a little thicker now, denser, and he was having a little trouble breathing. He shook his head to rid himself of the uneasiness he had started to feel when Bion recounted the dream. *That's all it was...a dream. Means nothing. Nothing. Won't happen.* And so thinking, Toby went to his tent and fell into an uneasy sleep.

And dreamed of sand and light.

Chapter Three

He stands in the desert, nothing but sand around him for miles. He is lost and the sun is beating down from directly above, without mercy. There is no way to triangulate his position and no way of knowing east from west, north from south. He stands, unsure and alone, and the heat is miserable upon him. He panics, whirling around in every direction, trying to make sense of his surroundings, and now he no longer remembers which way he was originally facing. He takes a deep breath and points in a direction. Surely if he travels this way, he will come upon someone.

He walks; he walks for a long distance, and still there is no one. There is no oasis, no cover from the sun. There is no camp, no road, and no trucks. There are no people. He hears no sound but that of the wind crying in his ears. He feels nothing but the wind and sun and sand crawling in every place on his body that it can crawl. It cuts and feels like steel wool against his skin. It chafes his thighs and genitals as he walks. It dries out his mouth and he tries to keep his lips pressed together, but he cannot for long. He cannot breathe because his nose is clogged with the sand.

Then, he sees it. The hole in the sand, large and black, and it is pulling him. He doesn't want to go, but the hole reaches out with an invisible hand and grasps him by his heart. He wants to stand still but he can't; he must move forward to the hole. He walks to it, and as he walks, his feet sink into the sand. Lower and lower, he goes farther and farther into the swirling sand. He is up to his ankles, and then to his knees. He walks and is in it up to his chest, and then he is swimming in the sand. The undertow begins to pull him down, and the sand fills his mouth. It fills his ears and his eyes, and he is blind, and he is afraid, and his heart is pounding . . . pounding . . . he is drowning in the sand . . . .

Toby jerked awake with a shout, wildly glancing around the tent to make sure he hadn't woke up his bunkmate. The lieutenant wasn't in, probably out with his current inamorata. Toby scrubbed his face with his hands, checking for sand in his ears. His mouth was filled with a gritty taste, as if he'd swallowed the desert in his sleep. He reached for the water bottle he kept by his bunk and drained it in three swallows.

Toby could hear the motor pool starting to stir. 0430 did come damned early in the morning, but Toby was a soldier. When Uncle Sam said get up, he got up; but that didn't mean he had to like it. He sat on the edge of his cot for a few minutes, trying to collect himself. That dream had been so real, from the smell of the sand to the taste of his fear. His heart was still pounding in his ears and he felt about ready to jump out of his skin. He knew he had to shake off the feeling of dread and get motivated.

Toby quickly packed his duffel with his things, including the care package of cookies and books. He'd come back and get that before his squad left for recon. The mere act of movement cleared his head and he started to calm down again. He remembered going to the beach once, off the Gulf Coast of Florida. He had stepped in some quicksand, as they were poking around a mangrove stand, and he remembered that feeling of panic when the sand crept up his ankle. It was the same feeling as he had in the sand of his dreams.

He stopped and mentally got hold of himself again, and sat down to lace his boots. It was his habit to make that the last thing he did every morning, his version of a good luck ritual. There was no rational reason for it; he just did it. He pulled his pants legs up and made sure that the flea collars were still around them. The heat and the sand weren't the only things that a soldier had to put up with; he also had the sand fleas. They were vicious little buggers that would burrow into the skin and make life even more unbearable. Flea collars had become the hot commodity and the current fashion statement. His were holding; he should still have another month before they'd need to be replaced. He put on his boots and laced them up. Boots tied and duffel packed, he grabbed his book and walked out of the tent.

The moment he was out of the tent, two things struck him with the force of a sledgehammer. The first was the unbearable heat, even this early in the morning. The sun was barely peeping over the horizon and it had to be an easy eighty five degrees. Toby brushed the tiny beads of sweat off his brow. He dearly would have loved to jack off all of his clothes and spend the rest of the day in his Army issue briefs, but that was only wishful thinking. There were female personnel in the camp – several that he was on very intimate terms with – and a handful of them would be the ones to scream sexual harassment to Colonel Wieczhalek. Toby sighed and decided against it.

A rumble from deep within was followed by a gnawing sensation, and Toby's hunger announced itself fully. Toby turned toward the mess tent. The intense heat and the walk channeled his thoughts elsewhere, the dream was forgotten.

By the time he'd reached the mess tent, he had convinced himself that hot coffee was the last thing he needed and he was going to drink water or canned milk instead. The moment he was inside the door of the mess, he knew that resolve was useless. The coffee was fresh brewed and he salivated for it. He got his mug and poured the first cup, and stood there, sniffing it. A deep inhale and a slow exhale, and his tongue was lusting for it. He took a tentative sip and tasted the elixir and called it good. There was nothing like that first cup of coffee in the morning to make a man feel alive and get the juices flowing.

He crossed to the next table and loaded up his plate. He took his cup of coffee and found a place to sit, near a few of the medics.

"Hey, Riordan, you look bright eyed and bushy tailed this morning. You got a hot date last night, eh?"

Toby gave the medic – a man named Cafferty – the finger and a smile, and took his first bite of powdered eggs and rehydrated bacon. The other three joined in with Cafferty's returning laugh and went back to their own meals. He chewed slowly but with determination – food was food, even if it was not quite as good as the cardboard it had originally come in.

"Tastes like dehydrated dog chow, don't it, Captain?"

Toby raised his eyebrows. "Well, Mendez, when was the last time you had dehydrated dog chow?"

This brought another gale of laughter from the men; every one of them, barely into their twenties, were all highly trained medical specialists. They were a good bunch of guys.

"You know what, man? This shit reminds me o' my old lady's cooking. She's always burning shit, man. Comes out tasting like this," said the other, a man identified on his 'camo' shirt as Davison.

"Then your old lady should come cook for the Army, man."

Mendez had a large grin on his face. "Because this shit can't get no worse. Ain't that right, Captain?"

"I think you are very right on that one. But it sure beats starving," Toby answered.

There was another round of laughter and the four men got up to go. Cafferty stopped just long enough to whip off a snappy salute and Toby returned it, and opened his book. He sat, lost in the story, eating his food. It wasn't until one of the mess workers came over and shook his shoulder that he realized that he was late for the "morning workout routine." He downed the last of his mug of coffee, left the tray on top of the others in the bus pan, and after stuffing the book in his back pocket, took off at a run.

0530 brought the sun, heat, and the exercise period for the day. The Army felt that all of its personnel should be razor sharp in mind and body, and calisthenics were the way to go. For the enlisted, it was mandatory to go and work out. For the officers, it was purely voluntary; if Toby had missed the hour, no one would have said anything about it. He didn't really mind, however, because the exercise kept him in shape. So, he did his jumping jacks, squats, sit-ups and assorted other calisthenics, grunting and sweating right along with the others.

After his exercise, Toby went to join the line to take his permitted thirty seconds of a shower. Normally, the water was ice cold from sitting all night in tanker trucks; this morning was no exception. By the time he stepped into the stall, however, he didn't care. But the little slice of heaven only reduced the heat for as long as it took to put his clothing back on. Once the clothes were on, and he had stepped back out in the sun, he was sweating again and walking on the sand produced more of a layer of sand that felt like a sugary cake frosting on his skin.

He desperately wanted to go get some water before the mess tent was packed up. Bion would have gotten several canteens filled for the day's excursion, but the water he got now would be nice and cold. He stood debating whether he should or not, when an internal sensor prompted him to look at his watch – he was late for the Colonel's morning briefing.

Shit, he thought, and took off at a fast trot, arriving outside the Command tent in less than a minute. He entered the tent, trying to be quiet, but no such luck.

Colonel Wieczhalek barely paused as Toby crept up behind another Captain, who was standing with his arms folded, intent on the Colonel's directives. A grid map was laid out on the desk and the aide handed Toby a smaller version.

"Alpha squad, you'll take grid G12. Bravo, I want you in G13. And Charlie squad will divide up and examine G14." Wieczhalek cleared his throat and with a forced cheerfulness, barked out, "Why, Captain Riordan, I believe that's your little group, isn't it?"

Toby gulped. "Yes, sir."

"Well, Captain, you're going to take your little company out and recon that sector. You can handle that, surely. After all, you don't have a problem with distances; it's just that time seems to escape you. I am correct in that presumption?"

"Yes, sir. Sorry, sir. We can handle it fine, sir."

The Colonel stared at Toby, no expression on his face, and simply said, "Dismissed, gentlemen. Oh, and Captain Riordan? Be late for one more of my meetings and it will cost you your rank. Am I clear?"

Toby did his damnedest to not flinch and kept looking straight ahead. "Yes, sir. Crystal clear, sir."

"Good," answered the Colonel. "Then I won't make you give me a lame excuse for your tardiness."

"Thank you, sir."

The Colonel surveyed the remainder of the men, standing in formation. "Is there a problem, gentlemen? Dismissed."

Toby scuttled quickly out of the tent. He went back and grabbed his duffel, then met his men at the motor pool. He assigned them into two man teams and sent them all on their way. Bion had managed to score a Land Rover, a smaller vehicle than they normally took. They got in and headed off towards their sector. They rode in silence for a few miles, Bion watching his side of the vehicle, and Toby handling the right hand side.

It was some time before the silence was broken. Bion was the one to break it.

"I hear you got on the Colonel's wrong side this morning. Somethin' 'bout being late," he finally said, a big grin on his face.

"Yeah, well, I wasn't paying attention to the time. The shower line was almost to Tehran."

Bion chuckled. "Man, I keep tellin' you, you need to start pullin' rank on these guys. Me, I do not wait for a shower. I do not dig this heat and I got me a whole lot of other reasons for wantin' the fuck outa here."

Toby snorted and shook his head, pulling the pack of smokes out of his pocket and lit one up. "Are you still serious about going UA?"

"I thought about it." Bion's voiced sounded as if he had done a lot of thinking on the subject. It almost sounded contrite. "Thought about what you said. You was right; I signed up for this gig. I guess I gotta stick around. Ain't got no choice."

"You have a choice, numb nuts. I just don't think it's the right choice."

"Yeah, you probably right."

"Of course, I'm right," Toby said. He sat back in the seat, propping his elbow in the window. He could relax about that little issue, anyway. Bion wasn't going to do anything that damned stupid.

"Well, we'll see, won't we?"

"I guess."

Both got quiet again, watching the desert. Nothing about the scenery changed as they went, nothing but dunes and sand as far as they could see. There were a few times that Toby was sure he saw something, but it turned out to be more of the shimmer of heat rising from the desert floor. There wasn't even a sign of an oasis anywhere nearby. They drove and watched the dunes and the sand, and Toby would keep track of the other squads by radio. They had a check in at 1000 hours, then got quiet again. After several more miles, Toby could finally stand no more, and decided to plunge in. But, he had to work up to it.

"So, did you have that dream again?"

Bion gripped the wheel a little tighter. "Hell, yes."

"And, did you try what I told you?"

Bion shook his head and stared out the windshield, watching the sand. "Only all night. It was like some kind o' loop in my head, same dream, over and over. I tried to control it, like you said; even knowed I was dreaming. Same thing happening over and over. Nothing changed, nothing stopped. I finally gave up around 0400 and read a book."

"Well," Toby said, "if it's any consolation, you gave me the same damn dream."

Now, it was Bion's turn to snort. Toby spared a moment to look over his shoulder, out of the corner of his eyes. Bion had an unreadable look on his face, not quite amusement but a corner of his mouth was turned up slightly.

"Man, that makes sense," Bion said.

Toby turned back to his side of the vehicle. "What does? What do you mean?"

"The only thing different about last night was that there was someone else in there with me, bro. Was you out in the middle o' nowhere? Didn't have no scrub, no nothing around?"

"Yes," Toby said, tentatively.

"Sun was right over your head? Like when you walked, it stayed on top of you?"

"Yes," Toby answered again, even more tentatively.

"And you, like, walk an' walk an' walk, and they ain't no people and they ain't nuthin' 'til you come to the hole in the sand and then you be walkin' and you be sinkin' in the shit?"

Toby felt his heart skip a beat and he struggled to get the answer to leave his mouth. "Yes."

"That's what I was dreamin' too. You sayin' you was dreamin' the same thing tells me it was you with me."

Toby went back to watching the unchanging landscape. "Coincidence."

"Maybe," Bion said, gloating a bit. "But, I don't think so. And listenin' to you right now, I don't think you do either."

Toby's breath came short and ragged and he camouflaged his growing panic by reaching down and getting one of the canteens. He took a long pull, filling his mouth and swallowing twice before he screwed the cap back on. "Coincidence," he repeated.

Bion took one hand off the wheel long enough to pull out a pack of cigarettes and lit one. He took a draw off the smoke before speaking. "You religious?"

It was the second time someone had asked him that in as many days. "Lapsed Catholic, so what?"

"Did I ever tell you 'bout Mammaw?"

Toby crossed his arms over his chest. "Who? Your Mom?"

"No, you stinking redneck," Bion said, the grin back on his face. "I said my Mammaw, not my Mama. You need a hearing aid, son. She was my Mama's Mama." He took another hit off the cigarette and blew out the smoke. "Well, my Mammaw? She was a voodoo priestess. She used to tell me about the old religion. I remember her telling me that when dreams was that clear, they was really visions. She said that if you dreamed the same thing three times, it'd come true."

Toby chuckled and shook his head. He lit a cigarette of his own, twisted his seating position again so that his head was against the headrest, and replaced his elbow in the open window.

"You don't believe that shit," Toby said. "Come on, this is the twentieth century, for Christ's sakes."

"Yeah, but I believe," Bion said. He had a big grin on his face. "I seen it happen, you know. I seen that old woman do some shit would scare you white. Well, whiter'n you are now."

"Ha-ha, funny, funny," Toby answered, returning the grin.

"All right, all right," Bion answered. "You can laugh at that, but don't laugh at the old ways. Or the old religions." He went back to staring back out at the barren landscape. "I think Mammaw had it right. That voodoo been around a lot longer than any them others. And there's older than that."

Toby took the smoke into his lungs, blowing it out as he spoke. "There are more things on heaven and earth, Horatio, than are dreamt of in your philosophy."

Bion furrowed his brow, and said, "Huh?"

"Shakespeare, Bion. It's a quote from Hamlet. Says there's plenty out there that we may or may not know about or believe; or can explain."

"Yeah, whatever. But, I know what I know. Mammaw kept tryin' to tell Mom and Dad that I had the shine. Mom thought it was bullshit, too. But that old woman believed. I used to tell my Mammaw 'bout my dreams."

"Yeah?"

"Oh, yeah," Bion answered, nodding head in emphasis. "I'd tell her about 'em 'because she said talkin' about 'em took the power away."

"And, this dream you've been having; do you believe it's a true one?

Bion glanced to his right, smiling as he did. "Do you think the sun'll be risin' tomorrow and today'll be hotter than Satan's asshole?"

But, Toby shook his head, muttering, "Well, I don't know about that, but I do know one thing. Your ass is going home in one piece. I am sincere about that."

Bion chuckled and snuffed the butt into the ashtray. "My ass ain't the part I'm worried about, bro. Can't let the enemy shoot off this purty face, baby."

They both laughed at this, and the sand kept rolling by. Further conversation on the subject seemed pointless so they went back to the business at hand; surveying sector 14, or at least their section of it. Toby could watch the surrounding landscape and let his mind roll on to wherever it wanted to go. He gave no more thought to Bion and the dream.

At 1100 hours, Bion pulled over to, possibly, the only oasis within 500 miles, and they had the afternoon meal. As Toby sat eating his packaged MRE, he told Bion about the earlier comparison to dog chow. Bion laughed so hard that he sprayed the air with a fine mist of saliva and crumbs. Toby was content to hear about Bion's recent letter from home; his sister was pregnant again, his father was laid off and rehired in the same day. Toby, in turn, told his friend about the care package. He had gotten a letter too, and his parents were nursing colds and his father was having some chest pains, but the doctor didn't find it serious.

They ate amidst the laughter. Then, while Bion relieved himself on the other side of the oasis, Toby radioed in their position. Command felt they should continue the recon in that sector and come in at 1600 hours. The unknown clerk who was speaking for command assured Toby that the new position would be radioed in at that time. Toby acknowledged and then swore at the thought of spending another four hours in the desert, baking like a potato. Bion was just as thrilled at the prospect, but both mounted up again in the Land Rover and continued on.

Toby checked in with the other squads on his team; all was well. The only thing to break the monotony was the passing of the occasional SCUD missile going overhead. In the distance, all they could see was the bright flare of light coming from the tail of the missile. Bion would bring the truck to a stop, and they would watch the missile pass overhead. Only when the missile was on top of them could they hear the thunder welling from the bomb. Everything within the truck would vibrate from the sound. Toby caught a glance outside and saw that the sand was vibrating also.

At 1600, true to the unseen man's word, command radioed for the teams to come on in and gave the new position. Both men were glad to hear it. They could now go back for the only decent meal they were going to get that day. After a quick debriefing, the rest of the evening was theirs to do with as they wished. Bion had plans to hang out with the guys at the cantina. Toby was going to just sit in his tent and be quiet, maybe pound out a letter to his folks. There wasn't much else to do. Bion turned the Land Rover in the direction of camp and silence returned to the cab. Toby watched the surroundings while Bion watched the horizon, looking for the new camp. It was at that moment that another SCUD flew in their direction.

Bion stopped the truck and they waited. This missile was flying lower than it should have, and as it came closer, the roar was deafening and the quake of the truck became violent. The truck shuddered so hard, that every screw, bolt, and weld began to scream in sympathy. A clipboard on the dash flew in the air and landed on Toby's left kneecap, causing an intense amount of pain. A radio that was held to the visor on the driver's side suddenly came loose from its clip and smacked Bion smartly in the forehead, leaving a trickle of blood as evidence of contact. And, just as it seemed that the truck was going to fly apart and leave them in the open, the SCUD flew by and every motion stopped dead.

Both men leaped from the truck and tracked the SCUD as it flew off into the distance. It suddenly took a downward arc and they could see the smoke cloud and ash of the explosion. As both men were standing in the open doors of the Land Rover, Bion looked across to Toby, who stood with his mouth open and looking right back.

"Muthafucka! Did that just land where I think it landed?"

Toby nodded. "If my calculations are correct, bro, thank whatever Gods you worship that the Iraqi didn't think to send that while you had your cock in your hands or you and I would be singing with the choir invisible."

"Jesus. H. Christ!"

Toby whistled through his teeth and muttered, "Amen to that, bro. Amen to that." He inhaled deeply and reached for the cigarette pack.

One jumped out, not because he was really trying, but because his hands were shaking that badly. He fumbled it to his lips, lit it, and then drew a ragged breath to inhale. He stood, mesmerized at the cloud, still rising up dark against the sky.

Bion's voice was urgent and demanding. "You comin', bossman? Because I'm thinkin', if we don't hit camp soon, I'm gonna drop a load in my shorts."

Toby felt his own bowels go hot and liquid in his belly. He gripped the door handle with one hand, the back of the seat with his other, trying to hide the fact that his hands were shaking hard. He stood still, his mouth hanging open, to keep his teeth from clacking together because his jaw was shaking as well. Too close. Way too close.

He turned to get back in the truck, when a flash of light caught his eye. The flash came from a nearby dune and kept twinkling in the sunlight, beckoning him. He rubbed his eyes, thinking that it would clear his vision, but when he took his hands away, the flash was still there.

Alarm bells were going off in his head. The dream, this was just like the dream. No, he told himself, no, this is not that damn dream. But it was. He knew it. He also knew that he had to go see what that was, what was making that flash. It couldn't be a sniper rifle; if it had been, he'd be dead already. He'd been standing out in the open long enough to have been a fairly decent target. No, he shouldn't. No, this was a bad idea. But that pull was too strong.

He slammed the Rover's door, giving in to the pull. He couldn't stop, not even if he'd wanted to. He had to keep walking, that compulsion to see what was there, what was making that flash. Even if the hair was standing up on the back of his neck; even if his mouth was as dry as the sand under his feet. He had to know. He had to keep walking. He had to keep moving. Even though a voice was calling his name, even if he could have turned around….

Toby had walked about thirty paces toward the dune when he saw the tunnel. It was a gaping mouth in the sand, rocks and something resembling stone beams around the mouth of the tunnel. The sand had formed a ramp to walk upon, disappearing down in the darkness. He kept walking, thinking that if he could see whatever was inside it, that it couldn't be that deep. He got closer, but there was no light inside this tunnel. He decided that he was going to need the torch from the back of the Rover if he was going to check it out.

He turned around and started back. He hated walking on these damn dunes because they always felt like rotten stone, crumbly and with no substance underneath. He made it back up the ramp and retraced his steps.

When Toby got back to the truck, he walked to the back of it and rummaged through the case of equipment. He found what he was looking for, two battery powered lanterns and started back toward the dune. He had gone a few paces from the Land Rover when he suddenly remembered Bion. He turned back to the vehicle and motioned the man to come with him, but Bion still sat in the cab, not moving and staring at the dashboard. Toby called Bion's name, but the guy didn't appear to have heard him. He walked back, going to the driver's side, talking as he came.

"Bion, you okay? Come on, man. We have to check this out."

Toby had gotten to the door, had his hand on the handle, when he saw Bion reach down between his legs to get the water bottle stored there. Bion's skin had gone pale, more a shade of gray than the dark coffee brown tone of his skin. Bion was panting like an animal too long in the sun, and the sweat was pouring down his face and soaking the collar of his shirt.

"Bion? What's wrong, man? Talk to me."

Bion shook his head. He opened his mouth to try, and quickly whipped open the door to puke on the sand below. Toby jumped back just in time to keep the spew from landing on his pants or shoes. He waited until Bion was finished and had sat back upright in the seat.

"Bion?"

Bion took another swallow of water from the bottle before turning to stare at Toby with eyes that were bloodshot and as wide as he could possibly open them. He looked as if he was going to burst into tears at any moment.

It hit him as hard as the heat from the desert's blast furnace. "Bion, dude! Come on, man. It was just a dream. It's cool. It's okay."

Bion just shook his head. "No, it's not. Please! Let's just get out of here."

"This could be a munitions dump and we have to check it out. You know that, man. Come on, let's do it while we still have daylight."

"No. No! I can't do that. Please. Let's just get out of here. We just keep beatin' feet like we never seen that and we forget about it."

Toby stepped back to the driver's side of the cab and kicked sand over the mess on the ground until it was covered sufficiently. He opened the door and gently pulled the man out of the seat until he was standing in front of Toby. He took Bion by the shoulders, and looked into his eyes.

"Listen to me. It was a dream. That's all it was. It was an anxiety dream. Nothing more, nothing less."

"But the sand, the hole – man, I am scared shitless."

"There's nothing there that can hurt us." Toby said. Once again, his voice became his father's voice, the one he used to keep Toby from being afraid of night monsters and boogiemen. "It's all right. Listen to me. That fear is natural after the dreams you've had. But, use that fear. Don't let it cripple you. Don't let it control you. Just be careful. I'm not going to let anything happen to you. I promised you, remember?"

"But the sand—"

"That is not going to happen," Toby insisted. He had to convince his friend. The problem was convincing himself now. "Not on my watch! We're going to be careful and, if there is trouble, we're going to split fast. Hell, you can stand right by the exit. You don't even have to go in. I'll go. You'll see; nothing will happen. Shit, this is probably nothing, but I have to check it out. Do you understand me?"

"I can't do it, man."

"Yes. You can." Toby had not let go of Bion's shoulders and was practically willing the man to go along. His voice was soothing but insistent; Toby never broke the eye contact. "You have to trust me. Come on, soldier. Let's get this done. The sooner we do, the sooner we're outa here. Nothing will happen. You'll see."

Toby stopped just long enough to radio their position in, let CNC know what was going on. When he'd finished, he picked up the two lanterns from the hood of the Land Rover where he had set them and started back toward the tunnel. Bion still didn't look convinced but he followed. They arrived at the entrance and Bion stopped. Toby debated trying to convince Bion again but decided against it. Toby turned one of the lanterns and entered the tunnel.

He had walked about ten paces inside the entrance before noticing that this was a fairly shallow cave. In the back, it split into two tunnels. He wasn't sure which one to explore first and mentally wished that Bion had not been so freaked out. It would have helped to have him in there; they could search both tunnels simultaneously. He pulled a quarter out of his pocket; heads, he'd go right and tails, he'd go left. He didn't have to make that choice; the crunching noises of boots on sand were insistent and came to a halt right behind him.

"You okay, man?" Toby asked.

"No. I ain't," Bion answered, his voice breaking in the middle of the sentence.

He handed Bion the spare lantern. "Well, we're gonna make short work of this. Then we're gone. Splitsville. Okay?"

Bion grabbed Toby's arm with his free hand and squeezed tightly on Toby's bicep. "We don't gotta to do this at all, brother. C'mon, let's make like trees and leaf. *Let's just go.*"

"Look. Stand right here, Corporal," Toby said, terse and formal. "Just stay here. If anything happens, you'll be able to run for the fresh air. I have to check this out. I *have* to. You stay here and make sure that we don't have any hostiles coming up on our asses and I'll check this out. I'll be as quick as I can. Okay?"

Bion was panting again, but answered with a curt nod.

Toby decided to hit the left tunnel first and began to gingerly make his way through the rocky opening. It was tough going because the lantern didn't seem to be cutting through the darkness much; he had to go more slowly than even *he* was comfortable with. When he had gone twenty paces, he called back to Bion, who acknowledged his call. So far, so good, and he continued his trip.

He hit a point where he could see that the walls were not just ordinary sand. They were hard packed – he remembered a trip to Florida when he'd been a kid. The family had gone to the beaches, arriving just in time to see a sand sculpture contest that had been sponsored by one of the local hotels there. None of the contestants had made the usual, boring sand castle; no, these were fanciful sculptures of fish and horses, of tableaus of nature and a film or two. But he remembered that they sculptures had sprayed the sand with some sort of substance so that it was hard packed and as rocky as concrete.

These walls were like those sculptures, hard and stone like but most definitely sand. They had been sculpted into almost smooth surfaces but with hieroglyphs of some sort carved into them. He couldn't make them out, but he could see faint characters of pictographs and something that looked like writing. He looked down at his feet and noticed that the floor of the tunnel was a mild rake downward. He hadn't noticed that he was going down deeper into the bowels of the cave.

He followed the passageway to its conclusion, a dead-end that had been carved with the same symbols. There was debris strewn over the floor of the tunnel; pottery pieces, glittery bits that looked like glass or jewels. One thing was certain; this was not a munitions dump. Or, at least, this part of it wasn't. He started back, slowly as before. It was at that moment that he noticed that the sand of the floor was vibrating at a furious pace. He couldn't hear the thunder, but knew it was a passing SCUD going overhead and stood still waiting for it to pass.

Suddenly, a feeling of great fear gripped him. *Bion!* The thought slapped him hard in the chest and he took off running, smacking into the walls every few feet. He came to the end of the tunnel, to see that Bion had stopped just inside of the tunnel's edge. He was standing gawping at Toby; his eyes wide open to show the whites. The thunder was louder and louder; the tunnel was now shaking like an earthquake. The SCUD found its target—the waiting Land Rover—and exploded with a fury.

The roof collapsed in a wave of sand. Bion was up to his waist in a pile before either of them could move; his screams filled the tunnel, the echoes dislodging more sand. Toby shouted his name and dropped the lantern, running to sandy flood pouring down. But, it was too late. The ceiling collapsed and Bion disappeared from view.

Toby scooped handfuls of sand away from the growing mound. He was going on blind instinct, scooping as fast as he could, first two-handed, then one hand at a time, then back to the two-handed. He called Bion's name, throwing the sand behind him and it flew across the floor. For every handful that he sent flying behind him, two more replaced it from the ceiling. It became harder and harder to breathe, and Toby was scooping so hard and fast, that he hadn't noticed that he was now sweating. Sweat mixed with the sand and became a streak of mud running down his cheeks and forehead.

The sand stopped falling but Toby kept on. He worked for what seemed like forever, and was finally making a dent in the pile, when a hand suddenly shot from the sand. It grabbed at his wrist, and he began to work harder and faster, moving sand with his other hand. The one poking from the mound gripped his wrist so hard, that he was afraid it would break from the pressure.

"Bion! Hold on! Oh God, hold on. Hold on, I'm coming. Please, God, please, God! *Hold on, Bion, please hold on!*"

But, it was not to be. Another SCUD passed overhead at that moment, bringing a fresh layer of sand as more of the tunnel's ceiling collapsed around the mound in front of him. The weight of the sand was immense; it had to be because the mound was as tall as Toby was. The hand released his wrist, grabbed it again, and then released it permanently. The dark skinned hand stood out in contrast to the white sand, and the greenish light from the lantern gave it an unearthly glow. Toby cried out hoarsely, and started scooping sand again. But the hand never moved. Toby scooped and scooped, and after a time, came upon Bion's head.

The eyes were still open, and there was a film of dust on the whites. His mouth was open and filled with the sand that had enveloped him. The look of unmistakable fear was on his face. The face was staring upwards as if unbelieving and terrified of the outcome. Toby couldn't breathe. He backed away, trying to gasp for air, trying to pull some into his lungs, until he tripped over the lantern. He landed hard on his butt, and began to moan. He continued to moan for a long time.

Chapter Four

Toby wrapped his arms around his knees and shut his eyes as tightly as he could, rocking and trying shut out the image of the sand and that hand still reaching out. His mind was racing in a million directions. The sand filtered down, sifted sugar from an unseen baker's hand to fall quietly around him. The lantern light turned the sprinkles into glittering phosphorescence, the mound of sand into a horror show of yellowish green. The exposed head and flesh of the man contained within the heap had another dusting of the silt, but the hand still reached out to Toby. The head was tilted back so that the eyes were still staring at him. This was too much of a freak show. Toby just couldn't look at it anymore. So he made himself as small as he could and closed his eyes to the sight.

Toby kept rocking, holding tightly to his legs, trying to grip something real and solid. He needed something to control, anything. He couldn't stop the pounding of his heart in his chest. It felt as if he'd swallowed the timpani section of an orchestra. He wanted to cry, but nothing would come. He wanted to stop and lay back, to sleep and just let it all flow over him like water, but his arms had locked now, and the rocking went on of its own accord. The deep guttural animal noise in the back of his throat moaned low in his ears and filled his mouth with terror.

As he rocked, he finally worked up the nerve to peek over his knees and saw the sand and the body as it lay. The sand fell on the exposed skin, a layer of dust that turned the skin ashen. He suddenly remembered those bodies that had been found in the ruins of Pompeii – they looked like this, that same grey color and sandy texture. Toby started to shake and he reached behind him to take the lantern, and turned it off, plunging the cave in complete darkness. He could take anything, as long as he didn't have to stare at that corpse.

. . . *crunch, crunch* . . .

He froze, arms wrapped tightly around his knees and he stopped his breathing. He heard something, the sounds of boots. He wasn't alone in here; someone was in here with him. Someone walking toward him. He felt movement, and was suddenly sure that Bion was coming to get him.

No, there's no one there. No one. It's all in my head. Where's the lantern?

. . . crunch, crunch . . . footsteps . . . coming . . .

He groped around on the sand, wildly reaching for anything, until his fingers closed on the familiar plastic shape and he snapped the light back on, throwing a sickly wash over the cave again. He clutched it tightly to his chest as his sight came to rest once again on the horror. He shook his head, slowly at first, then violently.

"You son of a bitch," he muttered. "You stupid son of a bitch, why didn't you stay outside like I told you?" He started panting now, drawing breath as fast as his lungs could inhale and exhale. "You son of a bitch!"

He raised the lantern, drew his arm back to throw it at the body, and thought better of it. In his frustration, all he could do was repeat, "You son of a bitch, I told you to stay outside. *I told you to wait outside.*"

There was no answer and he closed his mouth with a click of his teeth. He took another deep breath and blew it out slowly. He had to get a grip. He had to do something.

Toby put the lantern down and stood on shaky knees. He knew what he had to do, if for no other reason than pure decency. He took a tentative step. When it was obvious that his legs weren't going to give out on him, he made his way over to where his friend had been buried to his neck. He dropped to his knees, and took out a bandanna from his back pocket. He began to clean off the layer of soot from the skin, speaking softly as he worked.

"Oh, man, what the fuck did I do?" He chuckled softly. "Why the fuck did you listen to me? You know I ain't worth shit as a commander, you stupid idiot. Why didn't you just stay outside? You'd still be alive, you dumb ass."

He gently wiped the hand sticking out of the sand. "Oh, God, Bion," he whispered. "I am so sorry. I am so fucking sorry."

The eyes were still crusted with the silt. It was only right, so he ever so gently cleaned the dirt from them, and then closed the lids.

"I can't have you staring at me, bro."

Toby stuck the bandanna back in his pocket, and stood again. He bent over to scoop double handfuls when he could, pushing it over the other side when he couldn't.

"Well, we're both fuckered now, bro. That entry is shut off. Hell, I can see it from here. Why didn't you stay out there? You could be reporting our position. You'd be alive."

Toby had exposed the upper chest, both shoulders and arms. He lifted Bion's head and laid it against his own shoulder while reaching under the arms with his hands, then wrapped his arms around the chest. He tried to pull the body out, lifting with his legs, but it was a no go. The body was still wedged in there as tight as the cork in a bottle.

"Shit."

He carefully replaced the limbs as they had been and went back to his task. The more sand he scooped, the more silt was in the air.

"Goddamn sand fleas" He dug into his skin with his nails, which were mercifully short, but they left welts on his skin anyway. He grimaced as he scratched, sweat breaking out on his body. The sweat made the sand stick to his skin, the itch more furious. His scratching and digging became even more frenzied until the sweat also contained the sheen of blood.

In his gyrations, he wasn't paying attention to what he was doing, and Toby rapped his elbow against the skull, causing the head to sharply loll to one side, and there was a sudden pop. Toby jumped back and the itching was quickly forgotten.

"Oh, Jesus Christ. Oh God," he moaned.

He clutched at his chest as the pressure inside built up again. "I can't breathe, bro. Can you dig that? I can't breathe, oh shit. Man, I'm gonna die here. There's no air, and I can't breathe. Fuck a duck!"

The world was starting to get fuzzy and grey, so Toby put his hands on his hips and bent over, closing his eyes on the way down. The blood came rushing into his head and, little by little, he started to get control again.

"Okay, buddy, I'm gonna get you out of there. It's okay. We're overdue and they know that." Toby slowly straightened up again, wiping the sweat from his brow with the back of his hand. "It's okay. They'll come for us. We'll get out of here. They'll see the wreck outside, the cave in. They'll get us out of here. You watch."

His breathing slowed down to a normal rate and his skin slowly lost the clammy, sweaty shine. Toby was still warm, but he was losing the edge of terror. His heart was slowing down and his chest no longer felt like it was going to explode. He crossed back to the mound, and scooped the sand again.

"Oh, man, this was a balls-up operation, doncha think, bro? I don't think I can take too much more of this shit; I gotta be straight with you. Too much more of this shit and I'm gonna be a guest at the local laughing academy. Yup, drive me right over the edge, for damn sure." Toby stopped in mid-scoop and looked down at the head. "Yeah, you're right, bro. I'm talking to a dead man, I'm already there."

He scooped more sand until he had uncovered Bion's body to the waist. Once again, he squatted down and got a grip around the chest. He paused for a moment, looking down into the face.

"This is gonna hurt you more than it hurts me, bro. But then, I don't think I'm feeling a whole lot right now. Except maybe that I want a big glass of scotch. Yeah, big bottle of scotch would be real good." Toby tightened his grip. "Here goes nothing."

The body slid easily out of the sandy coffin. Toby half carried, half dragged it backwards for several paces away from the cave in. He tenderly laid the body on the ground and began to wipe the sand that had drifted back onto the face.

"There ya go, bro. There ya go. Get that shit off my man. Get you cleaned up. Can't let them find you here, not like this. Oh, man, what the fuck did you listen to me for? Why didn't you wait outside?"

As Toby knelt next to the corpse, he decided to pray. He wasn't sure he could do it, but he figured that it couldn't be that hard. But, the words wouldn't come. He had absolutely no idea of what to say or how to say it. For that moment, the right words were so important; this was his friend, his responsibility. He had to get the words right. Instead, he simply knelt there, feeling an agony that words couldn't describe.

"Sorry, bro." He gave up, plopping down on his ass again. Tears were streaming down his cheeks, leaving streaks in the dust on his skin. "Me and God – well, we're not exactly on a first name basis, you know. I wanted to do right by you, Bion. I am so sorry, man. I am so sorry. I shoulda kicked your ass back out there. I shoulda. I shoulda given you a direct order to *stay outside*."

He scooched closer to the body and absentmindedly started brushing off the uniform again. "Yep, this was a seriously balls up thing. What the fuck *are* we doing here? You were right; this was not the place to be. Well, I'll get us outta here, son. I will. You'll see." He looked around the cave, and his eyes rested on the other tunnel. "I wonder – I wonder if there's anything in there. I wonder . . . ."

He had a reason to move now, his original objective in coming into this hole. He had to do something, anything that would give him something to do other than sit and stare at the body. He would give himself over to duty. Then he wouldn't have to think anymore; wouldn't have to see that image of the rescue just out of his grasp. He wouldn't have to think about his guilt or remorse. He wouldn't have to stare at that dead man. He could just do something that would make it normal again.

"You wait right here, sonny boy, and I'm gonna check out the lay o' the land. Do me a recon. Yeah, yeah; dat's de ticket." He put his fists on his hips, striking a decidedly super hero pose. "Recon-man." He dropped them to his sides again. There was something so awkward and stupid about that, making a joke about it.

So, got up off the sandy ground and picked up the lantern. He had already explored the tunnel to his left and there was nothing to report. He would follow the road not taken; or in this case, the tunnel not explored.

It proved to be more difficult than he first thought. The mind was willing; however, the feet were not. He looked down and saw them staying put in the same spot. Stupid feet, he'd never get that recon done if he just stood there. It took him a few seconds to convince them that they really needed to move. His left foot stepped out and his right foot followed suit. He paused only once to gaze back at the body and then, he was walking.

He started down the tunnel making his way gingerly because the lantern was not throwing as much light as it should. There was light for an arm's length, and the darkness owned the rest. He took his time, pausing every few feet to examine the walls of sculpted sand, adorned with the same strange hieroglyphs. Some looked like birds, some like other animals but he couldn't tell what kind. They didn't look like any animals he'd ever seen; and having been raised on a farm, he'd seen a lot of them. After a few stops, he also noticed that the walls and floor were carved stone.

Wait a minute, stone? Carved stone? These are stone blocks? In the desert? Stone blocks?

He was spending far too much time looking at the stone at his feet and not enough of looking forward, so the change in the surroundings took him by surprise. He noticed that he could see things a little more clearly than he was before, and could actually make out the color of his boots . . . .

. . . brown boots walking . . . .

He stopped dead in his tracks, bathed in the light of a warm summer day. Toby shielded his eyes briefly. Above and beside him was the stone of wall and floor, but there was a strong sunlight ahead of him. Was this a way out of the cave? Had he been so wrong? He had to continue down the tunnel. He had to know what was there. And with every step he took, the light became brighter until he was absorbed in it. There was more than just light, it was a scent of spices, of cinnamon, clove, and something else.

Wait. This is fresh air. That must mean an opening back here. Where is this tunnel leading me?

There was something else, another scent was there underneath the spices. It was a something that he couldn't name, and it came on a breeze wafting over his face. *What the hell is this place?* He kept walking, now curiosity was getting to him. *Is that music? I hear music, I know it. That's it, I'm losing it. I'm coming unglued. So, this is what it's like to go crazy. Not so bad, actually.*

And without fanfare or prelude, he was no longer in the tunnel. He stood in the middle of a vast oasis. He looked around and saw date trees filled with fruit and in the distance, tents. They were the sort of tents that his Aunt Renee had read stories about – huge affairs in colors of purples, golds, and reds, resplendent in flowing banners and silk. They were gathered as a small city might be, in a cluster around one in particular. There was a huge pool of crystal blue water shimmered in the middle of the gathering and the trees around it were full of exotic birds, cooing and billing and squawking.

Damn, he thought, *when I hallucinate, I do it in style.*

The tent in the center was a huge sapphire affair, ornate in structure with what looked like silk banners waving in the breezes. There were patterns on the sides and the top but he wasn't close enough to see what they were, only that they sparkled in the sun. Somehow, he had walked from one desert to another. This had to be civilization; it had to be where he could find shelter and help. He'd find people here and that tent looked like the place to start.

As he walked along, two thoughts dawned on him. The first was that there were no camels, no horses, and no mode of transportation. Surely, they traveled. These were nomads, they needed some method to . . . well, *nomad*. But, there was nothing. Maybe they didn't go anywhere. But, wouldn't they have more permanent structures than tents? Maybe that's where the vehicles were, the camels or whatever animals they used to travel with. Maybe, these people *were* nomads but they kept their stock in the tents. That could be it. That had to be it. There really was hope.

The closer he came to the sapphire tent, the more ornate and rich it seemed. The material was of a rare silk, and the dyes were rich in color. There were banners of gold and silver flowing and flapping from the tent poles poking through the top. Whoever owned this tent was truly wealthy; perhaps a sheik with a Rolls or Bentley tucked in one of the other tents. Yeah, that had to be it; some eccentric sheik who didn't use camels or horses, but automobiles to move his caravan. It was the twentieth century, after all. This was a different breed of nomad. Probably had a computer in there and a satellite dish to reach the outside world. In that case, this mythical sheik had a radio. Toby could radio in his position and be assured of a quick recovery.

And so, he walked. But in the desert, distance is deceptive. What looked like a brief journey was a long distance. Toby was forced to stop several times to catch his breath when he realized that he had been hurrying along at a short trot.

After what seemed like hours, he finally arrived at the crystal blue water. Toby used his hands to dipper the cool water over his head and down his back. He was surprised to find that he was thirsty and used his hands again to drink deeply. The water tasted pure and clean; it refreshed him as no other water had done before.

He was now close enough to see the same strange markings from the tunnel walls were woven into the tent fabric. There were gold and silver trinkets hung as tassels around the seams of the tent, glittering in the sunlight. He could hear the music more loudly now, and was sure that it was coming from inside. The tune was unfamiliar, but the style was what he imagined an Arabian tune to be. The instruments were of a haunting flute or recorder variety, and he heard the taunt of cymbals and sitars. The song, hypnotic and lilting, called him inside.

He threw back the cloth that passed for the door and waited as his eyes became accustomed to the sudden dimness. He saw earthen lamps with neatly trimmed wicks set around the perimeter of the outer structure. Another smaller tent was inside; the material was a deep cobalt blue and also adorned with the strange markings. These glyphs and trinkets were of silver only, and the floor was covered with a lush Persian rug. Huge overstuffed silk pillows had been scattered on the floor, and lounging on one of them was a fat, white Persian cat with the truest china blue eyes he had ever seen.

He heard laughter coming from inside the inner tent. He threw aside the material and stepped through the opening.

Once inside, he was definitely not prepared for this sight. The inner sanctum was, *huge*. It, too, was much larger than it appeared from outside. The overstuffed pillows were strewn about the floor in here as well. The carpeting was plush and thick. He could hear the music distinctly, lulling him into its sensuality. The strange mix of spices was stronger now, almost cloying with the cinnamon and clove.

And something else, what is that smell? I know it; I can't quite put my finger on what it is.

The laughter brought him back to the sense of surrealism in the room. Lounging on the pillows were beings that he couldn't think to describe to anyone else. They were golden skinned and black eyed. Each one had a golden hoop in the lobe of one ear. Each being was thin and elfin in appearance, dressed in silks of rainbow colors. They were genderless and graceful. Toby could not take his eyes from them. Those that were not watching *him* intently were fondling and caressing one another. Some of them were smoking from great brass hookahs and clouds of fragrant smoke rose in the air.

Of course, opium. That's what I smell, opium. But, there's something else; what is it?

Toby heard laughter and he turned see one of them giggling behind its hand and pointing at him. He clenched his jaw in indignation and tried to ignore the pointing individual, but it was becoming difficult. Others were pointing and giggling, but he simply chose not to look at them. The room was filled with these beings, lounging and smoking, and now staring at him. He realized that he had been staring first, and didn't wonder at why they would find him such a fascination.

At the center of the sea of bodies, was another, dressed in cobalt blue silks, to match the inner tent. This being was radiant with pale, almost luminescent skin and the darkest eyes he had ever seen; the color of dark chocolate. It was painfully thin and reclined on a chaise of royal blue. Its lithe fingers were resplendent with jeweled rings of silver and precious stones. Its slender legs were footed in slippers that curled up at the toes; one was crossed daintily over the other. It waved another being over and whispered something in the other's ear, then sent the other scuttling off.

This pale being then turned its attention to Toby and when it spoke, a deep male voice came forth. Toby was caught off guard again, because he was thinking it was really female.

"You will forgive them for their amazement. It's been so long since we've had a guest in this hallowed hall that they seem to have forgotten their manners. You are most welcome. Please. Come and sit with me."

And so saying, the being uncrossed its legs and sat up in the chaise. It patted the seat in front with one jeweled hand, then reclined again.

"Oh, do come and sit. Please? I can promise you the most special of treats."

Toby no more wanted to sit on that chaise than he wanted to go back to that tunnel of horrors. But he was a guest. He crossed over to the chaise, still goggling at his surroundings, and sat at the end. The being leaned on one elbow and rested its chin against the fingers of its hand. There was a glee in its eyes that made them sparkle and a slight smile decorated its face.

It watched with amusement as Toby tried to collect himself. The young one that his host had originally waved over came to Toby with a solid gold goblet filled with wine of the most exquisite variety. He handed Toby a plate of dates and figs and confectionery. Toby realized that he was ravenous. He thanked this young one and began to eat.

It watched with the same mirth and glee as its guest ate heartily. If Toby's glass, at any time, was in danger of being empty, it clapped its hands and the same youth filled it immediately. All about him were watching intently, as was his host. No attempt at conversation was made until Toby finished his food.

"Thank you. It was wonderful."

The being smiled warmly and waved a jeweled hand as if the hospitality was Toby's due. "Of course, of course. We simply cannot have guests sit and not have them be fed or refreshed. We are so happy to have a guest after such a long time. Are we not?"

The staring faces nodded in unison.

"And so, now that you've supped, you must tell us a story."

The sea of smiles now became a chorus of "yes, yes, a story" and the beings gathered around closely.

"No, I couldn't. Really, I'm not a story teller," Toby felt very self-conscious. "I, uh, well, I really don't know any."

"Oh, but you must," the bejeweled figure implored. "You see, we must be amused. Call it the price of your repast. A simple story, some news of the rest of the world that can amuse us. Please, entertain us."

"But, I really don't know any stories."

The being sat back and sighed. "Well, then you must tell us of yourself. By what name are you known?"

"I am called Toby. My given name is Tobias."

The others started tittering and he heard his name repeated throughout the room.

The being beside him nodded. "Tobias. Tell us what has brought you here."

"Well, I'm here with the United States Army on the behalf of the Saudi Arabian government—"

The being interrupted him with a bored yawn. "No, no; that's not what we want at all. We want to know why you're *here*."

Toby looked away from the sea of faces to the being sitting on the chaise. "I don't understand."

As if speaking to a child, it spoke slowly. "You see, there's a reason we get so few guests. We have set ourselves off from the outside world so that only those who have a great need and are willing to make a sacrifice may find us. You must be in great need – and you've already made a sacrifice – so you are here for something. We wish to know what it is. What has brought you to us?"

Toby still didn't understand. "Well, there was a cave-in that killed my friend, and I'm—"

The being once again waved away his words. "We know all of this. What do you *want*?"

Toby set down the goblet. "Look, all I want to do is use your phone or radio and contact my unit. I need to let them know that I've lost a man, and then I'm out of here. So, if you'll just—"

"You have no idea, do you?"

It actually thought he should know all the rules of the game, whatever game he was playing. Toby decided he was better off admitting the truth than trying to cover with a lie of sorts. He couldn't be any worse off than he was at the present.

"No, I guess I don't," he answered. He tried to keep the edge of irritation out of his voice "Look, I don't mean to intrude, so if you don't have a radio, just point me to someone who does, and I'll go ahead and leave and let you get back to, uh, whatever it was you were doing."

This answer brought another chorus of giggles. Toby bit back a retort of barely suppressed anger, and stood up. This had become annoying and his patience was worn very thin. The being on the chaise patted the seat once again. Toby looked down into the being's eyes and felt the anger draining. His whole body seemed to be losing the tension and energy that was holding him erect. Without meaning to, he let go and simply sat back down. When it spoke again, it seemed to be speaking only to Toby, but his words were for the others.

"Please, *please*; we must be kind to our guest. He doesn't understand. So, let us explain."

"Please do," Toby said.

"Well, you know . . . . We are very familiar with your war. We are not *part* of it, but we are familiar with it. We have gathered here to get away from it and to get away from the *others*. And as far as going back to your – what did you call it, your *unit*? – well, that's impossible. You see, you're still in the cave."

"Excuse me?"

"This place is of my making, you see. I have created this oasis out of the darkness and the chaos. It is our place of peace, away from the dreary world of the *others*. Because it *is* different, you see. This is a magickal place."

Toby opened and shut his mouth very quickly. What was he – it – whatever – talking about? He had a weird feeling in the pit of his stomach.

It watched him as if it were waiting for something, then it went on. "Surely you know what a djinn is, do you not?"

Toby had no earthly idea. He checked his internal dictionary and pulled the closest word he could come up with. "Uh, a genie, right?"

This answer brought another round of giggles; Toby made a great effort to look only at his host.

"Well, yes and no," the elfin figure answered. "Same power, no master. You see, I travel where I wish and do as I wish. I answer to no one, and no one answers to me." The golden lips smiled. "No popping out of lamps and bottles for me. Not me! But, since you've found us, we are prepared to offer you the same thing a genie would. We offer you three wishes."

Toby took a deep breath and exhaled slowly. This was going to be their entertainment; provoking him, teasing him, and keeping him captive. His military mind tried to focus on solutions to this problem, but an identification of the problem was the most he could do. These beings had been sucking on that opium pipe a bit too much.

Out loud, he only answered, "Yeah, right."

It giggled, clapping its hands. "Of course, you think us intoxicated from the smoke. But I assure you that I am speaking most truthfully. Those who come here are specifically searching for us."

It stopped its narrative to drink from the goblet still clutched in one slender hand and then pointed to Toby with a manicured finger. "You, who have found us by sheer accident, will be given these three wishes freely. So, entertain us. What would you have? Riches beyond measure? Power? What?"

It was at this point, that another being nestled itself at Toby's knee. This being had china blue eyes and alabaster skin, its lips were full. Toby suddenly thought of the cat in the outer tent. As if it could read his thoughts, it began to purr and rub against his thigh. Toby found himself aroused as the hands began to caress his leg, working their way to his inner thigh.

Oh, dear God, that's what I smell, he told himself. *The musky scent of sex. Not only did I walk into an opium den, I entered into the middle of an orgy.*

Toby reached down and took hold of this being's hands. He had to stop the caresses; the reaction in his crotch was stiff and throbbing. He pushed the hands away, heard its giggles combined with sighs of displeasure. He took a few breaths to cleanse and focus, feel relaxation between his legs.

"Look, this is all nice and good, but I need to get back to my unit now."

The being on the chaise stuck out its lower lip in a childish pout. "You would refuse our gift? How ungrateful these *others* are, would you not agree?"

"No, not ungrateful," Toby answered quickly. "I just have to get back. No, I – I guess I accept your gift."

"Then, we will help you," the djinn answered, mollified. "But, first, you must have your wishes. Then you may be on your way."

"Look, thank you for the food and drink, but I really don't need anything."

"Oh, nonsense. You know . . . ," the creature started. It leaned forward, as if it were about to whisper some great secret. "The last *other* that was here wished for wealth and power. He, of course, was not like you, a seeker of knowledge. He was, well, simple. Insane. It amused us to give him this. I believe he is the cause of your little war, right now. Yes?"

The blue eyed being nodded, never taking its gaze from Toby's crotch.

"Yes, of course, I'm right," the djinn went on. "I always am. So, Tobias, you will now entertain us with your wishes. Tell us, what will you have?"

The wine bearer now appeared at the side of the chaise. He whispered in the djinn's ear and it nodded.

"Yes, yes, of course, we should tell him that, shouldn't we? You see there are some *restrictions* that we must make you aware of."

"Restrictions?"

"Well, yes," the djinn explained. "You see, we can't just hand you everything, you know. There must be some limits."

"Yeah, yeah, I saw that movie. Can't raise from the dead, can't make someone fall in love with me, all that shit."

The djinn clapped its jeweled hands with a triumphant look on its face and laughed heartily. "Yes, yes, yes. You have it. Will you have riches, Tobias?"

Toby shook his head. They weren't going to let him pass without their entertainment, such as it were. Not that he really believed this garbage but, at this point – in an effort to get the hell out of there – he might as well play along. He thought for a few seconds before he made his first wish.

"Immortality. My first wish is for immortality."

The djinn nodded in agreement. "A good start. And do you wish for immortality as a youth?"

"No, as I am is fine."

"Done." The djinn settled back into the cushions of the chaise, jeweled fingers tracing the arm. "What is your second wish?"

"Uh, I don't know. Time travel. I want to be able to travel through time."

The djinn nodded again. "Interesting. Why time travel?"

"Oh, hell, I don't know. I guess if you're passing out wishes, I can use one to travel through time. Not that I believe this shit, but what the hell, I'm entertaining you," he answered with a bit of sarcasm. "I guess it would be nice to travel in time and see the sights. You know, meet Einstein, Da Vinci, see the future and how it all turns out. That kind of thing."

"Yes, yes, I suppose someone such as you would want that. Done. And your third wish?"

Toby thought for a few moments more.

"Well, if I'm time traveling, I suppose I should be able to understand and speak the language of wherever I am. It would be a pain in the ass to go to early Rome and not speak or understand Latin."

The djinn laughed and nodded again. "Quite true. It *would* make you stand out in a crowd, wouldn't it? It might even cause some problems, mightn't it?"

"Yeah, it would."

"Very well, done. Now, the restrictions."

"Right. Restrictions," Toby agreed.

"Yes. I give you these gifts, but there will be sacrifice," the djinn said. For the first time, there was compassion in the creature's voice. "You cannot use them for personal gain. This little *accident* of yours is a good example. What has happened, has happened. You may not change it. It was this Bion's destiny to go as he did and when he did. It cannot be changed. And as for your immortality – well, I can promise you, it does not wear well for you *others*. But, you cannot die, so if you wish to leave this plane of existence, you will have to make that decision for yourself and then do it. For yourself."

The beings sitting around him were watching him more intently now, but more than that. They were chanting, low and steady.

Something was happening and Toby wasn't sure that this was going to be a good thing.

"And one more thing," the djinn said. "I will give you this also. In order to use these gifts and in order to pass beyond the veil when you *are* ready, you must pass them on."

"And, how am I going to do that?"

"These gifts I give you will be tied to a token."

The djinn lifted one jeweled hand, and plucked a ring from the thumb. It took Toby's right hand, and held it.

"This ring is of silver and selenite. Do you know what that is?"

"No, I don't."

"This stone is used for time travel. You must wear this always until you are ready to leave your existence. This will be your token. Do you understand?"

The chanting was growing louder, and Toby felt strange electricity building in the air around him. He was starting to grow dizzy from the wine, the opium, and the energy growing within and without his body. The more he sat and tried to focus, the more the chanting seemed to be coming from far away. His body had gone numb and everything around him was starting to melt away like a watercolor in the rain. It was a few seconds before he realized that the djinn was speaking to him, and that he needed to answer.

"Do you understand?"

"Yeah," Toby answered, his voice coming from that same faraway place as the chanting. "Yes, I do."

The djinn slipped the ring on Toby's right forefinger, and the feeling of vertigo became stronger now. "Good. My friend, Tobias, you are on a great quest now. I hope you find what you seek. We will not see you again. Allah speed you on your journey."

And no sooner had the words reached his ears, than Toby watched the world around him melt away, and the chanting, the music, the smells, and the colors became a swirl in his senses and he passed out.

When he awoke, he was back where he started. The lantern had gone out, but there was light. It took him a few minutes to realize that the light was coming from a hole above him. He squinted at the brightness of it, and then there was a shadow.

"Sir? Captain Riordan? Are you alright?"

He had no idea how long he had lain there but he knew he was dehydrated. He managed to croak out, "Yeah, yeah."

"Sir, lie still. We're going to lower some help down to you. You're injured. Don't move; we'll come to you. How many of you down there?

Toby struggled to sit up. "Just me." The sudden memory of what had happened caught up with him and he pointed towards Bion's body. "Wait, no I'm not; there's a body down here, medic. One of my men got caught in the cave in. He's dead."

"Sir, please lie still. We're coming down now."

Toby did as he was told, watching as two medics were lowered down. While they strapped him into the stretcher to lift him out, he was actually able to convince himself that he had just dreamed the whole incident.

Except for Bion. I can see his body again. Dear God, I remember it all. Even the dream.

It wasn't until they had lifted him out and he was watching the medic put an IV in his arm that he had a chance to look at his right hand.

He saw the ring. He hadn't been dreaming.

Chapter Five

Toby didn't realize how long he'd been talking until he took a sip of his coffee and tasted how cold it was. He spat the ice cold drink into the fire, sending up a hiss of steam into the air, and threw the remainder off behind him. He stared, dumbly, at the empty cup and tried to sort out his feelings. The telling had stirred up a hornet's nest inside his chest. He wasn't sure if the itch in his eyes was a memory or the tears that wanted to fall but couldn't. He wanted nothing more than to turn this whole thing off and just go, but he still had that little "restriction" to deal with. As he sat holding the cup in his hands, he tried to settle himself again by rolling it back and forth against his palms. After all of it, the stones he carried in his heart were still ice cold and hard.

Even knowing what he knew now, it didn't erase the guilt still within. He had been flown by Med-Evac to a local army hospital, where staff spoke in hushed tones around the patient. Toby had been buried alive for four days with no food and no water, and only the dead body for company. According to the prissy Army physician, Toby had spent most of it in shock and hysteria, that he'd been delusional when they brought him in. Toby knew better – he had the ring to prove it. The doctor had kept him in the hospital for a week, attached to IV's and machines, before finally releasing him back to his unit. But his heart wasn't in it anymore.

The coffee pot floated in front of his face and Toby's attention was jerked from his lap to the hand holding it. He held his cup up, watching John fill it for him. The other man replaced the pot on the grate and reseated himself. Toby held the metal rim to his lips and took a small sip from the steaming liquid, waiting for something.

John was waiting too. So far, the guy had sat there, watching the fire, and telling a long story about being in combat. That much, he could believe. The details were right, and his inner sense told him that the man had been through it. All he had to do was watch his companion's face to know that this wasn't faked. John had a fairly good sense of when he was getting lied to, and that alarm bell wasn't going off. But, did he *believe* it all?

Now, believing was another matter entirely. He could tell that the guy believed every word he was saying. But so far, John was unconvinced. He remembered a crazy who had been determined to prove that he was the reincarnation of John the Baptist. Fortunately, that particular nutcase had been thwarted and turned aside gently, but firmly. John didn't believe *that* story at all, because the teller had been a religious nut. So far, the man didn't seem to be a religious loony. It *was* a rational telling of a story. John just had one question about all of it.

"Tommy – "

"*Toby.*"

John held up his hand in an apologetic gesture. "*Toby.* Sorry. Toby, I need to know something. You said the Goddess or God told you to do this, to tell me this story. Why? Why me?"

Toby took a deep breath and reached up to scratch behind his ear. He blew it out with pursed lips before addressing the question.

"Well, there is an answer, but do you mind real bad if I don't tell you just yet?"

So far, John hadn't bolted. Toby wasn't sure if it was because he'd captivated the man or because John was truly lost. What he *did* know was that this had to come out in its own time and in its own way. Rushing to the end would be telling it badly.

He watched John chew on a corner of his lower lip, nod, and then take a sip of coffee. Toby pointed to the rock that was now under John's left knee, and drew the older man's attention to it.

"You found that for a reason, right?"

John nodded and said nothing.

"Then, I'll give you full permission to use it," Toby continued, "if I make one untoward move against you or if I haven't answered your question at the end. The reason I can't tell you now is because it's part of the story."

John nodded again and still said nothing.

Toby looked back from the large stone into John's eyes. The older man was giving nothing away and Toby was afraid for a moment. *What is he thinking?*

John just nodded a third time and relaxed, pulling his legs into a lotus position.

Toby leaned back against a large boulder and relaxed as well.

"So," John said, breaking the silence. "What happened next?"

"Spent time in a hospital from dehydration and shock," Toby answered. "They wanted me to see a shrink for a while. I knew all the head shrinker crap they were gonna lay on me. It didn't matter." Toby took another log and tossed it on the fire, sending sparks dancing in the air. "I lost a man on my watch."

"So, you didn't see a counselor? Why not?"

"Because I think they're a waste of time and money," Toby said with a snort of disgust. "I had an aunt went to one once. Jackass didn't do anything for her except pump her full of valium and new age bullshit."

"What happened to her?"

Toby rolled a small pebble between his fingers. "She went to his office for 5 years, spilled her guts out, told him all her fantasies and about how all the voices were telling her about the other side. She should have been in a hospital. He told her it was okay, and sent her home. She finally listened to the voices."

Toby drained his cup, set it down beside him, and listened to the fire crackling. He, now, tossed the pebble back and forth in his hands, sneaking a glance at John. *If that doesn't convince him I'm totally deranged, nothing will.*

John raised his eyebrows and then lowered them. He chewed that lower lip again before he asked, "So, you went back to your unit?"

"For a while. I didn't have the heart for it, to tell the truth. You know, when I first got there, I really felt that I was doing something worthwhile. After Bion – after the accident, it wasn't the same."

"What do you mean?"

Toby paused a moment to stare off into the darkness before he answered. "Oh, you know the rap. I went there to fight for freedom and democracy. Isn't that always the way? Go to war for God and Country?"

John nodded. "Yeah, that's usually the way. But, I know a lot of soldiers that come back feeling totally different, no matter how noble the cause."

"Yeah. See, that's exactly what I mean," Toby blurted out, staring at the pebble in his hand. "I was never really a soldier, but I enjoyed the dress up, the work outs, and the fact that I could score with the babes. The Army gives you great exercise facilities and the women are hot, man." Toby shook his head. "But, I didn't believe in the cause. Truth is, I didn't give a rat's ass about the crude oil in Saudi Arabia any more than I cared about what happens in China. But, I lost a good man, and I couldn't help but think it was my fault." Toby tossed the rock out into the desert night.

"How so?"

"I knew he didn't want to go in there. What it boils down to is I politely strong-armed him. I said I told him to stay at the truck, but the truth is, I gave every signal to the contrary. I did everything but dare him to follow me."

"So you felt guilty."

"Very."

John took another sip from the cup. "Sounds like you've been beating yourself up over this for a while."

"Oh, yeah. You could say that I did a lot of soul searching over that one."

"So, you left."

"Well, it wasn't that easy. You don't just walk away from the Army, you know."

"You didn't go AWOL. That's good."

"UA," Toby corrected. "In the Army, they call it UA – *unauthorized leave*. But, no, I didn't. I thought about it – and I wanted to – but I didn't. I signed up for the long haul, and I was my daddy's boy, responsible to the end. I didn't stay for the full hitch, though. I did get out a lot quicker than most."

"How did you get out early, then?"

"I got involved in a small skirmish a little later," Toby answered, pouring his third cup of coffee. "My unit was sent to secure a refinery and there was an enemy platoon guarding it. We got into a fire fight with them, and I got shot in hip and my upper chest. It was bad enough that I got another hospital stay, this time for two months, and then, I got shipped stateside and an honorable discharge. Uncle George decided to take me out of the game. I wasn't heartbroken about it."

"Did you get injured on purpose?"

Toby chuckled and shook his head. "I said I lost the fire for fighting that war, I didn't say I'd lost my sense of duty. No, I didn't get shot on purpose. I am many things, but I am *not* suicidal."

"So, where did you go?"

"I tried to go back to teaching," Toby said. "Tell you the truth; my heart wasn't into that either. I just couldn't handle those kids. Schools were a battleground, too. The little brats brought guns and knives to school. Sometimes, things happen there, too."

"You quit teaching?"

"No, I quit the public school system. The new school year had started, and every parent wants his little Johnny or Susie to have a head above the other little Johnnys and Susies. I spent the first two months of the new season doing private tutoring through the local library. Paid pretty good, but it was just the same crap. So I quit that, too."

"Where did you go?"

"Well, you could say I disappeared back into my past. I needed to be grounded, but I also needed something more. I needed my family. Actually, you could say I needed my parents. I needed to heal. So, I went home."

Chapter Six

The drive home had been a renewal of sorts. The moment he had crossed the state line from Ohio, a sensation of all things familiar filled his soul and he knew he was home. For a Saturday, there wasn't as much traffic on the road as he had expected, and it made the trip that much easier. He set the cruise control to sixty-five miles per hour, and let the old Accord do its thing, chugging along. As he rode through Florence, he reached into the black plastic case on the seat beside him, and grabbed a tape at random. He slipped the cassette from its case and stuck it into the dashboard player, and gave the volume knob a twist. Within the first verse, he was singing along with John Denver, wondering how he could leave the lady he loved; the lady in question being Denver's wife at the time, but the lady for Toby was as yet unknown.

Once he had given notice to the library, Toby had gone back to his apartment manager and turned in his notice there, as well. The man politely informed Toby of his lease and Toby told him what he could do with it. When the super threatened to keep his deposit, Toby told him what he could do with that, too, and turned on his heel and left the office. Three days later, there was a "vacate the property" order stuck in his mailbox. It got only a chuckle from him, and he went back to packing what few things he planned on taking with him. He was taking only what meant anything to him and what he could pack in the Honda. After that, and within a week's time, he had sold everything else, dumped what was left, packed the car, turned in his keys, and shaken the dust of Columbus off his feet. He had his last paycheck, his liquidated teacher's pension, the money from his possessions, and he was "outa there."

Another hour's drive and he pulled off I-75 and onto a smaller country byway. Before the interstate, there had been the state roads, and he was on Paris-Georgetown Pike. Driving through the vast array of horse farms, he watched the mares graze and the foals kick up their heels in the late summer air. He had his window rolled down and his hair was blowing in the breeze.

"Take me home," he sang to no one but the tape playing in the deck. He followed the series of country roads until he arrived at his parents' farm, turning into the driveway, and pulling up to the house. He honked the horn once, and turned off the motor.

Toby stepped out of the car, and stretched his long frame, letting the muscles relax from the long drive. He released a satisfied groan at the pleasure of it, and then sniffed the air around him. He could smell the roses of his mother's garden; the sweet fragrance of the clean air underneath it. The front yard was ablaze in colors of zinnia, clematis, and lobelia. The grass was neat and trimmed and Toby wanted to throw off his shoes and walk barefoot in it. A slight breeze was blowing across his face, and the gentle caress smoothed away some of the pain in his life.

He heard the screen door slam and turned toward the front porch and the small, slight woman standing there. She had a dishtowel in her hands, wiping them, and her face wore the look of surprise and relief. Both stood, Toby fighting the urge to run to her like the small boy that he felt like at that moment. It had been, at least, two years since he'd been home. He could do no more than gaze at her and wonder how she had gotten so old and he so young.

"Tobias? Dear Toby? Is it really you, my son? Are you really home?" One of her hands flew to her lips, to cover them.

Toby smiled and held out his arms to her. "Aye, Ma. I'm home."

With a shout of delight, the dishtowel flew into the air. The tiny woman ran across the yard, her dainty feet barely touching the grass, and Toby swept her up in his arms. Her giggles mingled with her tears, and she buried her face in his shoulder and wrapped her arms around his neck. Toby held her tightly to him, smelling her perfume and loving the giggles. The door slammed again, and a huge hulk of a man awkwardly came across the lawn. Toby set his mother gently to the ground, and turned towards his father, and was swept up in an uncharacteristic bear hug, for the man had never shown such a display of affection in all of Toby's life. Toby joined his father in the embrace, and felt the tears from his father's eyes as they met with his cheeks.

Toby's eyes widened and then he started patting his father on the back, "Da! Da, I'm fine. I'm home. It's okay." He heard sniffles from his side, and saw his mother shedding her own tears. He reached a hand to her, and the three stood for some time, holding each other in the homecoming.

There is a swirl of sand around him. Like a whirlwind, blowing around him and through him. He can't see anything but the sand. Somewhere, a voice is calling his name and he can't see the person, but he knows that someone is coming for him. He tries to run, but can't. He tries to scream, but no sound will issue forth. There is no sound; only the wind and the blowing sand.

And now he can break free. He is running blind, lost in the blowing sand. The sand invades him, rapes him, and he is groping his way through the sand. And the voice is still calling his name. Where is he? Where is help? Where is the end of that sand?

And now, someone is ahead of him. Someone small and slight, laughing, and he is running to that someone. The someone is never within his grasp. But the laughter is maddening and he can't escape it any more than the sand. It is only after he has stopped running that he is face to face with the djinn, who is calling his name.

...Toby...

...Toby!...

He jerked upright, throwing the covers back on the bed and his feet on the floor. He was almost out of the bed before conscious thought surfaced in his mind. His breath was fast and shallow, and his heart was racing. He put a hand to his chest, and let his gaze touch on all things familiar; his room, his clothes, and his furniture. It was okay, he was home. *This was home.* He was safe and it was just a dream. It was nothing more than a bad dream and there was no sand, and no djinn.

The door whipped open, his mother fussing, "Tobias Robert, did you not hear me callin' you!"

It happened so fast that Toby threw himself backwards against the headboard, his heart thumping. He moaned in the back of his throat, that animal noise again, and struggled to keep from screaming. He raised his eyes to focus on the figure of his mother.

Maeve Mary Riordan stood with one hand on her hip and the other on the door knob. She was dressed in her Sunday best, a small black veil neatly bobby-pinned on top of her head. She was a slight woman with steel gray hair that still had the youthful wisps of the red that it had once been. She was thin and elfin, a proper Irish mother.

As soon as he looked up in his barely concealed panic, her face changed and the demanding look was replaced with one of complete fear. "Toby, darlin', you look as if you've seen a ghost. Are you ill, boy," she asked, coming quickly to Toby's side to touch his forehead.

Toby gripped the sheet on the bed to keep from cringing away from her. "No, Ma, I'm not ill. Just a bad dream. I'm fine."

"Toby, you've had that same bad dream every night for the last two weeks. I'm starting to worry a bit about you. Maybe you should see Father and let him help you."

Toby reached out to her, and she took his hand in hers. She looked worried even as she tried to bury it under a smile, but he could tell that she was not happy about any of this. He really did want to comply but with his guts tied up in knots right now, it just wasn't a good idea. He didn't need a priest. He needed a stiff belt, but not in this house on a Sunday. He kissed the back of her hand, and guided her to sit next to him on the bed, and she did so willingly.

"I'm fine, Ma. I am. It's okay; I don't need anything but my family for a while."

Her brow furrowed and she spoke quickly, trying to allay what she thought was causing his fears. "Toby, you have us. Of course you do. You won't be losin' that anytime soon, and you know it. But, Father can help you—"

"Ma, please, not today."

She was truly unconvinced. "Come now. I'll be leavin' for Mass in a few minutes. You'll need to dress if you're going."

Toby shook his head, and answered, "Thanks, Ma, but I'm gonna pass. I really don't think I can handle that this morning."

His mother huffed and dismissed the thought with a wave of her hand. "Tush, boy, I'll wait. Just put on something that looks fair decent. But, you'd best be hurryin' if we're to make it in time."

"No, Ma. I don't want to go. I'm just not up for the church gig."

His mother stood up with lightning speed, and whipped around, both hands on her hips now. Toby had a brief moment of wondering if she was going to twist his ear until he got out of bed. It was like old times again, the ear twisting never failed to get him moving when he was a boy.

She didn't twist his ear, but she did shake her finger at him, and replied, "Tobias Robert Riordan! I'm surprised at you. After everything that's happened, that you'll be turnin' your back on your faith! Of course, you're up for 'the church gig,' as you call it. Now, get dressed."

Toby looked away from his mother's intent gaze, and stared at his hands as he spoke, "Mom. I know you're probably right. But, I'm really not ready for that. I can't face people yet. I'm gonna stick around and help Dad with the fence. I'll catch it next Sunday, Ma. Promise."

Maeve clucked her tongue and put the hand back on her hip. She softly sighed, shaking her head, but her stern expression softened. "Your soul needs some attention, sweet," she pleaded with Toby. "You need to come to Mass. You've been through so much. This will help you; I know in my heart it will."

"Ma, not today; not yet. I can't, okay? I just can't."

Maeve's philosophy of life began and ended with her faith, and she hadn't changed one iota in her life. Or his. "You can sit with Father Francis and talk this out. If there's anyone can help you find the answers to what happened, it'll be him."

Toby twisted the sheet in his fingers and clamped on with a tight fist. He had never been able to tell her no before, but when she was on one of these kicks, she made it a damned sight easier. "Ma, I know you care, and I know you mean well, but I'm not going. Please, let it rest. Next week, I promise."

Maeve held up her hands in surrender. She laid her hands gently on his face, and kissed his forehead. "You know I love you, my sweet son. I only want what's best for you. You do know that, I hope."

Toby took a hand to kiss the palm. "I know, Ma. I know. Say a prayer for me? Okay?"

"That I will," she said, and smiled her special smile for him. "Hurry up, then. Your Da is already downstairs and breakfast is waitin' on table. I'll be seein' you after."

She kissed his forehead again and patted his cheek, before making her way to his door. He waited until he could hear her footsteps down the stairs before getting out of bed to dress. When Mother said hurry, he hurried. It was funny; as soon as he had walked in the door, he had fallen back into old habits. Mothers were to be obeyed and

Fathers were for advice. Not that he had asked for any, but his Da was there. He knew that as surely as he knew that he would never again see a night where he slept completely at peace. But, it didn't matter anymore; he was home. And if his father looked a little too pale and his mother looked a little too thin, well, it wasn't important. *He was home.*

Toby went downstairs to the kitchen. His father sat in the usual place, head of the table, reading the newspaper and drinking his coffee. The cigarette was burning in an ashtray within easy grasp, the curls of smoke slowly rising in the air, dissipating in a breeze that flew in from the open window. Maeve never permitted smoking in her presence and frowned upon the practice at all. So, Toby's father waited until she left or he was outside, puttering on the grounds, before lighting up. It was a habit that Toby adopted.

He stepped to the cupboard, and found one of Maeve's old china plates, chipped and faded from the wear. The plates were a gift from her parents when she had married, and while they weren't good for company anymore, they were still used for family. He went over to the stove and loaded up with eggs, toast, sausage, sliced tomatoes, and grabbed a cup of coffee for himself. He brought everything to the table, sat down across from his father, and began to eat. His father barely lowered the paper to peek over the edge and acknowledge his son's presence. Both sat in silence for a time, as one ate and one read. Toby was content. This was the normalcy he had needed.

Brendan Michael Riordan was as tall and stout as his wife was short and fey. He was a big man – standing six feet tall – and broad shouldered. His hair had once been the dark blond; it was now white as snow. He'd worked this land as hard as he'd worked for the oil companies of Ashland, Kentucky. He'd loved his family as dearly as he'd loved the life around him.

So, father and son sat, one eating and one reading, and neither said anything. Toby reached over and grabbed the sports page from the top of the stack, and he heard the paper rustle. His father hated when he did that, he knew, but it was an age old game between them. Toby continued to eat, and caught up with the Wildcats and how they were faring. After a time, when he had finished eating, the two sat, still reading and smoking, as if the passage of time had never occurred. When the paper had been demolished, Brendan neatly folded it back to its original dimensions, and stood up.

"Well, I'm off. You coming?"

Toby stood and removed his dishes from the table, "Yeah, Da. Let me put these in the sink and I'll be out to help with that fence."

Brendan snorted and lit a fresh cigarette. "Boy, I just said that to your Ma to get out of goin' to church. I finished that fence last week. If she thinks I've got serious work to do, she lets me be. I'm off to the garden. Got some roses need tendin'."

"Well," Toby answered. "I guess I'll help you with that, then."

"As you wish, boy."

Brendan turned on his heel, and headed out the back door. Toby filled the sink with dishwater and put the plate in to soak. It was that desperate need for something normal, again. Toby's own philosophy had been "better living through machinery," and he had a dishwasher in his old place. Here, though, it was different. Here, doing the simple things like dishes, or sweeping the floor, made him feel grounded again. It took away that feeling of displacement. Toby picked up his father's ashtray and, after wiping it off with a paper towel, set it back in its hiding place. He refilled his coffee cup, and went into the back yard.

He came out to the flower garden, and sat in a nearby chair, content to stare at what his father called "the north forty." It was nothing more than a plot of forty by forty feet that was planted with vegetables that they would eat over the winter. One of Brendan's few joys was his vegetable garden, and what he could grow in it. The crops were not that varied, tomatoes and green been comprised the major amount of crops. He always grew at least ten or twelve rows of sweet corn, which Maeve would serve piping hot with plenty of butter and salt. From the first of June until the last growing day of September, they would feast on fresh food from the garden. His mother would begin the canning of the vegetables for the off season with the excess. They grew enough to sustain them, and they grew no more.

"Whatcha staring at?"

Toby looked back to his father and smiled. "Looking at your garden. It's looking real good."

Brendan paused to look over his shoulder, and nodded in agreement. "Does, don't it. We oughta get a damn good crop out of it this year. I'm real pleased. Your Ma's been canning tomatoes and beans since middle of July, I reckon. Gonna have bumper crop."

"Yes, I bet you are."

"So? Are you gonna help or not," his father said, the tone of voice gruff and stern. "If you are, get up off your lazy ass, and get out here."

Toby took a gulp from his coffee cup, set it down next to the chair, and got up as he was told.

His father working on the rose garden, his real pride and joy. Da had decided that he was going to learn to grow roses. After a couple of years of "learning," he'd finally gotten the right touch because his roses had started blossoming with a vengeance. With a few blue ribbons under his belt, Brendan had become something of a local celebrity for his roses.

He ladled a mixture into his spraying can, and was screwing the cap back on both containers when Toby came up beside him. Toby stuck his hands in his pockets and watched his father for a second. "Okay," he said. "What do you want me to do, Da?"

Brendan pointed over to a large metal pitchfork lying on the ground. Get that fork an' start workin' the soil." He stood upright, using the sprayer attachment to make his point. "Mind you, don't hit them roots. You'll kill 'em if you ain't careful." He made a half stabbing, half scooping gesture with his hands, fingers spread apart. "Just around 'em. Want you to work the soil loose, like this. That damn clay is worse'n cement."

Toby picked up the implement and stepped over to the outside of the garden. He stabbed it into the ground and started working the tines back and forth. "Da, you need to get some mulch or something in here. That would loosen it up."

"I got a compost pile back there," Da said, as he started at the other side of the roses and began spraying them. "I use that for the vegetable garden. Don't want my roses smellin' like shit."

"Come on, you're supposed to put that stuff around 'em."

Brendan stopped spraying and stared at his son, his face blank. "And you know all about growing roses, do you?"

"No, but—"

"Then don't be telling me what I'm doing, boy." His father dropped the spray can to his side and pointed with the sprayer again. "I've been doing this long enough to *know* what I'm doing. I don't need you telling me."

"Yes, sir," Toby said, immediately contrite. "Sorry, Da."

The family habit was to wave it away with the flip of a hand, and his father did so. "You just poke holes in that ground and let me spray this stuff on 'em. Gotta watch out for them damn bugs."

Toby continued with the pitchfork and did as he was told. Once, he got too close to a bush, and his father was quick to jump on it.

"Boy! I told you not to get too close to them roots. Mind me, now. Pay attention to what you're doing!"

Maeve's domain was the inside of the house and the front yard. Her real contribution there had been what flowers were planted but *Brendan* had chosen where to plant them. His father had always puttered about in the yards, since they had moved here when Toby was ten years old. Brendan had chosen the spot for "the north forty" and he had designed the rose garden that they now worked. His father had designed curving beds that were slightly raked with the country side. Every rose bush was easily seen and the spectacle of the blooms was breathtaking, year after year. Brendan always seemed more in his element working outside, than he ever had been anywhere else.

So they worked, one tilling the soil and one spraying the plants. It was quiet between them, but Toby wasn't in need of conversation if the truth be told. He was just content to watch his father and do his own job. It was another piece of normalcy and just the simple act of aerating the soil freed his mind to try and make sense of it all. He knew his father was sneaking worried glances at him because he could see it out of the corner of his eye. Every time Brendan stopped to wipe the sweat from his pale face, he would watch Toby working. Toby had seen that expression many times, and it usually precluded an attempt to bond, followed by a disagreement on the bonding method. He wished he could reassure his Da as easily as he'd reassured his Ma.

Brendan had his own recipe for the bugs that involved lye soap, which should have been very bad for the roses, but Toby noticed a loving relationship between man and plant. They didn't seem to mind or know what wasn't supposed to be good for the plants, and so, in spite of themselves, the roses flourished. They were Brendan's children, his pride and joy. The love he couldn't lavish on Toby, he lavished on his garden. Toby smiled in amusement that displays of affection for a child was considered unmanly, but gardening wasn't.

There was a bad joke in there, but then, that was Da.

Brendan sprayed until he had emptied the container of its contents, and then took to pruning some dead wood from the plants. It took a few minutes, but the moment that Toby was dreading arrived. Brendan had started pruning next to his son.

"You look like a man that has something on his mind, boy. Might as well spit it out."

"Just the roses, Da. Just the roses," Toby answered, a lot less than truthfully. "I'm not thinking any further than that."

"Well. That's probably a good thing. Too much thinking can hurt your brain."

Toby leaned on the fork. Maybe talking *would* help. "That's not the part that hurts, Da."

His father never broke the rhythm of the pruning shears, never looked up. "I figured as much."

It was quiet again for a few minutes and Toby retreated back into his thoughts.

"Your Ma was real upset about gettin' that telegram, you know. Worried her pretty bad. Took to her bed for a spell."

Toby had no answer for this, he kept working the soil. His father continued as if he hadn't expected a reply.

"Yep. Mighty worried. She took to her bed and stayed there for quite a spell. Until you drove up, she thought you was at death's door. You comin' home made it all right again, eased her mind."

Toby paused, staring at the ground for a few seconds. "Yeah, I know, Da. Doc said they were bad wounds. Said the one in my shoulder missed a serious artery by about an inch." He shrugged, remembering the doctor who'd had the misfortune to tend his wound. The man had been Greek and about two hundred years old. But he'd been patient when Toby was grumpy, insistent when Toby hadn't given a damn about the healing. And he'd cajoled Toby into living when he hadn't wanted to. "Well, that's what I was told, anyway. Bad enough to get discharged."

"So I heard," his father said, in a distracted voice. "That gettin' discharged didn't bother you none, did it?"

"No. It didn't."

"Sounds like it was the other thing that bothered you," his father said, still seemingly distracted.

Toby looked sharply at his father. "How did you know about

that?"

"Oh, I still got some contacts in the right places. A couple of old drinking buddies. One of them told me about your man got killed."

"Still?" Toby was more than a bit intrigued.

Brendan stopped pruning long enough to look back at his son. "Yeah. You know, when someone goes through something like that, you're buddies forever, especially when you put your life in someone's hands."

"Da? You were in combat?"

Brendan stopped pruning, and turned to his son. He absentmindedly massaged his left shoulder as he spoke. "Well, boy, it ain't somethin' I like to talk about much, but before I married your Ma, I did my spell in the Army. Went to Nam. Lost many a good man there, myself."

"You were in the war?"

Brendan went back to pruning the plant and kept talking. "I was there. I was a Looey." He stopped and tipped a wink at his son, and said, in a confidential tone, "That uniform made me quite catch with the ladies, you know. Took your Ma out to dinner night, wore my uniform. Proposed to her in that get up. Don't let anyone tell you it ain't true, but women do love the uniform." Brendan winked again, and went back to his pruning.

As he worked, Brendan went on with his story. "I remember one day, outside of some piddley ass jungle, and on re-con with my platoon. Got caught in an ambush and lost about twenty or thirty good men. They was shootin' out of them trees and we couldn't touch 'em. Hell, couldn't even see 'em. They just mowed us down like a knife going through hot butter. Took the medics the better part of the day to get in there for the wounded and dead. Longest day of my life."

Toby had completely stopped working the ground, captivated. "What happened?"

"Well, I reckon it was a case of bein' in the wrong place at the wrong damn time. Me and my men got sent out to survey a section o' jungle and secure it. I had me a feelin' it was wrong to do, but, you know." He shrugged one shoulder. "Only, we couldn't see nothin' when we got there. Goddamn bastards knowed we was comin', I guess. Set up an ambush, with them hidin' in trees and brush. Moment we was in position, they commenced to mowing us down like grass. Took me a bullet in the shoulder. Medic said the same thing to me, said that bullet missed my heart by inch."

"Why did you go? I mean, if you knew it was risky and all, why did you go?

Brendan cocked one eyebrow and answered simply, "You should know all about that. You go where they send you and you do what they tell ya. When your life is on the line, you follow orders to the letter and pray to Jesus that *someone* knows what the bloody hell he's doing."

"How come you never told me about this, Da?"

Brendan stopped and rubbed his arm again. "Well, wasn't nothing to tell a youngster like yourself. Didn't want to think about it then, either. And then, when you was old enough to understand, didn't want to talk about it. But I remember at the time, I felt as low then as you probably do about now."

Toby stared out over the tops of the roses, chewing on it. "Da, does the pain ever go away?"

"Oh, sure, son. Takes a bit, but it goes. And the guilt. That goes too."

"I don't know, Da. It feels like I should have done something, anything."

"Boy, in a war, those are the risks, that a good man in your command will die. You can't change that."

Toby plunged the fork deep into the grass and stood with his hands in his pockets. He turned away from his father as he struggled to get the guilt back under control. "But, Da, he didn't want to go in there. I could have left him outside."

"Aye, I reckon you could. But, from what I heard, he would've dead when that missile hit your vehicle. I heard tell there was powerful lot of shrapnel scattered for a long ways in any direction. Your friend was a dead man either way. Now, ain't that the way of things?"

"Maybe."

"Ain't no 'maybe' to it. Either he was or he wasn't?"

He had to stop again. Was Da right? Was Bion a dead man either way? As much as he didn't want to admit it, Da was probably right. Bion came in because of his sense of duty and the dream came true. But what if he'd stayed in the Rover? The SCUD took it out and left a crater that was about thirty feet deep, according to the report. He would have been dead there too.

"I don't know, Da. I just don't."

"Well, from what I heard, he was a dead man. The only difference woulda been his death wasn't gonna be on your conscience if he'd stayed out in the truck. Am I right?" Brendan straightened up and stretched his back out. He groaned slightly, and then, looked into Toby's eyes. "Truth is, son, the good Lord made that decision, and there wasn't nothing you could have done to stop it. And you takin' on the guilt don't change it neither. Seems to me like you *want* to feel guilty."

"Da, I don't," Toby insisted. But again, he had to ask himself if maybe, his Da was right about that too. *Do I?*

His father nodded, and then, in his practical and sensible voice, Brendan gruffly said, "Then stop kickin' yourself in the ass, son. You did what you did because it was war and you had orders. MacArthur was right, war is hell."

"That was someone else, Da."

"*Whatever*! It's still hell. Good men die. That ain't gonna change in your lifetime, boy."

Toby watched his father wipe the pruning shears and stick them back in the case. In that moment, he felt the reach of his father, and reached back. Da understood; it was something they could relate with each other on. Was his Da always this wise, this smart? He got it; he finally got it. "Thanks, Da."

"For what?"

"Just thanks."

"As you please, boy."

Brendan pulled the fork out of the ground, and picked up the can and, with Toby's help, put away the tools. Toby sat back down with his now lukewarm coffee, while Brendan inspected his rose bushes.

"Da?"

"Yeah?"

"Can I ask you something? Why didn't you go to church with Ma?"

Brendan pulled a pocket knife from his trousers, and cut some of the roses from the plants. He chose an assortment of lavender and pinks and yellows, Maeve's favorites among the whole garden. Toby watched a smile form on his father's face as he did it too. He thought, at first, his father wasn't going to answer, but Brendan finally did.

"Well, I'm just an old pagan, boy," Brendan replied, his face glowing. The smile he wore dropped years off of his face and he looked every inch the young man who'd fought in a war and come back alive. "I always found God in nature. I never saw no need to go into some stuffy buildin' so that some stuffier old fart could tell me I was going to hell. I figure, if I'm goin' to hell, then my being there wasn't gonna change that."

"I hear ya, Da. I hear ya."

"Well, I'm goin' in to take a nap. My chores are done, and I wanna rest a bit before your Ma gets home. I got pains on pains and my rheumatiz is botherin' me some."

Brendan put away his knife and gathered the blooms off the turf where he'd laid them. The assortment was beautiful. He saw Toby looking at them, and tipped another wink. "Your Ma's favorite, you know."

"I know, Da," Toby said. "I remember."

"Been long time I've been married to that woman," Brendan continued, lovingly touching the stems, his face lost in the memory. "Was the best day of my life when she said she'd marry me. When I said I wanted to put me in some gardens, first thing she said was, 'Bren, you put in a rose garden for me, you know I love the roses.'" He paused to look back up at his son. With the smile widening into a grin, he added, "I never could resist that faery woman. You comin' in?"

Toby smiled back. "No, I think I'm gonna sit here for a while and just enjoy the roses. They are beautiful."

"Yeah, they sure are." Brendan seemed to be pleased that Toby had an appreciation for his garden. He nodded to his son. "You know, tendin' that garden has been one of my joys since I got back from Nam. Well, you and your Mom have been my greatest joy. But I reckon the most peaceful time I ever had was working on them roses. That'll cure what ails ya."

Brendan gathered the roses in his arms, and started past his son, towards the house. As he got even with Toby, he looked down and said, "You know, this is where you really find God. He's right here, in nature." With that, Brendan left Toby to his thoughts, going back inside the kitchen.

Toby realized at that moment how deeply he loved his father and how his words had calmed something inside him. Of course, neither man would ever say the words outright, that wouldn't be manly. They were more alike than they would ever admit to. Toby stretched his legs out and just stared into the rose garden for a bit. He had had his share of problems with his father when he was younger. This man, who had always been so remote, was even more of a stranger now. Brendan had never really said the words of comfort before; that had been Maeve's job. His mother was the nurturer, and she had done it with the typical Irish panache. Brendan had just been there.

They had had their fair share of fights as Toby reached his teens. Brendan felt that the reading was a waste of time and that Toby was in danger of becoming "sissified." He was a practical man and never really felt too strongly about education as a whole except for what he could get out of doing. Later, Brendan tried to rule the roost in "making a man" out of Toby by the wrestling matches he held at whim. Brendan's idea of Toby's man-making was physical, but he usually fought dirty and Toby would end up cussing more than anything else. Which would upset Maeve, which would upset Brendan, which would open up an argument about where Toby's life was going.

Brendan was a man of his generation, whereby he didn't openly discuss or show his feelings. In his mind, that was a woman's nonsense and not a manly thing to do. Toby knew his Da loved him, even though he never showed it, but they never had anything in common. It was as if his son was such a mystery to him that he couldn't comprehend how to speak to Toby, so he spoke in his own way. Maybe they were a mystery to each other.

But something had changed. Had his father mellowed with age? He was still the big man but he was quieter. Something had happened, that was for sure. The Brendan of old would never have opened up like that, a shared moment of sorrow or guilt. Toby took a gulp of the coffee and tossed the rest on the ground. Something was definitely different.

And it was nothing he was ever going to figure out. So he sat and contemplated the roses instead. He was still sitting there when his mother arrived. She sat with him and spoke of the Mass and then they both went in to start lunch.

Maeve was a chattery thing, had always had been. She was never one to be able to stand silence, and so she filled it with the local gossip of what was going on in this sleepy little town. There was always something going on, someone sleeping with someone's spouse. Maeve had one failing that her son could see and that was gossip. Point out to her that this was considered a sin, and she would make her clucking noise with her tongue and only proclaim that she was just keeping up with things and that it wasn't meant in a malicious sense.

And so, she filled the silence. She refused to allow Toby to help her prepare the meal, and so he sat and watched her cook. It was a simple meal of leftover ham, green beans, corn, and sliced tomatoes; a good and hearty Kentucky repast. He did, at least, get to set the table for her. She slapped his hand away from the tea pitcher and poured it for herself.

"And if you're that desperate to do something, go and wake your father for dinner. I'll be getting everything on the table. He hates it when I don't have the meal ready. I can't disappoint him."

He kissed his Ma on the cheek, loving her giggle and the blush on her cheeks. "It's nice to see you two still in love, Ma. Gives me hope."

"Feh, enough with your hope. Give me grandchildren instead, you sot."

He laughed, kissed her cheek again, and left the kitchen. "Anything for you, Ma."

Toby went back to his parent's bedroom and knocked on the door. There was no answer, so he knocked a little harder. He stood there waiting, but again, no answer. So, he pushed on the door and it opened with the long remembered creak. Da had never fixed that. Said an old house always settled more and he would wait to fix it. He never did it. Toby made a mental note to take care of it later for him.

He saw his father lying curled on his side, and a wave of love swept over him. The earlier conversation came back to him now, and he suddenly realized that Da had been talking about his own fears. It caught him off guard for a moment, because he would have sworn that his Da had ever been afraid of anything. At least, he never showed it.

"Da?"

Of course, Toby wouldn't say anything either. It was enough to gaze upon the man lying there. He had often said that he would never be like his father and now, he realized how much of his father he had become. All in all, he was beginning to understand his father a little, and the thought made him smile.

Da sure was deep asleep; he must have been real tired. Toby reached down to take his father's shoulder, shaking it gently. "Da? Wake up. Dinner's ready." It was a few seconds before his fingers registered the coldness of the shoulder.

"Da? *Daddy!*"

He shook his father's shoulder hard enough to turn him over onto his back, and Toby looked down into his father's open and lifeless eyes. The way the body had fallen back, the eyes were staring up at the ceiling and one arm was outstretched, leaving one arm curled over the chest.

Toby was frozen to the spot, gasping hard and his mouth dry. "Da! Please, sweet Jesus, no. Da! Wake up! Oh, dear God!"

The malaise dissipated as quickly as it had set in, and he dropped onto the bed. He took his father's wrist, trying to find a pulse, but the flesh was cold and unmoving. There was no pulse, no breath. Toby screamed for his mother as he found the place just below the breastbone and began CPR.

Maeve appeared in the door, a dishtowel in her hand and her brow furrowed in confusion.

"Ma, call 911."

"What is it? What's wrong."

Toby turned around and saw her there and stopped the compression of his father's chest long enough to shout at her. "Ma! Call 911!"

She stood, frozen to the spot. She had the dishtowel in both hands, twisting and squeezing it, then holding it tight to her mouth as if to hold back the screams. She suddenly looked so small, more so than usual, so vulnerable and childlike.

"Ma!"

This pulled her glassy stare to Toby and she took her hands from her mouth then and they dropped loosely at her sides. He found himself speaking to her gently, as if speaking to a child.

"Ma. Go to the phone and call 911. Do it now."

She finally put her feet into action and left the room in a daze. Toby went back to CPR. He was softly crooning to the dead body lying there, alternating with the breathing into the mouth. Toby kept it up until his arms were tired and sore, and there was nothing.

He sat back and stared down at the corpse. He sat there for a very long time, rocking, until the paramedics and the coroner's wagon had come and gone.

Chapter Seven

"We have come to mourn the passing of our dear friend, Brendan Michael Riordan; to bid farewell to his spirit and rejoice in his communion with God."

They were gathered in the chapel, the friends that had worked with his father, and all of the living relatives of the Riordan clan. With a typical Irish Catholic family, there were a *lot* of living relatives. Toby lost count of the many aunts, uncles, cousins, and such that had given condolences or cried on his shoulder. Some of the cousins never even knew his father, but had come because of a sense of duty to the relatives. They wouldn't be attending the remaining drama to be played out later. The brothers and sisters, and a handful of aunts and uncles who had been close to Brendan would be a full part of the drama known as *The Funeral*.

The first act of *The Funeral* was subtitled, *The Service*; it would begin at the chapel and continue at the graveside. It would start with words of sympathy, move to platitudes of life everlasting and the Savior's embrace. It would segue into a narration on his father's life and accomplishments by someone who had never known who Brendan really was. It was a rousing first act, full of musical numbers, tears, and drama with an extravaganza of costumes and lighting, the pall bearers and the casket. It was a first rate piece of liturgical drama, right down to the extravagant set – a Broadway producer's wet dream. But not one damn bit of it came close to erasing the emptiness inside of him.

"Let us pray. Our Father, who art in Heaven—"
"Hallowed be thy name . . . ."

Toby sat in the pew, dressed in the only suit he owned, a deep brown three piece that he had bought to wear for his job interview with the Bourbon County school board. It was a little tight on him but he wasn't going to go out and buy a new suit. Brendan would have thought it frivolous and Toby would have agreed. It was a good suit. It would do.

Maeve's fingers were loosely entwined in his own. She had dressed in her prettiest frock of cobalt blue, absolutely refusing to bow to the tradition of wearing black. She got a few shocked looks but she was too far gone in her grief to notice. It wouldn't have mattered anyway. The dress had been Brendan's favorite and it would be what she wore to say goodbye to him. Her only concession to the dictates of the local hens was wearing her black veil, shoes, and hat.

She had been quiet all morning, and beyond getting dressed, her only activity had been to make coffee. He watched her now, glancing at her from the corner of his eye as she sat, her lips moving silently along with the prayer. She looked so thin, so frail, so lost. What was she thinking? God, he wanted to be that in love with someone; have someone that much in love with him. They had been so devoted to each other; it was a surprise that they'd had children at all.

She stared at the coffin, at the flowers on top. Was she as numb as he was? *It's not fair*, he thought. *Why? Why is he gone? What kind of numb nuts God—?* He bit the thought off as quickly as it had started. He felt his mother squeeze his hand, her fingers pressed against the ring with a little discomfort on his part. Could she read his thoughts, know the anger inside of him? He squeezed back, trying to reassure her that he really was there. That it was all right. Even if it wasn't.

"I have had the privilege of knowing Brendan for the last ten years of his life. When I came to this parish, he was the first to welcome me, with a hearty handshake, a clap on the back, and a bit of the Irish. He was a good host, a good husband, and a good father . . . ."

The eulogy was done: so many words and good deeds for all of them to celebrate, to say farewell and pray for strength for the family that lived on. Toby sat numbly listening, but the sentiments meant nothing. Strength? Why? What did it matter? He and his mother would go on whether those people prayed for strength or not. Whether he or his mother got any or not. Brendan had it easy; he was out of this hell. Toby and Maeve would go on, still dealing with this crushing emptiness.

He stared at the crucifix, bolted to the wall so that the man nailed there could look down on the congregation. Thin but well-muscled, the face held a look that was both agonized and beatific. Toby stifled the snort that had risen up the back of his throat and threatened to explode from his nose. *What are you looking at? Hmm? Like you really give a fuck. If you cared so fucking much, why? Why did you take him now? A year or two would have made the difference and you picked now? Why? Got a fucking garden needing weeds pulled?*

He didn't bother to swallow the sentiment this time. He twisted the ring on his hand. *I just needed a little more time.*

"Ashes to ashes, dust to dust, we commit the body of Brendan Michael Riordan to the ground and his soul to Heaven. In the name of the Father, and of the Son, and of the Holy Ghost, Amen."
"Amen."

Toby turned the key in the lock, and opened the door. It was different now, less . . . full? Noisy? Cheerful? No, it was because the house had a little less light in it now. Maeve had drawn the curtains to keep it that way. Her head hurt terribly, she said, and the dark helped it. He tiptoed about and did as she asked. He would take care of her from now on. He would do that much for his Da.

He took his mother's elbow and led her in the door, helping her remove her coat and veil. She hung it on the coat rack, and slipped off her shoes.

"Ma, you ok?"

A weak smile and a pat on his arm, "Aye, darlin'. I'm just a wee bit tired. I was thinkin' of layin' down for a nap."

Toby took off his jacket and started to loosen the tie around his neck. He hated the damn things, but he had been bound and determined to look good for the yokels who'd gossip about it if he didn't. "I'm gonna have a cup of tea, Ma. Would you like one?"

"Aye, sweet, that I would. I'll be getting it for us. I need to get the kitchen ready for the wake. You can keep me company."

He started to protest, but she'd already walked by him and down the hallway into the kitchen. He followed her, after hanging his jacket and tie on the stair railing. While she put the kettle on and set out the cups, he helped by clearing off the counters and dining room table. There would be food aplenty when the family arrived; the gathering for the Second Act of this little drama, *The Wake*. Toby checked Brendan's liquor cabinet; while it was a safe bet that anyone in the door would have a bottle in hand, he wanted a good start on the evening. For now, it was enough to sit with his Ma, drinking their tea.

"Ma, you look wiped out. Why don't you go take that nap?"

She gave a wan smile, and stared into her cup. When she spoke, she never raised her eyes. "Do you think he minded bein' in his uniform? Your father never liked the black. Said it made him look like a cheap undertaker."

Toby chuckled, "But he knew you loved him in it, Ma."

"Aye, he looked fetchin' in it, he did. Your father was a bit of a dandy when he was your age." She loosed a plaintive sigh and sipped her tea. "Still, do you think he minded?"

"No, Ma. I don't think he did."

Maeve nodded and was silent once more. He was able to persuade her to lie down when she had finished her tea. He helped her to her room, then covered her with a light quilt. He laid her favorite picture of his father in her hands so that she could have it next to her. He stroked her hair while she drifted off, sang to her while she slept. After a bit, he quietly stole out of the room. Everything was in readiness for the *Second Act*; the intermission was over.

The Irish never celebrated the death, only the life. They brought food by the bowls and pans, full of meat and vegetables and sugar and cream. They brought casseroles and cakes, fudge and filets. By the time the last person had come in the door, the counters and table were overflowing with all the food. Some had thought in advance and brought paper plates, plastic forks, and spoons. All had brought single malt refreshments, but there was also the scattering of brewed beverages as well. Ah, the Irish knew how to send a body off to the Eternal Reward and do it right the first time. It would be a long night.

Toby stood in the kitchen, acting as host for the evening. Someone had roused his mother from her nap; or maybe the she'd wakened on her own. Either way, he could see her in the living room, through the doorway that separated the two rooms. He kept an eye on her while keeping the liquor flowing. He was doing a good bit of drinking himself.

"Do you remember the dog?"

"You mean that mongrel tart he brung home, swearin' it was a pedigree of high virtue."

"Yeah, he loved that dog, he did."

He stopped trying to recognize voices and listened to the stories instead. There were so many memories and none of them familiar, none of them his. All of them were endearing to him, showing a side he never knew. His father had always been a strict disciplinarian, the rock wall that Toby had been forced to bounce off of.

"He was right proud of you, Toby."

Toby looked into the face of his Aunt Renee, six years his father's junior. She was the baby of the family, the only girl, protected by seven older brothers. She stood with a glass of whiskey in her hand and smiling.

"He was," she said, her voice quavering slightly as she spoke.

Toby took a swig from his own glass. "I never got to know my father, Renee. I don't think he ever knew me."

"Oh, he knew you were too much alike to ever live in the same house for long. But he *was* proud of you." She sniffed, wiping the skin under one eye with her forefinger. "He wrote everyone about you going off to Iraq, you know. Said you were off to fight for freedom. It was proudest day of his life; well, except for the day you were born."

Toby spared a small smile and nodded. "What did he say?"

"Told anyone who'd listen that you were off to be a soldier. He used to call us and regale us with your stories of being there. When you had that accident in the cave, he bragged about you but . . . we were scared it was happenin' *then*. Especially when you got shot soon after."

"*What* was happening?" He felt a kick in the ribs, the breath leaving his body faster than he could suck it into his lungs.

"You didn't know?"

"Know what?"

Toby watched his aunt's face change into one of embarrassment, as if she'd told tales out of school. In this instance, Toby thought, maybe she had.

"Had himself a small heart attack when the news came, Toby. I thought they told you. He was in the hospital for three days. Doctors wanted to keep him longer, but he told 'em he'd be healin' just as well at home as in the hospital. He told 'em it was because they wouldn't tell him how his boy was and he needed to know. Said he wanted to be home where he could take care of you if they sent you home sooner."

Toby held out his arms and his aunt walked into his embrace. He held her close while he mulled over this news. His father had been upset enough to have a small heart and he had never known it. It wasn't fair at all. Renee held him till they were interrupted by her daughter. Eleanor came rushing through the door from the living room, her rather ample bosom heaving.

"Mom, Toby," she blurted out.

His aunt stepped back, wiping her eyes and sniffing to clear her nose. "What's wrong?"

"Aunt Maeve fainted. She started to get up and just passed right out."

Eleanor stepped in between Toby and the archway to the living room, holding her hands up to catch him. "She's fine. Cousin Josh is tending to her. I just thought you oughta know."

"Thanks, cuz." Toby smiled at her. "Let me get her to bed. It's been a long day and she needs some rest. I'll be right back."

By the time he made it to the living room, his mother was awake again, and his cousin had her giggling a bit. She looked a little sheepish as he scooped her up in his arms.

"I'm that sorry to cause a fuss," she muttered weakly into his shoulder.

"It's alright, Ma. You look tired and stressed. Let me put you to bed."

As he carried her to the bedroom, he noticed that she weighed no more than a feather in his arms. As he stood, helping her undress, he also saw that her ribs stood out in contrast to her skin.

"Ma? Are you ok?"

"Oh, sure, darlin'. I'm fine. I . . . I just . . . I'm having a bit o' trouble pulling a breath is all. I'm just so tired."

"I know, Ma. I know." He reached out to help her, holding her steady while she fussed with the garment. "Here, let me help you finish putting your nightgown on and into bed."

Maeve stood, unmoving. Toby gently slipped the other sleeve of the nightgown around one thin arm. He eased her back against the pillows and pulled the blanket up to her chest. As he leaned over to kiss her forehead, he saw a tear roll down her cheek.

"Oh, Toby. What's to become of me now?"

He was so taken aback by the sheer heartbreak in her voice that he didn't know what to say. He took her frail hand in his and struggled for the right words to come out. "Come on, Ma. What kind of question is that?"

"I'm so alone now. I have no one."

"Ma! That's not true," he said, quickly. "*I'm* here. *I'll* take care of you. You'll be fine."

She didn't seem to hear him. "So alone. No one there anymore. What ever will I do now?"

"Go to sleep now, Ma. Get some rest."

"I *want* to sleep now. I want to dream."

Toby bent down and kissed her on the cheek and turned off the bedside lamp. He crossed to the door, pausing long enough to watch her lying and staring at the ceiling. "Good night, Ma. I love you."

There was no answer, so he turned out the light and closed her door.

He stood in the hallway for some time before he went back down to the gathering. Everyone was concerned, but not taking it too seriously as they each grieved in their own way. It was three in the morning before the last had left, drunk as a lord and singing folk tunes loud enough to raise the dead. *Too bad they can't*, Toby thought, and methodically turned out the lights and went to bed. It was a long time before he slept.

The sand is swirling around him and through him. He pulls his t-shirt up around his nose so that he can still breathe. He hears someone calling his name. He knows who it is now and he doesn't want to see this being, this djinn. So, he runs away from the voice, running as fast as he can.

He is back in the tunnel. He has no lantern to light his way, and so he stumbles in the dark. Tobias . . . .Tobias . . . *echoes throughout the tunnel and he is moving as quickly as he can. He knows that if he finds the entrance to the tunnel, he'll be back in the real world and away from that being. But where is it?*

He arrives at the tunnel entrance, but a shadow crosses in front of him and he turns toward it. Bion is still lying where he put the body. The eyes are open again . . . didn't he close them? How can that be? Bion is dead and he knows he shut the eyes. He knows he did. He doesn't want to go near that body, but he is drawn against his will. So, he walks to Bion and kneels down beside his dead friend.

Bion's eyes turn to him and focus on him. Bion's mouth opens and begins to work as if he has something to say. Toby is desperate not to hear it. He knows that it will be something horrible and bad, but he can't move away. And then, the voice of the djinn comes from Bion's mouth, "I give you these gifts, but there will be sacrifice; a sacrifice for each gift. You have made two, but now, you must make one more."

"No," he cries. "No, please. I don't want your gifts. No more."

"You have asked for these gifts. It amuses us to see that you have them. But, be careful what you ask for. You will most certainly get it."

Bion is laughing . . . or is it the djinn. Laughing wildly and loudly and the laugh echoing within the tunnel and the sound making everything reverberate and shake. He wants out, but he cannot run; he is drowning in sand.

It was the second time his mother fainted that Toby got the hint and took her to the hospital emergency room. Rather than take her to the little hospital there in Paris, Toby rushed her to Lexington. The nurse took her immediately into triage and left Toby to fill out the paperwork. He sat, scared silly, filling out the endless paper trail that was required of him and worried. All around him were signs of gunshots and stab wounds, and the more mundane fevers and broken bones. None of it could distract him from the gnawing feeling inside of his chest.

It was several hours before someone finally came to him. The young nurse took him to an office and asked him to sit, to wait for the physician to come to him. It was agonizing, that second wait. In his mind, he saw several scenarios and wondered which of them would come true. He was staring at his sweaty hands and trying not to think, when the tall man walked into the office and sat down at the desk.

"Mr. Riordan, I'm Dr. Parker. I'm the attending physician."

"How's my mother?" Toby blurted out.

Dr. Parker cleared his throat, silent for a few moments. He picked up a paperclip and twirled it in his fingers as he spoke. "There's no way to say this except to just say it. Mr. Riordan, your mother has large cell, non-small cell cancer and it's in stage four. At this point, I can't even tell you where it began, but she has a large growth next to her heart and according to the x-rays, it's spread to the upper lobes of her lungs and her liver."

Toby gulped loud enough that the doctor looked up at him. He shoved his hand out at the man, stuttering the words to push them out of his mouth. "Wait, wait. Cancer?"

"I'm going to run some more tests, to be sure, but I must be honest. There's nothing we can do for her. She is such an advanced stage that the prognosis is three months, four at the most. I'm going to give you some prescriptions for her and we're going to keep her here for a few more days. If you'd like, we can keep her here until the end. That way, you'll know that she's getting proper care and medications. But, of course, it's your choice."

"No . . . maybe . . . *shit*, I don't know," Toby ran his hands through his hair, trying to breathe, trying to absorb what he was hearing. "What do you mean, there's nothing you can do for her?"

The doctor licked his lips, and clasped his hands together over the chart that he'd been reading from. His voice was supposed to be professional and soothing, but to Toby, it was the sound of nails on a chalkboard, grating and condescending. What he had presumed was a certain amount of unwillingness to tell such disturbing news was actually Parker's reining in his temper.

"Sir, the extent of the carcinoma in her system prevents any usual therapies we can do for her. We can try radical chemotherapy and radiation therapy, but I really don't think it will do any good. In her weakened condition, the cure would kill her just as surely as the disease will. Why didn't someone get her in here sooner and we could have saved her."

"I . . . I didn't know."

"Well, not knowing has taken away any chance we might have had to save her life."

Toby bristled in a defensive posture. "Now, wait a goddamn minute," he retorted. "I have been out of the country . . . *in the Army*. How the fuck was I supposed to know? You're not going to make me feel guilty for this."

Parker waved away Toby's anger. "It is not my intention to make you feel guilty, sir. It is my intention to inform you as to my patient's condition. Guilt is your affair." The doctor closed the chart, and stood up. "We're admitting her now, and you can see the nurse at the desk for her room number. I would suggest you contact any family that she has and start putting her affairs in order. With the medications we'll be giving her, I doubt she'll be able to do it. Do you know if she has a will? Or a *living* will?"

His anger diffused as quickly as it had erupted, Toby suddenly felt lost. "My parents had wills drawn up a few years ago. I . . . I . . . don't know about . . . living . . . ."

"Well, good, that will help," and the doctor rose from his chair. "I'm going to tend to my patient. See the nurse at the desk. If you have any questions, she'll know how to find me."

Dr. Parker left the room as quickly as he'd entered it, no further words of any kind for the man sitting there. Toby didn't even watch him go. He gripped his knees hard enough to feel his legs shaking so hard that standing wasn't even an option. He didn't know what to think or how to feel. He barely had enough to keep breathing, keep holding on to the ground below him.

I give you these gifts, but there will be sacrifice. A sacrifice for each gift. You have made two, but now, you must make one more.

Toby sat for a time, just rocking. He needed to gather himself. He needed to do something, what was it . . . oh, yeah, see the nurse at the desk. For some damn reason, the intelligence factor had been knocked completely out of him, and he couldn't remember if he was supposed to see what room his mother was in first, or get the prescriptions, or . . . . *cancer.*

The word rocked him back in the chair. His fingers locked into the soft faux leather hard enough to slice small slits with his fingernails. He felt as if he were losing touch with reality and had to dig harder into the material to remember what sensation was. *A sacrifice for each gift.* Did someone just belt him in the stomach? Because he sure couldn't breathe and that sounded like a damn good explanation as to why.

The next week was a whirlwind of actions, diagnoses, and

medications. Her doctor was efficient and priggish about it; always polite to Toby, but always leaving the impression that he held Toby personally responsible. Only one thing was certain; his mother was in a great deal of pain and had been for some time. In her way, she bore the pain and never mentioned it to his father. Toby spent every waking moment with her at the hospital, every sleeping one dreaming of sand.

There was, of course, the long discussion of whether Maeve should stay in the hospital or not, and that was mostly of Toby trying to decide. Maeve said nothing, sitting in silence, her half smile as the only indication that she was still conscious. After a few days of various pain pills, the physician had opted for straight heroin. This left Maeve a little nauseated at first, but then euphoric and glazed over. Parker was right about one thing, she was not going to be able to make decisions for herself and she was going to need a caretaker. Toby wrestled with the idea that maybe he wasn't fit to take care of his mother, that maybe this was going to be a little more than he could handle.

But, Maeve did become conscious for one person, Father Francis. Toby had called him the day she was admitted and he had to confess that the priest had been an asset. When Maeve wouldn't talk to anyone else, she talked to Father Francis. They would sit for hours, discussing the parables and her life. They would pray or he would hear her confession. She was calmed and soothed when he was there, and silent and withdrawn when he wasn't. Toby was thanking God constantly for this man and his effect on Ma.

On the fourth day in the hospital, Toby came bearing gifts. Actually, it was Maeve's favorite picture of his father and her Bible. The picture was of a handsome young Brendan, in his wedding clothes. The leather bound Bible was one that she had painstakingly copied the family genealogy; the leather was worn and the pages crackled from use. Toby remembered her always getting it out for family dinners or for special times when a scripture reading was needed . . . or wanted.

Toby had both items in hand as he came to her door. The sign stated *No Visitors*, but the sound of voices floated through the door. They were too muffled for him to make out, but logic told him that one was his mother's voice. He stopped short of the threshold and took a deep breath. He wouldn't say anything in front of his mother, but he was going to take the visitor and ream the hell out of whoever it was..

When he walked into the room, he saw who it was. Father Francis was reading from his Bible, head bent over the scripture. Maeve's eyes were closed and she had a dreamy expression on her face.

"But I would not have you to be ignorant, brethren, concerning them which are asleep, that ye sorrow not, even as others which have no hope. For if we believe that Jesus died and rose again, even so them also which sleep in Jesus, will God bring with him. For this we say unto you by the word of the Lord, that we which are alive and remain unto the coming of the Lord shall not prevent them which are asleep."

Father Francis only acknowledged Toby's presence by a brief pause and a glance in his direction.

"For the Lord himself shall descend from heaven with a shout, with the voice of the archangel, and with the trump of God: and the dead in Christ shall rise first: then we which are alive and remain shall be caught up together with them in the clouds, to meet the Lord in the air: and so shall we ever be with the Lord. Wherefore comfort one another with these words."

The priest closed the book softly and reached over and patted Maeve on the hand. She opened her eyes then and smiled so sweetly that Toby could almost see the mother she was before.

"You see, Maeve," he said to her in that priestly calm. "There will be comfort for you, and you shall meet our Savior in the clouds."

"Oh, aye, Father, I do see. I'll meet my Savior and I'll be with my Brendan again."

"Yes, my child, exactly. We will continue to say Mass for Brendan, to make sure that you see him in Heaven. You can be comforted in that knowledge."

Toby hid a smirk; it was rather amusing to hear a man that closer to his own age address his mother as "my child." Maeve didn't seem to mind, she seemed comforted by it. The smile never wavered; her eyes shimmered a little more.

Or, is that the heroin?

Father continued to speak to her softly, as if talking to a child. "For if we believe that Jesus died and rose again, even so them also which sleep in Jesus, will God bring with him. You believe that, don't you, Maeve?"

"Aye, Father, I believe," his mother answered, acting every bit as the child. "I know in my heart the Savior died is risen. He went to his Heavenly Father, just as I'll be goin' too. Do you think Brendan'll remember me?"

"Yes, I do. I sincerely do."

The priest rose at that moment, and acknowledged Toby's presence verbally now. Toby stuck his hand out to receive Father Francis, who grasped it with a warm handshake.

"And how are you this fine day, Tobias? Your mother and I have been discussing . . . well, the situation. It's good that your son is here, isn't it, Maeve?"

"Oh, Toby," she said to him, clutching the new Bible in her hands. "I'm goin' to see my Brendan in Heaven. Isn't it a wonder?"

Toby smiled and sat gingerly on the side of the bed. "Yes, it is, Ma."

Her eyes glazed over, and Toby watched the transformation with a growing alarm.

"Did you know I've a son named Toby? I do, you know. I named him after my Uncle Tobias. He was such a wonderful man. I knew my Toby was goin' to be the same. I can introduce you some time."

"Ma, *I'm*—"

Father Francis stopped Toby finishing his sentence by laying a hand on Toby's shoulder. He gestured out the door with his head, and then leaned down to kiss Maeve's cheek.

"Yes, you must, Maeve; introduce them to each other. Children are such a blessing. As it says in Psalms, 'Lo, children are an heritage of the Lord: and the fruit of the womb is his reward.' Our Father gives us children as our mainstay and comfort. They are a joy and should be thought of that way."

"Oh, yes, Father."

"And with that, Maeve, I must take my leave," Father said in his pleasant voice. "We'll talk more tomorrow. Peace, my child."

The priest made the sign of the cross over Maeve's head before he took Toby by the elbow and walked him out into the corridor. He looked at Toby with sympathy, but Toby could almost see something else there. Whatever it was, Toby didn't care for it. It grated on him, but he would suffer it.

"Tobias, I didn't want to say anything in front of your mother. She's not doing well today. I'm sure you can see that. Pay it no mind."

"I don't understand. Is it the drug they're feeding her?"

"No, it isn't," Father replied, shaking his head. "I had a long talk with her physician about it. Good man. I think he's very caring of his patients. Just like Luke, the dear and glorious physician."

Toby opened his mouth and shut it again. In his mind, it was a little presumptuous of the priest to seek out *his* mother's doctor. Hell, Toby hadn't done that much of it after the man had insinuated that Maeve's illness was his fault. "And what did he say?"

"Oh, probably the same thing he's told you, that the cancer is slowly eating her brain. She'll be like this quite a bit. That doesn't mean she doesn't have her lucid moments, but she gets a little foggy sometimes. God bless her, she didn't know *me* at first. That passes after a bit. Just humor her."

"Yeah, right . . . humor her."

"I also wanted to talk to you about what comes after. Have you made arrangements for her?"

That feeling was coming over Toby again. "Meaning?"

"Well, I presumed that you would want to put her in a hospice," Father Francis said. "Surely you cannot care for her, and she *will* need care."

"I haven't decided yet."

Father Francis nodded. "Well, she surely cannot die here, away from her faith. I can put you in touch with a good home, a place very nearby. I can recommend it highly. They can give her the care she needs and it won't be a burden on you."

It was the patronizing tone that had set Toby off. He was desperately trying not to lose his temper, not here in the hospital. "Father, with all due respect, she's *my* mother. Her care is not going to be a burden. I can handle it."

"Tobias, she needs shots at certain intervals. She will fast become incontinent and you'll need to clean her up. Her meals must be specially prepared. You can't do this. You are not qualified."

Toby was bristling. "Listen, Father, I have had a little experience in giving shots, I think I can handle this. I'm just as qualified as I need to be."

Father Francis patted him on the arm and nodded. "Please think about it and let me know your decision. We can have her moved in as soon as she's able to be transported. I just need at least one day's notice and we'll have a room for her."

Toby watched the priest leave. *I'm just as qualified as I need to be. Damn it, I can take care of my mother and I don't need some frigging hospice. That's bullshit.* So, he decided that his mother should live the remainder of her days at home. He wanted her to be comfortable in her last hours and home was the place that this could happen.

But it was all right in the end. The hospice came to them; a nurse was on duty during the day at the house, the costs were picked up by Medicare. Toby would have the necessary syringes and would take care of her through the night. They had a routine at night. He would wait until the nurse had injected her meds and checked her vitals and then, leave for the night. Toby would put something in the CD player and they would have something to eat – as much as she *could* eat. But the heroin helped with that.

Most of the time it was classical music; she had a fascination for Bach and Vivaldi. But, sometimes, he would put something else on, and they would sit silent and listen. He would watch her as she listened to the music and dreamed her dreams and watched her fantasies. He would try to talk to her, but she never responded. She would only do that for Father Francis.

Toby would spend his time away from her in the rose garden. He needed something to hold on to his father; this was a natural conclusion. He would spend hours, weeding, spraying for the bugs, and tilling the earth. It wasn't the same, he noticed, because the roses didn't quite respond to him as they had for his father. They still grew and flowered, but not with the same intensity. He was sorry for that and tried harder, but the plants missed Brendan's love and care.

He found that gardening let his mind go where it wanted. He thought about the last time he has spent here with his father. He thought about everything his father had said to him, about the accident. He was coming to grips with Bion's death. It came clearer in his mind that what had happened was an accident, war at its worst. Da was probably right; Bion would have been dead either way. If he had stayed outside, the explosion would have torn him apart. Didn't mean he had to like it but it was closer to the truth than any other explanation Toby could come up with.

He was also coming closer to accepting his father's death. He had no answers as to why that had happened either, but, the coroner had told him that Brendan's death was the result of a massive coronary. Thinking back to the correspondence he had received, there were hints and whispers of a heart problem. Brendan was a heavy smoker and a typical Irishman in his drinking. Mother's cooking was simple and laden with fat and lard, particularly. He wasn't sure if there was a history of heart problems, but it didn't take a cardiologist to see that Brendan's lifestyle was a heart attack waiting to happen. It didn't help to ease the pain, but it helped to deal with the anger that he was feeling.

He was angry for having to go to some wasteland to fight a war that made no sense now. He was angry with his mother for her culinary deathblow. He was angry with this father for not taking care of himself. He was angry because they seemed to have been lost in a dream world, never thinking about stupid things like their health or their son. He was angry because they never spoke of the ills and everyone around them had to guess. He was angry with the doctor who wanted to place blame on him. He was angry, and then he felt guilty for being angry. And then he would be angry with himself.

He heard a car door slam, and knew it was Father Francis leaving. He looked down at his watch and saw that it was nearly 1700 hours. He was surprised that he had been in the garden that long. It would be time to give Maeve her meds. Funny, they didn't care that the medication would make her a junkie; she wasn't going to live that long anyway. At least it was killing the pain. At least, he thought it was.

He put the tools and elixir away, and went in to wash up. He would go up in time to watch Maeve get her shot and help get her settled. The, he'd walk the nurse to the door and go fix supper for them. At least, that was the plan. For when he walked into his mother's room, she was alone with her Bible in her hands. The syringes were laying where they were supposed to be but there was no nurse.

Maeve sighed and looked directly at him. For the first time since the diagnosis, her eyes were just as clear as rain. Her smile was so sweet and she appeared to be very lucid. He was turning to go call that nurse and give her a piece of his mind for not being here when he heard her speak.

"Wait," she whispered, her face beatific in a pale beauty.

He froze in place, one hand braced on the door frame. "For what, Ma?"

There was a lot of pain in her eyes; each word was taking something out of her. But her mind was made up. "I want to talk to you for a bit, and I don't want to be a blitherin' idiot while I do it."

Toby sat gingerly on the edge of the bed, but pulled the syringe closer. "Sure, Ma. Anything you want. Are you in a lot of pain? Because, if you are, we can talk later."

She smiled at him with her sweet smile. "There'll be no laters, my sweet son, and we know that. We've so much to say and it all needs to be said now."

Oh. It was going to be *that* kind of talk. He dreaded it. He wanted to avoid it. But he couldn't do that. He had to hear it out, no matter how much it ripped him apart inside. "Sure, Ma. Let me get you another pillow. Do you want some water? Anything to drink?"

She shook her head slowly and kept smiling her sweet smile at him. "No, I'm fine."

It took a while before Maeve offered anything remotely to do with conversation. She just sat gazing at Toby, as if she were memorizing every feature on his face. When she was ready, she held out one thin hand, and Toby took it gently into his.

"Toby, my darlin', it's been a long time since we sat this way. Maybe we shoulda, but we didn't."

Toby grinned in spite of himself. "I know, Ma. I was, what, eighteen? Right before I left for college, wasn't it?"

Maeve nodded. "Was, yes. We sat here and talked about whether or not you should go to school or work with your father. You were so scared, goin' off on your own. I wanted to hold you and make you feel safe. I wanted to keep you here."

Toby chuckled. "Wouldn't have worked, Ma."

Maeve's softly giggled as well. "No. It wouldn't have. You were always your own man. You always had to go your own way, no matter where it led you. I never told you how proud I was of you. How proud I *am* of what you've become and who you are."

Toby gently kissed the hand that he held and sighed. "I needed to hear that, Ma. I wish Da could have said it. I needed to hear that from him just once."

"Yes, I know. He couldn't, Toby. He just couldn't. Why, I would have given anythin' for you to know the man I married. He was was such a romantic. We used to go walking in the woods and sometimes, he'd take me to dance. There was this wonderful place in town where we could listen and dance. He was such a lovely man."

"I bet he was, Ma."

"He loved you so much, I hope you know that. The day you were born, he rented an ambulance to take you through the town, did you know that? He did. Had 'em blarin' the siren the whole way. You were his wee man, his favored son." Her face darkened for a moment. "I couldn't have any more children, after that. The doctors said it was just how my innards were, you know. I grieved it so badly, to not give your Da more sons."

"I'm sorry I was such a disappointment."

She frowned at him. "What are you talking about, Tobias? Disappointment? What put that silly idea in your head?"

His throat felt closed and tight. He shook his head in answer, afraid to try to speak – afraid that his voice would betray him and the tears would come.

She knew and squeezed his arm. "If he didn't tell you, he still felt it – he was proud of you. He always talked about you. Told anyone who would listen about what you were doing, how you were teaching young people. When you joined up in the service, just like he did. Gone to fight for your country. He was always talkin' about you."

Toby wiped the corner of his eye, clearing his throat.

"So like your father. The same thing he would have done, the sot. My men, so strong and sure. So deep with your feelings. But you didn't fool me, you know. I knew when you were scared or angry. I knew. And I always knew you loved each other. You just couldn't say it."

He smiled to himself.

"I'm goin' to be with him again, that old pagan. I know he's waitin' for me in Heaven. I know it."

Toby nodded, the only thing he could do. He wasn't ready to say it yet.

"Oh, Toby, Heaven must be such a beautiful place. I want to go there, do you understand?"

He found his voice again; she was looking at him and waiting for an answer on this one. "I understand, Ma. I just . . . I don't want you to go."

She breathed a soft sigh, and squeezed his hand with as much strength as she possessed. Toby felt her weakness and knew it would be soon.

"Toby, I wanted us to say the words we should've said before and never did. But, mostly, I wanted to talk to you about going back to Mass. You're going to need it, more than ever before."

He wanted to make it right for her. He would have promised to fly to the moon if she'd asked. "I will, Ma. I will."

Her face was so pale that she almost blended with the pillow that she lay on. "I'll be happy knowing' I'm going' to Heaven and that your Da is there, waitin' for me. I want to know that you'll be there with me when it's your time to go."

Anything, promise her anything. "Yes, ma'am."

"I never told anyone this, but when I were young girl, I had a vision. It was a man with longish hair and a beard. He had a lamb with him and I knew – *I knew* it was Jesus. He told me about your father and about you, and how my life would be if I lived it in his name. He looked so peaceful an' that was how *I* felt looking' at 'him. Whenever I was troubled, I saw that image in my mind and I'd be comforted."

Toby began to stroke her hand. "Sounds very lovely, Ma. Must have been a wonderful vision."

"Oh, it as. I carried that in my heart always. I want you to find that peace, my son. I want you to go back to Mass. I want you to sit with Father Francis and talk with him."

Anything, promise her anything. "I will, Ma, I will."

"Promise me," she said. She sat up rather suddenly, wincing as she did. "Promise me you'll find your faith, Toby. *Promise me.*"

"I'll go, Ma," he answered. It was painful to watch her like this. He'd say anything if it would get her to lay back. "I'll talk to Father Francis, and I'll find it in my heart."

She lay back against the pillows again, and relaxed. "You won't lie to your Ma. My sweet son, and my joy. You always have been, you know; my joy."

Toby kissed the hand again, and reached for the syringe. "Ma, it's time for your medication. Let me give you your shot; you need to get some rest."

"Yes," she said. She nodded her head very slightly. "You've

promised to find your faith, and that's all I need to know. I'm ready for my medication."

She lay still while he tied the tourniquet around her arm above the elbow. As he stuck the needle into the vein, she reached over with her other hand to touch the one holding the shot.

"I love you, Tobias. More dearly than you will ever know."

Toby injected her with the heroin and sat with her while the nausea took her. She vomited into a bucket he had sitting nearby, then lay back against the pillow. He only moved away from her to put some Bach on the stereo and held her hand until she went to sleep.

Chapter Eight

"Happy fuckin' Easter, boys and girls...*woo hoo*...."

Toby tipped the bottle towards the ceiling and gave a mock salute to the deity above. There was little more than two or three fingers depth left in the bottle of bourbon, but they disappeared in two gulps. Toby belched, tasted the gorge that wanted to rise up, and grimaced. He needed another bottle, but his legs didn't want to co-operate at that moment.

"Wait...where are my legs? I had legs. *Buuut*, they're gone. Who took my legs?"

Toby's drunken gaze swept around the room formerly known as his mother's parlor and saw no signs of his lower extremities. He remembered walking in the room, at least one bottle of bourbon ago, but after that, he couldn't remember sitting in the chair. He didn't recall seeing anyone enter but it was possible. He had shut his eyes for a moment when the room spins had gotten out of control, but that was just for a moment. No, someone had definitely stolen his legs and he had no vague idea of how it happened.

"So, who stole my legs? Hmm?"

Toby's bleary eyed gander across the parlor produced no clue as to the robber, and he slid to one side, trying to catch his jaw on the back of his hand. He missed several times, always jerking up short as the fist flew by the proposed spot until finally catching the target. He, unfortunately, hit his own jaw just hard enough to slam his teeth against his tongue and the air was blue with the profanities of his pain. He slammed the bottom of the empty bottle down and made contact with his knee cap, causing a fresh burst of pain and more obscenities. One thing was cleared up in his agony; he found his legs.

A week had passed since Maeve's passing. She had lived through Christmas and saw the New Year in with him. Of course, she'd been stoned off her ass, but, by God, they'd had gifts and a tree and champagne – and the pain. Her last few days left her lost in the maze of her mind, not knowing where she was or who the strange man with her was. Toby had been feeding her nothing more than baby food until the inevitable coma came. The only words spoken between them had been that day on her bedside.

The end had been nothing spectacular; she simply stopped breathing. There had been no last minute revelations, no heart stopping visions, no long walk down the tunnel. It was just a heart that stopped and a chest that ceased to rise. It was over. There would be no more days flirting with the nurse and no more trips to the doctor. There would be no more baby food jars, no more diaper changes. No more. Done. Finished. Toby was never sure what he had been expecting at the end, but it never happened. Nothing happened, and he felt empty and cheated of it, whatever *it* was. Mostly, he felt empty.

Again, there were the funeral arrangements; this one, Toby did on his own. The void inside made it easy for him to just do it and get it done. Of course, the liquid courage he'd started ingesting hadn't hurt one iota, thank you. Again, there was the wake and the family gathering, the ritual of food; the Greek tragedy was played out to a standing room audience. This gathering was different, however, because it was so subdued. They had all gone through two funerals in such close proximity that the second seemed an afterthought. Or, maybe it was just a continuation of the first, and no one had left yet. Either way, it was an obligation, and a chore to suffer through until he could be alone.

"And here I am," he said, cheerfully and to no one. "All alone. All by myself." He hadn't bothered to change out of his beloved Hawaiian shirt or shorts in the days passing. He didn't have to; his cousin came by to do the cleaning for him and he had all the food he needed in the house. He never had to leave, so why bother getting dressed? He sat, barefoot and in the same sweaty shirt and shorts, day in and day out. He let dishes pile up to give Eleanor something to do, but he never ate. It was a pretense, and soon enough, he'd let Eleanor know that her services were no longer needed. He found he really wanted the solitude.

The pain in his knee was gone, and he wanted another bottle. "But, I found my legs. There they are!" Another rambling perusal of the room, "Damn, it's quiet. Well, I'll just talk to m'self then."

Toby managed to pull himself out of the chair, and wobble on unsteady feet to the cabinet passing as his bar. The relatives had left him several bottles of extremely high-powered booze, in addition to what he had already purchased. He pulled open one of the doors and found a bottle of vodka. It wasn't bourbon, but it would do. He removed the cap and took a pull from the bottle. The vodka slapped him hard and burned on the way down, but it was his kind of fire.

"Whew," he blew out and his eyes watered from the sensation. "Damn that's good." He released another belch and, again, tasted the sourness, scowling with disgust, and he spat on the floor to relieve the taste. Immediately, the idea of Eleanor's disapproving face came to him. "Oh, man, *that's* bad. She's gonna see that and freak. *Damn!*" The idea of the weekly cleaning binges brought another grimace to his face. He looked at the bottle in his hand, and said, "Well, you'll do," and took another gulp. He tipped his head back in doing so, and the bleary gaze came to rest on the pictures on the mantelpiece.

Toby closed one eye to cut down on the double-vision, and staggered over to the gallery that his mother kept on the mantle. Scattered amidst the snapshots that chronicled Toby's growing, there were two other pictures and they were kept at opposite ends, like the bookends his mother had in her library. *My* library now, he thought, as he approached the pictures of his parents.

"*My* library, now, Ma. Sorry about that, but hey, you don't need it no more anyway, right?"

Toby's alcoholic gaze rested on the picture of the Virgin Mary, a sweet countenance of glowing purity. It had been Maeve's second favorite picture and she had displayed it with great reverence in the room. He could see the purity in the woman who had posed, her hands held out in open invitation to take the viewer into her arms. The smile was compassionate and her eyes could see into the soul. Toby put forth a finger to the metal frame and traced the filigree, losing himself in the woman's eyes.

"Tell me Mother-Mary-comes-to-me, is there an answer to all of this? Hmm? Is there a heaven? Do you really give a damn about what happens?" Toby clinked the lip of the bottle to the picture and then drank from it. "Yeah, right. Let me guess, you were just some hooker at Third and High. You needed a few bucks and this smooth talking dude says, 'pose and I'll pay ya.' Am I right?" Another drain from the bottle, another burning, nauseating burp, and Toby nodded. "You bet I'm right. You probably blew him while you were at it." Toby's chortle was both sardonic and angry. "The Virgin Mary does *not* show up on water towers or in chocolate muffins. Jesus, what a fairy tale."

His besotted gaze shifted to the picture at the opposite end, a framed picture of his Da and Ma. Her smiling face was glowing on the photo, but she wasn't looking at the camera. She was watching her husband, and the look of love on her face was almost more than Toby could bear. It was poignant and precious, and Toby could tell from his father's stance, that he had been whispering words of love back at his wife. He held her in a sensual embrace, and even without looking at her, he still never kept his hands off of her. Da had been beaming at the camera, with his arm around his wife, and a thumb stuck in the air. He had on his gardening clothes, and in the background, the fruits of his labor. He remembered that picture. Toby had taken it, on an infrequent visit. The garden had been prospering, the roses were impressive, and his parents had celebrated their thirtieth wedding anniversary. Thirty plus years, and they still couldn't stop touching each other, fondling each other.

"Tell me, Ma. Are you happy there? You and Da are together, like you should have been. Is it what you wanted?" He held the bottle to his lips and drank deeply, never taking his eyes off the picture. "Hey, Da, what's the word? Is it only just a heartbeat away? Hmm?"

He looked closer, looking at the intimacy of her hand on Da's chest with her fingers splayed and one of his hands on her ass. One of those things no one should have to think about, one's parents getting it on. The very idea of his old man putting it to his mom was just a bit gross and disgusting.

"Coppin' a feel, old man? The only love you ever showed was to her. Couldn't say it to me, could you? Son of a bitch." Toby took a hitching breath as his emotions started to run away with him. "Why don't you talk to me? Come on, tell me. Tell me what it's like"

If they could talk to him, if they *would* talk to him. "All I wanna know is why. I don't think that's such a big thing, do you?" He stifled the urge to chuck the bottle at the far wall, to take the damned picture of those two and slam it to the floor. *Just prove it to me...that there was a reason. Show me how it is when you die.* "Talk to me, please. Tell me why. Tell me something! Anything...*JUST TALK TO ME!*"

He tossed his head back and screamed, "WHY?" There was only

silence and he stared drunkenly at the picture of the Blessed Mother again. Toby shifted the vodka bottle to his left hand and reached out for the picture. His lip curled in a sneer, and he pulled the picture off the mantle and brought it closer to his face.

"You're a fraud, lady. You and that bastard kid of yours, all a fraud." He belched in the lady's face and spat on the floor again. "It's all a fraud. All of it, and it killed us all. Stupid tart." He let his temper take control as he threw the picture across the small room. It connected with the opposite wall, glass shards sprinkling on the wooden floor, and Toby staggered again. He reached up to wipe his dripping nose with the back of his hand, and something rasped against the tender tissue.

"What the fu..."

He held up his hand, and saw the ring, shining on his finger. He stared at it, his eyes glowing as he burped again, the acid burning his throat. His focus was on the ring and the stone, the filigree of the metal. He wobbled back to his chair, and dropped like a rock into it, a slosh of the vodka spraying against his leg. He didn't glance in any other direction, except at the ring.

"Time; I can travel through time. What a crock o' shit. Look, Ma, I can travel through time." He focused back on the picture of his parents. "See? I got this as a gift. See?" He held the ring up for their perusal and met only silence. The hand dropped back into his lap. "Yup, I got two rounds from an Iraqi rifle, a body count of one good man and two parents, and a ring. Not damn bad for one tour of duty, hmm?" He took a sharp inhale and another pull from the bottle. "Nope. Not bad at all."

He looked back down at the ring, sullenly staring at the selenite. "I can travel through time. Not that I believe in this shit, you understand." His vision was starting to blur again, and he tipped his head back against the back of the chair, letting the bottle rest on his thigh. *If it was all real, what would I do? You know, a couple of months would be nice. Just to get through this bullshit holiday. Yeah, I'd go a couple of months ahead, and get past this. You know, just to let everyone stop staring at me when I went into town. Yeah, they'd forget all about it, about me.*

He started to feel a strange vertigo, and Toby's stomach started to roil and flip. He gave one more hearty belch, and the free hand came up to grasp at his chest, which was starting to burn. His vision doubled and blurred, then tripled and blurred. Toby closed his eyes, trying to fight the spinning in his head. Everything suddenly felt out of whack and disjointed in him, around him. He had a strange *there but not there* feeling as if the world was dissolving around him, then it blacked out. Toby had no idea how long he had been asleep, but it felt like he'd never gone under at all, it felt like a mere second or two.

He jumped out of the chair and made a clumsy run down the hallway to the bathroom. He had just enough time to drop to his knees and fling the toilet seat up before the contents of a bottle of bourbon and one partial bottle of vodka came spewing out of his mouth. The flow was so severe that it came out of his mouth and nose and Toby barely had time to catch a breath before another bout of liquid regurgitated into the bowl. He vomited until he felt like he was turning inside out and every organ was going to fly out next. He vomited until there was nothing else inside. When he was sure it was over, he got on his feet, and braced himself against the sink while he washed the tears from his eyes, and the bile from his lips and mouth.

"Jesus, please us."

He slid along the wall, slowly making his way down the hallway, until he was back to the parlor. He barely made it into the room before he lost his balance and fell toward the chair. Desperate to keep his feet underneath him, he caromed across the floor, until his drunken dance dropped him, ass first, back into the cushion. The vodka bottle next to him had fallen in his haste to reach the lavatory, and his foot kicked it when he sat. The pain in his head mushroomed as he leaned over to pick up the bottle, but his fingers grasped the target and he quickly sat back up. He took the bottle in his hands, and tried to twist off the cap, but it wasn't there. He must have left it off when he ran, so he tipped the bottle back to his lips. Empty.

He set the bottle down on the cool, dry floorboards, and let his head drift back against the chair. The material of the chair felt soft against his head, and it, too, was cool to the touch. It felt good against the heat of his body, and he flipped his shirt off. He sat back, again, in the chair and reached to the table to get a cigarette from the dusty pack sitting next to the ashtray. He lit the tip and sat back, spent and sweating, and smoked it, letting his mind just be silent. His eyelids felt heavy and his stomach muscles were in agony from the vomiting, but he couldn't move another inch. He smoked his cigarette and stubbed it out, and just sat, breathing.

His eyes lit on the picture of Maeve and Brendan once more, and he felt a twinge of shame. That picture was almost like having them in the room, and he felt as if he'd been caught doing something nasty. And he never felt more alone than he did right then.

"I miss you, Ma...Da. God, how I miss you."

Toby passed out again, and slept, dreamless and empty.

He stood over the tiller, one hand on the throttle and the other on the pull, and yanked hard, again.

"Goddamn piece of shit!"

Here it was, the first day of May, and he had a vague idea that it was time to till the garden, but he couldn't get the damn thing to run. Toby had pulled the spark plug and it was fine. He'd checked the gas tank and it was full. He'd even cleaned the damn thing, and nothing. He pulled the choke open and closed it slightly, and once more pulled the rope. The engine would not turn over and refused to fire up. Toby slung the tiller to the ground in disgust. If he couldn't till, he couldn't plant. If he couldn't plant, there would be no garden.

He left it lying in front of the plot and went back to his chair sitting by what should have been a thriving rose garden. Something had gone wrong there, too. He had mixed the formula wrong and every bush was now just as brown as the soil. There would be no more roses, no more flowers, no more vegetables...there would be no more. *Fuck 'em,* he thought, and sat down with his glass in hand, and consoled himself with his current best friend. *What else can I kill? Hmm? Any idea?*

A car door slammed behind him and pulled him out of his reverie. God *damn it,* he thought and turned toward the sound. It was Father Francis standing by the car, and he immediately felt guilty for swearing, But then, he remembered that he hadn't done it out loud, so guilt was shelved. He stood up and walked towards the priest and stuck out his hand in greeting. Father Francis took it immediately in both of his hands.

"Hey, Father."

"Hello to you too, my son. I hope you don't mind, but I came to check up on you, see how you're doing. We've been concerned."

It was that look of pity and superiority that set him off. The priest with his piety, looking down at Toby and thinking himself so holy, so bloody pure. Francis didn't have the first fucking clue about anything Toby was feeling, about the pain in his heart. He wanted nothing more than to smack that pitying look off the man's face. He didn't show it though; he simply smiled and asked if Father would like to come inside for a glass of tea.

"No, thank you, Tobias. I'm fine. And if you don't mind, I think I'd like to sit outside and have our talk. You must be sitting out here for a reason."

"Sure," Toby said.

He and Father Francis walked back to the rose garden. Toby still went inside and got two glasses of ice and the pitcher of tea. He was going to be a good host, if it killed him. He poured the tea into the glasses and handed Father Francis one, and sat down in the opposite chair. The priest was right to the point.

"Tobias, we have not seen you at mass since you returned from the war. Why is that?"

Toby cocked his head and exhaled. To the point, alright. "Father, I am not ready to be around people. I just want to be alone and sort out what has happened to me."

"And you can't do that with people who know you and care about you?"

Toby shook his head, "No. I can't. Oh, everyone means well, but it's too much."

"And you feel that you are better alone with your grief, do you?"

"Right now, yes, Father. I...well, I guess I have doubts and I really don't think that being in church is going to help that. I just need to sit and think for a while."

Father Francis took a sip from his glass and barely held back the grimace. Toby had never liked sugar in his tea and forgot that some did. He made a mental note to go get the sugar bowl in a few minutes. The priest said not a word, just setting the glass down on the ground. He didn't set it on a stable place, and the glass spilled the contents on the grass. Neither man made note of it.

"It sounds to me as if you think too much, Tobias. Spending too much time within your thoughts can keep you in a depressed state far longer than you should."

"Father, all I have left is my thoughts. I've lost my parents and all I have is their memory. If that's a state of depression, then let me stay in it."

"Tobias, I think I know what you're feeling...."

"*You don't know a thing about what I'm feeling,*" Toby spat out. It was out of his mouth before he had even thought about it. He instantly felt a twinge of guilt for having been quite so forceful, but at that moment, he didn't think anyone *did* know how he felt. "I'm sorry, Father," Toby said, meaning it at that moment. "But, I really don't think you know what's going on in here. I lost a good man under my command in that stupid war. And now, in rapid fire succession, I've lost my mother and father. I'm still trying to make sense of this."

"And does 'making sense of this,' as you put it, also include the amount of alcohol you've been consuming lately?"

Toby shifted in his position. He felt guilty, a little boy caught with his hand in the cookie jar. But a second later, he felt angry. Why should he let this sanctimonious son of a bitch judge him?

"You've been spying on me, Father?"

"Not at all, my son. You forget; Paris is a small town. It's hard to keep secrets here. And so, I'm asking you, is alcohol the only way you have to deal with this?"

"It's the best way I have right now."

"Wine is a mocker, strong drink is raging: and whosoever is deceived thereby is not wise."

His head jerked up with a snap in his neck. "Excuse me?"

"Proverbs 20:1; Wine is a mocker, strong drink is raging: and whosoever is deceived thereby is not wise. What it means is that—"

"I know what it means, Father. I did spend my time in catechism. I am hardly an alcoholic."

The priest shook his head in such a deep sorrow that it practically dripped off him like rain. "No, my son, but you can be led astray by the drink. It can make you think strange thoughts, do strange things."

"And that's what you think I'm doing now?"

"Tobias, you've been through much, suffered much. It's natural that you'd be lost as such a time, but your answer is not in a bottle. I think...no, I *know* that's it's time for you to turn back to the church and away from the bottle."

"I am fine; I'm not drinking that much—"

"Charlie says you're ordering a case a week. This is not good, Tobias. That tells me that you are drinking far too much. You are not yourself and you need others of like mind to lead you back to the fold."

Toby sat back and gripped the arms of the chair. "You *are* spying on me. Why?"

"Let's just say, that while your mother was lucid enough to still make plans, she asked me to look after you. I keep my promises."

"Well, Father, you're not your brother's keeper anymore. I am releasing you from your promise."

The priest chuckled softly and replied, "It's not that simple. I didn't make the promise to you. Tobias, you need to come back to mass. And you need to be with people right now. As I said, you're not yourself of late. I'm going to set you up with a good rehabilitation hospital that can help you with your alcohol problem. You'll get all the help you need there."

"I am *not* going to some rehab when I don't need it."

"'Look not thou upon the wine when it is red, when it giveth his color in the cup, when it moveth itself aright. At the last it biteth like a serpent, and stingeth like an adder.' And you are being seduced by Satan's adder just as surely as I am sitting here."

Toby felt as if he'd been bitten by something all right, but it sure wasn't Satan that was doing the biting.

"Tobias, surely you can see that you need help."

"Oh, I need help all right, but not from the Church. Right now, that's the last thing I need."

"You *need* to reach out to God and let him heal your wounds."

"Oh, right. Reach out to God. That's a laugh. A God that thinks it is a real funny joke to take my mother in the most painful way possible. A God that gives me a chance to get to understand my father for the first time in my life, and then snatches him away from me."

"God was calling them home, Tobias, it was their time."

"*Bullshit!*"

"Tobias, I must stop you here. You are dangerously close to blasphemy, and I cannot allow you to damn your immortal soul," the priest said, and shook his head in his own answer. "I think the alcohol is speaking here or you wouldn't be saying these things. 'Thine eyes shall behold strange women, and thine heart shall utter perverse things.'"

Not only was the bastard insinuating...no, *stating* that Toby was not mentally all there, but was doing everything possible to piss

Toby off. And he was succeeding. Toby was panting, curling his fingers into fists and uncurling them just as quickly.

"Let me state this for the record, Father, I am perfectly sober. And as far as what's in my heart, you have no idea. I don't understand a God that can allow this kind of suffering to exist, so I'm asking questions. All you're giving me is platitudes and proverbs that don't mean shit."

Father Francis heaved a heavy sigh and folded his hands in his lap. "Tobias, the profanity is not going to answer your questions. And neither is the alcohol. Once again, I seem to be upsetting you and again, that is not my intention. I am only caring for you as one of my parishioners and as a promise I made to your mother."

"And, like *I* said, I don't need your concern. The church isn't going to help me, and as I see it, God is the reason my life sucks. When He decides to stop the pain and give me back a little of what I've lost, then I'll think about your church again. Until then, this conversation is over."

"As you wish. Tobias, I am here for you anytime you need me. And I want you to seriously think about the rehabilitation home. For your alcohol problem. I will make an open booking for you and you can let me know when you're ready to go in. They can help you, Tobias."

"Father, the only thing that's going to help me is to have my parents back. I don't think your rehab or your God can do that. Now, if you'll excuse me."

Toby picked up the pitcher and the two glasses and stormed inside the house. He had to fumble with the glasses and the doorknob to get inside, and didn't quite make the grand exit that he had planned. If anything, he was so angry that his hands were shaking and one glass slipped from his grasp and shattered on the floor. *I hope it's the one you drank out of, you asshole.*

He stood, torn between sweeping up the mess and actually throwing every glass object in his hand across the room. Everything was out of control and all he wanted, at that moment, just to destroy. He actually had the second glass drawn back to throw it across the room when he heard the car door slam. As quickly as the anger had come upon him, as soon as the priest was gone – he could hear the car backing out of the driveway now – he felt it drain from him.

He fell back against the doorway and slid to the floor. His feet pushed the shards of glass away from him, although he came very close to sitting on the broken bottom of the glass. His head tilted back to rest against the doorway and his fingers loosed the pitcher and remaining glass. He was limp and empty again.

"Why *God, why?*"

Toby felt his world falling around his feet in the shards of a life that he no longer had. His voice cried out why, but there was no answer. *Why?* Why did this happen? How could this happen to him? He called out to God to answer, but God would not, maybe because Toby wasn't worth answering. Maybe because there was no God to answer.

"*Answer me! Why?* Why kill them and not me? Why kill them at all? What did I do? Why are You doing this to me? *DAMN IT, ANSWER ME! WHY?*"

He sat for several minutes, waiting for that still, small voice that never came, that never gave any notice to him. He finally got up and cleaned the glass off the floor. He sat with a full bottle of bourbon and before the night was over, the bottle was empty. As empty as his soul.

Chapter Nine

Toby took a deep draw off of his cigarette and let the smoke tendril from his lips. After the first shock of the returning emotions, he'd managed to keep them in check, but he was still feeling them. He was still seeing the images again. In real, chronological time, five and a half years had passed from that day until the moment he sat in. A corner of his mouth crept into a wry smile and he mused that for some, five and a half years could be an eternity.

John was sitting quietly with his hands in his lap, and again, Toby wondered what was going on in the older man's mind. He had known *of* this man for most of his life. He had seen John cry in public many times, but now John was sitting with his head bowed. There was no expression, no movement from him at all. What to do, what to do. Was he getting through to John? This was really important; not just that this man believed him, but that he *understood* the story.

He sat smoking quietly, waiting. He got his answer moments later when John looked up at him, tears beginning to form in his eyes. Toby fished a handkerchief from his back pocket and tossed it to John, who gratefully accepted it. John wiped his streaming eyes and pulled himself together.

"You ok?"

John nodded. "My dad was in the military, an Air Force man. I didn't understand him, either. We fought all the time, when I was younger. All the time."

"Then, you know," Toby said, and took another drag off of his smoke. "What is it about the military that beats the feeling out of you? Why is that?"

"I don't know that the military did that to my dad. He was like that as far back as I can remember."

"Yeah?"

"Dad was a proud man, Toby. He was like his dad, too, I guess. You keep things close to the vest, keep your business private. It's not *manly* to show your emotions, to talk about your feelings." John rubbed a knuckle over his lips, frowning slightly. "My Dad was a strong willed man. Always made sure I kept my feet on the ground. Never let me forget where I came from."

"Sounds like he was a hard man," Toby said.

John shrugged, one corner of his mouth turned up. "Tough, maybe. Hard? I don't know. I know I couldn't touch him. I couldn't make him understand who I was inside, what my music meant to me."

"Dad was out of the Army by the time I was born. I just wish he'd talked about it when I was a kid. I could have understood him better, I think."

John shook his head. "I doubt it. Your dad sounds a lot like mine. Maybe that's just how they were raised."

"Maybe. Maybe not."

"The only time my dad talked to me, felt like he was trying to pick a fight. I never felt like I was good enough, like I could measure up." John got silent again, and started to play with the rock he had, staring at it. There was a melancholy tone in his voice as he continued, "There were a lot of things I never said to my father before he died. I'm sorry we never got to say those things."

"Would it have mattered, if you had?"

John looked up at Toby, eyebrows raised in surprise at the question. "Yeah, I think it would have. I really do. I spent so much time in therapy trying to understand myself, trying to create safe space for myself. If I had said those things to him, I think it would have helped us both."

Toby took one last draw from the cigarette and tossed it into the fire. He reached forward and picked up his cup again. "I was always closer to my mother than I was to my father. Sometimes I don't think she understood me either, but she always seemed to listen to me. More than he did. "

"Only child?"

Toby nodded. "Yeah. You?"

"Nope," John answered. "I have a younger brother, Ron. He's a good man. My best friend."

"I didn't mind being an only child. Most of the time, anyway."

"You miss out on a lot, though."

Toby shrugged and said, "Maybe. Too many shrinks say too many things, and what it boils down to, is that nothing matters except what you know and what you feel."

"And what *did* you feel?"

Toby steeled himself; time to admit it out loud and deal with it. "At the time? Anger," he said, simply. "I was angry with anyone who came near me. I can't tell you how many times I wanted to smash everything in the house. I was angry with God. You want to know the biggest reason I didn't want to back to that church?"

"Wanted to pop the priest in the mouth?"

Toby chuckled, and said, "No, but good guess." He sobered up again. "I just felt like the whole thing was one big hypocritical piece of shit."

"You can't blame God for one man's inability to say the right thing at the right time," John said.

"Oh, can't I?" Toby swallowed the remainder of his coffee, and held the cup in both hands, rolling it between them. "If you'd asked me at that moment if I believed in God, my answer would have been a big, fat no; I don't believe in any God that doesn't believe in me."

John smiled, and said, "Oh, a few years ago, I probably would have agreed with you. I've seen too much now."

Toby snorted, "You've seen poverty beyond belief, racism, hatred, hunger, man's inhumanity to man, and you can still sit there and be so believing in it all?"

"Yeah, well. Call me an optimist."

Toby nodded and fished another cigarette out of the pack. John paused long enough for Toby to pull a splinter, and light it from the coals. While Toby held the lit end to the cigarette, John voiced the thought in his head.

"You know, so far, I've heard a very sad story of loss. I still haven't heard why this pertains to me. And you haven't mentioned one thing about the time travel ability."

Toby inhaled and blew out a stream of smoke from his pursed lips. "Yeah. I know. I hadn't really thought about it yet. At least, I hadn't at that point."

"Why not?"

Toby tossed the splinter back in the fire and stared, point blank, at the older man. John flinched a bit from the hardness of the gaze.

"Tell me something, first," Toby said. "Do you believe this story?"

"You want the truth?" John asked, his stare just as frank this time.

"Yeah, I do."

"Some of it, yeah. Most of it, no. I don't think you're insane or suicidal any more, but I also don't think a lot of this is true."

Toby nodded his head. "But you believe that *I* believe what I'm saying," Toby said. "That's the same thing as believing, I guess." He poured himself another cup of coffee, and continued, "That's all right. To tell you the honest truth, I didn't believe it yet, either. You know, I never took drugs in my whole life, never did acid or peyote, nothing. I still would have sworn that the whole thing was just a flashback of some acidic variety."

"Something changed your mind?"

"Big time," Toby answered

"What was it?"

Toby reached up and scratched the back of his head, and said, "You might say, I decided to take my promise seriously. Not in the way that most people might, but I did it in my own way."

"The one about finding your faith?"

"That's the one." Toby blew on the steaming liquid to cool it and took a tentative sip. "I was angry at God, and I wanted, more than anything at that moment, to prove the whole Christianity thing to be a joke. I decided that I going to and I wasn't just thinking about the time travel/immortality gig."

"So, what did you do?"

Toby looked back down at the fire, took another drag of the cigarette, and answered him. "I sold everything – lock, stock, and barrel – and bought a one-way ticket to Jerusalem. I wasn't planning on coming back. But, I was going to find out for sure. One way or the other."

Chapter Ten

Toby stared at the Wailing Wall and stifled the urge to go up and spit on it. He wanted to very badly – for everything it was and everything it wasn't. Coming to Israel had been one colossal joke; it was nothing but a memorial to everything that was wrong with religion. Three of them had made this their personal ground zero and none of them had any tolerance for the other two. And if you gave any one of these zealots half a chance, they'd be shooting each other to get rid of the two that weren't a part of the third.

What the hell was he doing here? He took a drink from the bottle of water, swallowing slowly. These people, all of them gathered here in reverence for the Temple Mount and what stood on or under or around it. Muslims, Jews, and Christians came and went in holy garb, jeans and t-shirts, or business suits. All of them had their faith in their hearts, believing so strongly in gods and demons, in prophets and seers. Every one of them clutched so desperately to a reason for their existence, believing in that reason even if the reason didn't believe in them.

He swallowed another mouthful of the water. They walked aimlessly in the square, wandering in cheerful conversations or respectful silences. Men, dressed in black – rabbis, he supposed – bobbed up and down from the waist and chanted prayers. Voices rose and fell in songs of pain and atonement. He listened to the singsong rhythm of their voices and tried to imagine what it felt like to be that devoted. If he felt anything, it was disgust for the futility of the whole thing.

How could they be so deluded, so naive? Didn't they understand? Didn't they recognize reality? How could they pray to a deity that didn't care? Did they really think anyone was listening? Were they stupid enough to think that there was some great cosmic plan for their souls? Toby shook his head. Maybe religion really was the opiate of the masses; a communal and cosmic prank played on those who were too blind to see the truth.

No sooner had Father Francis left than Toby had lost himself in a drunken stupor. Why not; the priest called him a boozer, so he might as well live as a boozer. It was an easy thing, really, to make a phone call to the local liquor store. All he had to do was punch a few buttons on a hand set, say a few words and numbers into the mouthpiece, and a case of whatever was delivered to him. Food wasn't an issue, but the liquid fire that kept him from dreaming, kept him from feeling – *that* was important. So he pretty much lost the next two weeks of his life to a haze of whiskey. No one saw him or spoke to him. No one acknowledged his presence. He lost contact with family and priest alike. He found that he really didn't care.

The garden was dead and he hadn't planted a new one. The flower beds were filled with nothing but weeds and poison ivy; no reason to be out in the yard. Toby was left with nothing to fill his hours. But something niggled in the back of his head, so he began to invent things inside the house that he could do. However, his only attempt to follow through with one of the tasks ended when he took a tumble down the stepladder and narrowly missed impaling himself on a lamp. So, he went back to the family room and watched television. The glory of pensions and inheritances was that he could afford anything and for a long period of time. He had the satellite service. As the hours bled one into another, he sat in front of the television, amusing himself with several hundred channels.

And it landed in his lap so easily; it was almost as if he'd planned the whole thing.

Sitting in Brendan's favorite chair, he had his obligatory bottle of bourbon tucked in the niche of his crotch. One hand held the smoldering cigarette, while the other worked the remote for the TV. A channel would flash just long enough for his inebriated brain to register the content and then he would flick the button again. Any other day, he could find a ball game of some kind being played somewhere in the world. Any *other* day. Tonight, he sat ensconced in booze and religion.

The televangelists told him his soul was in danger, and he needed the Lord's guidance. "For, lo, the wages of sin is death," they exhorted at him. "Let us help you. Let us help you find your faith; find Jesus in your heart. If you're lost, we'll show you the way." His sole answer was a sardonic laugh, a wave of the hand, and a deep draw off the bottle. He wasn't lost. He knew *exactly* where he was and he was just fine and dandy, thank you for your concern.

He flipped to another channel and sat watching a desperate plea for money. They told him they needed his cash to help others. They told him they would pray with him on the phone. Yeah, he was tempted to call – for about two minutes. Another long slug of straight ninety-eight proof removed the thought. Toby looked to the picture of the Virgin, now propped up on top of his mom's bookcase. The frame had been smashed beyond repair, but the picture had survived intact. He had just set it up against the wall where she could watch him, where he could watch her.

"Tell me, oh Mother of the Ages, Mother of God," he said, his voice slurring over the words. "Tell me. All I gotta us pray and Sonny Boy will save my soul, huh? You gonna appear in my corn flakes and tell me how precious I am? Huh?"

No answer from the lady, her arms still outstretched to him. He plucked the bottle from his crotch and managed to get to his feet without dropping like a stone.

The liquid diet of single malt was taking its toll. He'd become gaunt in the face, his bones standing out in freakish relief as the skin sagged. He'd developed a paunch that might have been the beer belly or the lack of food. A walk to the kitchen or to the bathroom left him gasping – if he managed to make it the entire way. Some days, it was all he could do to make it half way before he was forced to lean against a wall, panting and spent. Even now, it was difficult, but he somehow managed to stagger over to the picture.

"I'm talking to you, damn it! *Answer me!*"

Toby had to hold on to the bookcase, leaning against it to keep from swaying as he stood. He wiped his mouth with the back of the hand that held the bottle and snorted.

"Yeah, just what I thought. When I'm *really* in need, you ain't nowhere around." He held the bottle to his lips and drank deeply, feeling the raw burn as it traveled to his stomach. He was burning all the time now but it didn't stop him. "I'm falling apart here, you stupid bitch. I don't want a friggin' hug, I need...you...*to talk to me!*"

The force of the last words threw him backwards, and he tottered back several steps before being dumped, unceremoniously, on his derriere. The bottle, clutched tightly in his fist, glugged a thimbleful of liquid on the floor. He blinked several times to clear his double vision, debating on whether he should move or not, when a flute melody floated through his haze.

"Wha—? What the fuck?"

The song was haunting, calling to him like a siren's song. The screen was full of images – desert scrub and sand, date palms waving in the breezes. He sat transfixed, one hand braced against the floor to keep him from falling over and the other still clutching the bottle. He stopped gasping, fully absorbed in the music, the images of a picturesque village of biblical times in the middle of a harsh desert day. He raised the bottle partway to his lips and then slowly lowered it again, no longer wanting the liquid within.

The music faded underneath the narration and he could almost swear it was that bald guy from *Star Trek*, with his crisp British accent.

"He was a simple man, a carpenter, born to simple folk, and he lived the life of an itinerant preacher. But his story is the guiding force behind a religion that has captured the ages. Who was this man, this carpenter's son, who created such a stir among the Roman government? Tonight, we will explore that question, with the archaeological findings. We'll explore the Bible, and we'll examine the unwritten teachings. Tonight...we'll find...The Historical Jesus."

The voice soothed him, calmed him. He wanted to hear more of it. He felt a pull begin to happen inside. Something about that place, about that time gnawed on him and tugged at his heart. He barely absorbed the narrative at first, only a word here and there making sense. But the longer he listened, the more fascinated he got until he sat cross legged with the bottle corked and laid aside.

Find your faith, my son. Find it in your heart.

The moment the program ended, the spell did too. It was as if an off switch had been tripped in his head.

"So that's it, ain't it? Want me to go find your sonny-boy, huh?" He clawed his way up the TV set until he was standing again. "Yeah, that's it. I'll go find this kid. Sure, find him and show them all what a fraud he is." Toby gestured to the TV. "He ain't no Messiah. And you ain't no virgin. You watch. I'll prove it. I'll prove it to all of you!"

For the first time in almost a month, Toby put the bottle back in the liquor cabinet. For the first time, he allowed himself to become aware of how far things had gotten. For the first time, he told himself that he needed to stop this. For the first time in a *very* long time, he pulled his soul up by the metaphysical lapels, dusted off the seat of his metaphysical pants, and gave himself a damned strict and overdue talking to.

He was going to need his faculties if he was going to do this. He needed to sleep and get moving, first thing in the morning. He turned off the TV, and walked to the doorway and forced himself to make his way upstairs to bed, another first in some time as he'd been sleeping on the couch. His hand hovered over the light switch and he turned back to the picture.

"You wait. You'll see. I'm gonna prove this whole thing was total bullshit. You'll see."

And with that, he had a reason to get out of bed in the morning. One look in a mirror woke up his ego in a hurry, and he took to walking in the morning, doing several miles a day. He "pumped iron" with old tractor parts, dropping the pounds he'd gained with the booze and lack of exercise. He stopped drinking, draining the few bottles of booze left down the sink and throwing all of the bottles in the garbage. Taking away the numbing influence of the booze had reawakened his appetite, and he made daily trips to the grocery to get vegetables and meats, eating balanced meals again.

The search took a bit more time than he'd anticipated, but thanks to the djinn, he had plenty of it. Toby haunted the libraries, both in Paris and in Lexington, reading book after book about the "historical Jesus" and finding an inkling of a place to start. He read anything he could find on the Israel and Jerusalem of the first century. He found information about the diet, the clothing, the day to day living. He pored over the Bible in his parents' bedroom until he couldn't see any more and had to put it down. He found a few books in his mother's bedside bookcase and skimmed through those.

He still couldn't bring himself to sleeping in that room. Oh no, that had been his parent's room and the pain was still too fresh to do that. Even the first time walking in the door brought him to a fresh spasm of heartbreak and the desire to crawl back into the alcoholic haze almost drove him mad with the want. But he took a deep breath and went in anyway. He swallowed that darkness again and let it rest, uneasy, in his belly. Distraction, he thought to himself. That's how to drive it back. Distraction and purpose. One day at a time. One step at a time. He dove into the research until the addiction became a small coal in a fireplace in a forgotten room in the recesses of his brain – still burning but no longer felt as the heat that would consume him.

But, time travel didn't especially mean *place* travel. And the resources of the public library were limited at best in what he could find. He decided that he would have to go digging in Israel to learn more. So, with little more than a decision, Toby contacted a realtor about the homestead and gave the antiques and the rest of the furnishings to the family. Of his own things, he sold or donated everything he owned except for two shirts and two pairs of jeans, a pair of sneakers, Brandon's pocketknife, and Maeve's cherished Bible. The only things, he decided, that he would or could ever want or need. The rest was just clutter.

The house wasn't on the market for long. One good thing about Brendan, he knew a good piece of property when he saw one, and the plot and house were prime real estate. One week to the day that Toby had put the house up for sale, some whiz kid professor from the University of Kentucky had made a bid and the place was sold. Six weeks later, Toby had signed the papers, taken the check and converted it into cash and traveler's checks, and had bought a one way plane ticket to Israel.

Arriving in Jerusalem had provided another sense of culture shock. The first thought that struck him was how anachronistic Jerusalem really was. So much of the city was full of bright shiny new buildings of steel and concrete. But the Old City was a mixture of old and new in architecture, with buildings older than any he had ever seen. They were made of roughhewn stone and simple mortar, buildings that reeked of history and ached to tell the stories of survival in a world of religious wars and trials. These blocks had been carved by human hands in a time when the streets were cobbled or just plain dirt. The newer buildings were so out of place with the old, so cold where the others burned with life.

It was jarring to be walking among these giants and see the automobiles and scooters traversing the same paths that he walked. The cars seemed to out of place. For that matter, so did he. He was awed by the temples and the mosques, testaments to human ingenuity and creation. Walking these streets was doing something to him, creating some kind of energy within him, and it was hard to fight that off.

He spent a week at the Mount of Olives, just walking amongst the ruins. He visited the Tomb of Mary and the Church of the

Assumption. He sat at the Dome of the Rock and stared out over the countryside, waiting for something to waken inside. He made his way to a place the locals called the Tomb of Jesus and walked inside, hoping against hope to see some angel, some scrap of something that would awaken the void inside of his heart. All he got was dirty and dusty, and he left for the sanctity of his hotel.

And still, he marveled at it, wondering how things could have changed so drastically. Everything in life was so complicated in this today of his, but it hadn't been for them then. They woke, slept, ate, and did whatever it was they had to do to survive another day. It was no wonder that religion was so important. They didn't really have anything else.

We created gods and then built monuments to our own creations.

The crowd showed no signs of thinning around the Wailing Wall. He shook his head, hands buried in the pockets of his jeans. The time was never going to be any better. He was ready; all he had to do was steal his nerve and just do it. He would go make his preparations and just go. But he wasn't quite as gung ho as he was when he left the States. His palms were sweating but he was cold in the heat of the day. Maybe this wasn't such a good idea; maybe this was all just part of his delusion. Didn't the VA doctor tell him he was suffering from some kind of low level PTSD?

Toby was so caught up in arguing with himself that he almost ran into a young man approaching the wall.

"Watch where you're going. Are you blind?" The figure was dressed in black, and the curls on either side of his head identified the man as Hassidic. He was a young man, could be no more than twenty-three or so. He was slender, almost ethereal, and his brown eyes looked serious and deep, as if they were hiding the thoughts that might solve the world's ills.

Toby raised one hand to his chest, the other to ward off the young man's anger. "Please, forgive me. I am a tourist here. You're right, I was not paying attention. Please. Forgive me." He bowed his head as he spoke, then looked up into the earnest face.

The young man smiled and nodded. "Understandable. The Wall is a great treasure and the prayers are heard here. You were distracted. Just be careful, my friend. You can get hurt that way." He nodded once more to Toby and then walked on to the Wall.

Toby watched him join the prayerful bowing to the Wall, and

turned back to resume his trek back to the hotel. Except that he got five paces into the journey before he stopped cold. He jerked his head to look over his shoulder at the young man, before turning to stare straight ahead again.

The young man had addressed him in Hebrew and he'd answered it the same way. But how could that be? He didn't speak a word of Hebrew; he had never been anywhere with anyone who did. He was panting again, sweating freely, but this time it had nothing to do with the heat. Or his anxiety. The sounds of the prayers, the conversations around him, everything faded to a dull roar as he replayed the conversation in his head – the young man admonishing him, his answer back in apology. And behind that, the voice of the djinn.

Now. I should do it now.

Toby went back to the hotel and changed into a simple tunic and pants made of homespun and woven wool. They had been crafted by a local artisan, who had assured him of their authenticity. He'd paid the man in the modern currency before taking the remainder to a small bank and putting the substantial remainder in an account there – of course, after finding an antique store with coins of the period and place. He'd also purchased a small bag to carry the coins in.

He'd had a simple bag made, also hand woven from wool. It was a natural color, from the sheep's wool as it had come from the animal, and was worn draped over his shoulder and over his hip. He stuffed a change of clothing, the bag of coins, and some fruit and cheese inside of it, and pulled the flap down. He thought about a small shaving kit but he wasn't very confident in his ability to use a straight razor and decided against it. After all, men wore beards in that day and age; a shaving kit would be Roman in nature and that would earn him the wrong kind of attention. No, he was better off with what he had.

He stopped for a moment and stared at himself in the mirror. What the hell was he doing? This was madness, all of it. That was it, he had to be nuts. Totally, completely nuts. Going back in time? Was that wise? To just up and go to a place and time that wasn't his own? Knowing no one and being so far from home? He stared at the face looking back at him and wondered who it belonged to, because that man was a stranger to him.

But he was too far in this to turn back now. There was no going back, only going forward. He disposed of his old clothing, the suitcase, and anything else that he'd brought with him. Threw it all in the trash, never to be seen or thought of again. He calmly went downstairs, waved goodbye to the desk clerk, and made his way out the door to the street.

Toby hitched a ride to Nazareth, enjoying the two hour drive with a young college student. They talked music, politics, women, books. The young man dropped him off in the middle of the city and, with a jaunty wave, drove off to his destination. Toby waved back and went back to his purpose. He just started walking. No idea where he was going, just that he'd know when to stop and do what he had to do.

He had no plan other than working up the nerve to give this a shot. He let his feet lead him where they would. He walked for another hour before a thought brought him up short and he stopped so suddenly, that a woman ran into him. Again an admonition of watching his steps. Again, an apology in Hebrew, and the answer back.

Wait a minute. How do I do this?

It suddenly dawned on Toby that this "gift" had come with no instruction manual, no warranty, nothing. He was left to fly blind. To say that the thought was a letdown was putting it mildly. It was bad enough that he felt like an idiot for half believing this whole idea, but to be left with no idea of how to proceed was worse.

How do I do this? What do I do?

"Shit," Toby muttered aloud, and looked around him. The people passing him looked right back and continued on their way. *I should have asked*, he thought, and sighed deeply. He combed a shock of hair back with his fingers. It suddenly dawned on him that he had meant to get a haircut before he left and had simply forgotten. His hand caught in some of it and he winced at the tug on his scalp. Toby disentangled his hand and held it out before him.

The silver ring. The selenite was glowing in the reflection of the sun and he felt the absurdity of the situation. Feeling even more like an idiot, he started twisting it, trying to remove the worthless piece of jewelry, but it wouldn't come off. He twisted harder and harder, and the knuckle started to swell from the activity. His mind raced with the thoughts of removing the ring and the idea of going to another time...focusing on how it might have been...thinking about moving backwards two thousand years to another time.

He hears laughter in the background and looks up, knowing it is the djinn laughing at him again. When he does, a strong wave of nausea hits him hard enough to make him reel. The world around him starts to waver as if a sheet of water is pouring on glass and running down it, right in front of his eyes. He can see the world beyond but the wavering is almost too much. He is dizzy and so close to losing his lunch. He feels as if he's going to faint.

The world is growing dimmer as if the sun is going out. The laughter grows louder and louder, drowning out any sound. The world starts to waver like some bad special effect in a cheap television show, the kind that has three hundred dollars to do the work of three million. It's like the desert heat rising off the sand, the same wavering. No more people, no more city, no more anything. The urge to vomit is so strong now and he knows that he's going to do it; it's just a matter of when...and where.

Toby closed his eyes and grabbed his stomach with one hand and his mouth with the other. The sound of voices came rushing back to him. He heard the rise and fall of men selling wares, of prices being discussed. He heard a woman shouting for a child, warning whoever it was to stay out of the way, to stay close. He heard animals lowing in the background and women bartering for goods and services.

Animals? Wait a minute....

The nausea began to subside, but he kept his eyes closed. Toby started to perspire and felt cool chills at the same time. He was sure that he was suffering from heat stroke and he didn't want to see that wavering. The voices were coming into perspective again, a good sign. But, the animals in the background puzzled him. A realization rammed into his head, and he sucked in a breath and held it. He wasn't standing in the middle of a barn; he was in the middle of Jerusalem. There shouldn't be any animals. He should be hearing the honking of car horns. *What the hell....*

A shout caught his attention and he forced his eyes open, waiting for the nausea again. A hand reached out and grabbed the back of his garment, pulling him roughly backwards and he stumbled as he came. He started to look behind him to see who had manhandled him in such fashion, when a loud stomping noise caught his attention and he turned back to face it.

At first, his eyes bugged out of his head and he had to shake it to clear his vision.

No, I'm not seeing this.

Not two feet in front him, the exact spot where he had been standing the split second before, a legion of Roman soldiers started to pass. He could see the metal of their shields and swords flashing in the sunlight. The sounds was deafening as the passing feet stomp, stomp, stomped in rhythm. There were so many of them marching, so many. The wave of soldiers kept coming and coming.

That's it, he thought, *I'm seriously hallucinating.*

He started forward and the same hand grabbed at his robe again. A passing soldier sneered at Toby, roughly shoving him back into the crowd and he stumbled again. At first, he was so shocked, he couldn't move. He couldn't even think. The men kept passing and the sun glinted off the metal of their armor. And all he could do was stare stupidly at them, almost drooling on himself with his mouth hanging open.

He felt the hand on his back and turned to see a boy, no more than thirteen years old, presumably the one who had grabbed him. The boy spat on the ground as the last of the soldiers passed by. The boy shook his head, making the curls at his ears fly back and forth, then pointed in the direction of the legion. It took Toby only a second or two to realize the boy was talking to him, and the words came into focus.

"...be in the way of the soldiers. They do not care for us. They will take you on the cross for stepping in their way."

Toby shook his head and grimaced at the voice. He understood this boy. He *understood* him. It took him a moment to see the look of concern on the young lad's face, as he put his hand on Toby's shoulder to steady the older man.

"You are not well. Do you wish to see the healer?"

"No, no...I'm all right," Toby sputtered out. "I'm just dizzy. The heat."

The boy nodded as if understanding. "Yes, the heat. It takes us all at one time or another. You are sure you do not wish to seek the healer?"

"I'm well. I need to sit. I...I...am lost. I...I...."

The boy looked thoughtful for a moment, sizing Toby up with a glance. "Yes, you are a stranger here. I can tell that by your speech.

You do not talk as one of us. I am called Yeshua ben David. By what name are you called?"

The force of what had happened started sinking in. He wanted to speak in a normal way, say normal things, but that seemed a bit too far outside of his grasp. All he could do was stammer. "Uh...*Tobias. I am called Tobias."

"Of what house are you, Tobias?"

"House? Uh...uh...no house. I...uh...why?"

"No matter. I am pleased to meet you, Tobias," Yeshua answered, seeming to pay no attention to Toby's sudden inability to speak. "If you wish, there is a well nearby to obtain some drink. You look as if a cool drink of water would help you."

"Uh...yes. It would. Thank you."

"You are sure you are well?"

Toby smiled as best as he could, trying not to look sick, and nodded. "Yes...yes, I am well. Thank you for your concern."

The boy again nodded gravely. "Then I must be on my way. I have a meeting at the temple to attend. I am most pleased to meet you, Tobias."

The boy reached out his hand, and Toby did the same. But, he didn't take Toby's hand, instead reaching out beyond and taking the forearm firmly in a grasp. Toby looked down at the gesture and did the same. When he looked back into the boy's eyes, there was a warmth and sparkle there.

"The well is twenty paces further in that direction," the boy said and pointed towards the way that Toby should go. "You should take that drink. I will see you soon. Take care until then, Tobias."

The boy released him and began to walk away. Toby watched with his mouth open and an unabashed stare; it was getting weirder and weirder by the minute. Whoever this kid was, he walked with confidence and as if he knew that Toby was watching. After a few paces, he stopped and turned back to face Toby.

"I will be in the temple. Ask anyone. Someone will tell you how to find it. You'll know what to do then. It is too soon. I must be at my Father's work."

And with that, he was off, still striding confidently and with haste. The crowd swallowed the boy and it was as if he'd never been there at all.

Toby felt his heart beating in his ears and he swallowed a few times, trying to get his control back. He was now on full sensory overload. He dug his fingernails into the palms of his hands and waited for the pain to rush into his head. That was enough to bring a sense of the here and now back, and he began to take in the surroundings.

The buildings were much the same, except they looked newer. No, not *all* the same, there were fewer of them. It dawned on him then that the city was smaller; still as many people, but smaller. Gone was the glass and steel, replaced solely by the hand carved stone buildings. There were no skyscrapers, no plate glass windows. These buildings had holes carved for windows and doors, and flaps of material over the openings. The streets were no longer paved, but covered in sand, packed by walking or marching feet. He could smell the animals, the cows and sheep and goats. He absorbed as much as he could until people coming and going finally caught his attention.

They were dressed much the same way he was, all of the material was handspun; Toby could see that. The colors of the material were earth tones and the men wore the locks of the Hassidic group. The women were heavily veiled with not much to show the gender, but Toby could tell. He could tell by looking at the eyes...and.... They scurried about him and ignored him. Oh, one or two would stare at Toby as he passed by in whatever great hurry he was about, but only the one or two.

Toby started to feel faint again, and more than just a little nauseated. His feet started to move of their own accord, more out of disbelief than an actual need to move. He simply directed them in the way that the young man had pointed, to the well. He never stopped looking around him; never let his eyes stop on one particular sight for long. He was beginning to wonder if he really had crossed the line into insanity and this was nothing more than a delusion. Maybe it was the heat. Maybe he was really here.

It was the cool drink of water from the well that brought him around quickly. Toby had tasted well water before, and this was just as he remembered, with the slight taste of the land and a smell of deep earth to it. But, it was cool and refreshing and went down easily. It settled his stomach and started to bring him back to the world of real things. He poured a cupful over his head, cooling him off instantly. He closed his eyes again, and let his hands rest on the cool stone. He had to breathe, get his shit together.

Toto, I have a feeling we're not in Kansas anymore.

He had done it. By God, he had actually done it. It wasn't a line of bullshit. He had traveled to a different time. It was true, all of it was true. He exhaled sharply and opened his eyes again. The well. The buildings. The animals. The people. All of it. He really was here. This was Jerusalem...in the time of....

Yeshua ben David! Something was coming back to him, something important. He chewed on his lower lip, trying to remember his catechism classes. What was it? Something about... about.... Yes, that was it. Something Sister Michael told him, about the common language of writing in the first century. That the name Jesus was the Greek version; the Hebrew name was Yeshua. From the House of David! Damn it! He'd been standing talking to the alleged *savior* and hadn't even noticed it. Toby slapped his palm to his forehead and started talking to himself, out loud.

"Son of a bitch! Okay, what was it he said? Temple, something about his father's work. He said anyone would point it out to me. Just ask. Son of a bitch! I don't believe I was standing talking to him."

A hand suddenly clapped him on the shoulder, and Toby turned suddenly, ready to let whoever it was have it for touching him. When he saw the Roman armor, he stopped short.

"You! You speak strangely. Who are you?"

The centurion was as tall as he was, but was broader in the shoulders and beefier around the middle. But that was most likely the armor he wore rather than the girth. The soldier's arms were not overly muscular, nor were his legs, but his thighs – what was peeking from the toga he wore – and calves were definitely solid. The man's hands looked as if they were made of steel and stone under the flesh; they were types of hands that could break a man, calloused and rough skinned.

The centurion was dressed in what appeared to be a plain woolen tunic underneath the armor, which was comprised of strips of brass that was tied with leather straps to form a shield around his chest and belly. Plates of brass had been tied together to form the shoulders of the armor that still left his arms free for movement. Under the brass strips and over the woolen tunic, the centurion wore an apron of leather strips that were attached to a belt around his waist. The strips were laid out in two layers, overlapping each other and giving protection below the waist. A short sword in a scabbard hung at the soldier's waist while he carried in one hand, a long spear that looked very sharp at the tip. An elongated shield was in the soldier's other hand, carried protectively at his side.

All in all, the centurion looked like a man that Toby did not want to mess with. Especially considering the look on the man's face was one of cold and brutal calculation. His eyes were squinted slightly as he sized Toby up and down, as if deciding whether Toby was a trouble maker or not and whether it was worth his time to put the spear to Toby and just be done with it.

The immediate shaking in Toby's hands wasn't an act; the shaking was starting to seep into his entire body. The water he'd drunk was now acid in his belly, burning and gurgling in a whirlpool in his middle. He had to do something, say something – anything – if only to quell his own fear. Toby took a deep breath, and ducked his head, trying to appear humble as hell. "I'm a traveler, sir. Just here to visit the temple. I wonder if you could point it out to me. I will be on my way."

The centurion frowned, his mouth tightened into a moue of irritation at thus being addressed. "Thirty paces in that direction, and turn towards the tent. That is the temple. And stay out of trouble."

Toby nodded, bowing slightly to the Roman and pressing his hands against his thighs to keep from balling them. "Oh, yes, sir. And thank you, sir. I'm sorry to have bothered you."

He bowed again and began to back away from the soldier. The centurion grunted and waved Toby off, pulling up the bucket to drink from the well. Toby knew he had better not stick around, and took off at a quick trot. To be honest, he wasn't even counting paces, he was just so glad to be away from that guy. The centurion didn't even spare Toby another glance as he drank from the dipper.

It was a few minutes before Toby realized he was totally and completely lost. Not only had he no idea of how far he had run, but he was nowhere near a building, let alone a tent. The heat was starting to get to him again, and he sat down in the shade of a date palm and just let his mind go quiet for a few seconds. Staring around, he started to shake with the fear and the realization that he was definitely *not* dreaming. He tried the old remedy of pinching himself and even pinched his cheek hard enough to make his eye water, but the images were not wavering. He leaned back against the palm tree and felt the roughness of the bark. He was convinced and then some.

Now what, he thought. He had to find that temple. He had to. What he would do after that, he hadn't a clue, but he was going to go that far. Hell, he was here. So, Toby got up again and retraced his steps. Finding the well was easy, just follow the voices. Finding the temple was a little more difficult, and he finally found an elderly man who walked him there. He felt rather stupid because if he'd been paying attention in his headlong rush to get away from the soldier, he would have known that he had run past it. Oh, well, hindsight being what it was, he was here.

He stepped into the outer tent, as he had done long ago in another age and time, and the sound of angered voices caught his ear. He stood there, quietly for a moment; so quietly, that the man who rushed out of the tent past him, didn't even notice Toby was there. He inched closer to the inner tent and stood outside as he caught phrases and voices, all speaking at once.

"...impudent child...."

"...to try and teach *us....* "

And, then, a louder voice spoke over the others.

"Come, brethren, *please.*

He wanted to hear more, but the voices started clamoring again and the yelling was too hard to understand. The voices melded together in one roar, droning like bees in a hive. For all he knew, maybe that's what they were. He stepped backwards away from the opening of the inner tent. It was all catching up with him. He was feeling dizzy and nauseated again.

A couple came running in, following the man who had run out. He was an older gentleman, of about forty or so, in a plain robe of homespun that was light in color. His hair was a wiry brown that had been bound back with a leather thong at his neck. His feet were shod in rudimentary sandals that kicked up the dust as he ran. Toby had a moment to register the man but it was the woman who caught his eye and who grabbed his attention.

She was a young woman, by Toby's reckoning; couldn't be more than twenty three or four. She was thin but not excruciatingly so. And she had the slight paunch at her middle, that said she had given birth to children – how many, only she and the older man who was obviously her husband knew. Her hair was plaited and then twisted in on itself to lay over her shoulder in a tight loop. She threw only a quick glance over her shoulder at Toby, long enough for him to see her face. She was so beautiful, so angelic, and her eyes were the deepest brown. They were sad, somehow, as if she, alone, knew some deep and terrible secret.

In a breath, they were through the slit in the inner tent and gone. But that one look was all it took. Toby felt as if she'd taken the air and light with her and, for the briefest moment, he thought he could fall deeply in love with that woman. He wanted to bend to her every whim, fall at her feet and worship her with all of his heart and soul.

He heard more shouting, more angry words, and then the cloth bowed out as if something had been thrown against it, followed by the sound of something landing in the sand. The sounds of anger never stopped, growing louder in fact. He stood, rooted to the spot. Should he go in? The man would protect the woman, surely. But there were too many in there, the cacophony of voices convinced him of that. Too many to protect her from. Maybe he should go in, do something.

He was still debating the idea when the couple came out, leading the young boy he had met in the marketplace. The woman must be the boy's mother, Toby thought, it was *her. The mother, the virgin. That was....* He grimaced at the idea that he'd just been daydreaming about Mother of God in a less than holy way, as if he'd been caught at it. He watched them as they started out the door. He had to follow them; he was *compelled* to follow them out of the temple.

When they set foot on the street, the older man reached over and ruffled the boy's hair. "You created quite a stir, young man."

"Yes, you did," answered the woman, her arm still around the boy, the look of fear and love still in her eyes. "What were you doing? What were you thinking? We were so worried, so afraid."

Toby couldn't see the boy's face, but could hear the solemnity in his voice, in his reply.

"You did not need to worry. I was about my Father's business."

The couple exchanged a look over the boy's head, and the older man was the one who answered. "Yes, Yeshua, I'm sure you were. But, did you have to be so *strong* about it. You know the Sanhedrin does *not* take kindly to being educated from a boy who has only seen thirteen summers."

At that, the young boy became the child, and stuck out his chin in childish indignation. "I am a man, now. I have been mitzvahed."

The couple seemed to relax. "Yes," said the older man. "Yes, you have. I am corrected in this. Yeshua is now a man."

"Well, my man," said his mother. "You still need your mother to cook for you. Come, both of you. The others are waiting for us, and it is time for supper. We must go home now."

They continued walking, and since he had nowhere to go, Toby followed. They seemed to have no notice of him, and he followed them out of the city and to a small place that was quite a hike in the distance. Toby reckoned it at half a mile, but they walked it quickly. They seemed to be talking the whole time, but Toby stayed far back to avoid being seen, and missed it. They came to a large enclosure and turned in.

There was a shelter of sorts that looked like it had more than just one room to it. It was too large to be anything else. That had to be where they slept, where they lived. To Toby's left was a shed that had a roof and three walls, but only bracing in the front. Toby could see tools across a bench and hung from the beams that supported the roof. There was a fire pit, and what looked like an anvil. He spotted saws and adzes, what looked like hammers, and some unfinished wood projects of wheels and such. Of course, it was a carpenter's shed and workshop.

He heard the laughter of children and as the family approached the shelter, several more came spilling out of the door. They were giggling and talking at once, interrupted in their play, the game of tag now dancing around the older members of the family. Toby smiled as he watched them be scooped up by their father, each in turn, until he came to the littlest of them. Yes, they had been at play and everyone was home. They stood, a lovely tableau against the sand, until the mother clapped her hands and shooed them all inside. Hiding behind a palm tree, he watched them enter the simple dwelling.

All, but the boy. He stopped at the threshold, turned around and came back outside of the door. It was as if he were looking directly at Toby, behind the tree. In fact, Toby was sure of it. The boy nodded his head, and then turned back to the hovel and went inside.

Chapter Eleven

The strength left his legs and Toby dropped to his knees in the sand. There was just a small amount of shade beneath the fronds to afford him a little relief from the relentless sun. The heat was dry but he was soaked from the perspiration which evaporated leaving little abatement. He reached beside him, taking the clay pot, and drank the rest of the water in it. *I'll have to go get more,* he thought, *but later, when the sun's gone down. I can do it then. I just have to hold on until then.* His head lolled against the husky bark of the trunk and he felt woozy.

There was a sense of irony to it all. Here he was, a soldier trained in desert survival and here he sat as if he'd never set foot in one. He'd been trained to live in a desert, how to fight in it, how to survive. The time travel seemed to have stolen his common sense as well as his nerve. Here he sat hungry while inside they were eating. Here he sat with a stolen pottery jar when inside they had plenty of water. Here he sat frying in the desert while there was cooling shade in the shelter. If he only could work up the nerve to go up to the door, release this unmanly hold on his courage and *do* something. *If only....*

It was now his third day in this time and place. He had lost track of the hours and minutes, but he could still track the days by the rising and setting of the sun. He'd spent the first day watching the children playing outside of the hut, listening to them sing songs and chant rhymes. He saw Yeshua only once more after they had returned, when the boy brought out the clay pot to the carpentry shed. He had left it on one of the benches, then turned around and gone back inside. The sun finally set on the first day, the children had disappeared inside the hovel, and Toby had gone exploring. The light went out in the openings, and Toby crept up to them, trying to see inside.

He walked around the outside of the home, picking up pieces of toys, watching the animals that had decided to come out in the cooling night air. He felt a chill creep into his bones as a light wind blew through the trees, lifting the edges of his tunic to play around his ankles. After the heat of the day, it was no surprise that the night had become cooler. Toby rubbed his arms and clapped his hands across his chest to stay warm, and when there was nothing more to see in the yard, he went to the shed to look at the tools. He saw the clay pot sitting there, and it had water inside. The water had evaporated a bit, but it was still mostly full, and Toby's thirst won the better of him. He drank of the water and took the clay pot back to the tree. He could refill it from the well, when he needed to. Toby spent his first night curled in a ball at the base of the palm tree, huddled to keep warm, and he slept, dreamless.

The second day threatened to be more of the same, but it wasn't. Toby watched father and son greet the morning by coming out and working in the shed. The children were still playing, but Toby was only interested in Yeshua and his father. During the course of the morning, they were visited by no less than a dozen men, carrying assorted wooden implements and wheels.

The father greeted each man, in turn, and listened intently as the object was displayed to him. He would nod and take the object, examining it and offering some words of assurance to the other. The boy would hand his father the tool needed, and attend to the small fire nearby. Together, they fashioned new wheels, new utensils, and fixed bowls needed for cooking, eating, or drinking. They worked as a team, with the father, occasionally, giving his son a gesture of affection by ruffling the boy's hair or clapping the boy's back. Some payment would be given to the father, the object carried off, and they would make ready for the next customer.

After the midday meal, the young man came out, carrying another jug. Toby had long since drunk his water, but had not gone back to the well, not wanting to miss anything. He watched Yeshua walk out of the enclosure, carrying the large jug on his shoulder, and Toby decided to follow him. He kept back at, what he hoped was a discreet distance, watching the boy walk jauntily to the town. He watched the boy approach the well and draw the water, pouring it into the pot. When Yeshua had done that, Toby followed him into the market. There, he saw Yeshua purchase packages of what looked like dried fish and fruit of some kind. The young man took his packages and his water jar and left the village. Toby noticed the stares that the young man received and saw yet others whispering behind veils to each other. At all times, they left Yeshua alone and cut him a wide berth. For his part, Yeshua didn't notice. *Or did he?*

Toby didn't know if the boy was all that oblivious, but the people were nervous about this young man. So he waited behind to find out why those villagers had reacted that way. Maybe it was his nerve returning, or maybe it was his curiosity, but he *had* to know. When he was sure Yeshua was gone, he went to the woman who sold the packages to Yeshua and talked to her. She was, understandably, less than co-operative at first, until Toby asked the right question.

"That family is an odd one," she said, with a glint in her eye. Her voice became hard and gossipy as she spoke. "I've heard talk that the eldest boy is not her husband's. That she became great with child before he had married her or knew her. I've heard that her child was born of divine intervention."

"And, did you believe the stories?" Toby asked.

The old woman spit on the ground, and said, "One has only to look at the child to see that he is not of the father."

"But did you *believe* them?" Toby asked again.

The old woman ignored the question. "They say he performs miracles. *Heh!* The only miracle I've seen that child perform is keeping from getting his backside bruised. He's a smart mouthed little know it all. Always knows more than anyone around him, always has an opinion about everything. His parents indulge him too much," she paused, waggling her finger at Toby in a gesture of knowing more than he did.

"What do you mean?"

"Telling the Sanhedrin about their business, as if he knows the mind of God. That boy only knows how to anger people."

"But do you believe the stories they tell about him? Is he what they say he is?" Toby asked a third time, more emphatically than before.

The yenta shook her head and waved dismissively at Toby. "That boy is just as you and I. He is a smart one, that is for certain, but no more divine than any of us."

Toby thanked her and left the stand. He walked aimlessly, no other purpose than the need for information. He got it from them. He would stop someone at random, and ask his questions about Yeshua. He would get the same reply from all of them. Toby noticed that they professed disbelief to his face, but they were always quick to make a sign against the evil eye. Oh, they believed this young man was different, but they also believed there was something wrong. *They're afraid of him. They're scared shitless. Why?*

He walked about for what seemed a long time before he came again to the well. The heat was starting to get to him again and he was thirsty. He pulled up the bucket, and filled his jar and then, took the dipper and began to drink the remainder. He drank, dropping the bucket back into the well once more, and filled himself with the sweet water. He drank until he could hold no more and his fatigue got the better of him. He had decided to sit down by the well and rest for a moment or two before the long walk back to where the boy lived. He had only meant to sit for a few moments, but his eyelids began to feel heavy. He let go and closed his eyes, letting it all fade away into the background as the darkness enveloped him. He leaned back against the well, and fell asleep.

He had no idea how long he had slept, but the voice woke him again. Two women had come for water. He was still groggy, the sleep slowly releasing him, but it was their conversation that finally penetrated the fog in his head. . He sat and listened to the splash of the bucket dipping into the water below and filling their clay jars as they talked.

"Avner says that he caused quite a stir in the temple," one said, with a hushed tone of someone who wanted to relate the gory details of a traffic accident.

"What happened?" the other asked, intent on hearing every single gory detail.

"Avner says that he told the Sanhedrin that they were wrong in an interpretation of Talmud, said that he spoke with the authority of his Father in Heaven. Heh! *A boy!* Telling the Sanhedrin they were wrong! Avner says that they were most upset."

"Avner told you what the boy said?" the second voice asked in shocked tones.

"Oh, no," the first replied in haughty, all-knowing glee. "That would be against the laws of the church. But he said that the Sanhedrin will meet to discuss the boy and what should be done about him." There was a splash of water to punctuate the declaration, and she finished with a malicious, "He is a *dangerous* child, Avner says."

"What will they do with the little brat?" the second voice asked. "And why do his parents indulge him so? Do they not teach him better?"

Toby suddenly had the urge to reach up and slap the two women silly. There was a self-righteousness in their voices that he didn't like. These were the same types who would be all too happy to ruin a young woman's reputation because of spite or jealousy. *Stupid bitches*, he thought, and kept his tongue in check.

"Avner would not say," the first answered, her smug tone almost more than Toby could take. "Perhaps he does not know. He says that something must be done. It cannot be allowed. *To teach the Sanhedrin?* It is wrong!"

The two voices carried on about other things, about someone's crop failing, someone's child having an illness, someone's interest wandering from the teachings of the Talmud into secular areas. On and on until they faded out of his hearing as the women left to go about their day. Toby stood up and watched them off in the distance. It didn't matter what he thought about the young man, these people were not buying into the myth of the Messiah.

Toby had taken his full jar and walked back the way he had come. His mind was buzzing now. He'd proved to himself and to his own satisfaction that no one was buying into this fable. No one had seen any miracles; no one had seen any messianic behavior. This young boy was nothing more than a tale told from one to another and in the telling, the story got bigger and bigger.

Hell, it was forty years before the Gospels ever got committed to scroll, he thought. *The mind plays tricks, forgets details, adds things that didn't happen. It was all blown out of proportion and like any good Grimm fairy tale, it scared the kids. That's all this is. Another fairy tale.*

But, something held Toby back. All he had to do was twist the ring and think his way back to his own time and place. If this fable he was living was true, all he had to do was give this curse to someone else and he could poof himself out of existence. A sanctioned suicide, and it was all over, he could just check out. He found he couldn't do it. The sun set on a second day, and he sat underneath his palm tree, hungry and cold, and stared at the ring in the moonlight. *All I have to do is twist it...think of my time and place...just do it...you've got the answer, just leave.* He curled up into his ball, wrapped around the jug, and fell into a sleep.

~*~

He wakes up, and it's still dark. He feels a presence next to him, and sits up in the night, and turns to his right. There, Bion sits.

"What are you doing here, man," he asks the dead man.

"You ain't done here, man, and you know it." Bion sits, calmly, and just watches Toby.

"It's a lie," Toby tells his friend. "Don't' you get it? It's all a lie. He's not a Messiah, he's just a kid. He's just a thirteen year old kid with an attitude problem and charisma up the ass."

Bion shakes his head and says, "You really believe that shit?"

"Yeah, I do," Toby answers with more conviction than he's felt in a long time. "I do and I'm leaving."

"Brother man, if you was really buying that shit, you'd done be gone by now. Don't be yanking my chain. You know different because you felt him. He knows you're here. He knows where you are."

"Yeah, so what?"

Bion shakes his head and snorts in disgust. "Man, how did you get to be captain and be so stupid? Maybe them Gospels was written later, maybe they wasn't. You ever think o' that? Some of 'em was written earlier. Some of 'em was written while he still was here. Don't you know nuthin'?"

Toby ponders this, lets it roll around in his head, before shaking it, dismissing the thought. "No," he says, "it's all a myth, made up by those who wanted to keep him alive. Hell, why not? You're my friend, I keep you alive. You're not here, you're dead."

Bion laughs, throwing back his head until he shakes with it. "Son, being dead don't mean I ain't here. You see me, don't you? Shit, brother man, you're sittin' in a desert two thousand years before either one of us was born. You believe that shit, don't ya?"

Toby is caught off-guard. He is here, in that long ago past that he has only read about, dreamed about, been preached to about. If he truly believes he is here, then he has to question the validity of his statement. No, that's too much. He starts to go into sensory overload again.

"Wait," he says, "those people say he's done no miracles. They think he's just a smart ass kid."

Bion rolls his eyes and shakes his head. "Come on, Captain, you *know the old saying, a prophet ain't never recognized in his own home town. Shit, it's like that always; don't believe in the homeboy. But how you know he* ain't *done 'em and them folks don't know about 'em? And why are they so scared of him? Hmm? Why they actin' like that if he ain't nuthin' but a fairy tale?"*

Toby takes a breath and says nothing. Bion just watches his silence, answering with his own. Toby feels the sleep beginning to overtake him again, and he leans back against the tree trunk. As he slips back into the darkness, he hears Bion say, "Go to him. Talk to him. See if it's true instead o' listening to a bunch of bullshit."

~*~

Toby had awakened, still leaning up against the palm, his hand resting on the jar. The sun had gone high into the sky and Toby could see it was too close to noon. He had slept late in the morning. It was the heat sapping his energy, taking away his resolve to move. The heat and his hunger made him lethargic and sleepy. He thought about the dream, and tried to decide if he should stay or go. Should he leave with Bion's questions still in his ears? Or should he stay and answer them?

He had decided to watch a little longer. He wished he really had the courage that Bion seemed to think he possessed. But he didn't. Toby wanted to go talk to the boy, but didn't know how. Sitting here, now, he was starting to feel out of sorts again. Maybe it was just a delusion; maybe he was still in that cave in Saudi and all of this was just a hallucination. Toby let go with the laugh of a madman baking in the desert. Well, that answered everything, didn't it? It was just a hallucination, nothing more.

The heat got to him and he slipped off again. He slipped into unconsciousness, with no dreaming, only the blackness. He was going crazy and this was all a lie. It was okay though, going crazy made it easier to bid the world adieu. He could do it here and no one would miss him. *It's not happening. I'm not real and he's not a messiah.*

He might have gone on believing just that, if the hand on his shoulder hadn't brought him back to reality very quickly. He jerked awake, slamming the back of his head against the rough bark, and sending sparks of pain into his consciousness. The sun had dropped down in the time he'd been asleep, it was almost evening or would be soon enough. The hand was cool on his skin and the touch was firm, insistent. He pulled himself together, gathering his wits, only to look up into the equally cool brown eyes of the boy.

"And have you come to the way of things?" Yeshua asked and he squatted down beside Toby. The expression on his face was one of concern or understanding, or both.

Toby just sat there, not knowing what to say.

Yeshua just nodded. "Or you have sat here, watching, and you are still not settled. Why is that?"

"You...you...*knew*," Toby managed to croak out, suddenly incredulous, and then answered his own question. "*Of course*, you knew. You left me the jar. You knew I was here."

Another nod, and the boy answered, "I have known these things, seen you watching me. I have waited for you to come to me. You did not. And so I waited more. And still you did not come. Did you get the answers you sought from Lydia?"

Toby flushed with guilt, and answered, "Yes. How – how did you know?"

"It would be the only reason you did not follow me back," Yeshua answered. "To ask questions of others. But you do not ask those questions of me."

Toby shook his head and looked down.

"Why?"

Toby looked back up into his eyes again. They were calming, those eyes. From such a young boy, this calm, this assuredness, and yet, he was still a child. Toby could tell that at once. "I don't know," he answered slowly, and then in a rush of words, blurted out, "Look, I'm not here to hurt anyone. I just...I wanted to—"

The hand never left his shoulder, and now, it squeezed lightly and softly, cutting off the flow of words. Yeshua interrupted him, "I know. But, you have kept me waiting when you should have come to me. I have my destiny to fulfill and it seems that you are part of it."

"Am I?"

Yeshua responded only with a laugh, and stood up. He held his hand out to Toby. "Come, Tobias. You are here, now. You must come. Surely you have had nothing to eat and you thirst. Come and break your fast with us."

Toby still didn't move. He looked into the calm face once more and took a deep breath. It *was* the reason he had come to this time and this place. What the hell was holding him back? Was he afraid that this kid would know who he really was? Was he afraid that this boy would know he was a fraud? Was he buying into this Jesus myth? What was the problem?

"You are afraid."

Toby opened his mouth. The boy read his thoughts so easily, or was it that Toby was telegraphing what he felt. Yeah, he was afraid. He was afraid that he was going to buy into all of this and not do what he had set out to do. "Yes," Toby answered.

"Don't be," Yeshua replied. "You are a guest in my home."

Toby took his hand, and was pulled off the ground. Yeshua was strong, probably because of helping his father. The grip was firm, but not unpleasantly so. Yeshua smiled and Toby smiled back. And then, the thirteen-year-old proved that he was still a boy in his show of exasperation.

Yeshua put his hands to his hips and said, with a distinct lack of patience, "*Come!* Will you stand here all day? You are late as it is. Come; *now!*"

He turned on his heel and started off towards his home, never looking back at Toby. Because Toby had to go *somewhere*, he followed the young man into the courtyard, and through the sea of children. Halfway to the door, he stopped with a jerk and whirled around again to look at the children. He saw their faces up close and noticed the resemblance to the young man. It wasn't a strong resemblance, and wouldn't be – except from having the same mother. Of *course, he had brothers and sisters*, he thought. There was another myth destroyed.

Yeshua stepped inside the house, and Toby followed him into the dim, cool interior of the clay building. As his eyes became accustomed to the darkness, he started to get a sense of the layout. He stood in what appeared to be the main room of the home. To his left were a fireplace and a table and chairs. There were shelves of plates and bowls, and there were more clay pots and pitchers hanging from fashioned hooks. To his right, there was a small seating area and a very large pallet lying against the wall. It was about the size of a queen size bed, Toby noticed, and he blushed. There was a ladder that was propped up against the wall, and it led straight up into an attic of sorts. Toby couldn't see what was up there, but he had a feeling it was where the children slept.

He heard a polite cough, and turned back to his left. There, by the fireplace, the woman from the temple sat patting a pancake of some kind, back and forth between her hands. He could really see her now, closer and not rushing away with her son. She was beautiful, in a plain way, with a face that had seen too much sun and too little pampering. Her face was tanned and oval, framed by her hair. She was a bit frumpy from the ravages of time and childbearing. Her eyes, however, caught Toby; her eyes that were the deepest brown. The smile she had on her face lit up those eyes and yet, held the faintest sorrow with small crinkles in the corners of them. The silver in her hair sparkled in the firelight and the corners of her mouth had the beginnings of the lines of age.

He couldn't take his eyes off her. This wasn't the beatific woman in the picture on his mantle – what *used* to be his mantle. This woman didn't have that otherworldly glow of silver and moonlight in her skin. She was real, this mother of Yeshua. He thought about the time and people he'd left behind; would they still follow this woman or hold her in such high esteem if they knew that she wasn't what those card and pictures and cheese sandwiches made her out to be.

Her smile broadened as Yeshua's lips met her cheek. "Well, my son, have you found what you were seeking?"

"Yes, Mother, he is here. You will prepare extra for him, yes?"

"I have done so, my son. And now, we will welcome your guest into our home." She stood and crossed the floor to stand before Toby. Both of her hands came out to clasp his and her soft cheek pressed against his in welcome. "Welcome to our home," she said, her voice warm and soothing. "You must thirst. Yeshua, get your guest some water from the jar. Please, come and rest yourself. I am Miriam. Yeshua is my son. My husband, Yosef, is from home at present, but will be joining us shortly for meal. Please. Come and sit."

Toby did just as he was told, and Miriam *(Mary)* crossed back to the fire and began her patting of the cakes again. She took each pancake she created and laid on a hot stone until she had created several. She turned several more that had already browned. Yeshua brought a clay cup of water and handed it to Toby, who drank until he drained the cup. Yeshua went to fetch more.

"Thank you...Miriam."

There was a returning smile as she answered, "You are quite welcome. You've been out there for several days now. I am not surprised that you are thirsty and hungry."

"Well, my Mother always taught me to give thanks when a kindness was given. I thank you."

As Yeshua handed him the cup again, she answered again. "You are most welcome. Now, by what name are you called? Yeshua says it is...Tobias?"

"Yes, ma'am," he answered in a sudden humility and awe. "My name is...Tobias."

"You are far from your home, Tobias. How come you to be here?"

"I...uh, well, my parents died. And I...um...wanted to travel a bit, I guess."

Miriam looked up at Toby with her kind eyes and sweet smile on her beautiful homely face and he saw it – he saw *her*; he saw the picture. He saw the compassion in her eyes, heard the caring in her voice.

"They have gone to God, Tobias. It is a better place that they are in. But, I do grieve for your loss."

Toby swallowed hard, trying to keep his voice from breaking around the large lump that had quickly grown in his throat. "Thank you," he managed in a hoarse whisper.

"It is a hard thing, to submit to the Father's will. Even with the knowing, it is a hard thing."

"Yes; yes, it is."

Miriam was silent for a moment before changing the subject. "And so, you travel?"

"Yes," Toby answered, grateful for the change. "I've, uh, always wanted to travel, learn about other places. It seemed like the thing to do."

Miriam began to pull the cakes from the stones and pile them on a basket. "Ah, men and their need to search the world. Yeshua has been speaking of travel."

Yeshua, who'd been completely content to let his mother speak for a time, now spoke for himself. "I have a destiny to fulfill, one that was appointed by my Father. In order to fulfill it, I must travel. It is He who wishes it."

Toby looked at first the mother, then the son. He was beginning to see why the others were a bit wary around the young lad. He was self-assured, bordering on cocky. He had an air about him that Toby could see was easily interpreted as "know it all." "Then...I suppose you should do it."

Yeshua nodded and, with an enigmatic smile, said, "You'll do."

Toby's mouth opened and then snapped shut. *You'll do?* What did *that* mean? Before Toby could ask, however, there was another arrival – the man from the temple.

The older man lifted the tapestry from the door of the hovel, striding in. He was a cheerful man, looking to be in his late forties. His hair was gray, but the former black was still evident in the beard on the man's face. He was stocky, well-muscled, and when he saw Toby, this man crossed the floor quickly and took Toby's arm in a strong embrace. "I am Yosef. You must be our watcher. You are welcome in my home."

Miriam stood and greeted her husband with an embrace, then went back to attending to the evening meal. Yosef gestured to the seating area and poured them both a bit of wine to enjoy until the meal was served.

This was not what he had expected – but then, he wasn't sure what he expected. Maybe what he had looked for was something more...*divine*? Here they were, a perfectly normal family preparing for a perfectly normal meal by washing their perfectly normal hands and sitting down in front of a perfectly normal fire. And here he was, in the middle of it all – out of place, out of time, and out of his mind. But, he took the wine as if none of this was remotely unusual to him. And they talked of wood and carpentry and furniture.

Miriam called the children in to eat and they came rushing in, a ravening horde of laughter and teasing. They all sat around the fire, and Yosef asked blessing of the food they were about to receive. Toby noticed that Yeshua raised his face where the others bowed their heads. His eyes were open, as if he was listening to some unseen voice. The food was shared around, the parents filling plates for the little ones before filling their own. Miriam had prepared the flat bread, and with it were the cheese that Yeshua had purchased, some figs and dates, and the wine that Yosef had shared with him earlier. He hadn't known how hungry he was until he had bit into the first piece of fruit.

Toby polished off the figs and dates on his plate, stopping for a few sips of wine and to catch his breath. Reaching down for the cup, he noticed that Yeshua was watching him with a look of amusement. They all were, to his embarrassment, and the little ones, seated on the floor, began giggling and pointing. A quick clicking of her tongue and Miriam brought that to a halt. She simply dropped a few more figs and another piece of cheese on his plate. Toby looked up at her smile and returned one of his own.

When the evening meal was finished and the wine was gone, the sun had disappeared from the sky. Miriam cleared away the dishes and brought another skin of the wine they had been drinking. She filled their goblets and then ushered the children up the ladder – he'd been right about the room. She returned to sit by a lamp and tend to the needlework that she pulled from a nook. Yosef sat back and began to whittle something with a knife, a small animal from the appearance of it. It was a comfortable routine, Toby could tell, and he slipped into it as well. He sipped his wine and felt the warmth of the fire and for the first time since he'd arrived, the first glimmer of normal washed over him.

Yeshua seemed to be stewing on something, his face a study in thought as he too stared at the fire. It was some moments before he finally broke the silence.

"I will be leaving soon, father. Tobias and I will be traveling to meet my destiny."

Toby took a quick gulp of the wine, but Yosef just chuckled.

"You will, my son? And has Tobias agreed to this?"

"He has."

"I have?" Toby sputtered. He met Yeshua's gaze and felt another piece fall into place, a small click inside of his mind. He answered his own question with full assurance of the truth, "I have."

Yosef blew some shavings from the piece, never looking up, but continuing on. "You know my mind on this, Yeshua. I feel that there is no need of this trip. You can learn all you need here, boy."

"No, I cannot. My Father has need of my leaving this place. He has told me that there are places that I must travel. I will come back to my people, but first I must be *away* from them."

Yosef's voice was calm, never rising above the conversational tone. "And if I do not give my permission for this journey of yours? I suppose you will go anyway?"

The thirteen-year-olds stubbornness came full force, "Yes, I must.

I must spread my Father's word throughout the lands, and His need for me to go to these people is great."

"And what says Tobias of this?"

Toby cleared his throat and thought for a moment. Nothing like being plunked in the middle of what was obviously a family squabble. Maybe, if he agreed to this, it would put the family's fears to rest – at least they could trust him. Besides, this was the perfect opportunity. Travel with the boy and see what the kid was made of. If he was going to prove this was all nonsense, it was the perfect way to do it. He met Yosef's steady look with one of his own and answered honestly, "Sir, I am agreed to this. I am alone. My family has gone to God and I have nothing keeping me here. I think that escorting your son on his journey will suit me fine."

"My...son, yes," Yosef said with a touch of amusement in his voice, but with something different in his eyes. "Well, then, my *son,* you must travel and spread the word. When will you go?"

Toby answered that one for the both of them. "Tomorrow, sir. We'll leave tomorrow."

Yosef nodded, and then looked towards his wife, "Well, Miriam, it would seem that our travelers leave us on the morrow."

"Yes, my husband, so it would appear," she answered her husband. "Then, I shall get your packs ready. You will need food and skins of water."

Miriam rose and busied herself doing just that. Yosef stood and walked out of the hovel, leaving Yeshua and Toby sitting by the fire.

Yeshua looked from the doorway to his companion at the table, and said, "Do not fret, my friend. He fears for the future, and what is coming. He has dreams in which God tells him of what must be. He wishes to avoid it, and yet, he knows that I will be well. He knows that I will be at my Father's work."

"Well...then we both will be, won't we," Toby answered, still feeling like a bit of a jerk for his part in this. He was taking their son away; he knew exactly how he would feel in that situation. They were just better at hiding it than he would have been. He turned his attention back to Yeshua. "Can I ask you a question?"

"Most certainly."

"Why me?"

Yeshua smiled and ducked his head before answering. "You have a good heart, Tobias, but more than that, you have come searching for answers to the riddle of your life." The boy's face was so serious, even with the smile. "You think that you can take away your pain by removing the cause of it. But, you cannot remove the cause, my friend; you can only search more deeply for the answer of why things happen. Sometimes God allows small answers to help us. I think you *and* I shall find our answers on this journey."

Toby drank off the remainder of the wine in the cup he held. There was a sudden surety in his own heart of what the boy was saying. "I think, my friend, that you are right."

Yeshua stood at that moment and followed Yosef out into the night. Toby had no strength to do so. It was just as well, because he watched Miriam prepare the packs and set them by the door. She said nothing for the entire time and Toby couldn't disturb the quiet. It wasn't until she had finished that she again acknowledged his presence. She spoke only five words...no more, and no less.

Her hands pressed against her belly, sniffing back the obvious tears, she couldn't meet his eyes. She simply whispered in her husky voice, "Take care of my son."

Toby found the strength to get up, then. He walked over to Miriam, and taking her hands in his, he kissed them—a formal gesture, but one that he felt was necessary. He held them to his heart and answered, "I will, Mother of God. I will."

The evening came to a close and Toby was given a bedroll next to Yeshua in the attic. The other children were fast asleep didn't rouse them when the two came up. Toby was surprised at how exhausted he was after having slept most of the last twenty four hours, thanks to the heat exhaustion he must have had. He curled up, his head resting on his shoulder, and was fast asleep.

Bion was there, scared. He heard the buzzing of the scud and he felt the ground shaking. Bion was screaming and he knew that the next thing was the cave in. He tried to shout at Bion to move, to get the hell out of there. But, nothing came from his mouth. No words. Bion just stood there, screaming, and the ground was shaking.

But, no, it was the djinn – not screaming but laughing; those were the sounds of laughter. The djinn was laughing at him. It wasn't the ground shaking; it was Bion shaking him. He turned and saw Bion's huge hands on his arms and he was shaking Toby hard enough that Toby's teeth clattered. Shaking, shaking....

~*~

"Wake up, Tobias. Please *wake up.*

No, it wasn't Bion. Toby abruptly and rudely jerked himself into a sitting position, with Yeshua grabbing tight to his shoulder. The boy's face was strained and tight.

"What...*what?*"

"We must leave! Now!" Yeshua was satisfied that Toby was fully conscious and raised a finger to his lips. "Shh, do not wake the children."

"What? Leave?" Toby was still groggy, nothing was making sense. His eyes were feeling gummed together and

"I have had a vision." The boy stood, still whispering. "My Father came to me. The townspeople are coming to take me. They are afraid of me. They cannot do this." He turned and started down the ladder. He spared one more glance at Toby as his head was just above the floor, illuminated from below by the firelight. "We must go," the boy repeated, the urgency stronger in his whisper. "Come, Mother has our packs ready. We must leave this place *now.*"

The boy's voice was enough to make Toby jump from the floor and bolt down the ladder. Miriam and Yosef were also awake and they hugged the boy tight in their arms. He could see the tears in Miriam's eyes as she held on to Yeshua. Toby became a bit embarrassed at the sight and just muttered his goodbye before walking out into the crisp night air. It was a bit chilly, but not uncomfortably so. Toby took a deep breath of the night air; how sweet and clear it was. No, he wasn't going to miss the pollution of his time. This was beautiful. He could smell the clean desert air. He could see the desert night sky. He could almost reach up and touch the stars. He could hear...*he could hear....*

Toby heard voices – far off and indistinct, but voices, they were, and they were *not* happy. He trotted down to the dirt road that lead to this place and in the distance, he could see flames. *Torches.* He knew what that meant, a mob. *Looks like Avner and his ilk decided what to do after all. Whatever it is, it's not going to be pleasant.*

He had barely turned around when a pack was shoved in his

hands, and a quiet voice uttered, "Come, we will hide in the dunes. Mother and Father know what to say that will make them think we have left. They will go off in the direction that they think *we* have, and we will leave."

"We'll need to go to the well and fill the water skins," he answered, just as quietly.

"Yes, but they must go off in the opposite direction. They must think we have gone and that they can catch us." He gripped Toby's arm, tugging gently but persistently in his eagerness to get away. "Come with me. I know where to hide."

Yeshua released his arm, and they ran across the dirt road and another thirty paces to a dune beyond Toby's tree. They got behind it and waited, watching the mob close in on the homestead almost as soon as they were hidden. They watched as Yosef came out of the building and spoke to them. One man in front seemed to be the spokesperson for the mob. Yosef stood, with Miriam at his side, and talked to the man. *Was that Avner?* They talked for a bit, and he must have been very convincing, because, Avner – or whoever he was – turned back to the crowd, which uttered a roar and then left. They came to the dirt road, and instead of turning left to go back into the town, they turned right and continued until they were out of sight.

Toby felt the hand on his arm again, and heard the soft voice. "We leave now. Come. Quickly."

When Toby stepped out on the road back into the town, he stopped long enough to look towards the retreating torches. Well, he wanted the journey. He had desperately needed the trip. All he had to do was take the one step and he was on the way. One step – taking that one step.

"Come, Tobias. We must hurry. They will see that we have not gone that way and will be coming back. We must make for the well and be gone. Come. *Come.*"

No, he had something to prove. He was going to prove it. He took the step towards town.

He took the step.

Chapter Twelve

The first night of the journey began at the well. The two ran into the village with Toby looking over his shoulder every other minute. Yeshua filled the skins as quickly as he could while Toby stood watch. The plan was to find some place where they could hide and finish the night sleeping, to wait out the mob's tenacity. And they *were* tenacious! Toby and Yeshua had gotten the skins filled just in time to hear the shouts of the mob again. The crowd hadn't been fooled for long, and they were coming back to the city. Toby was intensely grateful for the desert air, carrying the threats and epithets to his ears well in advance of the returning horde. He grabbed the boy's shoulder and pulled him along, not even leaving Yeshua time to drop the bucket back into the well. If it was a mistake, they'd pay later, but for now, they had to leave.

Toby let Yeshua take the point, and the boy certainly knew this part of desert like the back of his hand. Yeshua trotted for what would have been a mile or so before he turned off the path into the night. A gentle breeze quickly covered their tracks as Yeshua led his companion through a series of small dunes. They walked until they were sure that they were alone and had lost the mob. After several minutes, hunkered down against a sand dune, the quiet remained and there were no torches. Yeshua seemed satisfied enough to grunt and nod at the ground. They spread out the bedrolls that Miriam had provided and laid down on them. Toby would've sworn that he'd be out as soon as his head hit the ground, but he couldn't sleep – not yet, not until he asked one question.

"Was this because of what happened in the temple that day?"

It was a full moon over the desert and Toby could see the boy very clearly. Yeshua raised up on one elbow, his face a study of contemplation. To tell it all or only some.

"Some of it, yes. But not all."

"It's because you're *different*?"

"Different?" The boy paused for a moment and then shook his head. "No. It is because I offer them change, Tobias. I offer them a freedom that we have not known for a very long time. It is hard for them to accept that change."

"But you told the Sanhedrin that—"

"I told the Sanhedrin that the day of the One True God is coming and that they must prepare. They want repayment for the wrongs, the pain and humiliation they have suffered, but they do not think that I can lead them there."

"They want someone older? More seasoned?"

"They do not know what they want. Or who. But they want an eye for an eye, a tooth for a tooth. They want revenge. I bring them justice."

"How will it happen?"

The boy's voice sounded weary as he answered, "Another day, Tobias, another time. For now, we sleep. I am weary enough that I cannot move any farther."

"One of us should stay up then, to keep watch."

The boy's voice was sharp as he answered, "Tobias, has anyone ever told you that you think and talk too much?"

Toby smiled in the dark, remembering all the times his father had said just that. "Far too many times to count. Is it safe, do you think?"

Yeshua had settled back down on his pallet and his arm was curled under his head for a pillow. He sighed, a soft sound that floated in the darkness. "It is safe, Tobias. If it were not, I would not have been directed here. Please, get some sleep now. I do not wish to discuss it anymore."

Toby yawned, his jaw painfully cracking with a loud pop. "Good night, Yeshua."

"Sleep well, my friend."

And with that, the boy turned over on his side and didn't move again. Toby couldn't fall asleep that quickly. He lay there, thinking, wondering. What would happen? Where were they going? Did it matter? He was here and this was whom he'd come to find. What was the next step? It was during a conversation with himself that he drifted off.

He sits by a campfire. Bion sits with him.

"Toby, man, what are you doing? You been hanging around with your thumb up your ass, man. What's wrong with you?"

"I'm lost, Bion. I thought I was going to come out here and find

out the truth, ya know?"

"So? What's stopping ya?"

"I like this kid, Bion. How the hell do I do this when I like the kid?"

"You came here for the truth, Captain. First, you act like you ain't ever been in the desert before, and now, you act like this is some recon mission. You came here for the truth. Find it!"

"Find it? Easier said than done, my friend."

But the djinn answered, "But, we thought you were a seeker of knowledge? Now, you question the method of how this learning is delivered to you. Are you afraid? Still? Always?"

No, not afraid...no! But he feels something for the boy. How do you shatter the myth and not shatter the boy...the man? And in the background, his name is called again.

"Tobias, find it. Tobias, you must find the truth. Tobias—"

"*Tobias*! It is time to wake!"

The hand that shook him awake was firm, but friendly. Toby's eyes opened to find his companion kneeling over him, and the sun rising over the horizon. Toby smiled and sat up. He saw that Yeshua had already packed his sleeping roll, and was ready to go. A small amount of food had been laid out for breakfast, and they had little time to eat it and be off. They ate a meager meal of dried fish and figs before Toby packed his roll and they were ready.

He and Yeshua walked back to the path and stood there. To turn left would be to return to the village, and *that* was not an option. Toby now saw that they had stopped at a fork in the road. With no idea of where they were, they needed to choose where they were going. One path went toward the east, the other toward the west. *Which way? Which way do we go?*

"Tobias, perhaps we should go that way."

Yeshua was pointing in a direction, but Toby had a feeling. Yeah, he had spent this trip with his thumb up his ass, letting the situation rule him, instead of the other way round. It was time to take control, take charge, and start commanding. It was time to start following what his gut told him.

"No, that's not a good idea."

Yeshua turned and watched Toby, who stood checking the wind, watching the surrounding area. Something was telling him that the west path was the right one. *Yes, the desert can fool a man—the heat rising can be mistaken for water; the distance can be more than it appears.* There were unmistakable signs that Toby recognized, but in the end, it was his intuition that won out. If they went west, there would be civilization and a new path, the path to wherever they were meant to go. In the west, there was water and shelter. It was almost as if he could smell or taste it. This was a well-worn path. He knew which way to go.

"No," Toby answered again, and pointed off down the left path. "We take that direction, to the west. We follow that way, we'll get what we need."

Yeshua glanced in the direction Toby point out and nodded. "Yes. There is a village in that direction, and my Mother has family there. We can stop and get more supplies. They might give us shelter for an evening. Yes, this is good." He clapped Toby on the back. "You have chosen well for a visitor. You have traveled this road before?"

Toby grinned and shook his head, "No, just what my heart tells me."

"Then, it is the first step of your destiny," Yeshua answered. "Come, we have several days of traveling and I wish to be away from this place."

It took them three days to arrive at another town, but there was water, a place to sleep out of the elements. There was food. Miriam's family had taken them in and treated them well. They couldn't stay long because there was the threat that they might have been followed. Toby didn't really believe that they would be, but it was always possible. After all, the main purpose was to get the boy out of the town. Since that had been accomplished, Toby didn't think the mob would want any more.

They stayed a night in the town and left. The two put three towns between them and the sands of Nazareth before they finally felt safe enough to slow a bit. The next place they stopped, they stayed a few days longer. Toby took the time to start watching the boy. Something was changing, and Toby wasn't sure if it was Yeshua or his own perception of him. The boy was confident, yes, but he was starting to be a little more than Toby had expected. It was a journey north and west that finally helped Toby put a finger on what it was.

"The time is coming, Tobias. You will see it come and it will be a great change on the land, on the people. I bring that change. I am the sword that will cut the Romans from our home as a healer would cut the disease from a body. You will see."

"I don't understand, Yeshua. What do you mean, you 'are the sword'?"

Toby had never asked about the boy's mission in life and hadn't wanted to. He liked the kid but that was all he was – a kid. Yes, Yeshua was strong willed, stubborn most of the time. He had a tendency to be a little arrogant but what teenager didn't? They never discussed religion, never delved any more deeply than that day's meal or place to lie down on. They stayed to the safe subjects and Toby was content with that. But he'd broached the subject and it could no longer be avoided.

"It is the prophecy, Tobias. I am come to fulfill the prophecies of Isaiah and David. God has spoken to me and told me that I am His Son. I am to lead His chosen people to freedom and He will be with us."

"Freedom? Freedom from who?" Toby was confused for a moment, until he remembered the day he met Yeshua, and the arm that pulled him back. "Rome?"

"It is as such," the boy answered, a cocky tone creeping into the young voice. "Rome has invaded the body of Israel. Our lives, our health, our very souls have been tainted with Roman stench. They oppress us and we are nothing more than conquered territory."

Toby walked for a few paces before he answered. "But Israel has gained from them, haven't you? The aqueduct, the roads, the markets...."

"Minor conveniences that have neither hurt nor benefited us."

"Hardly *minor*, Yeshua, those 'conveniences' helped to – uh, *will* help revolutionize the world. The Roman sense of law is amazing in its structure." He chuckled under his breath at the thought, and a sudden chill in the air forced his attention back to his companion, who was glaring at him openly.

Yeshua's voice was equally frozen as he replied, "They take from us *much* more. Rome has stolen our homes, beaten and starved our children, made our mothers and fathers into slaves. We owe them nothing and they have demanded everything." The boy's eyes narrowed as he added, "You do well to remember that day I saved you from them. They would have trampled you to the ground and never thought of cleaning your flesh from their sandals."

If looks could kill, he thought to himself. He'd pissed off the Savior. But did he really want to press the issue? But his feelings about the boy had slipped a little along the way. Suddenly, he wasn't all that sure that he liked Yeshua at all. He turned his attention back to the road they traveled and Toby decided to change the subject...a bit. "How will you do that?"

Yeshua didn't seem to hold a grudge, and answered, "An army. I shall lead an army of men against them, as Joshua did, as Saul did, as my own forefather David did. Israel shall take up the sword and fight for her freedom, by driving them from our homeland. And if we must, we shall annihilate them. I shall lead my people as the Son of the One True God, as God's Chosen. I shall fulfill the scripture written by Isaiah." A look of sheer ecstasy came over the boy's face as he recited from memory, *"Of the increase of his government and peace there shall be no end, upon the throne of David, and upon his kingdom, to order it, and to establish it with judgment and with justice from henceforth even forever. The zeal of the LORD of hosts will perform this."*

Toby stopped dead in his tracks, shocked beyond his own wildest dreams. *This was the Messiah? This* was the being whose message was peace? Love? Do unto others? Preaching annihilation of the Romans? Calling for an armed resistance of bloodshed and homicide? Before he could comment, before he could even absorb this, Toby watched the serious young boy before him suddenly turn on his heel, give a glorious shout, and run off toward an approaching traveler. In the blink of an eye, a child ran to greet a possible peddler, and the would-be warrior was gone. Toby could only stand and watch, mouth open.

He tried to take in the brief conversation. Take up the sword? That didn't sound like the Messiah he remembered from childhood. What happened to lying down with the lamb? He supposed he might feel the same in Yeshua's shoes, but still, this was a far cry from the pacifist his mother had worshipped. And who was this arrogant brat that had replaced the endearing young man he'd been travelling with?

He was still thinking when Yeshua came back with some dried

fish and figs, paid for with the last of their money. "Tonight, we will feast well." The brat was gone again, the charismatic boy out to see the world had returned.

Toby nodded. "Yes, we will. Let us go further. I wish to be closer to the next village before nightfall."

Yeshua quickly fell into step with Toby and they walked in silence. Toby's mind turned over the conversation in his mind, as he tried to examine it, over and over. He was coming up with no answers, trying to reconcile the two. It was a long time before anyone spoke, but someone always started a conversation. It was that way between them.

"You are troubled."

Toby smiled and curled his lip in rueful agreement. "A little."

"Why?"

"Oh, I guess I just didn't expect that kind of an answer."

"What answer, Tobias?"

"Taking up the sword against Rome, leading an army. I always heard that you were – what the hell is this?"

Yeshua stopped, turning toward Toby. He opened his mouth to say something, but Toby didn't give him the chance to say it. He stepped around the boy.

A man ran toward them, looking over his shoulder after every few paces before continuing his headlong rush. He was a handsome man in his early twenties, with long, reddish-blonde curls framing his pale face. His jaw was square and his eyes, a dark blue. The man was lithe and agile, and his running reminded Toby of a cat's gait, grace in every step he took.

As soon as he reached Toby and Yeshua, the man dropped to his knees and, clutching his chest with one hand and struggling to breathe. He dropped the other hand to the ground to support himself, as if he were afraid of collapse on the hot sand. Toby noticed, under the disheveled curls on the man's forehead, there was a lump of healing scar tissue – in the shape of an "x" with a circle around it. Toby dropped to one knee at the man's side, and opened a skin of water, offering it to him. He looked up at Toby, and with another gasping breath, took the proffered skin. Holding it to his lips, he drank deeply. After several gulps of cool water, he handed the skin back to Toby, and nodded his thanks.

Toby asked, "What are you running from?"

"Romans," the man answered. "And it's your help, I'll be asking for. Please!" He swallowed hard and finished breathlessly, "You have to help me. They'll kill me if you don't."

That was all Yeshua had to hear. He clutched Toby's sleeve in a desperate fist, and shook the arm roughly. "Tobias, we must hide him. But how? Where? There's nothing but sand around us."

Toby's quick glance around him confirmed that not even an oasis or scrub of sorts was nearby. At the same time, he heard shouts from a distance. Whoever was chasing this man was coming fast and there was little time. What to do? An idea came to him. *Of course, their one big fear in these times. Of course, and I can use that.* Toby helped the man up.

"Well, then," he said, smiling. "We can't let them take you. I know what to do. Just follow my lead and do what I tell you, and you'll be safe."

Toby reached into his pack and pulled out a robe that Miriam had stored there. He motioned to the man to remove his own garment, and when he had done so, Toby threw the robe to him. Taking the man's garments in hand, he tore them to strips and quickly wrapped them around the man's head and hands. Yeshua, immediately understanding, reached into his own pack and pulled some dried berries from a wrapping. He chewed them quickly, spat them into his hand, and smeared the red gelatinous mess against the bandages on the man's head. The disguise was almost complete, and Toby took his sleeping rug, and wrapped it around the man's shoulders.

The shouts had been getting steadily louder as the force grew closer. Toby and Yeshua had finished the makeup job and turned the man around, in time to take a few steps, as if they were continuing a journey. And just in time, he saw. They came in crack formation and trotting along in this unbearable heat. He counted at least twenty soldiers running toward them. With a silent prayer, Toby hoped that this would work. If it didn't, they would all be taken.

"Now, then," he said, muttering of one corner of his mouth. "*You* don't talk. Neither one of you say anything. Let me talk for all of us. Agreed?"

Both of his companions nodded.

"Good. Let's keep walking."

They hadn't gone ten paces before a burly man as broad as he was tall, evidently the leader of the band of soldiers, stopped them. "You, halt. What is your business?"

Toby dropped his shoulders into a slump and let his head forward. He walked slowly toward the commander and bowed slightly to the man. The reaction was exactly what Toby had wanted, one of disgust and boredom. They wouldn't pay a whole lot of attention to the three men because they were looking for *one* man who should be fleeing in the opposite direction.

"We are simple travelers, sir," Toby replied, his voice equally subservient. "Nothing more."

The leader of the squad looked Toby up and down with a practiced eye, as Toby would have done. He knew the soldier was looking for weapons, but didn't expect to find any. "Where are your papers?"

Toby was enjoying playing the 'ignorant hayseed' role. "Papers, sir?"

"Papers, trash," the centurion replied with a growing disgust in his voice, and he grabbed Toby's shoulder in his ham sized fist. "You are required to carry papers at all times, as the Roman Governor has decreed."

"We have no papers, sir," Toby replied, and gave a penitent dip of the head, until he was staring at the ground. Inside he was laughing, but he was also scared shitless. If this didn't work....

The centurion released the grip on Toby's shoulder, and looked to the other two, and asked, "Why is that one bandaged?"

Toby struggled to stifle his grin; that was the question he had been waiting for. He did remember a *little* of his biblical history to know what one of the greatest fears of the time was. Now, if they didn't get too curious, curious enough to look deeper beyond the makeup job.

"Leper, sir. I fear he has the leprosy and we were told there was a colony near here."

Toby got the expected reaction as all of the men stepped back and winced as they did so. The commander, himself, took several paces from Toby. It was becoming harder and harder *not* to smile at these idiots. This was Rome at its finest?

"Yes...yes, there is," the centurion stammered and he rubbed his hand – the one he had touched Toby's shoulder with – under his armor against the cloth of his tunic. "On the other side of the next village."

"Thank you, sir," Toby said. "Then we shall be on our way." He motioned to Yeshua and the "leper" to follow along, but before he could move two paces, a hand flew up in his face.

The commander wasn't quite ready to let it go. He moved to take Toby's arm again before he stopped himself, obviously remembering. "One moment, the soldier said, letting his voice do the intimidating. "We are chasing an escaped slave. Perhaps you've seen him. A male with red-gold hair." He held one hand even with the height of his shoulder. "Standing so high, and the markings of a slave, a brand on his forehead."

Toby knew what to say. "Yes, sir. He asked for some water of us, and ran off." His hand was shaking a little and he made a fist to quell it. *Hang on, Toby, you can do this. We're almost there.* "We didn't know he was a slave, sir," he whined. "Please don't hurt us, sir. We didn't know."

Toby stepped forward, and put his hands on the forearm of the commander. With a look of disgust, he shoved Toby back, knocking him winding. Once again, he scrupulously scrubbed the hand to cleanse the foulness of the beggar before him.

"Get moving," the soldier sneered in complete disdain and disgust, "before I forget the one I'm after and take you instead."

"Yes, sir," Toby said, and bowed so slightly again.

Toby motioned to the "leper" and they both went forward, the runaway even managing to put a limp in his walk as they went. Yeshua followed, and the trio ambled along past the soldiers. Toby watched with hidden amusement as the entire group stepped back as far as they dared to keep out of arm's length of the three men. The three no sooner cleared the last soldier, than the small attachment formed up again and took off in a jog to find the missing slave. Toby and his companions kept going, with Toby looking over his shoulder periodically to be sure they weren't followed.

It took at least a mile before Toby was sure that the soldiers had bought their little charade. He exhaled with relief and grinned for the first time since they'd gotten away. "Well, I think that did it. Keep the disguise on 'til we get to the other side of the village, but I think we're clear anyway."

The man took Toby's shoulder in a gentle grip and then patted it. "Thank you. You've saved my life and I'm that grateful. To the both of you." And the man put his other hand on Yeshua's shoulder.

"Aye, I was a dead man to be sure. I shall owe you both a great debt."

"You are most welcome," Toby answered.

Yeshua smiled said, "I am called Yeshua ben David. This is my companion, Tobias. We have come from Nazareth and are traveling through the country."

"Traveling where?" the man asked.

Toby chuckled. "Well, we've not decided that yet. What are you called?"

The man laughed in reply, and answered, "I am called Gwydion. I'm from the island of Ir."

It took Toby a moment or two, because the name wasn't familiar. *Ir? Of course! He means Ireland! That accent, how could I have missed it?* The man was a long way from his home, if he was Irish.

"How did you get here," Toby asked.

'Well, that is a good question," Gwydion answered. "You see, it was a case of being in the wrong place at the wrong time. Shall we walk? And I'll tell you my story."

They fell into a comfortable walk and Gwydion went on.

"I was traveling through Gaul, you see. That'll be how I make my living, bringin' the news of the land and tellin' pretty stories for the women," he added with a lecherous wink. "Well then, I stopped for the night in a place and was planning to trade my services for a room, a bath, and a bite." Gwydion shrugged his shoulders and added, "My mum always said my mouth would get me in trouble sooner or later. Aye and it did."

Yeshua was totally confused, and asked, "How did it do this?"

"I'm a bard, boy," Gwydion answered, proud to say so. "I sing the songs of the goin' and comin' of the world and I sing the truth."

Toby snorted and crossed his arms over his chest as he walked. "In other words, you told a story that someone didn't want told?"

Gwydion laughed hearty in answer. "Did that, did I not? 'Twould seem that there be a great deal of secrets bein' passed in the bedroom, as it were. I wove a tale of love and tyranny...."

"And, they grabbed you?" Toby finished

"*Grabbed me*? Here now, what sort of thing is this to ask? I'm not knowing what you mean by *grabbed* where you're from, but I was taken prisoner for tellin' the tale of the' local governor and a servin' wench."

"They took you prisoner," Yeshua repeated.

"Aye," Gwydion answered, "they did. The local gentry thought he was doin' me favor by sellin' me into slavery instead of havin' my head cut off."

Yeshua's only answer was to spit on the ground.

Gwydion's rejoinder was a bit of Celtic profanity.

Toby's response was, "Well, we shall stop in the village and rest a while. I suppose you'll want to travel on, to put as much distance between you and the Romans as you can."

"Aye, that I'd like more than I can say," Gwydion answered, a wide grin on his face. His sunny smile was infectious. "Though, there is something else I'll be saying. You saved m' life and it's a debt I'm owin' you. Surely, there must be somethin' you'll be needin' from me."

Toby shook his head, and held up his hands. "No, thank you. We will be fine."

The Celt was insistent, turning a stubborn look on them with his hands on his hips and the cheery smile hidden under a furrowed brow. "Now, I'll not be takin' no for an answer. There must be some way I can repay you for it."

"No, thank you," Toby said, just as insistent. But his resolve was definitely wearing out. Who was this man, with the smile and the friendly manner? He had no earthly idea but he was drawn to the man. He felt a certain kinship with Gwydion.

"Wait! Did you not say you were travelin' with no destination?"

Yeshua suddenly gained a glow, eagerness in his face. "Yes, we did."

"Well, that's it then." Gwydion clapped his hands together and rubbed them together in obvious glee. "You'll be comin' with me."

"Coming with you?" Toby asked, confused. "I'm sorry, but I don't understand. Coming? Where?"

"Back to Ir." Gwydion threw his arms wide. The man was a bard and he had a showman's flare for the dramatic. "You'll be comin' with me," Gwydion continued, becoming more and more in love with the idea of taking them with him. He seemed to sense Toby's reservations, because he rushed to continue. "You said you have nowhere to go. Then, you must come to Ir and let me show you my home. Let me repay you for your kindness." Gwydion paused for effect before he played his trump card. "And besides, the Romans'll know you've tricked 'em badly. They might be lookin' for *you* as well. Come with me."

The stubborn look was back on Yeshua's face, a look that said he would have what he wanted in this instance. "Yes."

Toby took the boy by the shoulder and turned Yeshua to face him. "Yeshua, are you certain of this? You will be traveling far from home. This is not a short journey and we know nothing of this man or his people."

The solemn brown eyes faced his and the features of his face eased. "*We* do not, Tobias, but *I* do. It is a right thing. My Father has told me that this is right. You know it in your heart. You feel the same way, I can tell."

The trouble was that Toby *did* know it. He was torn between wanting to go to the land of his own ancestors and walking away from this whole affair. He'd answered the question he came to answer, and he just wanted to be back in his own time. But, he liked Gwydion. He liked the man's free manner and easy charm. Gwydion was personable and warm. Toby was drawn to that. He found that he really did want to go, if only for Maeve's sake, to see the old sod of the Emerald Isle.

"Are you sure, Yeshua?" he asked again, wanting confirmation of how he felt.

Yeshua smiled, and said, "Yes, my friend, I am sure. You will see; this will be an experience for both of us. Our destiny lies on this pathway." To Gwydion, he said, "We accept your offer, Gwydion. We will travel with you. Now, come, I have family here. We will dine, rest, and set off on our journey to...where?"

"Ir," Gwydion answered. "Let me tell ye all about my home."

Toby watched the two walk off, Gwydion's arm around the boy's shoulder. He remembered a book he'd been given when he was a boy, full of legends from the early Catholic Church. There was a story in it about then young Jesus traveling with his uncle Joseph of Arimethea to England, Ireland, and France – *excuse me, Gaul,* he corrected himself ruefully. Joseph was supposed to have been a wealthy merchant. *I'm hardly a wealthy merchant or Joseph of Arimethea,* he told himself. He'd dismissed those stories as folk tales from the Dark Ages. And it now appeared they might have been true.

Either way, they were off to Ireland...*to Ir.* Toby shook his head and caught up with the other two; one telling the stories of his home, and the other, listening to them as if his life depended on it.

Chapter Thirteen

Toby pulled a splinter off one of the burning logs and reached into his pocket for another cigarette. He lit the end and blew out the smoke slowly and deliberately. He sat, waiting for it all to absorb again, lost in his own thoughts. It wasn't until he heard the voice that he realized he had a captive audience. Literally.

"Coffee?"

Toby nodded, and John filled both cups. He watched John replace the pot on the stone, but the older man didn't sit down right away. Toby watched him stare off into the darkness, give a quick glance at the pot, and look back into the desert night.

"John?"

The older man appeared to blush in the firelight. "Ok, I know you're not gonna kill me. I know I'm lost out here. I trust you. Ok?"

"Ok."

"Then, you won't mind if I get rid of some of this coffee, will you? I swear I'm not going anywhere."

Toby smiled down into the fire and nodded his consent. John was already reaching for the zipper of his pants before he had reached the periphery of the light, and stood for several minutes, his back to Toby. Soon, the urge would strike him, too. It was the simple things that he would miss in wherever he was going next. Things like coffee and food, and relieving the body's excesses were things always taken for granted and simply annoyances before. Here he was, on the edge of becoming something different, and they weren't so annoying anymore. Would John know that?

Toby heard the zipper again and the soft footfalls as John turned back to the fire. The older man got back into his cross legged position and picked up his cup. Toby sat watching the smoke rise, seeing this from the corner of his eye but not paying close attention to any of it. His mind was focused on the remainder of the story. It would only get harder from now on. He was going to be facing things he hadn't faced in many years, whatever that term meant anymore. It was good to get it all out again, to let it go. It was time to throw these stones away, get them off his heart.

Toby drew another hit off the cigarette and returned his focus back to his companion, who was waiting and not so patiently.

"Well?" John asked, gesturing with his cup.

Toby felt the corner of his mouth begin to twitch and forced it to still, seeing the seriousness in the other man. "Well, what?" he teased.

John gave a huff and shook his head. "Was he or wasn't he? Was he the Messiah or not?"

"That's the story, my friend. If I tell you that, you'll miss out on the rest. It wasn't just that he was or wasn't, but what happened on that journey."

John's thought about it for a moment before he nodded.

Toby hoped John understood why he had to tell it the way he was going to do. He wasn't sure if he completely understood but it had to come out in his own way and time.

"So, what was he like," John asked. "The boy. Did he *seem* like the Messiah?"

Toby took another hit off the butt and tossed it into the fire. He blew out the smoke before answering. "Truth? No, he didn't." He took a sip of coffee, delaying as long as he dared before continuing. "I was having a hell of a time trying to decide whether or not I liked this kid. One minute I did, the next minute I didn't. He was the most infuriating child I'd ever been around, and yet, he was the most endearing."

"How so?"

"He had this naïve thought that he was actually going to lead an army of rag tags against an entire Roman force. He was just bound and determined that he was going take shepherds right up to a seasoned and trained army and take that army down and hard."

"Do you think he could've?"

"At that moment, no. I don't think he could have. I don't think this kid knew the first thing about being a soldier or fighting against them. But, he was going to do it, and he was going to have his God with him."

"And did you believe him?"

Toby took a deep breath, held it for a moment, and released it. "At that moment, I wasn't sure. I didn't want to. I was...."

"Confused?"

Toby mulled the question. Was that it? Confusion? Was it that simple? He was confused about the time and the place, about the boy that was supposed to be a savior of men's souls? Was that it? Or was it something else?

"I was *comfortable*," he finally said. "It was a routine and it was comfortable. And I had no place else to be than where I was."

John shook his head and barked a short laugh. "Man, how could you be comfortable with this? You're in another time, you speak the language, you understand it – I would have been freaked out."

Toby nodded, "Yes, I was for a bit. It took me a few days when I got there, and after that, I was just...just...*caught up* in it. I don't know why. I just was. I stopped thinking about it, stopped wondering, and just did it. I never thought about it again."

"I don't know if I could have," John replied, shaking his head. He leaned against a small boulder to his side. "I wonder what I'd do if I could do what you do."

Toby smiled at the man. "You believe my story, don't you."

John's jaw dropped as he realized that Toby hadn't asked a question – he'd made a statement. He really *had* started to believe this whole story. *When did that happen?* He looked across the fire and saw that Toby's eyes were steady and true. It wasn't just a case of whether or not Toby believed what he was saying; it was that John believed it too. No wonder they always called him gullible. He would believe stories of UFOs in Roswell if they were well told. He had another realization on top of that one – that he was starting to feel comfortable with Toby. Maybe *that* was the reason he was believing it.

John took a minute and said, "You were there, you were comfortable..."

Toby nodded and answered, "I had this *gift* and I went back with the sole purpose of destroying this myth once and for all, and when I got there...."

"You couldn't do it."

"Oh, I could," Toby said, working through his ambivalence about it all. "I just didn't want to. He was a good hearted boy. He had a charisma that you couldn't walk away from. He was easy to talk to. I had to be careful or I was gonna tell him everything."

John just nodded, and made no answer.

"And he was quick," Toby blurted out. "Yeshua wasn't stupid. Ok, he couldn't read, but...well, take the language thing."

John settled back again against the stone, bringing his knees up. "I was wondering about that," he said. "*You* could understand the Celtic language, but how did Yeshua?"

"He didn't, at first," Toby explained. "You see, Gwydion had been with his master long enough to pick up Latin and they'd been in Israel long enough for him to learn Hebrew. We spoke in Hebrew for Yeshua. As the three of us traveled, we started to learn the Celtic language."

"Started?"

Toby smiled, sheepishly. "Yeah, I got it right away. But, Yeshua – he picked it up so fast that by the time we arrived in England, he was pretty good at it. By the time we made it across to Ireland, he was fluent in it."

"Yeshua sounds like a remarkable young man," John said.

Toby suddenly looked back down at the fire and felt a start of guilt coming. "Yeah, he was. But, you want to know the sick part? I wanted to slap this kid sometimes." He took a deep breath, shaking his head. "We'd have a great time laughing and talking and then he'd go off on his Roman domination rant, and what he and his God would do to them. We finally stopped talking of anything to do with the subject."

"What did you talk about?"

"He wanted to see the world," Toby answered, and leaned back up against the stone behind him. "See what was there." He smiled at the memory with a sense of amusement. "He wanted to learn to read. He wanted to be a good father. I guess you have to be married and have children to have the name of Rabbi."

John shook his head and said, "Do you know that everything you're telling me—"

"Oh yeah, I know." Toby took a deep gulp of the coffee. "Flies in the face of what I was taught, too. That Mary was untouched 'til the day she left this world, and yet, he had brothers and sisters in that house. That he was chaste and pure all his life, and here he was talking about being a father at thirteen!"

"Man, he wasn't talking about taking on Rome, about war," John blurted out. "You have to be remembering that wrong. I mean, the New Testament—"

"—is full of pacifism and turning the other cheek, I know," Toby finished for him. "I know; I remember. But you forget, there was no New Testament for him. He was steeped in the Talmud and the book of law. An eye for an eye, man."

John shook his head in answer.

Toby continued on with the story, "Well, with Gwydion, we had a threesome. He and Yeshua hit it off, right away. Hell, Gwy and *I* hit it off. Gwy made it all right. It was like we were waiting for him to join us, make us complete."

John was curious about the other man that had joined them, "What was he like?"

"Gwy?"

John nodded. "Yeah. You called him Gwy?"

"Yeah, I called him Gwy for short," Toby answered. "Gwy was...well, he part of us. He sorta stepped in as if he'd always been there and always would be. He was comfortable to be with, easy to talk to, and had this way of making you feel like he focused on you alone, like you were the only one in the universe at that moment. He was funny and friendly, and a big kid."

John laughed into his coffee cup, a sort of whuffing noise that bubbled the liquid in the container. He peered up over the rim, seeing Toby's expression, and took a quick sip of coffee. When he had swallowed, John explained, "He reminds me of...never mind."

"Yeah, I know," Toby said. "Reminds me of you."

John shrugged amiably and nodded for Toby to go on.

"Anyway," Toby continued, "We headed off for Ireland, the Isle of Ir. Ma would've loved that."

"She wanted to go?"

"Oh, yeah. Since I was a kid, I remember her talking about it. I made that journey for her."

"Where was it? Gwydion's village, I mean."

"Well, later, when I had a chance to look at a map, I decided it was right around the Kildare area of Ireland. I remember Piper's Stones. That's what Gwydion called them, but they're called the

Athgreany Stone Circle. The stones were a two day hike from the sea, and his village was another half day's journey from there. Took us a long time to get there, but we did."

"How long?"

Toby sat, thoughtful, for a moment. "Let's see. Yeshua was a few days past his thirteenth birthday when I met him. When we landed in Ir, he had passed his fifteenth birthday. We walked most of it, took our time. Well, it's not like we had any place to go."

Chapter Fourteen

Toby stoked the fire, making ready for the return of his companions. They were off in the bowels of the forest, leaving him behind to keep to his own counsel and prepare for what they were bringing back for supper. Toby had done his bit of collecting, finding the tubers, wild onions, and fruits that would round out the meal.

For Toby, it didn't matter the time frame he was in, he was still caught up in that old fashioned – to him, anyway – thinking that he had to have vegetables with his meat. It was an old habit, but a piece of his past (*present? future?*) that he could still hold on to. Most of those habits had been left to the wayside, like the need to brush his teeth after every meal. He'd had to make do to compensate for that by finding the mallow roots along the way and chewing on them. Gwydion had shown him what to look for. Doing without vegetables with his meal was one of the few he couldn't. *Besides*, he told himself a little petulantly, *I happen to like vegetables and what's wrong with that? Nothing*, he answered himself, *nothing at all*.

After the desert, coming into the hills and greenery of Europe had been a bit of a shock for Yeshua but it had been a homecoming of sorts for Toby. The Roman roads were easy to walk upon and full of travelers. With so many languages, the young boy was not quite shocked into silence but certainly into his best behavior. He picked up those languages as easily as he'd picked up the Celtic.

They'd found companions easily enough, shared food and stories. Gwydion practiced his trade and even collected a few coins for his troubles, along with the stories and news from the others. They made their way across the continent before booking passage on a ship bound for England. Once there, they booked passage on another ship. They finally arrived on the shores of Ireland and slowly began to make their way toward Gwydion's village.

They'd fallen into a routine in all the days of travel. Yeshua was the one who chose camp, set it up, and then broke it down on the morrow. Toby set the fires and was the cook for them all, preparing delicious meals according to his companions. That left Gwydion to hunt for meat and keep them entertained with his delightful stories and songs. They were free to keep to themselves or enjoy the company of each other. It was companionable, comfortable.

Gwydion had become more to Toby than just a runaway slave dragging them to the home of his birth. He was a good hearted soul with a wicked sense of humor. His stories were more than just the gossip or news of the day; he could add a slant that would have Toby laughing until his sides ached. Even Yeshua would roar with laughter over Gwydion's antics. He would be just as quick to listen when one of them needed to unburden his soul, give advice if he felt a story could answer a question. In that way, he was like Yeshua and his parables.

Toby felt closer to Gwydion than he ever felt possible. It was like having the best friend he'd lost when Bion had died, or the brother he'd never had when he was growing up. Yeshua, for all of his faults, was a brother too – although he was more the bratty brother you wanted to ship off to the movies or sell to gypsies – but not like this. This was almost destined to be.

With a good fire going and the tubers and onions to the side slowly roasting, he sat back and let his mind wander. He took a rare moment to wonder at why he wasn't more surprised at his surroundings, where he was. He should have been sitting next to a tree trunk, drooling and foaming at the mouth. He wasn't. He was in another time and every new day was living and talking to another person from another place, speaking another language. He'd taken the giant leap of faith and every day just brought one more day. If anything, it was surreal to him because it *wasn't* surreal to him.

He heard laughter and the sounds of brush being swept aside. His reverie was put aside and he took the skin of water and poured some into a small metal pot. They had gotten the pot for a trade of furs that Gwydion had collected. It was big enough to make three or four cups of cider or a decoction made from herbs and flowers. Toby had the mix ready, adding them as soon as the water was boiling. He spared one more thought to how his father would be proud of him for living, for going on. He could hear Brandon laughing in the back of his head, encouraging him to not let the grief get to him, to take it and use it to make his life better. There was comfort because of it, but was he really doing that?

A laughing Gwydion and Yeshua broke through the underbrush

around the grove of trees they had camped beside. Gwydion carried something over his shoulder and as they approached, he waved at Toby with his free hand. Yeshua, laughing shyly at Gwydion, turned his gaze to the scene by the fire and did likewise. Toby waved back.

Gwydion reached the campsite and slung the lump he'd been carrying to the ground. "Here you are, Tobias, two lovely coineán to dress and spit. 'Tis a grand meal we'll be having this night, for sure."

Toby joined the laughter with real gusto, shaking his head and holding his hands out, palms first. "Aye, we shall feast well, but *you*, Gwydion, will have cleaning of them. If you think I'll be turning those two rabbits inside out, you are daft, indeed."

Gwydion's laugh was hearty and infectious. "Aye, 'tis a fair bargain." He reached over and ruffled Yeshua's hair, and put his arm around the young man's shoulder. "And only because his cooking is far better than mine; do you agree, my friend?"

Yeshua nodded emphatically and made his way to a nearby log to watch.

Gwydion separated the snares from the rabbits and began the messy business of removing skin from the bodies. He did it with a practiced hand, taking the knife from his boot, and making the slit through the belly of the first rabbit. The Celt ran his fingers under the hide and over the musculature of the body to separate the two. If there was interference, his knife was at the ready to cut the sinew or the membrane that held pelt to body. It was a fascinating process to watch.

But what made it fascinating wasn't the skinning; it was Gwydion murmuring as he worked. He spoke so softly that it was impossible to make out what he was saying, but it was said in a sing-song rhythm as the voice rose and fell. It was not quite musical, but not quite a chant either. Toby strained his hearing but with no success. But there was something about it the he couldn't turn his attention way.

Toby also saw that he wasn't the only one fixated the process. Yeshua had become entranced in the procedure, too. They watched Gwydion expertly remove the skin, then rub sand into the fleshy side of the pelt to remove fat and the like. It was a few moments before Gwydion noticed his audience.

"What, and you've never seen a hare bein' skinned?" He grinned and went back to work on the second hare.

Yeshua picked up a stick and poked the pelt, examining it for a moment. He used the stick to turn it this way and that, staring at the newly cleaned skin side, and then the fur. When he finally spoke, it was a voice of awe and wonder at a newfound talent that seemed to have never been in his realm of possibility before. "What is it that you are speaking, Gwydion? Why do you do it?"

Gwydion smiled as Yeshua poked at the pelt again. Toby watched them both, recognizing what was happening. *He's teaching. He's got that same voice that I always had, trying to explain a term to young mind.*

"You see," Gwydion began with his voice soothing and gentle. "The creature gave of its life to feed us. So I honor it by giving thanks to the spirit."

"You give thanks?"

"Aye, I do," Gwydion said. "Was a brave thing to give their lives as they did and the giving of thanks honors that, sends their spirits to the Other Side, ye see."

"Oh," Yeshua answered, still in his trance.

"And, there's another way we honor the sacredness of life and that's by not wasting the gifts given by the creatures."

Only then, did Yeshua look up, the look of wonder still on him. "Not wasting? I don't understand, Gwydion. Explain this to me."

Gwydion held up the carcass in one hand and used his other to point to the part he was speaking of. "We use the bone for meal, mix it with the plantings. That'll be good for the soil, give food to the plants. The blood can be used in puddings and such, but we'll put it in the ground, too. The hides will make fine gloves or boots. They'll keep you warm in the winter months by makin' a sturdy coat for you. They'll make a set of clothes for you. To tell you the truth, I've the need of a bag to carry my herbs and anythin' else we'll be needin' for our trip." Gwydion tipped a conspiratorial wink to the boy and leaned in closer to him. The Celt gestured with the knife back to the carcass and said, "You know, of course, the rabbit's feet are good luck charms, do you not?"

Toby snorted, helping to break the seriousness of the moment. "Surely not for the rabbit, now."

He and Gwydion burst into hearty laughter. Gwydion threw his head back and began to sing with a clear tenor.

As I was a walking one morning in Spring,
For to hear the birds whistle and the nightingales sing,
I saw a young damsel, so sweetly sang she:
Down by the Green Bushes he thinks to meet me.

With a voice, pure and true, he sang a tale of an Irish lad out for a turn around the country who fell for a lovely lady. It was a story of love that ended too soon.

And when he came there and he found she was gone,
He stood like some lambkin, forever undone;
She has gone with some other and forsaken me,
So adieu to Green Bushes forever, cried he.

When the last note cleared, they sat in silence, neither wanting to break the spell that the bard has cast. Gwydion, for his part, simply sat with his head tilted back as if smelling the air. Toby broke the silence with his applause, slowly at first and then picking up the tempo. Yeshua blinked his eyes a few times and joined in with a full gusto. The bard laughed again, stood up and took his bow, pleasing his audience further.

"You have an incredible voice," Toby said, finally.

"Well, thank you, Tobias," Gwydion answered as he reseated himself and went back to his task. "Comes from me màthair's side of the family that I've the gift."

He nodded at Yeshua, and said, "And it was her seanair, her *grandfather*, that kissed a faery girl, ye know. We've all been blessed with the gift since."

"The gift?" Yeshua asked.

"The gift of singing, of spinning a yarn. The gift of the bard, my boy."

"Spinnin' a yarn?" the boy asked again, his brow wrinkled in confusion.

Toby was trying hard not to laugh at the young man with his oh, so serious expression.

"Tellin' harmless stories, Yeshua," Gwydion answered, still grinning. "That will be what a bard does, you see. It's pleasing those who would hear you with a bit of storytelling. Have you never told a bit of a story, then?"

Yeshua took a deep and audible breath, the look of understanding coming to his face as the brow relaxed, and he nodded at his teacher. "Ah, I see. No, my friend Gwydion, I have not. Nor will I. I must tell the truth at all times. The Father does not need me to spin stories. The truth shall be the guide for my people and I must show it to them."

"Must you, now?"

"Yes, I must." The boy jutted out his chin, giving his face a stubborn cant. "I know that one day, my words will mean great power to my people. I have been shown this. This means that I must speak the truth at all times so that they might find the path."

Gwydion continued skinning the second carcass. "Well, 'tis not but a little weavin' of a tale. There is no harm in it. You take life too serious, my friend."

The boy rose up in indignation and the serious look turned to one of haughtiness. Before Toby could speak or do anything to intercede, Yeshua had balled up his fists, his face red in a fury.

"It is lying. *Lying*. My people have been fed enough of the lies and deceit of the Roman oppressors. I will not insult them – *or my God* – by spreading more." Yeshua's eyes narrowed; he was working up a full religious fervor.

Toby rolled his eyes. *Oh, shit, here it comes.*

Gwydion seemed to be genuinely surprised; he stopped what he was doing and stared for a moment. "I was not meanin' to insult, Yeshua," he blurted in a rush. "It was just my way of having you on a bit, that's all. I apologize if I've insulted you. I truly do."

The boy backed down again, the anger left his voice. He dropped back on to the log as if exhausted. "You do not understand, my friend. I must take these things seriously. I lead my people on a path to salvation and freedom. It is a path that I must not turn from and it is a hard path. I must not make it harder by the disrespect of what I do."

Toby wanted to reach out and throttle the boy. The zealot had returned; there was no place in the peaceful atmosphere and the beauty of the day for it. He swallowed the urge and threw a pine knot into the fire, instead. The resulting pop brought the attention back to him for a moment. He hadn't meant to draw focus, but since he had it, he chose to use the moment.

"What path is that?" he said, trying as hard as he could to keep his anger out of his voice. The expression on their faces told them that he hadn't, but he was in it already. "Tell me; what path?"

Yeshua cocked his head to one side, confused. "Tobias, you should know the path I mean. The truth that I offer my people to do my Father's will, the path of the righteous."

"And the truth shall make you free, is that about it?"

"The truth always makes men free, Tobias," Yeshua replied in earnestness, his brow furrowed as if he were speaking to a child. "The truth that His love is without reservation, without prejudice. The path of salvation and freedom is there, and I have the means to lead my people to that path and beyond."

Gwydion held up his hand to silence Toby before he could say anything in response. With a nod, he said, "Then, lad, you should do it. Never let anyone steer you from the course you've chosen."

Yeshua seemed mollified and he nodded in response. "My way is ordained by God, my friend – it was chosen for me. I will help my people drive the Roman scourge from homeland."

Toby gave a silent snort. The more he kept his mouth shut, the better off they'd *all* be. With Gwydion, it was hard to tell how he would approach the discussion. Certainly, the Celt had no love of Rome, given his recent bondage. Toby was becoming more curious as to how this conversation was going to go.

"Aye, lad, will you?" Gwydion dropped his gaze back to the second carcass.

"Yes, I will," replied the boy, and the tilt of the chin and haughty tone returned. "We will take arms against the Roman armies and, with the help and blessing of the God of Israel, they will be defeated."

Gwydion pulled the skin from the last body. He took to cleaning it as he spoke, "My seanair used to tell me stories when I was a wee lad. He told me about *his* àthair – *his* father – going to war." He sat back for a moment, a wistful smile playing on his face. "Aye, I remember the stories of how the Celts once conquered Rome. Oh, they called us barbarians then but I hear it was a grand sight to see."

Yeshua's face became all eyes in astonishment as his head jerked up. "The *Celts*? The *Celts* conquered Rome?"

Gwydion nodded at Yeshua, "Oh, aye, my friend, that they did. The Celts had the sacking of the Roman Empire. Such as it was at the time. My seanair on my athair's side told me that the Celts stretched over the known world and back again. He said to me, 'Gwydion, ye couldn't set foot on the land without steppin' on Celtic toes."

"What was it like, Gwydion? The sacking of an enemy?" Yeshua's words rushed out in a flurry.

Gwydion settled back against the log behind him and cleaned his boot knife as he spoke. "Oh, I was not there, to be sure, but I hear it wasn't as grand as you'd think. *I* think 'tis why the Romans drove 'em back out. Conquering isn't always the way, Yeshua. Peace is the answer."

"But, what was it like?"

Gwydion looked into Yeshua's eyes and answered, "Do ye not know, boy? Are ye not conquered as they were?" The knife clean, Gwydion replaced it back in his boot.

Toby watched the boy's face blush. He could see Yeshua trying to steer the conversation back away from himself. He felt torn as to whether to rescue the young man's innocent lapse of sensibility or let him just continue to wallow in it. The suddenness of the next question took the decision from him.

"You are not a soldier?" Yeshua finally asked.

"No, that I am not. And never wanted to be. I'm a bard." Gwydion rested an elbow against the bark of the fallen tree. There was sadness in his voice, but a look of peace on his face. Whatever had taken Gwydion from his home, he was content to resume his former life, to find that place and return to it. "I sing the songs and invite the world to sing with me. I tell stories of the day and tell the news, nothing more." Gwydion waggled a finger at his audience. "Now, that is not to say, I'm not above giving someone the wrong end of a verse if I see the ignorance of tyranny. But I'll not take up sword against them. My father's father was the soldier in my family. When the Caesar came – *Julius*, he was – he fought against that sod."

Toby perked up at this one. "Your grandfather fought against Julius Caesar?"

Gwydion nodded again. "Did. Word spread that the sods weren't content with just drivin' out the Celts from *their* land, but were comin' to drive us out of ours. Many a man of Ir an' Scotia went to stand against 'em. They went to Albion, crossed the great sea to make their stand. Caesar never came this far because the best that

Rome had to offer was stopped in Gaul. Which will be why Gaul is still under Rome's skirts."

Toby smiled, remembering a bit of history class. *Julius never came to Ireland, but he conquered England. Claudius finally captured the Emerald Isle, if I remember correctly and Hadrian after him.* But he kept those thoughts to himself.

With that, Gwydion wrapped the pelts carefully, to store them, and put them to one side. He had the rabbits on makeshift spits in a thrice and handed them to Toby. Toby placed them over the fire at a distance that would cook but not burn the meat, and the smell of roasting food soon filled the air.

With the food safely cooking, Toby, with an air of mischief, took a sniff of the air. "Lads, if I'm to have a good hot meal such as this, I fear I must beg you to go to the river and bathe."

With a twinkle in his eye, Gwydion said, mockingly, "Such a silver tongue on you, Tobias. Have *ye* kissed a faery?"

"No, Gwydion, but I do know that both of you have the stench of the road. I can vouch for the power of cleansing a man, body and soul, in the waters of Ir."

Gwydion stood up and with hands on hips, bent slightly, and said, "Well, then, that is what we'll be doin'. Come, Yeshua, we'll leave the cook to his charges while you and I shall have a wash in the stream."

"And I must find suitable food," Yeshua said as he stood up.

Both men passed a questioning glance between them and then at the boy, but it was Gwydion who spoke. "Ye don't like rabbit, lad?"

The haughty brat had returned with a snort and a shake of his head. "You lived among my people all that time and you never learned anything? This flesh is forbidden. To eat it would be to damn my soul. It is enough that I touched it, would you condemn me further?" With that, Yeshua turned on his heel and disappeared back into the brush and trees.

Toby plucked a rock from the ground and threw it off, with all of his might. That was it, he was going to smack that kid a good one. The zealot was bad enough, but the bad manners were too much. He closed his eyes and began to rub his temples, trying to calm down. When he opened his eyes again, he saw Gwydion still standing by the log. It was a moment before he noticed that Gwydion, reaching behind a stone, had plucked several plants.

"What is that?" Toby asked.

Gwydion held up the weed. "Soapwort, my Mum calls it. Does a fair job on your skin without removin' it." He held the plants, gazing at them with a smile and a loving look on his face, "I'll be that glad to be home, to see my Mum and Da again."

"I know you are. You've been gone many a month, now."

"Aye. Too long and I'm missin' it somethin' fierce." Gwydion replied and sat back down on the log. "Tobias, may I ask you a question?"

"Aye. Always."

"I watched your face while the lad was talkin'. I take it you hold none of his thoughts as your own."

Toby answered with a curt bark, "No, I do not!" He stopped, chastising himself for his harshness. It wasn't that simple. "Gwydion, right now, I don't know what I believe, but I do know one thing. Yeshua – he's a good boy for all of his going on and on. I do like him oft times. But he is childish and arrogant. And he is wrong."

"Well, he is a bit of a dreamer, to be certain. But why do you call him childish?"

Toby shook his head at the question, gesturing as if the lad were still with them and in sight. "Gwydion, he thinks he'll be takin' the sword and plowin' through the Roman army as if they were weeds. He thinks he is the Messiah foretold by prophets and angels."

"And you do not agree?"

"That he will lay waste to the best army in the land? No, I do not agree." Toby threw his stick in the fire and just sat, his hands folded in his lap. "That he is their Messiah? I don't know. Sometimes I think he is. Mostly I think he's a spoiled brat who needs a good smack on the bum." He looked across the cook fire at Gwydion. "One thing is for certain – he is not what I expected."

Gwydion's expression of concern turned to one of thoughtfulness. He crossed a leg and folded his hands on his knee. "It is amazing where the holy ones come from, sometimes from places you'll never expect. Sometimes, in *ways* you'll never expect."

"And what do *you* think, Gwydion?"

Gwydion smiled and stood up again, and held the weed before his face. "Well, Tobias, it is not what I *think* but what I *know* – and 'tis two things I know. That, this time on the morrow, we'll be sittin' with my àthair and màthair as we dine on a good meal and sleep in a good bed. And, t'other is that all things are possible in the sight of the Goddess. We've a saying, my people; *the paths are many, the truth is one.*"

"What does it mean?" Toby asked.

Gwydion grinned broadly, sniffing his armpit before he answered. "It means that I need a good washing if I'm to have a bite of supper tonight."

With that, Gwydion gave a short bow at Toby and turned to follow Yeshua. As he disappeared into the brush, he started singing.

> *"Ye brighten up my morning*
> *With the kiss o' morning's dew*
> *With the golden touch of sunlight*
> *With a breeze that whispers through*
> *With the scent of tender lilac*
> *With the breath of gentle rain*
> *You brighten up my morning*
> *Come, brighten with your grace"*

As the lilting tenor faded into the brush and forest, Toby sat back to absorb it all. He liked Gwydion, his easy charm, and his ability to put everyone around him at ease. Gwydion was a good listener, and a gentle man. There was something familiar about him, something...*kind, but fiercely proud...something good and decent.* Toby ran his fingers through his hair, as if the act would clear the mystery from his mind as easily as it swept the shock of hair from his forehead. Maybe he was right. Maybe he should just let it go as the boy's youth and immaturity

...with all that's happened, maybe I should....

Toby gave it no more thought. This night, with less than half a day's journey to their destination, they sat and ate the splendid feast – with Yeshua joining in with only the vegetation and fruits, having caught a fish from the river while he bathed. They watched the stars and listened to Gwydion as he sang one tune after another. He sang a story of an old man's love for his son in a song he called *The Dyin' Rebel*. He sang sweet and tender songs of love for his lady. When the moon had finally fallen behind the trees and the fire had been stoked one last time, Toby laid back against the rock that served as his pillow and went to sleep. He slept dreamlessly, for the first time since the journey had begun.

True to his word, the journey to Gwydion's village had only been a half of a day's walk through the brilliant green countryside. Toby was caught up in the beauty of Ireland's rolling hills and gentle breezes. The wildflowers growing in the fields had been heather and lavender and daisies of every kind. The sky was so blue, so brilliant, contrasting with the richness of the earth. The path had been beaten down by countless feet and the traveling was easy. Toby was content to think no more on the previous day's foolishness and just enjoy being here, today.

Yeshua was even more captivated by the Irish countryside. He fought to take in everything, to miss nothing. It was almost funny watching Yeshua's head whipping around, his eyes landing first on the field of heather, and then the golden eagles flying in the distance. *Almost* funny because Toby was in the same straits; he'd never been here either. He had, however, been treated to the sights of grass and meadow, field and stream. Yeshua had never been out of the desert, though, and this had to be blowing that mind of his. *It's blowing mine*, Toby thought.

"Well, lads, here we are. My home."

They came up over a rise to see the village ahead. The round cottages and shelters were in a large circular clearing, with the forest around it. There were squares marked off and plowed gathered in sections according to each cottage. A roadway meandered in a rude circular path, passing by each farm. In the very center of the village stood a stone circle inside of a field, also in a round shape. Toby guessed that it had to be at least two hundred or so acres across at any one given point. Smoke rising from the chimneys brought the smell of fresh bread, and stewing vegetables and meats. As they stood, shoulder to shoulder, Toby watched some children in the distance, running and tossing some object. He could almost hear the shouts of joy, the giggles.

There was a mixture of love and relief in Gwydion's voice as he repeated, "Aye, lads, I'm home. Where I belong." Gwydion put a hand on the shoulders of his mates and said, "Welcome to Fireun Sidhe, *the Eagle Folk*. We named it for the nestin' pair out in the forest. This is where I grew up and where I shall spend the rest of my days."

Yeshua's eyes had gotten as large as saucers again,

Toby nodded in appreciation. "I see why you love this place. I could love it too."

"And so you shall, Tobias. Come, Yeshua, let me show you my home. I promised you a hot meal and a good night's rest. And you both shall have it."

As they approached the stone fence, a great clanging began as a man standing nearby began to toll a huge bell. He started the shouting and the banging of the gong began to reverberate through the village. People ran out to see what the cause was and picked up the shout.

"Gwydion, he's home. Aye, call Niamh. Where's Liam? Gwydion has come home!"

As they walked, faces would peer from doorways, and then the men and women would come dashing out to greet their friend who had been gone so long.

Gwydion was quick to clap a hand on a back, or kiss a face. "Seamus, you devil, are ye still carrying the torch? Sean! Kaleigh, darling, you look like a spring flower." He greeted them all; he took offered hands and waved at those who stood in back of the crowd and couldn't touch him. He never let Toby and Yeshua get lost in the crowd, keeping them with him as he walked on.

The crowd followed them as they passed onward. Toby noticed that no one ever asked a question, just kept passing on bits of welcome, and *where've ye been, boy*, and *we've a good harvest come this year, we have.* By the time they'd reached what Toby presumed was the intended destination, it seemed that every man, woman, and child had, in some way, spoken to Gwydion. They had all taken time to touch his hand or his shoulder. As the three men walked, those who spoke to Gwydion also followed along, until there was a homecoming parade behind them.

A dark headed woman was standing by the gate of the house that they had been slowly making their way towards. She stood there, a look of worry on her face that furrowed her brow and made the corners of her mouth go down. It quickly faded, replaced with the sunshine of homecoming the moment that Gwydion came into view. This small, elfin woman clapped her hands to her mouth and the tears streamed down her cheeks. The crowd stepped away and

Gwydion stepped forward, his arms outstretched, and she came to him.

"Ma! Màthair! I came home, I did."

Her hands came away from her mouth and clasped against her breast. She appeared to be calm, but it was obvious that she was moments away from bounding into her son's arms. She took a hitching breath and said, "Aye, my sweet son, ye did. Ye did, indeed. *Liam, our son has come home to us.*"

The tiny woman reached up to take Gwydion's face in her hands, and he bent down to her. Her fingers cleared the shock of hair that had fallen down, and her eyes opened wide at the sight of the brand. The tips of her fingers gently touched the wound and she started to cry again.

"Ma," he said, gently. "It is over. 'Tis naught."

But her hands made a systematic search of his body, touching almost every square inch, murmuring his name and blessing his soul for the insult to her child. When she had touched every inch of him, searched every place, touched the scar, and wept harder.

Gwydion took her hands in his and kissed them. "Shh, Ma. I tell you, 'tis all over."

With that, she launched herself into her son's arms and the two clung to each other; she sobbed as if her heart had been broken and was broken no more. Another shout of joy went from the crowd, and the sound of applause and huzzahs rang in Toby's ears.

An older man came from around the back of the house. He threw aside a tool of some kind and ran to the crowd. "Gwydion, lad, you've worried your mother no end."

Gwydion looked away from his mother, who was weeping into his chest, and looked rather sheepish. "Ay, Da. I know. I'm that sorry about it."

A beaming smile came over his father's face as he shrugged and waved a hand absently in Gwy's direction. "Well, 'tis no mind now. You're home where you belong, my boy. 'Tis all I need now."

With that, Gwydion was swept into his father's embrace and the three of them stood crying. The crowd took this as their time to go and they began to disperse. Toby watched parents take their children by the hand or hold them close as they walked away. There were tears in many eyes and, to be honest, Toby was starting to mist up a little too.

He was also starting to feel a little uncomfortable, like a voyeur at the bedroom window. He couldn't leave, even if he wanted to. It was a scene he had been part of once, so long ago in another lifetime. It was painful to watch them and not see himself and his own parents. He stood watching, anyway, feeling the tears slip down his cheeks. He heard a sniffle next to him and noticed Yeshua was wiping his eyes furiously.

Gwydion broke the embrace to turn back to his companions. "Màthair, Àthair , these are my friends. They saved my life, rescued me. I asked them to come with me. If you don't mind, may they stay here a while with us?"

She stopped sobbing at this, and unburied her face from Gwydion's chest. She wiped tears from her eyes with one hand, sniffling as she spoke. But, she never released her hold around Gwydion's waist. "Saved you? How did they do this, my sweet son?"

"Aye, when I took my freedom back from the bastards, Tobias and Yeshua hid me and sent 'em on their way. They kept the soldiers from takin' me back. And they made sure I came home safe, they did. Aye, I owe them my life."

The tiny woman released her son's middle and, after taking a few tentative steps in their direction, she scurried to Toby. Without thinking, he bent down to her. She threw herself in his arms, wrapping hers around his neck. She kissed his cheeks, this time her tears mingled with her giggles of delight. Toby was so taken aback that he just let her do it. It had been so long since he'd been held that way that he was touched by her gratitude. He'd almost forgotten what it was like.

Gwydion's father came bounding over and made the same overtures to Yeshua – although, to Toby's amusement, he didn't kiss the boy. Yeshua was just as astounded at the treatment as Toby. *Poor lad never met an Irishman; I probably should have warned him.* Gwydion stood watching his parents, that same smile fixed to his face.

When the couple had kissed and hugged both of them, Gwydion's mother took one of Toby's hands in hers, and then one of Yeshua's.

"Well, anyone who saves my son and brings him home to me safe and sound is a part of this family. You both are welcome in our home, boys. Come on in now and have a rest. You look as if you have not eaten a good meal in forever. Come now, you're all home."

She led them into the gate and from there, the little party went inside.

Chapter Fifteen

If Toby had had any concerns about the evening, they were soon removed and dispelled. Niamh had run between them during dinner, mothering all three. She would stand next to Gwydion, touching his face, his hands, playing with his reddish-gold locks, and crooning in his ear. Then, she would be up, fussing over what Yeshua was eating and was Toby eating enough. The meal was simple – dried fruits and fresh vegetables from Niamh's garden and a dried fish stew. She would set another bowl before Yeshua and pat his shoulder. She would refill Toby's mug with the fine Irish ale, dark and full bodied, and make sure he was enjoying it. Then, she would return to her son and resume crooning his name as if she dared not believe he was home again.

She was a small woman, like Maeve had been, with the same thick black hair, same laughing green eyes. The black glimmered with strands of the purest silver and she wore it braided over her shoulder and tied with a leather thong. She wore a simple dress, woven from wool. She was what he had always imagined an Irish lady to be, a faery.

Toby could tell, however, which parent Gwydion favored. Liam was the same tall, lanky build as his son. Liam had the same red-gold hair, the same blue eyes, and the same sunny manner that he had passed on to his son. He was quiet, as Brendan had been, and Liam had the same intensity as when it came to his family.

Liam simply sat and beamed throughout dinner. His smile was so large, his elation so obvious, that Toby was afraid the man would explode from his happiness. He would occasionally ask Gwydion a question of his captivity, or whether or not Toby had been in Israel long, or when Yeshua had begun his journey. Then, Liam would lapse back into his silent jubilation and just watch his son.

When the time came for them to turn in, Gwydion had taken his place where he had always slept – in the loft. But Yeshua and Toby were led to a sturdy lean-to shed behind the house where they would sleep. Liam had apologized for the makeshift lodging, offering another option the next day, but Toby had not cared at that point.

This was going to be a luxury for him and he intended to revel in it, wallow in it.

Since he'd arrived, Toby had slept either on a blanket under the stars or on a hard pallet in someone's home. Either way, he'd slept on the ground. Liam had taken the shed and turned it into a spare bedroom by shredding two bales of hay and making bed-like shapes of them. Niamh had brought out two spare down ticks and placed them on the straw. She'd also given each of them an extra quilt and kissed them good night, stealing away with the lamp. He was asleep before his head hit the pillow. No dreams, no nightmares, no thinking – just blessed sleep and welcome darkness.

When he woke the next morning, the only clue he had that it was morning was the open door. The sunshine streamed in and bathed the shed in beams that sparkled with the dancing dust motes. Angels dancing in the sunlight, his mother had told him when he was little. He watched them whirling in the sunbeams, glistening in the air, and smiled at the memory – his mother on the bed next to him, snuggling him close as they watched the sparkles. He scrubbed his hands over his face and, turning over on his back, looked around at his surroundings.

The shed's walls had been meticulously hewn smooth, impossibly square at the corners. They had been whitewashed to a milky white, highlighting the natural texture of the wood. Someone, presumably Liam and Gwydion, had carefully hung tools on pegs and hooks. Each scythe, adze, and spade had been carefully and logistically grouped in order of the purpose they served. A bench had been shoved back in order to make way for their sleeping arrangements but Toby could see that the bench had been well worn in places, indicating that this was also a tool for the farm.

He finally convinced himself to get up and moving. This was a working farm, after all, and there would be a lot to do. Even if he was a guest, he could still earn his room and board. Gwy's family had been very kind in allowing them to stay in their home. The least he could do would be to help out. Toby dressed quickly in his tunic and sandals, made a tentative attempt at making his "bed", and went out to find his way to the home of his hosts.

When he stepped out of the shed, he had to stop for a moment to take it all in. Once again, he was bowled over by the green of the grasses, the color of the sky, but he was seeing more in this light. It was autumn, and the colors of the trees were breathtaking, with the golds, reds, and oranges of the leaves. The air was crisp and clean with the smells of the good earth and the loam of it, of the fall crops in the fields and the fruits of the trees. He stood there, just breathing it, seeing it, until his mind threatened to collapse from the overload. *So, this is what it was like before the machines, before progress.*

Another scent attracted him, this time from the house. He sniffed the air and smelled baking bread, herbs and spices – the smell of food. His stomach growled in a perfectly Pavlovian response. *Pavlov isn't even born yet, and here I am proving his theory. I'm even salivating*, he thought and reached up to wipe the corners of his mouth with the back of his hand.

Toby suddenly remembered Yeshua and turned back to the shed to make sure he was awake. The young man, however, was nowhere to be seen. Toby raked his fingers through his hair, wondering exactly how long he'd been asleep. He had that question answered when he looked towards the sky and then the shadows on the ground. They were shorter than they should have been. Toby reckoned it had to be about nine in the morning, long after he would normally be up.

He found Yeshua as soon as he got to the house. He had barely reached the front door when he heard a shout from the fields. There were Liam, Gwydion, and Yeshua, laughing with each other as they came. Yeshua waved at him, a huge grin on his face. Toby waved back but right now, he was more interested in investigating those wonderful aromas than he was in finding out what the men were doing.

Walking in the door, the smells were stronger. *Is that cinnamon? My God, it is. How did they get cinnamon here?* He followed on to the kitchen and just stopped, closing his eyes and breathing it all in.

Niamh clucked her tongue, startling him for a moment. He sheepishly turned his head, smiling as if he'd been caught at something he shouldn't have been doing instead of appreciating her cooking. She didn't appear to be too upset as she stood at the brick oven, taking out loaves of freshly baked bread. His stomach growled again, and she giggled.

"And there's our savior, awakened at last. You slept a good time, Tobias. You must've been so weary. Well, you settle down at the table and we'll feed you proper. You must be famished."

"Aye, that I am."

Her smile was just as sweet as the jams and jellies she began to place on the table in front of him. She brought an entire loaf of bread that had just come from the oven, and set it on a wooden tray, and then placed that in front of him, as well. In no time at all, a knife and a pot of butter joined the array, and Toby tore into the meal with a vengeance.

"Will you have a spot of cider to wash it down, love?"

"Aye, ma'am," he managed to get out around the mouthful of bread.

She dipped a gourd ladle into a smaller cauldron and poured a golden liquid into an earthenware mug. When she put the mulled cider before him, he smelled the wonderful spices and apples in the drink and polished it off before he could stop himself. She just laughed again and poured another mug for him. This one he sipped as he ate.

"The cider is wonderful, ma'am; all of this is wonderful. Thank you."

"No, Tobias, 'tis I should be thankin' *you*. For the returnin' of my son."

Toby paused, his mouth full again, and looked at her. Niamh's eyes were brimming with tears, her hands clasped to her bosom.

"You have given us the greatest gift any man could and we shall be forever in your debt."

He felt the flush in his cheeks and he ducked his head, pleased but still a bit embarrassed. "He would've done the same for me. It was the right thing to do."

"Aye, our Gwydion always did care for those who were downtrodden and friendless. He would have. But, 'tis you that saved *his* life."

Toby smiled up at her. "Well, ma'am, you have given Yeshua and I a place to sleep and fed us well. I'd say the debt is paid. I think he and I owe *you* that debt now."

"We'll have none of that. You both are our guests, our honored guests." She nodded, ending the discussion of debts and changed the subject. "Well then, and how long will you boys be stayin'?"

Toby took another swallow of the delicious cider, and said, "I don't know. But I like it here."

She clapped her hands in almost childish delight. "Then, you'll stay with us for as long as you like."

"We don't want to put you to any trouble—"

Her brow furrowed at that, her hands slipped to her hips and the mother stood over him. *If she starts twisting my ear, I'll really know I'm home.* But, she didn't.

"In the first place, I don't know what 'ma'am' will be but one thing is I will insist is that you'll be calling me Niamh! Not ma'am, just *Niamh.*"

Toby's eyes got wide and he gulped in answer.

"In the next place, you're not any trouble, do you hear? And there'll be no more of this foolishness about trouble and inconveniences. You're home! And this will be your home for as long as you want it."

Toby grinned sheepishly, nodding back at her. "Yes...Niamh."

The sunny smile returned and she said, "Thank you. Now, when you've done eating, you can help me put the bread away. I s'pose they'll be wantin' you in the fields to help with the hay, but they've plenty of hands for that. And I'm grateful for the company, to tell you the truth."

"What can I do to help you, Niamh?"

Toby was not the baker that his mother was, nor this woman, but he could grind the grains for her. He worked steadily, seated in front of the stone, and watched her make dough in batches, the new set aside to rise while she worked with the ones that already had. Through it all, Niamh kept a steady stream of conversation, stopping only to correct Toby's technique or ingredients. He was grateful not to have to do more than nod or grunt an answer. The remnants of the stew were added upon and another boiling pot added to the mixture of smells in the room.

There were two dozen families in the village, most having been born and bred to the area. Some had come and settled; some had married into families and started their own. Niamh proudly announced that the population had reached a little over two-hundred souls this past spring, and several more ladies were with child. They would spend the next spring clearing more land for the homes that would be built for the new families. There were four handfastings planned for Yule and they'd need new homes.

It was communal living at its best. They lived by barter and they helped each other when there was need. The village now had an apothecary added due to a recent handfasting, and now that her Gwydion had returned, they had a bard again. She was also quick to point out that Gwydion was an herbalist, learned from the High Priest and Priestess, a thing she noted with pride.

"Niamh?" Toby interrupted her.

Her chatter stopped and she looked up at him from the current batch of dough she was kneading. "Aye?"

"Niamh, what is a handfasting? What is a High Priestess?"

For a moment, she had a confused look on her face, and then an understanding rushed over her features. "Aye, of course. Oh, do forgive me, Tobias. You're a stranger and not knowin' our ways. A handfasting is when two join as man and wife."

"A marriage," Toby clarified.

"Well, not completely. A handfasting comes before the marrying ceremony." She went back to kneading the dough while she talked. "You see, a couple handfasts for a year and a day, to live as husband and wife, in what you call a trial. Should the couple find any opposition in themselves, they can dissolve the union with no harm done. But should they find that they both are meant to be together, they will have the marrying ceremony. Which will be mating them for as long as love lasts, mostly for life and beyond if 'tis meant to be."

"And, what's a High Priestess?" Toby continued. "I know what a High Priest would be. I think."

"Well, the Priestess would be his mate and partner. They are Goddess-chosen to lead us, help us in our path."

"Goddess? You worship a Goddess?"

"Aye, we do. We are the children of the Lord and the Lady. Do you not worship a Goddess?"

Toby ducked his head again, scratching at the back of his head. "No, ma'am – I mean, Niamh. I had always heard of such people, but I was taught to believe that...that.... I was taught that it was wrong."

Rather than be insulted, Niamh seemed more amused than anything else.

"Aye, so I've heard. There was a traveler came to the village once. Said he was a – oh, what did he call himself...*a Jew*, aye, that was what he called himself. He said he believed in the one true God and there were no others. Ne'er saw him again, but I remember his ways were strange."

"Yeshua is a Jew."

"Oh, aye? Well, then, we'll be learning a bit more of them, I suppose. Aye, 'tis good to learn." She began to shape the round loaves of the soda bread, using her knife to cut an X shape on the top. "And what of you, Tobias? Are you a Jew, as well?"

"No, Niamh, I'm not."

"Do you follow that of the Romans? Or the others?"

Toby stopped grinding the grain, just sitting for a minute. *I don't know what I am...or who I am in this time.* He went back to his grinding before he answered. "I follow no Gods. I don't believe anymore."

Niamh's smile of pity almost broke his heart. How very much like Maeve she really was.

"Oh, Tobias, I'm that sorry for you. We all need something to believe in, something to keep our faith alive. If you have no faith, how can you be happy?"

Toby couldn't answer that one, so he didn't try. Which was fine because Niamh didn't wait for an answer.

"Well, then, you'll have to come with us to *Alban Elfed*, although some have taken to callin' it *Mabon*. You'll not be permitted in the circle but there'd be no harm in your watching. You can learn of our faith, as well. Would you like that, Tobias?"

"Aye, I think so. What is *may-bun*?"

"Well, 'tis our celebration of the harvest. All the grain has been gathered, all but the winter crops from the field, all the harvests put away in storage. Aye, and this season has brought us a fine harvest. The Mother has blessed us, surely.

"We'll be celebratin' with the grains and the new wines. And we've so much to celebrate this year. My son is home from his journey. You've saved his life from slavery. Aye, we much to celebrate."

The last loaf popped in the oven, and she removed more, done to a turn. Cookies followed. In the short space of time that Toby had been grinding, she had baked several dozen loaves of bread, and had them cooling on shelves and window ledges. The fragrances of stew, bread and cider made his mouth water and his stomach growl again. Niamh laughed and put a hand on Toby's shoulder.

"'Tis time to eat the midday meal, Tobias. Will you do me the courtesy of calling in the hungry workers in the field? They'll be wantin' their supper as sure as I'm standin' here. Be a dear and ring the bell for me."

Her laugh was so infectious, he joined her and the sound filled the small kitchen. Then he did something that he never expected himself to do. He took the hand on his shoulder and kissed the back of it ever so softly. He looked into her green eyes and smiled.

"Tobias, what is it, my darling?"

"I was just remembering times like this with *my* mother," Toby answered, with a catch in his throat. His eyes misted up again as he stared down at his hands, folded in his lap. "I miss her so much, Niamh. You're so like her."

Her other hand came up to his hair and caressed it gently, smoothing it away from his forehead. Her gaze was kind as she did it. Then, she leaned forward, and kissed his forehead.

"Then, I'll be your mother, sweet Tobias. You'll call me Ma. 'Twill be well, my boy."

Toby rested his forehead against her bosom and she cradled his head, running her fingers through his hair, softly speaking his name and calling him her son. He cried for the first time since it had all begun. He cried until his body shook with the force of the tears and the agony. He cried while she held him. She never rushed him, never stopped combing her fingers in his hair. She simply waited till his tears had abated. Then she wiped his with the corner of a handkerchief that she pulled from her sleeve and kissed his cheek.

"Go," she said, in her gentle way. "Call the lads in for their meal. Go on, now, my son."

He did as he was told, feeling a bit lighter than he had since Maeve's death. He was still sniffing as they came in but she never told them he had cried. She had just served up the stew with the freshly baked bread, and waited on her men.

And, how they ate. Between the four men, they demolished five loaves of her bread, an entire pot of blackberry jam, most of the fish stew, and a whole pot each of cider and ale. Toby listened to the chatter between the three men as they discussed the baling of the hay and how to preserve the tubers in the root cellar. Wooden spoons clapped against earthen bowls and the sounds of slurping stew and ale accompanied the conversation.

Toby watched Yeshua the most. The young man had blossomed; even more, he was *smiling.* Yeshua had lost his oh-so-serious demeanor and looked every inch the teenage boy he really was. Toby watched him toss back an entire mug of ale, wipe his mouth with his sleeve, and give a deep trumpet blast of a belch. Yeshua grinned and laughed with the rest of them, then held his mug out for more. Life was good – for just this moment, it was good.

"Liam, you'll have help with the addition to the house. Moiré came by and said they'll be happy to give you a hand. She wants to know if you want the other men in the village as well."

Liam pushed his bowl back and lit the pipe that Niamh had placed beside him. When he had it going to his satisfaction, he sat back against the wall and blew a smoke ring.

"Aye, 'twill do fine to have the extra hands. With the lot o' them, we'll have a roof before sunset. Aye, I'll tell 'em."

"Nae, husband, I'll tend to it. Moiré has some linen to embroider and I'll take it in with my own as payment. We'll be feeding those lads for the effort. I'll walk over after you're all back to your work."

"Aye," he answered, and puffed more smoke into the air.

"Addition to the house?" Gwydion asked his parents. "What'll you be needing that for?"

"Well, lad, you've brought guests to the house," Liam explained. "That old shed was not for the sleeping of anyone. Besides, you're a bit old to be sleeping in the loft, you know. Your màthair and I discussed it, and we've decided to build another room for you three to sleep in."

"Aye," Niamh replied, in agreement. "'Twill be good for you to have a place for yourselves. And I'll be getting my loft back to store my quilts and herbs again."

Toby and Yeshua locked gazes for a moment. Toby began, "Niamh, Liam, please—"

But, Niamh, standing beside Liam, with her hand on his shoulder, simply raised one finger in the air, silencing him immediately. She pointed it at him, her eyebrow cocked with the stern refusal of any objection he was about to give.

He grinned and nodded at her, finishing instead with, "—let us help you with the building. More hands to raise the roof and you'll have it done all the sooner."

"Thank you, boys; that is a fine idea." Liam glanced sideways at Niamh, smiling his understanding at her.

She turned her attention back to her son. "Gwydion, dear, Declan is askin' you to sing at the ritual. Can you be prepared by then?"

Gwydion looked thoughtful for a moment. "Aye, with Elfed but three days away, I can prepare and have a few tales for the ready. Has he said what he wants?"

"Well, perhaps you'll go speak with him and he can tell you."

"I'll have my harp tuned and some stories ready. I'll see him after we've done with for the day."

"Wait," Yeshua blurted out. "I don't understand."

Niamh patted Liam on the shoulder. "Liam, do you remember the traveler that came upon us that time? Yeshua is the same faith as he."

Liam took the stem of the pipe from his mouth, and looked toward the youth. "Are you, boy? You're not of the Goddess?"

Yeshua straightened in the chair, sitting as if a rod had been bolted to his back. "I worship the One True God of the Jews, Liam. He is my Father and I am his son."

Toby took a long draw of air into his lungs. *He'll tell them how they're sinnin' against the One True God and damn them to hell. I like these folks...and the shit storm starts.*

Liam replaced the stem of his pipe in his mouth and nodded. Yeshua watched him with an eager look on his face, waiting for something.

Gwydion was the one that explained it to him. "Yeshua, our celebration is the last harvest of the season. We'll gather together to thank the Goddess for Her blessing of the food we've received of Her bosom."

"You see," Liam said, taking the reins of the discussion. "*Dana* is the Mother of all of Her creatures here on the land. She is the Mother of the Gods. She represents the land, the earth."

"Do you have no Father?"

"Aye, Yeshua, we do. The *Dagda* is the Father of the Gods, the *Eochaid Ollathair* and the *Ruad Ro-fhessa,* the Father of all and the Lord of Perfect Knowledge."

Toby struggled to say the names again in his head, twisting his mental tongue on the Celtic. But he was fascinated by what Liam was saying and let it go for now to hear more.

"The Dagda keeps the Cauldron that can never be emptied and from which no man goes away hungry. He is the seed we plant into the ground and Dana is the mother; her womb gives the seeds the place to grow."

"Are there other Gods?" Toby asked.

"Oh, aye," Gwydion answered. "There's *Lugh*, the God of the harvest. 'Tis He that we thank for the help bringing in the bounty. There's *Angus Og, the God o' Love,* and *the Morrigan*—"

"Gwydion," Niamh hissed. "Don't be calling Her if there's no cause. You know She's a harsh one for the men."

"Sorry," Gwydion answered, and to his credit, he did look contrite.

"Who is the Mo—? Uh, that one?" Toby asked.

"She's the Goddess of War," Liam answered. "And no friend to the man who is not fair with his women."

"Aye," said Niamh, and she ruffled Gwydion's hair to help remove the repentant look on his face. "She is that. If you call her with no cause, She is like to cause you ill luck if you're a man. If you care for your women and respect them – and you should – She is like to treat you well. If you're in battle, She is your champion."

"I see," said Yeshua. "But there is only one God, the God of the Israelites – the God of us all. He cares for all of His children, and knows when there is need, to provide."

"You only have the one, Yeshua?" asked Niamh.

"Yes, and He is all that man has need of. He feeds His children, clothes them, protects them."

"And what do you call him," Liam asked.

"*I* call Him 'Father'. As *you* all must call Him 'Father', but I may truly call Him 'Father'." Yeshua sat upright, closing his eyes as he recited, "'For behold, a virgin shall conceive, and shall bear a son.'" He looked back to his audience. "I am that Son, the Son of my Father."

Toby watched the family and waited. But he was surprised when each one nodded, accepting the story at face value. They each seemed to take the fantastic statement as truth and embrace it.

"Aye," said Gwydion finally. "You'll tell us the story someday, will you?"

Yeshua seemed satisfied and nodded. "I will tell it."

"I'd like to hear more of the Celtic Gods," Toby interrupted.

"Would you, lad?" Liam took the pipe stem from his mouth again. "Gwydion, when you go to see Declan, see if he's accepting any new pupils. Perhaps our guests would like to meet him and discuss learnin' of the Celtic way. Would you like that, lads?"

"I know I would," Toby answered.

All eyes turned to Yeshua, who sat in a thoughtful state. His eyes were focused on the wall above Gwydion, who sat opposite him. After a few seconds, the young man blinked a few times and returned his gaze to the family sitting around him.

"As would I. I have come to learn of others, see others, and my Father has said that I should start here. I would like to meet this Declan and talk with him about...Gods."

"Well, then, 'tis settled," Niamh confirmed with her no-nonsense tone.

"Aye, that it is," Liam announced, grinning again at his wife. "Now, I'll be takin' your cookin' partner with us to help in the field. Another hand balin' the hay will make it over all the sooner and on the morrow, we can build that addition with no guilt. Are you ready, boys?"

Liam stood up and the rest followed. For the rest of the afternoon, Toby baled hay and thought about Gods and Goddesses, of earth and sky. He worked with his hands and wondered if there could ever be such a thing as a God. He finally decided that there must be for such beauty to exist.

The hay baled, another night spent with the family. They lived simply, from what they could grow in the land and the animals they raised. They worked hard during the day and the nights were spent in simple pleasures. Toby sat and watched Niamh take up the linen handkerchief she was working on, as she made tiny stitches to create a geometric design on its corners. Liam sat back and smoked his pipe, talking about the day's work and how happy he was that his son was home to help. When all was said, Gwydion took his harp from the wall and played songs. There was music and laughter.

A larger crowd turned out to help put up "the addition," as Liam called it. In fact, the entire village came for the event. They gathered, as Liam had asked, as soon as the sun had crested the treetops, bringing tools and food. The women used Niamh's tiny kitchen or set up cook fires in the back of the house and the aromas of stews and breads and cakes soon filled the air.

The men set to work with a will. Some took the clay and made the mortar to fit between the logs. Others began to tie up the thatch that would soon cover the roof. Still others began to cut down the logs and hew them to the right thickness. Some of the logs would make the walls and some would be the roof. Liam walked what he wanted to be the perimeter of the new room, marking the exact dimensions with sticks. His eye was precise as the lie was again perfectly square. When he was finished, still more took axe and pick to the ground and removed the sod and laid the stone foundation. Liam, himself, took an axe to the existing wall, and carved a doorway that would lead to the new room.

Yeshua had carpentry experience, so he worked with the men in hewing the trees. He worked the adze against the wood, often stopping to help someone with another log or show someone a better grip to the tool. He would periodically run his hand across the surface of the log to test it. Then, he would wipe the back of his hand across his forehead and get back to the work at hand.

Yeshua had stripped the robe he still wore down to his waist and had tied it with the sleeves so that it wouldn't fall off. So Toby did the same with his robe and continued to help make the mortar. He collected the mud and mixed the right measure of straw into it. The conversation with the other men made itself but he listened more than he joined in. The men talked of mixtures and dimensions, of crops and seeds, and the stuff of their lives.

Only once did Toby's attention waver from his task, and that was when the women began to put the food out. Several of the men had left stumps out and laid several of the hewn logs on them to act as tables, and the women were laying the food out upon them. They worked diligently, laying out bowls of vegetables, legs of beef and lamb, steaming pots of stew, loaves of bread. She was moving among the other women, the most beautiful sight he had ever seen in his life.

She was dressed in dyed wool and she moved like the grasses when the winds have kissed them in the field. In a sea of blonde and black haired women, her long red hair shone like copper down her back. When she pushed an errant strand of burnished red back out of her face, Toby felt like he could no longer breathe. She was curvy in the most pleasing of places with a full swell of her bosom that tantalized. She stood taller than the other women. He saw her lean towards one and toss her head back, laughing. He caught the sound of her laughter from where he was and found it sweeter than any music he had ever heard.

Try as he might, he could get no closer. When they stopped for the noon meal, she was off with another group. She floated through them with a huge pitcher of some liquid, and Toby felt his mouth dry up on the spot. He watched her stop and chatter with Gwydion, but she never came Toby's way. When she kissed Gwydion on the cheek, he felt a stab in his chest and wondered if she was promised to him. When he saw her kiss another man on the cheek, he knew that this one was promised to no man and became more determined that his friend was going to introduce them.

After the food, while the women cleared the leftovers and parceled them out to be eaten later, the men finished thatching the roof. Once done, there was more ale, more celebration, and Gwydion brought out his harp. They sang and drank until the sun left the sky. Each family left after congratulating Liam on his good fortune in a son returning and wishing the family well. Liam thanked everyone personally, shaking hands as they left and making sure each had a good pot of ale to take home with them.

They sat up for a while, moving the bedding into the new room – it would be several days before the mortar in the fireplace was set enough that they could light a fire, so Niamh made sure they had plenty of quilts to keep warm. She also brought in bundles of cloth.

"There, lads, you'll be needing these. Some new clothes for you. I noticed you slavin' in those things you've been wearing and I knew they were makin' you uncomfortable. And I said to myself, you'd be needing some good and proper clothin' to wear."

Toby took the clothing from her and kissed her on the cheek. She giggled, and turned to hand Yeshua his clothing, as well. The serious young man took the package from her, and then her hand. He kissed the back of it and laid his cheek against it.

"Bless you, Mother, for the kindness will never be forgotten."

Yeshua held her hand to his chest for a moment, long enough for Niamh to get a little misty eyed and pat his cheek, resting her hand there.

"Enjoy the wearin' of the clothes, lad. Good night, my strong sons. Sleep well."

She left quickly and they were left alone to try on their new finery. Niamh had sized them up well, because the clothing was a perfect fit.

"Well, you'll blend in now, for sure." Gwydion lay on his bedding, leaning on one elbow with the hand behind his head. "They'll be comfortable and warm, if I know my Ma."

"They are." Yeshua ran his hands over the material, tightly woven to keep body heat inside. "It is soft against my skin, and these leg coverings…what do you call them?"

"They're called trews."

"Trews," Yeshua repeated thoughtfully. He smiled. "Yes, they are most comfortable as well. A fine leather."

"Deer hide," Gwydion offered.

"We'll have to do something for her, to thank her," Toby said, lying down on his own bedding.

"Not at all, lads. 'Tis in her nature do to it. Besides, if you try to thank her in any way than you've just done, you'll embarrass her. You need do no more."

"We have to do something."

"When you're shown a kindness, you pass it on. 'Tis not in payin' it back. You treat those around you as you'd want to be treated and the energy you send comes back to you."

"When someone does a kindness for any of my friends, they do it for me, Gwydion," Yeshua replied soberly.

"When you do a kindness for *anyone*, you do it for us all, lad." Gwydion turned onto his back, his hands pillowing his head. "Now, are you ready for sleeping, boys? I'm fair used, I am."

The other two pulled blankets over themselves and settled down as well. As Gwydion reached to douse the candlelight, Toby finally gathered the courage to ask about the red haired woman he'd seen. He described the woman and Gwydion grunted, half asleep.

"Aye, that would be Siobhan. She's the daughter of Cieran. A handful, that one is. But, she's a good girl."

"Is she...well...is...she....?"

With a broad grin, Gwydion watched Toby, who was squirming just a bit. "Is she what, lad?"

"Is she en— Uh, I mean, is she spoken for?"

"No, Tobias, she's not spoken for. She's never promised to any man. I take it you fancy her a bit."

Toby sat up with a sigh. Why was this so hard to admit? Was he afraid they'd make fun of him? And what if they did? With a deep breath, he finally admitted the truth. "Aye, my friend, I do. She's a rare beauty, she is."

Gwydion laughed from his toes, his head thrown back and a hand on his belly. "Aye, she is that. She's spirited, our Siobhan. Yeshua, do you think I should be introducin' 'em?"

Yeshua rolled over on his stomach. "Don't tease him, Gwydion, when you know you should."

"Aye, you're right, I should," Gwydion agreed, still laughing. "All right, Tobias, I'll introduce you to the fair Siobhan. We'll be goin' into the field soon enough for the ritual. Would you like to meet her then? That's supposin' you can last that long."

Toby took a handful of straw and tossed it at Gwydion, and, of course, it came nowhere near him, dispersing across the floor. But, it brought gales of laughter from the other two and a stern warning from Liam in the main room of the house.

"Aye, lad, 'tis her acquaintance you'll be making soon enough. Now sleep, lads. Good night to you and sleep well."

Gwydion extinguished the candle and they lay back down to sleep. Toby slipped his arm behind his head and stared into the darkness for a bit. His thoughts were wrapped around the red haired lady, and he saw her face painted against the black ceiling. *Siobhan...Sha-vawn....* Her name was as musical as he imagined it would be. Well, he would have to wait for a day or two. He thought he might burst before then but he'd hold on.

He fell asleep, repeating her name, imagining the meeting, and praying he didn't screw it up.

Chapter Sixteen

The seed brings forth the flower
The flower brings forth the fruit
The God that brings the shower
To seed and stem and root

We gather in the harvest
The grain that She has given
Blessings from the Mother
The gift of life from Her

They slowly filed into the stone circle, dressed in white robes of wool and cotton. They came silently; some with hands clasped in front of them, some with their arms to their sides. They entered through an arched gate that had been fashioned from corn shocks and dressed with ribbons of gold and brown. They entered in a line, walking in a slow clockwise circle. The only exception was a single figure; he was helped to the altar and left to lean against it.

Another circle had been laid out just inside of the stones. This one was made of dried corn shocks, wheat fronds, and other dried, harvest plants. Up near what appeared to be the headstone, a table had been set with more of the corn shocks and wheat fronds. On the table, someone had placed two goblets, two clay pitchers, and two plates of bread, along with assorted other dishes and what appeared to be a rudimentary broom. There were two lit torches on either side of the table, thrust into the ground. An old tree stump, leveled at the top and the roots neatly hacked off the bottom, had been plunked down near it, with Gwydion's Celtic harp propped up against it. At each quarter mark in the circle, two more blazing torches, approximately two feet apart from each other, rose from the ground. In the center of of the circle was the beginning of a bonfire. The wood, neatly stacked in a pyramid shape, was dressed with the same dried plants.

Gwydion deposited Toby and Yeshua outside of the circle, where they could still see the ceremony but not be involved in it. Liam brought a bench from Niamh's garden for them to sit on and left it to one side of the headstone where they would have an unobstructed view of everything. He and Niamh waved to them and went to take their place in the circle.

Gwydion waited until his parents were on their way to address his friends. "You'll be just fine here, boys. You're close enough so you can hear it all and everyone's making sure you can see everything. Now if you have any questions, just save 'em; Declan will explain it all after the rite at the céilidh."

"Will he lead the ceremony?" Yeshua asked.

"Oh no. He's the High Priest. Declan has the charge of teaching the wee ones about the history of our people and the Gods, counseling those in need, and leading the village. *Aiobh* will lead the ritual as the High Priestess."

"Her name is *Eve*?" Yeshua asked with a concerned look on his face.

"Aye," Gwydion answered. "She is the spiritual leader of our village, our midwife and healer. Why do ye ask?"

"The first woman was called Eve and she did eat from the Tree of Knowledge after she was forbade. She tempted Adam, the first man, and he did eat also. For this reason, God cast them from Paradise and that was the original sin."

Gwydion chewed on that for a few moments, rolling his tongue in his cheek. "Cast out for eating a bit of fruit. 'Tis a hard God you have, Yeshua."

"They disobeyed Him, Gwydion. They were not to eat of that tree, the only one they could not touch. Eve is the cause of the suffering."

"Well, our Aiobh is a good woman. She's helped many in this village with her herbs and potions. She's been helping women birth their children for as long as I can remember. She's been a good spiritual guide to us all. I doubt she's anything like your Eve, friend. You'll meet her later. You'll see."

Yeshua nodded and said no more.

"Well, lads, I must be off. I'm getting called to start the singing. I'll be back to collect you when 'tis over." Gwydion had walked a few paces before he had stopped and turned back to the two on the bench. "Eve, you say. Hmm. I wonder why it was so wrong for her to know. Maybe we can talk about it sometime; you can help me understand."

Gwydion, still smiling, continued on to the arch and through it. He sat down on the stump, balancing the harp on his knee. Closing his eyes, he plucked at the brass strings. Toby listened to the sweetest strains coming from the harp, the clear notes and the soft melodies. Gwydion's fingers were lithe and graceful as the notes and chords drifted from the harp. When he sang, his tenor wafted across the air like the smell of the lavender flowers.

"He sings beautifully, does he not? I remember the stories of David and his harp, how he sang."

Toby took a deep breath, and turned to Yeshua. He didn't want to break the musical spell but now that it had been, he was going to address the subject. "You were rude to him."

Yeshua crossed his arms, jutting out his chin. He sat with a straight back, raising himself to his full height and glaring at Toby. "I spoke the truth."

Toby slowly reached down to grasp the bench, pressing his fingers to the underside of the wood. "No. You spoke *your* truth. You insulted his religion and his High Priestess. You had no right."

"Tobias, even you can see these people are damned to the eternal fires of hell."

He's a young man now. But he's still that militant kid. Toby bit his lip, trying to keep his temper under control. It would do no good to lash out. "You don't know what hell is."

"I do, Tobias, I do" Yeshua insisted stubbornly. "It is to be separated from the love of the One True God."

He snapped, barely raising his voice above a conversational tone but still seething as he spoke. "No, boy, hell is to be caught in the middle of want and need, to be without the rope to hang on to when you're drowning." Toby caught himself, turned back to the circle. He was panting, gripping the bench so hard that he thought his knuckles going to pop apart.

There must have been something in his voice that made Yeshua really look at him for a moment. The young man's eyes narrowed, his head cocked to one side. "Tobias, is there something you need to say to me? Please say it."

Toby forced himself to breathe more slowly. His heart was pounding and he swallowed, struggling to keep his voice even and low. "Look, I'm sorry I got angry. I just...you said you were sent to journey and learn. How much do you think you'll learn if all you do is...*never mind.*"

Yeshua swiveled on the bench until he was facing his companion. "Tobias, say it."

Toby waited until he had control again before he turned his head. In genuine bewilderment, he asked, "Are you so right and everyone else is wrong? I didn't say anything when you refused to eat the rabbit or some of the other food you were offered. You were rude about that, too. And now, you insult their beliefs. Do you even listen to yourself? Do you know everything there is to know? You sit there in judgment and you don't even know these people. How can you do that?"

"I know what I know, Tobias."

"You know what's right for *you*, not for these people," he hissed in exasperation. "Try coming down from Heaven and Mount Ararat, and listen to them, *be* one of them."

"I am the Son of God, Tobias. I must be who I am."

"You're the son of a man and he raised you to be better than that. You're supposed to be kind and forgiving. You're supposed to be a man, like us. You're supposed to be human and understanding." His hands were shaking again and he laid them flat on his thighs to still them. With a steadier voice, he asked, "Look, why don't you just listen to them? Stop worrying about whose God is right and who's going to hell. Just be one of them, accept them as they are. You might be surprised. They might be more like you than you know."

"They might not," Yeshua answered, his lips primly pressing together after he'd spoken.

"You'll never know if you don't stop being so judgmental. What—"

They were both interrupted by a woman's voice and their attention was drawn back to the circle and the altar. She was small – if she was five feet, Toby would have eaten the grass she walked on. She had thrown back her hood and her hair was the purest of silver, hanging down loose around her hips. She addressed the villagers with her arms outstretched to them. Her voice was powerful and lilting and at that moment, she owned the circle and all within it. He knew in an instant that this had to be Aiobh.

"We celebrate the harvest and the blessing of another season. We have been most fortunate, for another year of abundance has been given to us and a son has been returned."

The woman turned back to the altar and picked up the broom. After a brief nod to Gwydion, she walked behind the gathered villagers and began to lightly sweep behind them, around the perimeter of the circle. Gwydion played softly as she walked the circumference, slowly and methodically. When she had gone fully around, she came back to the altar and replaced the broom in the same spot it had occupied before.

A man came forward from the altar and handed her a staff. Toby wasn't close enough to fully see wooden surface but he could tell it had been carved intricately. The woman took it and, facing the altar, twirled it like a baton. Three times she twirled it and then, holding the staff close to her body, she turned and walked to the circle's rim of corn shocks.

She approached the first of the torches and stood before them. The man had followed her, carrying a dish of something. She held out the staff now, as she stood before the torch, an end in each of her hands. Again, she twirled the staff three times, and then took it close to her body.

"Guardians of the Watchtowers of the East, of the Air, I do summon, stir, and call you forth, to witness our rite and protect our circle. I welcome you and Blesséd be."

The gathered repeated the welcome and again she twirled the staff three times before moving to the next quarter. The man following her took a small sprig of some foliage and dipped it in the bowl he carried. Removing it again, he shook it in the space between the torches and drops of liquid flew from the leaves.

Oh, I get it, Toby thought to himself. *It's a doorway of sorts. I get it now.*

The villagers turned to follow her progress, turning to face the same direction as she faced it. Many held out their hands in a gesture of welcome, while some raised a hand to the sky and lowered the other to the ground. No matter the gesture, they all repeated the blessing of welcome, and then, turned to follow her.

She went to each of the torches and entered the invocation of the directions. The next was the South and she called it *fire*. Then, came West and *water*, and finally, North and *earth*. She invoked each one, twirling the staff thrice before and after the invocation, and moved on. When she came to the last torch, and called the last Guardian, she continued in the clockwise direction until she had reached the altar again.

The man that Toby assumed was Declan walked with her, always two steps behind her and with a reverent gait. She crossed to the altar again and Toby stood up to see better. He watched the man as he came to stand on the woman's left side. Again, the twirling of the staff, yet this time, she stood with the staff raised over her head.

"Mother Dana, You have given us the bounty of your bosom. You have given us another season of fertility and have fed Your children. We call You forth to celebrate with us, that we may thank You for Your blessings. We call You forth to witness our rite and protect our circle. Welcome and Blesséd be."

She turned to face the man, turning clockwise, and handed him the staff. He took his place in front of the altar and, with a deep mellifluous voice, entered the invocation of the Dagda.

"Father Dagda, You have given Your blessing to this earth, and You have given the seed to the ground. You brought us the strength of the harvest and we celebrate with You and thank You for Your blessings. We call You forth to witness our rite and protect our circle. Welcome and Blesséd be."

The staff twirled again, and he turned to face the gathering, pulling back his hood at the same time. Toby was surprised to see that Declan was at least ten years younger than the woman he stood beside. He had thick black hair and a handsome face. He was a muscular man, fit and lean, and taller than the rest of the villagers. He was also just as commanding a figure as his lady, and Toby's eyes were riveted to him.

Aiobh stretched out her hand to Gwydion who ceased his playing and laid the harp down beside him on a quilt he had brought. She motioned him forward and Gwydion came to kneel before the Priestess.

"For we have great reason to celebrate this day. A son who was taken has been returned safe from harm."

She stepped back to the altar and Declan spoke next, taking her place in front of Gwydion.

"Gwydion ap Liam, we rejoice in your freedom and we celebrate the returning. For while you were gone, we were as incomplete as the cutting of a limb from the body."

When she had turned back, she held a small dish in her hand, running her right forefinger in it. She replaced the dish on the altar and stepped back to Gwydion. Cupping her left hand under his chin, Aiobh lifted Gwydion's face up and, with her finger, traced a shape on his forehead.

"You have been Goddess-blest, my son; She has brought you home to your parents and to us all," she proclaimed. "And so I do anoint you, in Her name, as *Bard of the Goddess*, Her true poet. As you pass from lifetime to lifetime, you shall sing Her songs and speak Her words, care for Her children. Her sign on your forehead will tell all that you are Her child and carry Her protection. *So mote it be*."

Again the gathering repeated the final sentence. Toby could see Liam and Niamh beaming as they watched their son receive his accolade. They, too, had pulled the hoods back from their faces and Liam put his arm around Niamh. At that moment, everyone in the circle had done the same, except the one who stood silent, leaning against the altar. He had stood there for the ritual thus far, no movement, no acknowledgment of anything. Toby's curiosity was about to get the best of him.

"And let this talisman be a reminder," Declan said. "This necklace of malachite has been cleansed and purified by the elements, sanctified by the Dagda and the Dana. Wear this as your protection and the badge of your office."

Declan slipped the necklace around Gwydion's neck. The High Priest helped Gwydion from the ground, and he and Aiobh embraced the new Bard of the Goddess. Toby grinned broadly, feeling a sense of pride and affection for the man. Gwydion, for his part, seemed to stand a little straighter as he walked back to the stump and reseated himself.

Aiobh stepped out into the circle, carrying the staff again. This time, she used it to help her make way around the center, walking slowly and methodically. As she walked, she began to tell a story in her beautiful voice and Toby got another answer – where the children were. As Aiobh spoke, the young ones ran into the circle and began to act it out in front of the villagers.

"For it was in the time of the Tuatha de Danaan, when they walked among us, that there was a village. And the folk there had gone through many hard times and were sore starving. They prayed and gave their sacrifice to the Gods of Ir to help them, to feed them. And every day, they worked the fields and never brought forth the fruit."

Toby watched the scattered young ones mimicking the work, one or two getting into the part a little too deeply. He smiled at them; it was probably their first ritual to do something like this. *The parents must be busting*, he thought, knowing he would be doing the same.

Declan removed his robe, folding it neatly and laying it on the grass. Underneath, he had been dressed in a pair of trousers and a shirt that had been dyed a deep, rich forest green. Declan bent down and, from under the altar, pulled a small wreath of what appeared to be oak leaves and placed it on his head.

Aiobh had not stopped her narrative of the starving village, but she had come to the part where Declan was to become part of the story. He stepped forward when prompted in the narrative. When he was required to speak, he did so.

"And so," Aiobh went on, "the Dagda came to them in his form as the Green Man. They fell before him and cried, 'Help us, Father, for we starve. We can't feed our children, or our livestock. The crops won't grow in the field, and there's not enough water to sustain them, or us.' The Dagda saw the peril of the Children of Dana, and He bade them rise. They did so, and He said to them....'"

"If I help you, what are you prepared to give me?" Declan asked in his rich, deep voice.

"'To the Gods, we are prepared to give a portion of the bounty we have,' they said to Him. 'We are prepared to give anythin' They ask of us.'"

Declan, acting as the Dagda, walked amongst the "villagers," as they surrounded him. His hands came to touch them in a familiar and affectionate gesture, touching shoulders or stroking hair.

"The Dagda said to them—" Aiobh started

"I will help you. I will bring the rain to you. I will cause the fields to be prosperous and fertile. You shall mark the season by the birth of the Sun, Lugh. And you shall see it end with His passing. As he grows ever stronger, so the season shall bring the prosperity.

"He will make His sacrifice for you by giving his life for you at the end of the season. I will ask only this – that when the season has ended, you will give a portion of the crops as sacrifice. You will take the shocks and fronds and make a man.

"And this man shall represent Lugh and be your sacrifice to the Gods. If you will do this and allow Us to come to take what We need when We need it, you shall have the bounty you ask for."

Aiobh resumed the narrative, "And they agreed. For it was a fair bargain, everyone knowin' that the Tuatha de Danaan never took much but that they gave more. And the harvest was very great. The villagers came to the end of the season and had more than they could have ever hoped for.

"And true to their promise, they built a man, a Wicker Man, from the leavings of the grain and vegetables. A great Wicker Man he was, and they built a bonfire and burned the Wicker Man as their sacrifice. In thanks to the Tuatha de Danaan, to the Dagda, and to Lugh, the God of the Sun and Harvest."

Declan walked back to the altar and took one of the torches, while two of the teens went to help the man, who had been standing at the altar. Toby was going to see who this was now. Declan walked behind them, brandishing the torch.

To Toby's surprise, it wasn't a 'who', but a 'what'. The boys carried the figure to the center where the wood was waiting. His brow wrinkled in confusion until he saw them pull back the hood from the figure's robe; it was a man fashioned of the same shocks and stems that surrounded the people and decorated the fire.

"We have had a fine harvest this growing season," Aiobh continued. "And we celebrate with the festival of *Alban Elfed,* the end of the harvesting. We have plenty to feed us all and we must give thanks to the Gods, to Lugh. So, it comes to the burning of the Wicker Man. And so that you may all give thanks, take a bit of the harvesting behind you, and feed it to the fire, to send our sacrifice along."

Toby watched the High Priestess wave her hand, and the two teens carrying the wicker form balanced it on top of the pyramid. When one raised the hem of the robe, Toby saw a pole running from beneath, going into the center of the pile of wood. They all re-joined their families now, leaving Declan and Aiobh alone in the center.

The Priest put the torch to the wood and then the fronds. The dry kindling caught at once and spread to the wood beneath it. A flicker from the center and the red-orange of the flame was kissing the woodpile, and soon making its way to the figure. The hem of the Wicker Man's robe was soon smoking, as the heat became increasingly intense.

As the hem caught fire and began to spread to the whole figure, first one family and then another turned to gather handfuls of the fronds behind them. They took the plants and each tossed every scrap on the fire, sending sparks to fly upwards, swirling and dancing. When each family had gathered and thrown the entire amount of debris on the fire, they stood for a bit and watched the blaze.

Toby could feel the warmth of the bonfire from where he and Yeshua sat on the bench. The sun had set behind the trees and the breeze carried the beginning of the evening chill. Toby felt the comfort of the fire's embrace around him. His thoughts wandered to Maeve and Brendan, and how they would have fit in here. His mother probably would've been in ecstasy. His father might not have wanted to give up the comfort of his time, but he might have enjoyed the simplicity and camaraderie. These were his people. He had a tie here.

A polite cough to his side reminded Toby of Yeshua. The young man hadn't said another word after Toby's outburst. Toby sneaked a glance to his left and saw that his companion was now watching with an intent look on his face. At least, he no longer looked disapproving and condescending. *It's a start.*

Aiobh and Declan crossed back up to the altar, walking in clockwise fashion again, and Gwydion picked up his harp again. The silvery tones of the plucked strings were the perfect accompaniment as Declan now picked up the plates of the bread, one in each hand. He turned toward Aiobh, her staff back in its place on the altar, and she held out her hands over them. Her head tilted back and the silver hair caught the last of the sunset rays and the fire.

"Oh, Mother Dana, You are the body from which the fruit is born, from which the feast is given. We are Your children. Bless this bread from Your bounty and let it nourish our bodies and our souls. For when the bread is eaten, we carry the Goddess within us; carry Her blessings and Her teaching. So mote it be."

She took one plate from Declan and he walked away from her, to the opposite end of the circle. She held out the plate to Gwydion first before stepping to the folks standing in the circle. She and Declan offered the plates to each person, who broke off a piece from the loaves and nodded thanks. When each had been served a piece, they ate the bread with the exception of one bite. Then, each person took that bite and crumbled it on the ground, wiping the crumbs from their hands as they did so.

The plates were set back on the altar, but one of them still held a portion of the bread. This was certainly interesting. Everything had a purpose; so what was the purpose of this?

Declan now lifted the two pitchers, one in each hand, and held them out.

"Father Dagda, You who sent Your son to help those in need, we thank You for Your bounty and strength. In the passing of the Sun God, we drink to Him who leaves us for the time and will return in spring. We drink the ale of Your givin' and we ask You bless it. For as we drink it, we carry the God within us; we carry his strength and his courage. So mote it be."

He handed one of the pitchers to Aiobh, who carried it to the opposite end of the circle, and once again they shared with the group. Each person had a cup that had been concealed in the robes and the Priest and Priestess poured into the cups. This time, they all waited until each had been served before they drank, pouring a last swallow on the ground.

The cups were replaced in folds and pockets of the robes, and the pitchers were replaced on the altar. The fire was beginning to show signs of burning itself down to the embers. The light of the sun wasn't completely gone, but there was a deepening gray over the treetops and the rosy glow of the sun was fading. The chill of the September air would begin to pervade in earnest.

Aiobh picked up the staff again, and faced the altar.

"Mother Dana, we do thank You for Your presence this day. We thank You for the blessings of the harvest. Go if You must, stay if You will. Peace and Blesséd be."

Declan followed next, with an almost word for word release of the Dagda. Toby watched the pair walk *counterclockwise* now, as they uttered the release of the Watchtowers they had called.

Toby watched, so many questions forming in his mind. *It couldn't hurt to ask about it, learn a bit about it, would it? Surely, it couldn't. I want to know. I do. There's something about this that calls to me.*

Declan has stepped to the center of the circle, near the fire that was still burning. "All of you, we need more celebrating!"

A chorus of male 'ayes' greeted him, and the women and children gathered clapped their hands in agreement.

"Well, then," he continued, "you'll all be invited back to our barn. 'Tis plenty of hearty fine ale and good whiskey for the drinking. The ladies have made a fair feast to be devoured and we should be eatin' of it. And the young ones will have fresh milk and heather tea for drinking."

The cheers went up again and Toby now saw the redheaded vision he'd wanted to see. She stood there, close to the fire; how could he have missed her? She had a sweet smile on her face, her arms crossed over her bosom and her hands rubbing her upper arms as if she was chilled.

"Aye, Declan, will you be providing the hay for the poor sods who celebrate a bit too heartily?" she asked with faint amusement in her voice. "They'll not be walkin' home this night, 'tis for sure."

The remark brought another chorus of laughter and cheers, but Toby could hear only her voice, her laughter. He had never heard a sound so captivating in his life. For him, the others simply faded back into the drab colors of the night, the voices to whispers. For that moment, he saw and heard only her.

He was still staring at her when their eyes met. He was locked to her gaze, the green eyes glinting and sparling in the fading fire. Her smile widened and her teeth were pearls in the shadows of her skin. Her face was angelic and softly shaped. Her lips were ripe cherries, plump and sweet. Oh, how he wanted to taste the nectar of her kiss.

A hand clapped his shoulder and his attention was jerked back to Gwydion, standing with a smile of amusement on his face. He turned back to give another glance to Siobhan as she was led off by a couple that he presumed were her parents. Toby sighed deeply, disappointed, and turned back to his friend.

"Well, Bard of the Goddess, you played well."

Gwydion looked a bit embarrassed as he laughed. "Thank you, Tobias. We're all of us children of the Goddess but 'tis a special title in the Bardic Circle. I've been given a special honor, I have. I'm glad you were here to see it."

"I am, too," Toby said. "Congratulations, my friend."

Niamh and Liam joined them, at this moment, and Niamh hugged her son about the middle again. Liam took his son's forearm in a strong grasp, and clapped him on the shoulder.

"Son, you've done well," he said. "And I'm that proud o' you."

Niamh looked up from her embrace, tears in her eyes, and reached up to touch the side of Gwydion's face. The brand had healed nicely, with only the faint marking on his forehead.

"Ma, you're runnin' at the eyes, again."

"Aye, lad, I am. It will be a màthair's privilege and you'll say naught about it."

Liam turned his gaze back to Toby and Yeshua, who had stood silent through all of it. "Well, boys, what did you think?"

"It was a beautiful ceremony," Toby answered. "Are they all like this?"

"No, Tobias, this was a special one for Gwydion's return and because we've had an unusually good harvest this season. But, they are good ones."

"You see," Gwydion interjected, "this was a High Rite. We have eight of them in the Wheel of the Year, and that's when we gather like this. We also celebrate the Moon Goddess in Her time, but those are done at home with the family only."

"I see."

"I wish to learn of these ways."

They all turned to look at Yeshua who was standing with his back to then, staring at the fire. The young man was watching the remainder of the Wicker Man fall away into the last of the fire. His brow was furrowed in serious contemplation of what he'd seen. Toby, alone, was the one who realized the seriousness of the statement.

"I wish to learn of your religion," Yeshua repeated. "Do you think this Declan will teach me, an outsider?"

Niamh released her hold on Gwydion, and reached a hand out to Yeshua, who took it in his.

"Well, I don't see why not, but you can ask him at the barn. You'll be invited, too, you know. Come and eat, dance and sing, and you'll talk to Declan. If he's takin' on pupils, he'll teach you."

"But, I am an outsider," Yeshua said.

"No, you're not, lad." Liam still beamed, standing at his son's side. "You saved my Gwydion and you are part of this family. Your ways are different, but that will be of no matter. The learning is for anyone who wants it. Tobias, too, if he's of a mind."

"I would like that," Toby answered.

"Well, then," Gwydion threw in. "We'll be off to the barn for some fine food, drink, and song. I know of a certain lady that's been askin' about our Tobias, wantin' to make his acquaintance. And 'tis fortunate that he's been making cow eyes at her, too."

Toby's jaw dropped so quickly, he felt the hinge by his ear pop. "*What?* What did you say?"

Gwydion was having too much fun again, a big kid in a romantic candy store. "Well, whilst you've been moonin' over the fair Siobhan, she's been noticin' you, boy-o. Declan said she's been askin' around for some information about you. I think 'tis time to put you two together."

Toby laughed and put his hand on his friend's shoulder. "This has been an interesting day and a good one. We're off to the barn then. I shall meet the fair Siobhan and see if there's a spark for that fire, as well." He put his other hand on Yeshua's shoulder, smiling down at the young man. "Aye, all of us. And we'll see if there's learning for you and I."

"All of you wait here whilst I fetch my best plate and then we're off."

While Niamh went up to the altar, he heard a rustle and turned to see who it was. Aiobh and Declan had come down to the fire, carrying the other plate and one of the pitchers.

"What are they doing?" he asked no one in particular.

"They'll be making the offerings to the Gods," Liam answered. "There's always a piece of bread left aside and a cup of ale, as well. When the ritual is over, they'll offer it up to the Gods as thanks."

Toby watched Aiobh crumble the bread into the fire and then dust the crumbs from her hands, as the others had done earlier. Declan took the pitchers and poured the remnants of the ale at the base of the fire, now just embers. Niamh rejoined them, giving him no further time to reflect on it. Toby made up his mind to ask about that too. After stopping long enough to drop off her plate at home, they hurried to the barn.

Toby wasn't quite sure what he had originally expected, but he was still surprised when he saw it. He heard the laughter and the music when they were still at the front gate. The closer their little party came to the barn, the louder it got. When Liam opened the door, the sounds of the party came rolling out like the smoke from a fire.

As Toby crossed the threshold, he smelled the most incredible aromas of cooked meats, fresh corn, and baked breads and pies. He caught the same spices he had smelled when Niamh was baking that day, cinnamon, clove, and his stomach growled in the same way. He watched a man walk by with a plate of food and backtracked with his eyes to where the man might have come from. Sure enough, there were the tables laden with food. Toby saw crocks of what he presumed were ales and ciders. There were also jugs that Toby was sure held the offered whiskey.

He felt a brush against his arm as Gwydion dashed past him, harp in hand, towards the other musicians. One of them gave a shout and a cheer at Gwydion's approach, and the new Bard of the Goddess sat down and joined in the song. Another soon joined them with a drum and the group seemed complete. Several couples had gathered in front of the make shift orchestra, and were dancing a lively jig, cutting in and around each other with laughter and merriment.

> *Aye, aye, the farmin' lad am I*
> With hoe and rake,
> The devil take
> The city life to try
> Aye, aye, the farmin' lad am I
>
> I work the fields all day
> At night, I sit and play
> M' harp and m' fiddle
> Sing a hey diddle diddle
> Aye, aye, the farmin' lad am I

Niamh and Liam joined the dancers. He would hold her close and spin her off, and then would take her back. Each spin would bring a spate of giggles, as if she were a young girl again. Each embrace would see them gazing into each other eyes as if no other person existed in that moment. Toby watched them dance and again, it reminded him of his parents.

Yeshua still stood at his side, watching the party, but his eyes were darting around the room. Toby waved his hand in front of Yeshua's gaze; the young man flinched and blinked furiously. When he realized it was Toby, he smiled and relaxed.

"So, where do we go, first?" Toby asked.

"I look to speak with this priest. If he is accepting pupils, I wish to become one."

Toby shook his head, laughing. "Yeshua, you can have a good time, you know."

"Yes, I know. But, you were right. I was judging these people without knowing them. I came into the world to reach it, be a part of it."

Toby smiled at him. "Being part of it means enjoying the pleasures of the world. There are many pleasures, my friend. We have all night to learn of religion. For now, let's learn of these people. I suggest a good feast should never go to waste."

Yeshua grinned, the child peeking out from the serious eyes again. "I agree. And I believe I would like to try a little of that rabbit. Surely, the Son of God will not be sent into the fires of hell for feeding the body from the gifts of God."

Toby leaned sideways, winking in earnestness and putting an arm around Yeshua's shoulders. "And I happen to know that Niamh made an excellent rabbit stew. Come, my friend, we feast."

Reaching the table, the two picked up plates and wooden spoons, and helped themselves to the foods before them. Niamh had made her rabbit stew and Toby found it was just as excellent as Liam had said. There was a corn pudding that had a hint of sweetness, and wheels of cheeses and plates of fruit. Yeshua helped himself to the latter, but Toby was pleased to see that he did have a small portion of the rabbit stew. He watched Yeshua take a bite and then stand for a moment, as if he were waiting for a strike of lightening to come down and incinerate him. When it didn't happen, the stew must have been to his liking, Yeshua ate the rest of it. He didn't go back for seconds, but it was enough.

They stood and ate the repast and the conversation seemed to take care of itself. So many folks greeted Toby that he forgot names quickly. They all wanted to know the story of how Toby and Yeshua had rescued Gwydion from certain death and Toby graciously told it. He hadn't seen Siobhan and each passing minute made him surer that she hadn't come.

"Lads, I've someone I want you to meet,"

Toby had been in mid-sentence with another group who wanted to hear his tale when Liam took his shoulder. He turned around to Liam standing with the High Priest. Yeshua turned around as well, watching the older men.

"This is Declan," Liam said, beaming. "He'll be our High Priest and Archdruid. Declan, I'd like you to meet our guests and new friends. That strappin' young lad is Yeshua and this is Tobias."

Toby quickly wiped his hand against his trousers and extended it to the man, who took it with an ardent embrace. Toby noticed that he clasped Toby's forearm instead of his hand and did the same to Declan.

"'Tis a pleasure to meet you, Tobias." Declan turned towards Yeshua and made the same gesture. "Aye, 'tis a pleasure to meet you both." Declan beamed warmly at them. "You brought our Bard back to us and I hear 'twas because you saved his life?"

Toby, who had told the story with pride to everyone else, now felt the flush in his cheeks. "Well, all we did was hide him well. Gwydion had saved his own life by escaping."

"Don't be so modest," Liam interjected. "They rescued him from the bastards trying to take him back. If they'd not happened along, our Gwydion would be rottin' away in the prisons or worse."

"Well, then," Declan replied, "we've got to get you boys a drop o' the whiskey to celebrate. Seamus, bring that jug over here and give these lads a taste."

Declan took the jug from a tall young lad and handed it to Toby. "Now, I made that batch myself. That's good whiskey, turned out quite smooth. Drink hearty, lads."

Toby saluted the man with the jug and tipped it back for a taste. It had fullness and body. Toby could taste the oak it had been aged in. The moment it hit his stomach, he was filled with spreading warmth. He took another sip before handing the jug to Yeshua

"Aye, that is excellent whiskey." To Yeshua, who was hesitating, he said, "Go ahead, have a drink. You had the rabbit; this won't damn your soul if that didn't."

"A sip," Yeshua agreed and took a quick taste. He grimaced and shuddered, which caused the men to laugh loud and hearty.

"Not a drinker, are you," Liam teased, a kind smile on his lips. "He'll be better with the cider."

"Now now, don't tease the poor sot," Declan admonished with a nudge to Liam's ribs. "He'll never have had the whiskey before, I can tell. Give him time and it'll be mother's milk to him. You watch and see."

Yeshua simply blushed and smiled.

Liam sobered up a bit, tilting his head at the High Priest. "I told Declan that you want to learn of our grove, Yeshua."

"Yes, I do."

Declan nodded, crossing his arms. "Well, I'm finishin' up a class right now. I won't be starting another until Yule. Will you be staying that long?"

"I have nowhere else to go," Yeshua answered.

Declan turned to Toby, and said, "And you? Will you be joinin' the learning?"

Toby opened his mouth to answer, but didn't get a chance to do so.

Gwydion interrupted him, thrusting a hand out for the jug. "Where's the whiskey? I hear you made it, Declan. If you cooked up your usual fine batch, 'tis a good whiskey, indeed." Gwydion took the offered jug and drank deep from it. When he finally took it from his mouth, he gasped and clapped a hand to his chest. "That's a damn good batch, Declan. I think 'tis your best yet."

"You quit playin'." Toby interrupted.

"Aye, the lads needed to take a break. And I've come to fetch you. The fair Siobhan has been naggin' at me to introduce her. She's fair chompin' at the bit, boy-o."

At the mere mention of her name, Toby's pulse quickened and his mouth dried up. He grabbed the jug from Gwydion's hands and knocked back a few good swallows. He put the jug down and wiping his mouth with the back of his hand. That set the men to laughing again and this time Yeshua joined them.

"Well, have you worked up your courage?" Gwydion asked.

Toby handed the jug to Yeshua and said, "Aye, I have. Come, lad, before I do lose my nerve."

"Make sure you pretty up for the girl," Liam yelled out.

"Aye," said another who'd joined them for the whiskey. "Pinch your cheeks and bite your lips."

Toby turned to the last man who had spoken and did exactly that, which sent them off on fresh gales of laughter.

Gwydion rolled his eyes, grabbed Toby's arm, and led him toward the musicians' area. They'd been sitting on bales of hay off in the back corner. As Toby was led closer, he kept looking at the milling crowd to see if he could find her. It wasn't until he got within a few feet of the musicians that he saw her.

She was dressed in a simple frock of wool, a soft brown in color. She had thrown a lace shawl around her shoulders and her auburn hair had been pulled back and tied by a thong. She seemed to sense rather than hear their approach and she turned to them.

"Siobhan, I want you to meet my friend, Tobias."

She put her hand out to him, and Toby clasped it gently in his own. He was sorely tempted to kiss her hand and decided against it. For a moment, he couldn't even talk; the air had left his body. All he could do was gaze into her eyes.

She made no move to break the silence, either. She gazed back with boldness and Toby thought he would melt at her feet. Gwydion broke the silence for them.

"Siobhan, this is the one I told you about, the man who saved my life."

She licked her lips and crossed her arms over her bosom again. "So, you said. Is that true, Tobias? Our Gwydion is a fair one with the stories. Tis hard to tell when he's tellin' true or when when he's tellin' another one."

"You've hurt me to the quick, you silly girl," Gwydion answered in mock dismay.

She just laughed and continued to watch Toby with her deep green eyes. Toby longed to get lost in those eyes.

"Well, Tobias? Is it true?"

"Well, miss, for once his stories are true. Aye, my friend and I did hide the poor man from certain death."

"Well, I suppose I should be grateful for bringin' him home. Niamh was fair beside herself."

"Like you never cared," Gwydion teased.

Siobhan turned to Gwydion, her mouth pursed with a stubborn cast. "Were you plannin' on playin' another round with the boys? I would like to dance, I think."

Gwydion bowed deep from the waist, and said, "Then, we can't disappoint the lady."

He gave a shout and a whistle, and the musicians were back to their instruments. They began to play another jig, but Siobhan made no move except closer to Toby. For the first time in his life, Toby was positively tongue-tied. He'd been with other women, plenty of women, but this one was different.

"So, tell me, Tobias, who are you?"

Toby was taken aback at the question. He opened his mouth to close it just as quickly.

"Tell me about yourself," she insisted. "Where are you from?"

"Oh, here and about. Everywhere and nowhere. But, my family hails from the, uh, north country."

It sounded good for the moment and wasn't too specific. He left the sentence there and she accepted it.

"Well, did they teach you to dance in the north country?"

"Aye, lady. That, they did."

As the musicians struck up a slow ballad, Toby placed his hand on her slender waist, tracking her hip until his hand rested in the small of her back. One of her arms came around him, stopping on the back of his shoulder, and she stepped closer to take his free hand in hers. He could smell her scent, the soapwort and lavender. Toby took the first slow step and she moved in time with him, their bodies never separating.

They danced, eyes locked to each other and no one else existing to them. Her eyes had small creases in the corners and the smile she wore made them dance. As one ballad flowed into the next, she danced with him. Neither spoke, afraid to break the spell of the night. Only once, did she look away and only to rest her cheek against his. When she did, he thought he could fly and take her with him into the night sky. She fit against him like a hand in a glove.

"Girl," a rough male voice said beside him.

It was enough to break the spell that had been woven around them, and she stepped back from him.

"Àthair?"

"Come, girl, your màthair's poorly."

"Aye, I'll be there." To Toby, she said, "I must go."

He started to panic and took her hand. "Will I see you again?"

She laughed, that beautiful face lighting up again. "Oh, aye. Is a small village we have."

"May I call on you?"

She began to walk backward, as if she wanted to retain that picture of him in her memory. He wanted to hold onto that sight of her as well. Her hand slipped from his as she stepped away from him.

"May I call on you?" he repeated.

"Aye. You may," she answered and turned on her heel, running after her father.

All he could do was stand and watch the air where she'd been. He played the sound of her voice in his head, felt the shape of her body against his. That night, when he slept, he dreamed of Siobhan and how it would be to make love to her.

Chapter Seventeen

"No! You cannot do this! It cannot be permitted and I will not allow it! No!"

Toby turned away, shaking his head hard enough for his hair to fly into his face. *Damn it*, he thought. *What the hell is that kid's problem? He's going to piss everyone off before this is over!* He put a hand to his forehead to get a grip on himself before he did or said something he knew he'd regret later.

Gwydion laid a hand on Toby's shoulder. "Easy, Tobias, steady on. I agree, the lad is a bit too strident in his speaking, but let's at least hear what he has to say. Aye?"

Toby nodded, unclenching his fists and blowing out a long breath. He hated to admit it but there was always the possibility that Yeshua had a good reason for this outburst. He clapped a hand to his friend's shoulder and smiled at him. "You're right, Gwy. We'll hear him out."

In the month or so since the harvesting ceremony, they'd been helping Liam get the farm ready for the winter. There was so much to do with bringing in the rest of the crops, finish the last of the haying, splitting wood and digging the peats for the fires that would keep them warm. Long days in the cool, crisp Irish air and all of the hard work had kept his days busy and his nights full of dreams of Siobhan.

Yeshua had changed in that time. He'd done what he said he would, becoming part of the village and getting to know the people. When they weren't working in the fields, Yeshua went to each house, breaking bread and talking to them. He would always be in the fields the next day, smiling and sharing what he'd been learning. His grasp of the language had improved immensely and he was starting to become human, a glimpse of that savior Toby had learned about in Catechism.

That is until he pulled this stunt today.

Toby turned back and saw Yeshua standing with a look of stubborn determination on his young face. His fists were resting on his hips, his face darkened in anger.

"And I tell you, *boy*, you'll have no right interfering with the cullin'." Liam was rigid, back straight as a rod and his eyes narrowed. He snapped at the Yeshua in clipped sentences, waving one hand at the animals around him. "We'll be doing 'em a favor, all the ones we cull from the herd. If we cannot feed them, they'll surely starve."

"That is not the point," Yeshua barked.

"Well then, perhaps you'll be tellin' me what the bloody point is," Liam growled back.

Gwydion glanced at Toby with raised eyebrows and shrugged, steeling himself. With a deep sigh, he stepped between the two, holding his hands outstretched to push the two men apart to keep things from getting physical. Yeshua was angry, but now Liam was *furious*; even Toby could see that fisticuffs were on the horizon.

"Alright, you two," Gwydion said, his voice conversational and reasonable. "Da, there's no reason to get your dander worked up. The lad doesn't know our ways is all. And you, Yeshua – Da is right. This is for the good of us all. We'll be savin' the beasts from starvin' over the winter months."

Yeshua glared, thin lipped and rigid. Liam returned the look, his arms crossed over his chest. Gwydion stood between them, looking back and forth. Toby watched, waiting for the inevitable.

It had started the previous day while they had been settling the cattle in the barn. Liam was doing a head count, then he and Gwydion could begin to choose which of the cattle would be slaughtered. There was a whistle from the gate and Declan had joined them in the barn.

"I'll not be keepin' you, Liam; I see you've started your cullin'. But I need to be askin' you a favor and this will be the right time. If you've a mind, that is."

Toby and Yeshua had stopped spreading the hay in the stalls and came out to listen.

Liam was immediately conciliatory. "Aye, Declan, you've but to ask. If 'tis within my power, you know I'll be happy to oblige."

"I know you would. The Samhain feast and rite are coming soon, at the end of the cycle. I was wondering if you'd be willing to offer up one of your cattle for the feast. Everyone knows you raise the best on the hoof and it would be a rare treat for the Ancestors. If you've a mind, that is."

Liam nodded his head very strongly and took Declan's forearm in an embrace. "Oh, aye, I'd be that honored. You'll have the best of my stock for the Feast o' the Ancestors. The *very* best of my stock!"

"Thank ye, Liam, I knew we could count on ye. It'll be a right proper feast, then."

They had chatted a few more minutes and Declan had left, after making sure the beef would be at the site the next afternoon and attaining Gwydion's promise to play his harp at the ritual. It was after he left that the two outsiders began their questions.

"Liam," Toby said, putting his fork back into the bail he had been spreading. "What's he talking about? *Sowwen?*"

"Aye, Tobias, 'tis called *Samhain*. The day when the Veil between the worlds is at its thinnest. 'Tis the day we celebrate with our ancestors who've gone before us. We can speak to the spirits that walk among us."

"We have a Feast before the Rite," Gwydion continued. "The village gathers together in Declan's barn and brings all manner of foods and sweets and cakes, and we have the Feast of the Ancestors. 'Tis a dumb feast and we share a plate with those who've crossed over."

Toby cocked his head in a sudden dawning. "Dumb feast? As in you don't talk throughout the whole dinner?"

"Aye, 'tis exactly right," Gwydion answered, pleased that Toby had grasped it.

"I do not understand," Yeshua said, putting down his own fork and joining the conversation. "You *worship* your dead ancestors?"

"No," Liam corrected, "we *celebrate* our ancestors. There is a difference. These are the members of our families, long past, our grandparents and their grandparents. Aye, we do ask 'em to intercede with the Gods on our behalf but this time o' the year, we celebrate their wisdom that they shared with us."

"You *thank* them?"

"Aye, Yeshua, we *thank* them." Liam smiled. "We have their wisdom from ages past, of raisin' the beasts and tillin' the soil; and for the knowledge of the Old Ones. We celebrate the earth they passed on to us, with all the creatures on it."

Toby nodded, he understood it all. More than that, though, he felt right with it. This wisdom, this culture, was part of him. How many of his ancestors had passed on that wisdom and tradition so that he was here today, each raising children until one had become his mother and one had become his father. Maybe he was too Catholic to believe in a Goddess, but he understood the need for intercession from the saints. It was a short step to the Pagan belief that his family long gone, and fathers and mothers he'd never met, would do the same. After the brief conversation, even Yeshua was looking forward to this night of nights.

But when it came time to do the actual slaughtering and Liam was pointing out which of the cattle, sheep, and pigs were to be slaughtered, things turned out to be a bit more complicated. Yes, they'd had an excellent harvest this past season, but there had been an abundance of animals born that year, as well. Liam explained, patiently, that there was no way they could feed them all.

Toby knew that Liam was right. It would be more humane to slaughter the excess animals. It's not like they were going to waste the meat. The carcasses would be salted or smoked and preserved to feed the family during the winter months. Since they'd picked up two extra mouths to feed for this winter, it was all the more important to have a successful slaughter.

Liam was methodical in everything. Gwydion and Toby had gone to cull out the sheep in the back barn, and Liam had taken Yeshua to pick out the cattle. Gwydion had selected a good mixture of males and females, leaving just the right amount of each for breeding the next litters. He marked each with a ribbon, patting it on the rump to send it back into the herd, and moved to the next. Toby just followed him, listening to the stream of gossip or natter, but not really following everything. His thoughts had been mostly on Siobhan.

He had made a point to see her at least once a week. They would meet in front of her parents' cottage or take walks through the village. Always chaperoned by her family, they had carried on a polite and chaste courtship but never had a chance to discuss anything more than the gossip of the day, never a chance to touch. It was frustrating for Toby. Fortunately, Liam's farm kept him busy enough to distract him from practically living on her doorstep. But it couldn't silence his thoughts or his heart.

Once the sheep had been selected, the two men had crossed back to the cattle barn. There, Toby saw Yeshua standing, fists on hips, squaring off against the taller Liam. The tone of the younger man was again the haughty prideful tone that he had heard throughout the journey to Ir.

"We'll be needing a moment of calm here, now," Gwydion continued.

Both of the warring parties backed off and took deep breaths to calm themselves. Toby relaxed, too, but kept up the watch. Just in case.

"Now, Yeshua, you say the cullin' is not the point," Gwydion went on. "What do you mean then? You must forgive us, but we don't know your ways. If you'd be so kind as to help us understand...."

Yeshua seemed to realize this at the same time and raised his hands up to Liam in a gesture of peace. "I see that, now. Please forgive me for my hasty anger. But, it is *my* law, you see. And there is no reason why you should know that law."

Liam also relaxed and nodded for the young man to speak.

When he spoke again, Yeshua began to use a different voice, reaching out to explain. "Liam, my friend, I have no objections in the slaughter for what you have said is good and true. It *is* a cruel thing to starve them when there is need of the meat. I must argue *how* you choose to do it."

"What do you mean?" Liam furrowed his brow in concentration.

"In my tradition, we have particular laws on how an animal must be slaughtered, to make the meat sacred; as we call it, *kosher*. It is done in such a way that the animal must not fear or feel pain. It must be quick and sure."

"Aye," Liam answered, "for 'tis our way, too."

"It's more than that," Yeshua continued, gesturing to the cattle. "For you see, these animals that you've chosen have given birth, these animals have all been raised together. You wish to slaughter the chosen ones in the sight of the others. How can you feel when you have seen your child or your neighbor put to death before you?" He put his hands together in a prayerful gesture, tapping the fingers lightly against his chin. "It is the Hebraic law that if you must slaughter the animal, it must be purified and blessed by the Rabbi. Then, it must be slaughtered away from the others, to prevent the hardship or the sorrow of the other animals. It is the only proper thing to do."

Liam chewed on his lower lip, looking around and taking it all in. When he'd surveyed the herd, he turned back to Yeshua and nodded. "When you say it that way, I must admit that you're right. I call myself a good soul with the beasts, but you've put me to shame. 'Tis true what you say; they'll suffer the pain along with the chosen ones."

"Where were you going to slaughter them?" Toby asked.

"Here, in the barn," Liam answered. "But after what Yeshua has told us, I'm thinking that will not be the proper place."

Gwydion added, "It'll need to be close enough to carry on the slaughter and take the meat to the smoke house."

The men fell silent for a moment, thinking of how they could work out the logistics.

"Wait," Yeshua interjected. "Of course, if the animals are inside the barns and the barns are closed, we can do it near enough to the smokehouse that none of them will hear the slaughtering sounds."

Gwydion grinned at the young man. "That's true, Da. Once these doors are closed up, the cryin' of the *beàn sidhé* will never penetrate."

"The *bayn shee*?" Toby asked.

"A cursed spirit, Tobias," Gwydion answered.

"Oh," he said abruptly, "of course. The *ban*shee."

"The *beàn sidhé*," Gwydion corrected gently. "Aye, the cursed spirits that can drive a man mad with their caterwauling. 'Tis the time o' chaos with the Samhain season on us. You'll hear them screamin' if you're not careful."

Liam rested a hand on his son's shoulder, admonishing Gwydion with one finger raised to punctuate. "And you'll not be callin' 'em, if I have aught to say." He turned to the other men, and said, "Aye, Yeshua, you speak true. And the smokehouse is the perfect place for the slaughter. We'll lead 'em out, one by one, and it'll give us time to do a proper job over the next few days. A grand idea, it is."

Liam held out his hand to the young man, who took it, and they laughed with each other. The tension was released, all was well again. Toby released the breath he'd been holding and dropped his shoulders in relief.

Gwydion leaned into him, grinning from ear to ear. "Not the same lad we traveled with, is he?"

"No, he's not at that, Gwydion."

"He'll come around, Tobias. Be patient with him. He's a good lad, just young and headstrong. Reminds me of myself when I was his age. 'Tis amazin' what a bit o' travel will do for you."

Toby never got the chance to comment on what had happened, thanks to the arrival of Aiobh and Declan. The bull Liam had chosen for the sacrifice was taken to the smokehouse, and Aiobh blessed it. With the men of the family watching, Declan slit the animal's throat, quickly and painlessly. It was over in a brief moment and the men went to work with a determination.

The blood was collected in huge crocks. It would be mixed with the other byproducts that couldn't be eaten and mixed in the compost pile. It would be spread over the ground to fertilize next year's harvest. The liver, heart, stomach, and other internal organs that could be eaten were taken to Niamh, and she set about making a good sausage of them. The intestines were cleaned of any fecal matter and, after repeated rinsing to clean them thoroughly, they were set in brine and would be used as casings for the sausages.

Liam and Gwydion stripped the carcass of the outer skin with a practiced hand. The leather would be used for clothing, shoes, and whatever else was needed. Liam explained that the bones would be kept back from the feast and ground up into powder, to be mixed in with the compost. As Gwydion had once said, nothing was wasted for it would be an insult to the animal's sacrifice for the people.

The beef carcass was taken to a pit near Declan's barn. Several men had helped build the pit and set a fire to burning in it. When the fire had turned to coals, they had placed coverings of wet branches and herb plants on top, which set a fragrant smoke wafting out. The beef, wrapped in water soaked skins, was lowered into the pit. Several more layers of herb plants, then more skins covered the package, before a final layer of dirt was spread out over it all and covered the pit. Gwydion explained to Toby and Yeshua that the large carcass would now take the rest of the time to fully smoke to doneness.

The day passed with preparation for the ritual. Aiobh had given permission for Yeshua and Toby to attend inside the circle as watchers but not participants, which suited Toby just fine. At least he'd be closer to seeing and hearing. Whatever Yeshua felt about it was never spoken of. Niamh set about making robes for the pair and her nimble fingers had the simple clothing done by morning. The morning of the ritual was spent either preparing the dish they would take to the feast or preparing for the butchering that would begin the next day.

Niamh wanted to arrive a little early to help with the setting up, but Gwydion jokingly confided that she had really wanted to find the best place to set up their blanket. Whatever the reason, Toby had excused himself and was outside enjoying the crisp autumn evening when Siobhan arrived.

She was with her parents; her hair tied back and her shawl hanging off one shoulder. As soon as she saw Toby, her face lit up and she quietly excused herself to join him.

"Why are you not inside helping out with all the heavy things, a big strappin man such as yourself," she teased.

"And miss an opportunity to catch the loveliest lady here? I think not."

She blushed, waving her hand at him. "Lovely! Pah! You keep that up and they'll all know you're daft."

She stepped closer and Toby caught the intoxicating fragrance of the lavender water she had sprinkled through hair and on her skin. The touch of her hand on his arm almost sent him reeling.

"Siobhan...."

"Do you really think I'm lovely?" she asked, her voice barely above a whisper.

Her breath tickled his skin in the most tantalizing way. He reached up to brush the fingers of his hand against her cheek, smoothing a lock of hair from her temple. She leaned her cheek against his palm and continued to his gaze with her own.

"Oh, aye, lady. I truly do."

A chorus of giggles broke the moment and she stepped back, a flush spreading across her cheeks. Toby looked over her shoulder to see several children, cupping hands over mouths and giggling precociously. He laughed with them and squatted down to join them.

"Here, now. And what'll you be doing, spreading your mischief?" he teased.

"We saw you," tittered a little girl, about the age of seven.

"Aye, we saw," the others echoed.

"We're gonna tell on you, Siobhan, for being a bad girl," another child teased.

Siobhan's musical laugh floated to Toby's heart and he stood up as she joined him, putting her arm around his waist and the other hand in the curve of his elbow.

"Aye," she snickered with them. "Will it be the trick or the treat?"

The sea of chuckles answered her, the little ones swarming around her skirt in anticipation.

"Well," she continued, "I believe I have a few sweets in my pocket. Who's wanting one then?"

Grubby little hands reached out and she pulled out shapes of all sizes and dropped them in the palms. The pieces disappeared into chubby, smiling faces and the children gave satisfied smacking noises of delight.

"Now, off with you," Toby said. "The lady and I are doing just fine without you. Get along before I give *you* the trick."

The children disappeared into the barn, laughing as they ran. Toby laughed as well, waiting until they'd disappeared before he turned back to his lady.

"The trick or the treat?"

"Well," she answered, "you've not been hearin' the wee ones about your house yet? If not, they'll be there soon enough. Our tradition, you see. 'Tis all harmless fun for 'em."

The stray lock had crossed her temple again and it was all he could do not to kiss it away from her face. She stood so close to him that his whole body was close to being hard.

"Aye, I remember the tricks," he said, remembering Halloweens from his own childhood. "What tricks do the children do here?"

"Oh, 'tis naught more than removing your gate or eggin' your front door wi' the rotten ones."

Too bad they don't know about toilet papering someone's lawn. That was a great one. "Ah."

She nudged him with her shoulder, smiling up at him. "Tell me, Tobias, you never egged a door?"

He put his arms around her waist, pulling her close to feel the warmth of her body against his. With a laugh, he answered her, "No, my lady, I was never that brave. I was the kind to pour salt in your water glass or run your knickers up the chimney."

"Run m' knickers?" she repeated, an amused smile playing on her lips.

Toby stopped short and snapped his mouth shut with a jerk. He had the decency to blush at that point and the gales of laughter poured from her until she shook and tears streamed down her cheeks. He beamed, watching her.

When she'd gained a bit of control finally, she laid her hands against his chest and played with the folds of his shirt. "Tobias, you are a wonder. I've never had so much of a good laugh in my life. You're a special one. I've become a bit smitten with you."

His sobered, the breath had been sucked out of him. His heart began to pound again and he felt like he could burst at any given moment.

She talked on, not waiting for a response from him. But she did get brave enough to hazard a glance at him. "I am, you know. I'm quite smitten with you."

She really had said it; he really had heard her. He opened and shut his mouth a few times but couldn't work out the words to say. She raised two fingers and placed them on his lips and stopped his feeble attempts.

"No, please. Don't say anythin', Tobias. Please. You'll surely break my heart if you feel naught the same for me. Just let it lay there."

"Siobhan—"

"I'm too forward, me Da says," she went on, not even listening. "He tells me I'll die an old maid or handmaid to the High Priestess. But I know what I feel, Tobias."

He tried to open his mouth again but she leaned against him and kissed him so softly that for a moment he thought he had dreamed it. It was a breeze that blew across his lips but it was enough to drive whatever thought had finally entered his mind back out. She pushed her hands against his chest to separate them and took several steps back.

"No hurry, my dear one. You've been visitin' me quite a bit and 'tis good enough for now. But, I want you to think about it. 'Tis how I feel about you."

She smiled and turned, running into the barn. Toby watched her go and then turned around to grab onto a nearby post. His knees had suddenly turned traitor and he was dangerously close to dropping on his butt. She was *smitten*? Hell, he was in love with the woman. At that moment, he wanted her so badly that his body started to shake.

"Tobias!"

He practically jumped out of his skin, whirling around. "Yeshua! Uh, what?"

Yeshua stood in the doorway with an all *too* knowing grin on his face, leaning against the threshold. Toby grabbed himself by the mental bootstraps and pulled it back together quickly.

"What do you want, you grinning loon?" he managed to croak out.

Yeshua didn't seem to take it personally, just smiling the enigmatic smile and answering, "Niamh wanted me to fetch you. The feast is about to begin."

Toby ran his fingers through his hair, praying that the shaking wasn't obvious from ten feet away. "Oh, yeah. I'm with you, lad. Lead the way."

Toby made his way to the door, but Yeshua didn't move. He just watched Toby, waiting. His eyes never wavered; he just kept grinning at Toby. For a moment, Toby had the impression the young man was looking deep inside of him. The young man's grin deepened and Yeshua nodded his head. *He knows. Oh my God, he knows.*

Yeshua said nothing, just taking Toby's elbow and leading him through the door and over to the spot that Niamh had chosen. She handed Toby a wooden plate and he went to the table to get his food. He made sure to get a good-sized helping of the beef that was carved and resting on a platter. After taking a mug of ale with him, he sat down on the blanket with the rest of the family.

Niamh had set a place at the head of the blanket, the plate was full of the wonderful food they were about to eat. She sat on one side of the empty place and Liam sat across from her. Gwydion sat next to his father, and Yeshua had taken the place at the other end of the blanket. Toby sat down next to Niamh, watching those around him. They were waiting.

Aiobh stepped to the center of the gathered and put the waiting to rest. "With the night of Samhain upon us, the Veil between the worlds is at its thinnest. 'Tis the time of the Chaos when the spirits among us can be seen and spoken to. So, on this night, we welcome you Spirits of our Ancestors to the table. We set the feast before you and we thank you for your presence with us. Welcome and Blesséd be."

She sat down next to her mate and the feast began. For the next hour or so, the only sounds were those of eating and drinking, of wooden spoons and metal knives clattering against wooden or earthen plates. If anyone wanted more food, they got up, walked over to the table and got more. There was no ceremony but a reverence and deep meditative feeling.

Toby was caught up in the ambience of it all. He enjoyed the feast but he was remembering his parents and what they had given him. He ached for the company of his mother and her quiet sweetness. He missed her hands on his face as she told him it would work out. He missed his father's quiet cough and gentle reasoning voice. He even missed his father's bullheaded stubbornness. *Maybe when I have my answer*, he thought, *I could go home for a little while*. Just to see them again, talk and laugh.

The longer he sat, the more he lived in his own head. He thought about what he would say to them, how he would be with them. He thought about how he could seal the breach with his father and get to know him better. He thought about sharing this experience with his mother, somehow. The more he thought, the more he craved them, and a single tear dripped down his face. It was as if he could feel them near and he wanted to see them; *really* see them.

A cool hand touched his arm and he looked to see Niamh watching him, a wistful smile on her face. She patted his face softly, never speaking a word but somehow letting him know that she understood. He saw Liam from the corner of his eye and the older man lifted his mug in salute to Toby. Toby felt a balm on his soul.

With the feast eaten, they all rose as one. Each family took empty plates and mugs, folding up the quilts. Niamh picked up the full plate and mug from their place, as did every matron of every family. Toby took the folded up blanket and carried his plate, getting in step with the other men and they were off.

Niamh led them back to their cottage, straight to the tall oak that sheltered the home. There was a small box set there with a silver plate. The plate was covered with ornate scrollwork, a series of knots formed from a continuous line. Niamh set the plate down on top of it, setting the mug next to it. She stood before the box for a few moments, her hands outstretched to the oak and the sky before turning and walking away.

They all followed her back inside the house and Niamh passed them their robes and helped them dress. No one had yet broken the stillness by speaking. Toby wanted to ask questions, make some notice of the feast but it felt wrong to do so. Niamh helped him into his robe and she pulled the hood over his face. When she had them ready, she dressed in her own robe and led them to center of the village.

This circle had been set up with torches and stones. As others joined them, they gathered quietly. Toby and Yeshua took their places in the back of the circle and stood reverently. Aiobh and Declan came into the circle to stand at the altar. When the last person had joined it, they began the process of calling the Quarters, as before. Toby could see nothing that was any different. Maybe it would be in the rest of the ritual.

Aiobh had begun to call the Goddess when a shout from the dark interrupted her. Toby pulled his hood back, turned toward the noise, and saw three men running as if the devil was chasing them. The men reached the circle, dropping where they stopped and gasping for breath.

Declan came down to them, steadying each in turn with a touch of his hand. He pointed to one of the men in the circle. "You! Get these men something to drink." To the fallen men, he soothed, "Breathe easy, lads. Take your time."

The tallest of the three shook his head, raising up on his knees in as dignified a manner as he could. He gulped in several quick breaths and put a hand on Declan's shoulder. He tried to speak but wasn't having much success.

"Does anyone know these men?" Declan scoured the gathering, hoping for an answer.

Liam pulled back his hood and step forward. "Aye, I know them. They're from the Grove at the Piper's Stones. You are Conor Tiegue."

The tallest man nodded at the recognition, starting to breathe a little easier now that he was motionless. One of the villagers returned with three stone bottles of ale, giving one to each man. The one identified as Conor swallowed hard before he finally answered. "Aye," he puffed, "that I am. I know you as well. I also know your family."

"What are you doin' here, Conor Tiegue, when you should be celebratin' Samhain with your own folk?" Declan asked.

"We come with news for you. If you are the leader of these folk, we've need to speak to you." Conor turned back to Liam and pointed at him, "And we've need to speak to you. And your son."

Liam cocked his head, stealing a quick glance at Gwydion before addressing the man. "Why do you need to speak to Gwydion?'

The men struggled to stand, and Liam and Declan helped them.

"Soldiers comin'," Conor wheezed. "They're almost to the Stones and promise to be here tomorrow."

The villagers had thrown back their hoods and the announcement of the soldiers' impending arrival brought a spate of curses and questions. Declan threw up his hands and called for silence.

"Why are the soldiers comin' here?" Declan asked.

"Are you chief?'

"I am the leader of this village; now answer my question. Why are they comin' here?"

Conor appeared satisfied. "They come for the runaway slave. We've had spies on 'em as soon as they landed ashore, and one of them spoke the name of this village and of Gwydion."

There was more uproar from the crowd, more confused shouting. Aiobh began to work the crowd, calming as she came through them. Toby wanted to hear more and stepped forward until he was standing by the other two runners. They weren't speaking, satisfied to let Conor do all the talking for them. *They must have been back up, in case not all of them made it.*

"Now, wait," Liam broke in. "How did they know to come here?"

"Does it matter, Liam?" Declan said. "They know to come."

Gwydion joined the small knot as soon as he heard his name mentioned. "They know because I had to tell 'em where I was from. Bloody Romans are more concerned with their record keepin' than any other I know. They set great stock by the letters and papers they keep."

Several more men joined the knot, now. Toby recognized Seamus, one of Gwydion's friends. They now joined the conversation.

"Why are they here?" Seamus asked. "To take Gwydion back? The Gods preserve us, lad, why are you so important?"

The men turned to face Gwydion, who was looking rather embarrassed.

"C'mon, lad," Liam insisted. "Out with it. Why are they so bent to get you back?"

Gwydion sighed, obviously not wanting to make the admission, but it was obvious that the crowd wasn't going to be put off. Rolling his eyes, he admitted. "I was the personal slave of the Roman puppet, Herod. The bastards are after me to set an example to the rest of the lot. No one ever runs from the likes of *him*, I reckon."

Toby's jaw dropped in astonishment. "You were King Herod's personal slave?"

Gwydion said nothing, just nodded his head and looked down.

"Well, they will not take my son," Liam said emphatically.

A chorus of "ayes" greeted him, more than a few female voices as well. He felt her presence at his side, smelled the lavender, and reached down to take her hand.

"Da, I know this lot." Gwydion had to shout to be heard above the din. "They'll come for me and if they can't find me, they'll take others. We can't let them near the village or none are safe here."

The entire village had now closed ranks around them. Declan called for quiet and received it. But it was clear that the entire village agreed with Gwydion.

"Well then, it is decided, we can't let them arrive here." Declan paused until the crowd grew quiet again. "We'll go to them and drive the bastards back out of our home. We'll teach the Romans that they do *not* own this earth and they cannot take who and what they please."

The shouts of agreement turned into a roar of approval and when Declan asked for silence again, he got it quickly.

"Gwydion, you'll stay here and keep your head down. It is possible we can lose this battle and I don't want them findin' you again."

"I can fight my own battle," Gwydion insisted but his father's hand on his chest quieted him again.

"Aye, lad," Liam agreed. "But you're my only son and you carry the family name. You stay. 'Tis my wish that you'll take care of your mother."

"The eldest and the youngest o' us will remain behind, and the rest will go," Declan declared. "We'll leave with first light."

Toby stepped forward, shouting to be heard. "Wait!"

Declan waved for attention. "What is it, lad? You may go, if you choose, but 'tis not your fight. You and Yeshua need to stay behind."

Toby nodded vehemently. "Yes, Yeshua will stay with Gwydion, but that's not it."

"I want to go," the young man protested.

"No," said Toby, his hand against Yeshua's shoulder as if to root him to the spot. "You'll be needed here. You don't know anything' about fightin', lad. 'Tis better you stay here. Your màthair would have my hide if I let you get in this."

"I want to drive the Roman—"

Declan spared Toby from having to be the bad guy. "No, lad, no. If Tobias says you know naught of soldierin', then he's right about one thing. You need stay behind."

"Declan." Toby turned away from Yeshua, making up his mind about his role in the coming skirmish. He did have experience and he wanted to put it to good use. "I'll go with you, I can fight and will. But we'll need to know what you have planned for 'em when we get there."

"What do you mean, Tobias?"

"I can help you. You don't know the Roman army, Declan. You can't throw stones at 'em. They'll come with armor and long spears. They'll come marchin' like a rock and you'll not be able to touch 'em."

Gwydion entered into the discussion again. "Aye, he's right. I have seen them. If they know you're comin', they'll get in formation and use the shields to make the turtle. You'll not touch 'em."

All the voices spoke at once, suggesting throwing fireballs or pots of oil set ablaze. Declan listened to each of them and would nod or shake his head if he thought the idea had merit. Toby tried to shout over them, he knew the suggestions were worthless. Declan saw this and called for silence again, nodding in Toby's direction.

"None o' this will work," he said.

"You're a soldier, Tobias?"

"Aye, Declan, I am. I know the enemy and I know how to defeat them." Toby let go of Siobhan's hand and stepped to the center of the group. "My friends, listen to me. The only hope you have of defeating this army is if you surprise them. Don't wait until first light. We must leave *now*." Toby turned to Conor. You told Declan that they were at the Piper's Stones, aye?"

Conor nodded, "Aye, I did. They were settin' up their camp as we left."

"Declan, that's half a day's journey. We can run to them, attack them before they can get ready. If we catch 'em before they have chance to don the armor, they'll be fightin' like we are – with bare skin."

Seamus shouted out in glee. "Aye, bare skin is more to my likin'.

If we catch 'em before they have chance to do more than stir, the plan could work."

"Aye," Gwydion said. "It *will* work. You can take the lot."

"Conor, how many o' 'em?" Declan asked.

"We counted no more than forty," Conor answered.

Toby nodded in agreement. "We can take 'em. I'd feel better with more of us than them, but we can do it if we catch them *before* first light."

"We'll have more'n enough," said another man. "A good matched fight it'll be."

Toby looked around at the gathered and said, "I count only twenty men of fightin' age."

There was an answer of laughter, and Declan reached up to scratch his neck in amusement. "We'll *all* be going that can fight, Tobias. You'll see," he said. To the rest, he shouted, "All right, you know who'll be goin' in the party. Tobias has said we can take 'em if we take 'em by surprise. Then we shall. Go and fetch your weapons and we'll meet here before the sun is gone from the sky."

"Will we be wantin' torches, Declan?" another voice asked from the back of the crowd.

"No, Deirdre," Declan replied. "We'll need the cover o' darkness. The moon is full enough to give us plenty of light. Now, hurry, we'll be leaving shortly."

The crowd quickly dispersed, each running to make ready for their battle. Aiobh took Declan's hand and told him she'd have his weapons and armor ready. Liam and Niamh moved off and Gwydion came to Toby.

"Tobias, 'tis a brave thing you're doing."

Toby shook his head, giving his friend a sideways look. "You were Herod's personal slave?"

"Aye," Gwydion answered, laughing in reply.

Toby chuckled along with him. "Well, my friend, I'll never be lookin' at you the same way, now."

"Tobias," Gwydion said soberly. "I'll be that honored if you'll carry m' sword and dirk as your own. You've no weapons and Da has declared I shan't be going. So, you'll do me the great courtesy of fightin' for me."

Toby touched his heart, bowing slightly from the waist. He knew what he was being offered and he was not going to refuse it. "No,

Gwy, 'tis *I* will be honored."

Gwydion nodded, touching his heart in return. "Then, I'll fetch 'em for you."

Declan had finished discussing last minute information and the runners started on their way back. He came to Toby and Yeshua as Gwydion started off to pick up the offered weaponry.

"Well, we'll have a bit more help in the next village. Conor said they'll give us all we can use and more, if needed."

"It can't hurt," Toby replied. "I want all the hands they can spare. You don't know this lot; they're crafty and almost invincible. You can beat them, but you need do it with more than they have and bein' crafty at it, too."

"Aye. Go get you ready and meet back here." Declan turned and ran off in the direction of his home.

"Tobias, I want to fight." Yeshua stood as tall as his five foot, six inch body could be with his chest puffed out in manly fashion. He was quite serious, quite adamant, and it was clear that the word *no* was not going to be taken with any good grace.

Toby swallowed his smile, but he couldn't help seeing a trace of the boy still within the growing man before him. "I know you do, Yeshua," he said as kindly as he could. "But I can't allow it."

The young man looked soberly at Toby. "They are my enemy as well. And Gwydion is my friend. I can do this."

Toby took the young man's shoulders in his hands and felt a surprising wave of affection. "Listen to me, Yeshua. We all have our destiny to fulfill. Yours is elsewhere and mine is on the battlefield. It's what I do."

"But, Tobias—"

Toby cut him off adamantly. "No. I can't let you have blood on your hands. You are the Son of God. Pray for us. That's what *you* do. That is far more important and what we need desperately, my friend. Please? Will you?"

Yeshua was mollified, soberly agreeing with the request. "I will. Be safe, my friend."

The first surprise that Toby had was after they reassembled and Toby saw that the women were also going, just as eager and prepared for battle as the men. He had a moment to talk to Gwydion, who laughed at Toby's suggestion that they be stopped from accompanying the male warriors.

"You don't know the women of Ir, my friend. They'll sooner gut you as look at you," Gwydion remarked. "I'll tell you true, I'm that glad they fight on our side."

Toby's next surprise was seeing Siobhan at his side. She coyly came up to him and nodded. They were all dressed in trousers and leather battle armor. Her armor fit her like a glove and showed off the curves of her body.

"What are you doing here, woman?"

"I come to fight, same as you," she replied. "Gwydion is my friend too, has been for far longer."

Toby peered around to make sure no one was listening in on their conversation. "I wish you would stay. I can't bear to think of you getting hurt in this."

Siobhan placed a hand on his forearm, stepping closer to him. Looking up into his face, she said, "Tobias, I can't bear the thought of *you* being killed. I'll go to fight for my village and my friend, but I also go to watch your back. Then, I'll know you're safe."

He wanted to kiss her, take her in his arms. He wanted to make love to her here in the common. He wanted to wrap himself in her soul, like a blanket, crawling inside her warmth and her beauty. He wanted to do all of these things. Declan gave the signal and they were off.

They took off at a fair clip, jogging most of the way. Toby was grateful for all of the hard work that he'd been putting in on Liam' farm. They stopped at intervals for water and food when needed and covered the distance in less time than Toby thought they would. They were still covered by night when Declan saw the first sentry. He gave a low *hoo* that sounded like an owl, which stopped them before they could be discovered.

Declan touched one of the women on the shoulder and she ran off in the darkness. He touched another, a man, and pointed off in the opposite direction. Both ran off in the directions that he'd pointed. The rest of them retreated to a safe distance and faded into the forest.

A cooing noise let them know that they were not alone and Declan gave the return call. Another forty men and women joined them in the cover of the trees. Declan crossed over to the chief from the other village, greeting him as Niall. They spoke in low whispers, their conversation sounding more like the wind in the trees than warriors discussing the routing of a garrison of Roman enemies.

"We've scarce had time to get here, Declan. But, we're here."

"Aye, Niall, thank you. Thank you all and I'll give a proper welcome and thanks when 'tis over. For now, we'll need a plan."

Toby rose up to see the new arrivals better and Declan waved him over. He was introduced and Declan told Niall what Toby had said about the small legion.

"Well," said Niall, "We have the element of surprise we do, but how do we attack 'em?"

"We have to move before they have time to put on armor and shields. If we catch them while they sleep, we can do it."

Declan snorted, and said, "Cowardly to do such. You fight a man like a man, to his face."

"Aye, Declan," Toby agreed. "But you don't know what they can do. They'll fight; we'll make enough noise and they'll be able to fight, just not put up the shields they use. If they do such, we'll have no chance."

"Well, then, what's your plan?"

Toby knelt down in the path, and began drawing a diagram of the area of camp that they'd seen. "We can do this in several groups. I say use that road we were on as a diversion. I'll take a small group of us that way." He made an arrow on what he'd drawn of the path they'd followed. "They'll think we're too small to be a threat, and will relax."

"The scout I sent will have taken care of the guard there," Declan interjected.

"Aye," Niall said, "it'll work. And I'll take the bulk of my people round here." He pointed off to the left side of the drawing and jabbed his dirk in the ground. "There's plenty of tree cover and we can blend in with it."

"All right, then," Toby said. "Declan, you lead the rest o' our people on the opposite side. I'll give the signal when 'tis time to join in the fight. And don't be late; we'll be takin' the brunt of the fight 'til you get there."

Niall raised a fist in answer. "We'll be there, you need not worry. We'll take the bastards and we'll do our share."

"I know you will," Toby answered. "Questions?"

A voice behind him said, "Who'll be providing the whiskey when we've done pickin' off the lot?"

Quiet laughter broke the tension, and Declan answered, "Seamus

Caugheigh, you'll get your whiskey when the work's done and not before!"

"Aye, then," Seamus answered. He came to Toby's side as the three men stood up again. He looked at Toby, and said, "I'll be watchin' your back, Tobias."

"Good, Seamus, and I'll have it no other way." To the rest, Toby said, "Are we ready? Dawn is breakin' and we need to be at it."

Toby picked out a dozen men and women to go with him. The remainder split up with Niall and Declan, and they took off to their respective points. Toby felt her hand on his elbow and turned to Siobhan. She stood by his side, dirk in one hand and sword in another. Toby saw her looking fierce and proud in the moonlight, almost animalistic.

"Seamus can watch over someone else. I told you, I'll be here on your back," she said, the fading moonlight giving her serious look a faery glow about it.

To hell with it, Toby thought, and pulled her to him. He wove his fingers in her hair and lowered his face to hers, kissing her deeply on the lips. She pressed harder against him, and the tip of her tongue teased against his teeth in answer. When the embrace finally released, both were breathless.

"You be careful, woman," he whispered in her ear. "In case you haven't noticed, I'm quite smitten with you, too. I'll not have your death on my hands."

"Come on then. Let's finish it."

Toby and his small band took off at a trot. As they approached the gate again, Toby saw the body of the slain guard lying off the road. The woman who had been sent to do the deed fell in with his group and they ran on. With no guard, there was no warning shout and Toby was at a loss for how to draw their attention. He needn't have worried because a centurion coming back from relieving himself in the woods saw the party and gave the shout.

In the next few minutes, the result was pandemonium and that suited the Celtic warriors fine. They thrived on the chaotic stirrings in their opponents and even fomented it. They were met by another twelve centurions and the fighting was matched, sword for sword. Toby was right; the Roman force didn't think them worthy enough for battle armor because of the size of the group. With the dozen that were holding off Toby's group, the other thirty were content to stand back and laugh. They made bets on how long it would take to dispatch this knot of barbarians.

They didn't laugh for long when Siobhan gave the yell for Toby. Her scream was blood curdling, ululating like a hot knife through butter. The Celtic army poured from the woods, returning the screaming cry. The fighting was in earnest and the unprepared Roman force fought just as hard as the Celts.

Toby and Siobhan stood back to back. They were able to fend off any attacker, and Gwydion had been right. She was a vicious opponent to those that came near her, slitting the throat of a hapless Roman and growling as she pulled his head back to let the blood gush from his body. Toby would not make the same mistake about her again. He saw another of her opponents fall to the side, his belly slit from groin to breast bone and the entrails spilling out of the gaping hole.

"You bastard!"

The shout of pain grabbed Toby's attention and he saw Seamus, in the growing light, had been stabbed in the abdomen. Seamus had lost his sword somehow and was trying to fight off the attacker with his dirk but the blade wasn't long enough. Without thinking, Toby ran away from Siobhan and closed the distance between himself and the Roman soldier. He jumped on the man's back, and with a quick motion, buried his dirk to the hilt in the man's shoulder. They both went down to the ground and Toby struggled to remove the knife before his opponent could roll over. Buried to the hilt, it wouldn't budge and the blood was gushing everywhere, making the handle slippery. He'd struck the vein in the man's neck and the blood spurted hot in his eyes.

He felt the thump against the side of his head as another soldier came to help *his* fallen comrade. Toby tried to raise his blade as quickly as possible, but the fallen soldier had rolled over now, and the two of them were about to make short work of Toby, who had finally pulled the dirk from the flesh. The resulting thump of the sword butt against his head caused his vision to blur and he was stuck between two blades. He fell back against the standing soldier, and pushed off against the fallen one.

A sharp piercing scream broke through, followed by a grunt and a thud. He looked to his right and saw Siobhan sitting astride the body, stabbing continuously as hard as she could and screaming. The soldier he had stabbed had risen to his knees, sword blade on the upswing, and Toby pulled his forward and drove it through the man's heart. More blood poured from the soldier's mouth and he fell backwards off the sword, dead before he hit the ground.

Siobhan vented her anger on the soldier who had attacked him; she was covered in his blood as she stood up. She reached a hand down to help Toby up and he raised himself off the ground.

"I told you, I'd watch over you, didn't I?"

"Aye, you did," he answered, grinning.

Around them, the sounds of the battle were diminishing. Toby surveyed the sight and saw the entire legion had been defeated and soundly. There were Roman corpses littering the ground. They had lost a few, one of them was Seamus, but they had done what they set out to do. It was over and his friend was safe. They were all safe.

Chapter Eighteen

"So, what happened about the Romans?"

"Conor and some of the others took the battle armor and dispersed it out through the English countryside, and I'm told some made it to France. We burned the campsite and removed any trace of ships or anything else they might have left."

John thought about this for a moment before asking, "But, what about reports? They would've sent reports and that would've have alerted somebody about where they were."

"Declan thought of that and searched the commander's tent before they torched it. He found correspondence that gave the exact whereabouts of the village and where they could find Gwy. We burned that too, along with the tent."

"And no one in Rome ever found out what happened to them, let alone where they were," John said.

"Yeah. That's it."

"And you all...?"

"We took our dead and wounded home. Life moved on."

"But I thought Rome never attacked Ireland."

"Rome never *conquered* Ireland," Toby corrected. "And they still hadn't. This was just one unit coming to reclaim a runaway slave and get a few more in the bargain."

"And Siobhan?"

Toby got up and crossed over to the woodpile he'd made earlier and picked up several logs. He came back and arranged them on the dying fire, and the flames lit up again. A pleasant glow cast a rose color on John's face and Toby watched the older man hold out his hands to warm them.

"Siobhan saved my life. She earned my respect and my gratitude that morning. She already owned my heart."

"You had a thing for her," John teased, a broad smile on his face.

"John, I had more than *a thing* for her." Toby closed his eyes at the memory of the lady, seeing her in his mind as she was that day – clad in the leathers of battle, her auburn hair tied back in a braid, the fierce look of her face. "I have never since met a woman who made me want to live in an ice cold lake. She was smart, sexy, beautiful, witty; she was everything I wanted in a woman and more. My friend, it was a lot more than *a thing*."

John chuckled at the comment, and held up the now empty coffeepot, giving it a little shake.

Toby pointed over the man's shoulder. "The water's behind you in those jugs. I have the coffee here. Hand me the basket out of the pot and you can fill it with water."

"You came prepared," John said.

"Yes, I did."

John dumped the used coffee grounds in the fire and handed Toby the basket. He unscrewed the lid from the plastic water jug, and filled the coffeepot as he talked. "You ran a big risk, you know."

"How so?" Toby asked as he measured out the coffee.

"I could have told you I wasn't coming. I could've called the cops."

Toby looked up from his task, one brow raised. "Why didn't you?"

John had filled the pot and paused, staring into the fire. He took a deep breath and set his jaw. It took a moment or two before he was ready to answer. "I don't know. I just know that...well, you didn't seem crazy. I felt like I could trust you. I don't know why, but I do."

"Oh, there's a reason," Toby said. "But, not now. Later. Ok?'

"Sure," John agreed.

Toby handed the tin basket to his partner, and John put it all together and stuck the pot on the flame.

"I loved her, John. I was so head over heels in love with that woman; I could feel it inside of me." Toby stopped for a moment, remembering, and began again. "You know, it was more than just Siobhan. It was those people and that place. Do you know anything about the Celts?"

"Practically nothing."

'Did you know they were the first environmentalists? They prized this earth above all other things, constantly working with zero impact on their surroundings. The Druids learned the cycles of the earth and worked with them. They knew about conservation of resources and living with in the 'need vs. want.'"

"Did they practice it?" John asked.

"Yes, they did. It was amazing – water reclamation, land

conservation; they even practiced animal husbandry with their livestock. The children were taught that we do not own the earth so much as we are the caretakers, placed here by the Gods. And they taught that message to their own children and on and on."

"I want to teach *my* children that," John said, wistfully. "I was always more comfortable with nature. It was my first and my best friend."

"I know," Toby answered. "I remembered hearing you say that once. At a Choices symposium. I went to one."

John was astonished, staring wide eyed at his companion. "You did?"

"I was there in 1995. A very powerful weekend, as I recall. I walked away with a lot."

"You were a member of the Conservancy?"

"Still am," Toby said. "I kept my membership going, but I never made it to any more symposiums. You really got to me that year."

John chortled and reached up to scratch his head. "I got to me too. It was a lousy summer for me that year."

"I know. I remember that, too. I'm sorry you went through that hell. You know – you do that a lot, always a slave to something."

"Yeah, well. It runs in the family, I suppose."

Toby reached down and checked the pot, which was just beginning to boil. He could see the bubble in the lid and the water was still running clear. "A few more minutes on that coffee."

"Good," John replied. "I could use another cup, I think."

"Can I ask you a question? Did the two DUI's make you check into the clinic?"

John pulled up one knee, and wrapped his arms around it, leaning forward slightly. "That and my son. He was going through some issues and I needed to set an example for him. I didn't want him to make my mistakes."

"He had a problem?"

"Coke."

Toby sat back to watch the flames and keep an eye on the pot. "That stuff'll kill ya."

"That's what I tried to tell him. He kept lookin' at the old man and seein' what I was. You know, it's different when it's your son. You do what you have to do for your children."

"Yes, you do."

"So, I told him I had a problem and I wanted him to go with me. I told him I knew *he* had a problem and we'd solve it together."

"You're a good father."

John dropped his leg back to the ground, picked up his rock, and turned it over in his hands. He hedged for a moment, juggling the stone between his hands. "I was a shit as a father, okay?" The intensity of the statement was forceful, the look on his face almost feral. He threw the rock off in the distance and looked back over the fire to his partner. "I was. I was a shit as a father. I was never there when they needed me. I had absolutely nothing to do with raising them. Annie did it all."

"You were on tour, how were you supposed to? You came home, didn't you?"

"Yeah, I came home," John answered, with a measure of disgust in his voice.

"Were you with your kids when you were home?"

"I tried to be."

"*Were* you?"

"Yeah, when I was there. But, I wasn't there enough."

"Then, quit beating yourself up over it," Toby told him, trying to be reassuring. "You did the best you could. That's all any parent does. You make mistakes but you love your kids. You were making a living and that's the nature of the business. You should know that."

"I know it. But they suffered because of it."

"Did they? I don't know about that. I saw your son at that Symposium. He looked okay to me. He's a good kid. You did fine. No, you did better than fine."

John gave him a wry smile. "I suppose I did. But the credit still goes to my ex. She made sure they grew up in a normal household."

Toby shrugged and said, "Hey, give credit where credit is due. You gave them a roof over their heads and the ability to get a good education and everything else money can get you."

"Except a stay home father."

Toby reached over to the coffeepot and pulled it off the fire. The water was now running a dark brown and there was a definite aroma of the coffee. He motioned to John's cup and John held it out for him. Toby poured them both a fresh cup and they settled back again.

"Let me tell you something," Toby said. "A stay at home father is highly overrated. You have three great kids there and they didn't get that way by growing up in a vacuum. Okay?"

John smiled and nodded. "Okay."

"Good."

Toby sat listening to the crickets for a few moments. It was his favorite music. "You know, I wanted to make a difference. I wanted to do what you did with Windstar, with Alaska. I never got that chance."

"Why not?"

"Just never did. Why did *you* do it?"

"I had some powerful friends," John said. "They taught me everything I know about this planet. And I wanted to do something, take some responsibility. I knew I could with every record I sold."

"But *why*?"

"At first, it was because it *felt* like the right thing to do," John remarked. "But, I met David Brower and I *knew* it was the right thing to do."

"I've read his books," Toby said, taking another sip of coffee.

"A smart man. And Bucky was too. I've been very fortunate. And Tom. Tom was the one who helped me get started with Windstar. I wanted to have some sort of a think tank, and Tom helped me get it moving."

Toby crossed his legs again, bending over to stretch his back a little. "Well, I know I learned a lot there. It was a good idea, a good place to go to learn what to do and how to do it."

"Thanks."

Toby watched the older man for a moment. "The land...the earth...the people. It always comes down to that, doesn't it?'

"It always does," John mused into his cup of coffee. He took a sip of his drink and then a sudden look come over his face. "Hey, wait. What about Yeshua?"

"What do you mean," Toby asked.

"You said he was changing. Sounds like they were some pretty serious changes."

"He was, in appearance and demeanor."

"Good, because I have to tell you, he sounded like a stuffy little brat for a while there. If there's any part of this story I really don't buy, that's it."

"John, what do you know about the Catholic Church?"

"Not a lot. I was raised Presbyterian, actually."

Toby nodded and said, "Well, there was a teaching I remember from catechism, one of the unwritten stories that had been passed down. Sister B taught us that the reason the gospels didn't mention Jesus between the upset at the temple and when he started his ministry was that he was traveling. I remember she told us that he was a strict Essene, 'an eye for an eye' stuff. She said, He had traveled with his uncle Joseph of Arimethea all over Europe and India before he returned home. And when he'd returned, he was changed."

John grinned. "And does that make you—?"

"Well, I was not Joseph of Arimethea, but he was changing, all right. Physically, he'd grown a few inches and put on a little muscle from all the labor he was doing. He cut off those curls he had around his face and was letting his hair grow. He was starting to look more Celtic than Hebrew."

"What about his beliefs?"

"Well, those were changing too. He started earning his keep doing carpentry for the other villagers, taking it out in trade. He helped Liam a lot. He worked hard on his people skills. You know, I think he started viewing them differently. He wanted to befriend them, I guess." Toby shook the thought from his head. "Oh, hell, I don't know what he thought. I just know that he really started to change after the battle with the Romans."

"Was he still serious about learning the Celtic way?" John asked.

"Well, he wasn't damning them, so I would say yes. He was serious. I know I was. Declan agreed to take us on as pupils after Yule. He said he'd be free at that time. And it was the time of newness, the New Year of the Wheel."

"Christmas. There's an irony in there, you know."

"I know."

"And you?"

"I was never more serious in my life. It was at that time, that first day of the learning, that I knew I wanted it. Because it was the first time I thought about staying there in that time."

"With Siobhan."

Toby smiled, blowing on the hot liquid to cool it. "Yes, with Siobhan. For the first time in my life, I was thinking about marrying. I wanted to marry her and spend the rest of my life with her."

"So, what happened at Yule?"

Chapter Nineteen

Declan welcomed Toby and Yeshua into the home he shared with Aiobh and set about making them feel at ease. He served mugs of heather ale along with thick slices of fresh bread covered with homemade butter and honey. They talked of nothings for a brief time, just enjoying the food and company. At a nod from Declan, Aiobh excused herself to go to a neighbor's cottage. She was off to help with some spinning, she told them. With a smile and a wave, she wrapped up in a thickly woven wool cloak and left them to their own devices.

"I hope you won't mind if we just sit here at the table," Declan said to them. "We'll just have an informal gatherin' – just to talk and get acquainted, give you a chance to finish your sweets." He smiled, a cheerful expression that set his eyes twinkling. "I want you lads to be sure that this is truly what you wish."

Toby was still feeling unsure about this whole thing, this learning of the Celtic religion. He considered himself a lapsed Catholic since Maeve's passing and he wasn't even sure he would even consider himself that. He thought himself open-minded enough to recognize that other religions did exist, but there was enough of catechism left in him to believe that learning of them was just this side of blasphemy. Practicing one was enough to earn him a place in the deepest pits of hell. And yet….

He had taken a stand with Yeshua, something he couldn't take back. He had berated the young man into being one of them, opening his mind and heart, and exploring this world. For Toby to do anything less would be hypocritical and he was not going to give anyone (Yeshua) the satisfaction of calling him one. So, he was here to do what he demanded that Yeshua do. He still felt the twinge of guilt but he knew he'd get over it.

"So, tell me, then, about your own beliefs."

Toby looked up from his mug to see that Declan was waiting on him to answer. He shrugged, leaning on the table with his elbows. "I have none, Declan. Maybe once upon a time I believed in God but not anymore. I believe there are some strange things in this world, but as to whether a God makes them happen? I don't think I believe anymore."

Declan nodded, let the words sink in. Toby looked out of the corner of his eye. Yeshua had a look of...what? Pity? Concern? *No. Sorrow. For me?*

"Tell me, Tobias, how did all of this—" Declan gestured around him to indicate not just the cottage they were in, but the great outdoors as well. "—come to be? Do you never wonder?"

"No," Toby answered, staring into his mug again. "I don't wonder. It just did. Millions of years of evolution, single celled microorganisms coming up from the sludge of being another ingredient in the primordial soup, growing into birds and cattle and who knows what else." He heard the deafening silence and his jaw clamped shut with an audible click, realizing that he was talking of things that wouldn't be debated for hundreds of years. *I sound like total lunatic and why not. Darwin doesn't exist yet and evolution isn't even a concept. Nice job, Toby; prove you're nuttier than a fruitcake and see if they don't serve you up as the next Wicker Man.* "No," he finished lamely, "I don't."

Declan nodded again and turned to Yeshua. "Yeshua, perhaps you'll tell us what *you* believe."

The young man answered quickly and soberly. "We have but one God, Declan. He is called by the name that only the Rabbis may speak. He is called *JHVH*, the *Lord Jehovah*, and He is the *Lord God of Israel. He* created Heaven and Earth and He created man in his own image. It was He who gave life to this world and He who put man on it to rule the earth and the creatures." He had said all of that on one breath, stopping now to take another before he finished. "He gave the stone tablets to Moses to guide the children of Israel to the path of righteousness. He has sent His only Son to this earth to lead them to salvation, to protect them from evil, and to free them from Roman slavery."

Yeshua took his mug and drained it after the long speech. Declan refilled the earthen container and offered to do the same for Toby, who shook his head and placed his hand over his own.

"Yeshua, you say none but the...what did you call them?"

"Rabbis."

"Aye, *Rabbis*," Declan repeated. "That they alone may speak this name of your God?"

"Yes, Declan, for it is the holiest of holies, His name. To speak His name is such power."

"But *you* can speak this name?"

"Yes, I may. As His Son, the representation of the Lord God on earth, I may speak my Father's name."

It was as if there was no doubting what the younger man was saying. Declan seemed to accept Yeshua's claim without question of any kind. Toby wasn't sure what he expected but maybe a little skepticism would have been nice. "Declan," he said, "you take that as a truth."

Declan cocked his head. "And you say that as if I should not. Why?"

Toby cleared his throat and shifted in his seat. "Well, because anyone else would think Yeshua was not right in the head."

"Does he seem as such to you, Tobias?'

Yeshua sat, his hands clasped around his mug. He watched Toby with a deep interest; he wanted to know the answer too.

"No, I don't think Yeshua's insane," Toby admitted, never breaking eye contact with the young man.

"Well, if you don't find him daft, then his story must be true. Have you cause to doubt it?"

Toby addressed Declan again. "I believe that *he* believes it. I guess that's the same thing, isn't it? But that doesn't make it true, just because one believes it."

"Aye," Declan agreed amiably. "It surely doesn't. But, then, Tobias, there are many things that can't be explained. And you ask how I can hear his sayin' he is the child of his God and never blink an eye. Is it not the way of the Tuatha de Danaan?"

"I don't understand," Toby replied.

"Perhaps, this will help you. Let me tell you a story."

Assured of an audience, Declan settled back in his chair and his listeners did the same.   "In the beginning was the chaos and the darkness. There was no shape, no form. It was empty and alone.

"From the void of chaos came a seed of light, and from this seed, the Goddess was born. She had no name but was the Maiden in Her creative form. And She took the chaos and the darkness, and began to make sense of it. She shaped the form of the universe and made the life in it. She took the seed of light from which she came and formed the light of the day.

"And She was lonely. She took from the light and from the earth, and created Her equal, Her mate, the Dagda. He was mortal, created human. Together, they were in love and created that love in the form of Her children, the Children of Dana – the Tuatha de Danaan. Her face changed to that of the Mother. "

"Is that when She was given a name?" asked Toby.

Declan clapped his hands, nodding in approval. "Aye, it was. So, Dana gave birth to Her children and because they needed further guidance, She created another face, that of the Crone, the Grandmother of Time. She became the three faces of the Goddess. These faces were of the same One, but they became their own. Brighid was the name given to Her face as the Maiden, the creator and virgin. Dana was the mother face and She is the Mother o' us all. Anu was the name given to the Grandmother, the Crone, the voice of experiences and the keeper of the memories.

"But there was one thing missing. For in the creation of life, there had to be a gateway to the growin'. For you see, you can't live forever, never aging, for then you will never grow in spirit and learn the lessons of your existence. The One loved Her mate so much that she gave Him the Godhead, and created one more – a God of passage to the other side of the Veil."

"A God of Death."

Declan nodded, sipping from his mug. "Aye, Tobias, if you wish to view it as such. He is called Balor, the God of the Underworld; where all souls go to refresh and learn the lessons of this lifetime and make ready to be reborn."

"Declan," Yeshua interrupted. "You say *reborn*?"

"Aye, boy, reborn. We come to this earth incarnate, as caretakers and to learn the lessons of life. When you pass beyond the Veil, at the end of life, you go to Annwn. And when time comes for you to be reincarnate, you come back. 'Tis that way with all creatures."

"What is *uh-noon*?"

"Annwn is the place where all souls pass into, the other side of the Veil."

"Heaven," Yeshua said.

Declan cocked his head to one side, raising an eyebrow. His face was a study in curiosity. "Heaven, you say?"

"Yes, Declan, *Heaven*. The realm of God that was furnished as a paradise for those who...pass beyond the Veil, as you put it."

"Do your own people teach of the Circle?"

"What circle?" Toby asked.

"The *Circle* is how we connect, the Wheel of Life," Declan explained. "All things move in circles, Tobias. Even life is a circle. You have the circle of birth, death, and rebirth. The Wheel of the Year begins with Yule and ends with Samhain. Can you not find circles everywhere?"

Toby sat back, his brow furrowed and racking his brain. Were there any *circles* he could think of? And that quickly, he remembered back to college. He had taken it for the easy grade but *Rocks for Jocks*, as it was commonly known, was a science credit for his requirements. He'd signed up for Geology 101 and went into class with his coffee and bagel every morning. One morning's lecture was about the theory of plate tectonics and had only mildly raised Toby's interest. The thought that the earth was covered with plates, constantly moving was absurd. Or so he had thought at the time.

Of course, the land – circles, creation of new land mass in the Atlantic Ocean, sliding into itself in the Pacific, turning back into the molten lava that recreated in the creation of new land mass. Wait – birth, death, and rebirth. Of course, it makes sense.

Declan was smiling at him. Toby had it; he could see the circles – the seasons moved in circles, ever changing and ever returning to the same. The plants began as seeds. The seed slept in the ground until water and nutrients helped it grow to a plant. The plant produced fruit before its life was over. The fruit produced more seeds and the cycle began again with the new plant. Of course, birth, death, and rebirth, it was so simple.

He was pulled from his thoughts by Yeshua's question. He found that he wanted the answer as well.

"Is that why you worship in a circle, Declan?" Yeshua asked.

"Aye, Yeshua, 'tis why." Declan motioned with his hands as he talked. "The circle represents many things – how all things move in their own way and in their own cycles, always returning to the beginning."

"The Talmud teaches us that when all pass from this earth, they go into a deep sleep. They will remain that way until the Day of God's Judgment. On that day, they will all awaken and come unto God, for He shall decide who shall be worthy of Heaven."

"But, Yeshua, did your God not create these souls?"

Yeshua paused a moment before answering. Toby could almost see the question turning over in his mind.

"He did, Declan."

"Then, how can they not be worthy?" Declan queried.

"Because of the original sin," Yeshua answered with a definitive tone.

"And what is this *'original sin?'*"

"In my belief, my Father created the heaven and the earth. And He created the Garden of Paradise, of Eden. The original sin was when first woman, Eve, doubted God and defied Him by eating of the fruit of the Tree of Good and Evil after God said she could not. It is this sin that taints all of God's children and makes them unworthy."

"Aye, the sins of the fathers do visit upon the children. Will be a sad thing, but true. But are you responsible for their sins?"

Yeshua smiled. "No, man is not responsible for the original sin, just tainted by it. For man is frail and full of failings."

"Then, surely, there is redemption, aye?"

"Yes, Declan," the young man agreed solemnly. "There is redemption – in asking God's forgiveness and doing your best to never sin again."

"Aye, you've said that word many times," Declan observed, resting his hand on his chin. He was going somewhere with this. It was fascinating to watch. "Sin, eh? What is that exactly, Yeshua? For my knowin'."

"Sin is separation from God, in pretending to know His mind. Sin is the act of defiance of God."

"Separation, is it?"

"Yes...." Yeshua's answer seemed uncertain. From the look on his face, it seemed that he understood that Declan had a point to make but wasn't sure if he wanted to hear it.

Declan laid his hands, palms down, on the table. "How can you be separated from your God if he is part of you?"

"As man was given free will, so he can separate from God's grace by choice."

"Hmmm," Declan said, running a finger along the grain of the wood. "So, would be your choice to separate from your God?"

"When man must do his own will and not God's, it is a choice."

"But do you not carry your God inside your heart? You say you are His son, but is not every child of God *His* child?"

Toby saw it. He wondered if Yeshua did.

Yeshua frowned. "I don't understand."

"Then, I shall explain." Declan sat back in his chair, once again smiling. "We all carry the Goddess within us, Yeshua. We are part of Her and she is part of us. We are the Children of Dana, how can we not be worthy? Surely, it'll be the same for your God. You say you are the Son of God. Truly this is so, but is not every man, woman, and child His children as well?"

"I understand, Declan," Toby broke in. "You're saying we are not damned unless we choose to be, aye?"

"No, Tobias, I'm saying there's no such thing as a God givin' eternal damnation to a soul. There is always forgiveness and a way of paying the debt to those you've wronged."

"But what about...what about sin, what about...?" Toby stuttered a bit, not sure what question he was asking.

Declan understood. "You are are just as much a Child of God as Yeshua is. Perhaps, not in the same way as he is but you are. Dana and the Dagda had Their children and they were the First Ones placed on the earth. And the First Ones had their children and so on and so on, and here you both are, Children of the Gods."

"But, Yeshua—"

"—is a direct descendent of his God, 'tis true." Declan poured another round of ale for them as he talked. "It'll not be an unusual thing for the Gods to be pulled to the likes of us. The Dagda was known for visitin' those mortal women He was attracted to and matin' with 'em. 'Tis how the other Gods were born, that are not part of the Sacred Five."

Toby shook his head. It was still a little farfetched to him. "So, you really do believe him when he says he is the Son of God?"

"Aye, Tobias, I do." Declan nodded his head at Yeshua and took a sip of his ale. "You have but to look in his eyes to see the truth. You have but to listen to him to know that there is a great power within him."

Declan put out his hand to the young man. Yeshua looked down at it and then held out his own hand. Declan clasped it in both of his.

"Aye, boy, there is great power here. You have a good heart," Declan said in a dreamy voice. He sounded disconnected and his head lolled back, making his expression unreadable. "You're a healer, a man of vision, and you hear the Voice. You have the makings of a Shaman for sure."

Toby watched the two as they continued the clasp of hands. It was almost electric; the air was thick and heavy in the room. Yeshua was lost in the spell, a glow about him that radiated through his whole being. Declan was almost vibrating from something; Toby could see the waves coming off of the man. Whatever was passing between them, Yeshua had the look of understanding on his face.

The High Priest came out of his trance and released Yeshua's hand. He closed his eyes, sat back, and shook his head as if to clear it. Yeshua simply sat for a few moments, his eyes crossed and clouded over. When he did come back, his eyelids fluttered for a few seconds and his breathing became less labored. The spell passed quickly but Toby still felt the tension in the room.

"Aye," Declan continued, "you have great power, son. You are what you are and I've no doubt of it."

Yeshua smiled and nodded. *You are what you are and I've no doubt of it.* Maybe it was true all of it. And if it was true, Toby was more determined than ever to see out the remainder of this lifetime. *But, then, again, the mind can play tricks on us all, can't it? Maybe Declan just saw what he wanted to see. Maybe this is all just a self-induced trance. Maybe....*

Declan clapped his hands and rubbed them together, grinning as he did so. "So, my friends, are you still interested in the teachings of the Goddess and the Tuatha de Danaan?"

He had no more reservations. "I am," Toby answered.

"What about you, Yeshua? Although, there seems to be little I can teach you."

"No, there is much you can teach me," Yeshua answered. "And I would learn it all. I am ready to learn."

Toby did a classic double take. He stared at Yeshua openly, his mouth hanging open. "Okay, who are you and what have you done with Yeshua ben David?"

There was a split second when both of the men stared right back at Toby. And then the room erupted in laughter as Declan and Yeshua got the joke. Declan threw his head back, clapping his hands as he laughed. Yeshua was bent over double, the curls of his now long hair bobbing up and down from the thong that held them back. Toby giggled at first, but it was just too infectious and he was guffawing along with them.

Declan wiped his cheeks and managed to say, "Then the day after Yule, we'll begin your lessons. You'll come here and I'll be teachin' you the ways of the Druids, the path of the Old Ones."

When Toby recounted the afternoon's events to Siobhan, she sat with her head canted to one side, listening intently. They sat on the bench, watching the moon beginning to rise over the treetops. She sat half in moonlight and half in shadow, dressed in her finest gown of homespun and a blanket draped around her slender frame. Bathed in the gentle radiance of the soft light, Toby wanted to take her in his arms and make love to her. He dared not, with her parents just inside the door. It was the first time they'd been permitted to sit without some chaperone in attendance. Toby didn't want to screw that up.

He leaned back against the rough wall of her parents' cottage and told her the story of the afternoon.

"Sounds as if 'twas a good beginning you had, then," she said, in her practical way.

"Aye, 'twas."

"You think the lad is changin', do you?"

"Aye...." His answer trailed off, his mind so wrapped up in her that there was no reason to finish the sentence. In fact, words completely failed him at that moment.

She sat forward just enough for the light to play across her hair. Toby was close enough to reach out and take a strand from her breast and he just held it in his fingers. The copper glow warmed his hands and felt as fine and soft as silk. Siobhan smiled and traced the back of his hand with her fingers before twining them in his.

He found his train of thought again and finished what was in his mind. "Aye, I do. He's not as arrogant as he was when we arrived."

"Well, then, you both have that in common, do you not?" she teased, her teeth white in the moonlight.

He squeezed her fingers a little too tightly making her yelp and then laughed along with her. "You're saying I'm arrogant, are you?"

"You sot!"

He kissed her fingers and sat back again. "Well, he has changed. And so have I. I'll never admit you're right, you know. But you are."

"Declan is quite taken with him. Said he felt the lad's spirit and 'tis a good, strong one."

"And you?" Toby grinned. "Are *you* taken with the lad, too?"

She flapped one end of the blanket at him, mock slapping at him. "Whatever are ye blatherin' on about?"

"I see the looks you throw his way. Do I have a rival for your affections, miss?"

She sat back in the shadow and her face became the mystery again. Her fingers never left his, however, and he was content to let his hand lay against her thigh.

"None that I know aught of, sir. And *I* would be first to know."

Toby glanced back over his shoulder at the open door to the cottage. No one in sight, he lifted her hand to his lips, and kissed each finger in turn. He turned the hand over and gently touched his lips to the soft skin of her palm, giving soft kisses there. Toby felt her shiver, heard the soft sigh, the mist of her breath trailing off in the crisp winter air.

"Good," he whispered against her wrist, where his lips had traveled next. "I would be sore in pain to know you did."

The hand caressed his cheek, and she whispered, in return, "As would I, Tobias."

The moon rose high over the treetops, neither one wanting to break the silence. The air was crisp and snow would be coming soon – a matter of days. They would have no more nights like this until the spring had returned. His skin was starting to chill and still he didn't want to leave her.

"Tobias?" she called softly.

"Aye, lady? What are you thinking?"

"Why do you do this?"

"Do what, lady?"

She was watching him, looking for something in his eyes. She was so serious as she studied him. "Learn of our ways. Why?"

The honesty was right there; he couldn't deceive her. "Well, it would not be a lie to say that I'm doing this for you, to make you happy."

She shook her head, the hair glinting and reflecting in the moonlight. "You don't have to do that to make *me* happy."

"Yes, I do," he said. "But 'tis more than that. I do it mostly for me. I feel at home here, with you and the people. I feel like I belong here. I want to belong, lady."

"Tobias," she said, reaching out to touch his face again. "Of course you belong. Always." She sat back again, giving him a sideways look and one corner of her mouth going up. "Does that mean you've decided to stay then, does it?"

Toby stole another glance over his shoulder. When he had reassured himself that no one was watching, he leaned forward until his face was less than an inch from hers.

"Aye, lady. That is my way of tellin' you that I have become besotted with you. It'll be my way of tellin' you that I love you truly and always shall."

Her tongue crept between her teeth and stole to the corner of her mouth. Suddenly, all Toby wanted to do was taste her lips, the sweetness of her tongue. The pull towards her was fierce and he didn't want to break the spell. So she took the step, leaning forward to kiss him. She came so close that she was almost in his lap, her arms wrapped around him. His hands found her hair and were lost in the sea of copper.

When the kiss broke, they were breathless and Toby wanted her so badly that his entire being was shaking. She knew it; he could see it in her eyes. He was never more thankful for the lambskin coat that Niamh had made him wear. But Siobhan's mother came to the door and called her inside. Toby bade them goodnight and watched her go inside. He sat there for some time, mostly to control the shaking and the part of his body that was still hard and throbbing.

He would have sat there forever, savoring the tastes and sounds of her. But his ass was almost frozen to the wood and he was pretty certain that his balls were turning blue with more than the need to be inside of her. Dragging himself to his feet, he could hear the wind whispering in the trees, the sound of the eagles screaming as they hunted. He hadn't lied at all; he wanted to stay here. He had fallen in love with the place and the people, with her. This was home.

She stood at his side during the Yule ritual. They were gathered in the henge, erected generations before any of them had been born. There was little snow, only an inch on the ground. Yeshua stood on his right, a most enigmatic smile on his face. Gwydion and his parents stood on the other side of Siobhan, and they all looked immensely pleased with themselves. That was fine; he had a few surprises of his own in store.

The Quarters called and the Gods invoked, Aiobh turned to the gathering and held out her hands to Toby and Yeshua. The two came forward to her and she motioned them to kneel before her. When she spoke, it was to the group, but her gaze was for the two.

"We were blessed when the two of you saved our bard and friend. We are now twice blessed that you request to learn of our ways. These two have come to our High Priest to receive the learning of the Druids."

She stepped to the altar and picked up two thongs; they had been tied at one end, and each thong had a quartz crystal that had been wrapped in leather and attached to the thong. She stepped back to them. As she spoke each one's name, she placed the tied leather around their necks.

"Tobias ap Brendan. Yeshua ap David. You are welcomed to the Grove of Dana, and you are students at the first level. We are more by your addition and do call you brothers. Welcome and Blesséd Be."

She anointed each with oil that smelled like cedar, drawing what he now knew was a half moon surrounded by a circle. When she had finished, she stepped aside and Declan came forward.

"Tomorrow, you start your learning in earnest, but for tonight, you are welcome to the circle as part of it. You need not stand back to watch. To show you're part of the Grove, there is one more gift for you."

Declan pulled something from his pocket and held out his hand for Toby's. Toby gave him his left hand and Declan slipped a ring of purest silver on his forefinger. The ring looked as if it had been beaten by hand, and there was a design etched in it. The design was a Celtic knot.

He did the same to Yeshua and said to them both, "The knot you see represents the family and Grove you are now part of, for we all are joined as one. There is no beginnin' and no endin', only the circle of the ring and the weavin' of your lives within ours and ours with you. Welcome and Blesséd Be."

Declan helped them to their feet and motioned them to return to the circle. It was now official. Toby felt as if his face would crack wide from the smile that he wore. He watched Siobhan's face as he walked back to her and her smile matched his own. When he was closer, he saw the tears in her eyes. He passed a glance at Niamh, who also had tears. It was Gwydion's beaming face that touched his heart, for he had his own tears and beaming grin. *I am home.*

When they were again at their places within the circle, Aiobh continued. "It is the birth of the Sun King, the return of the light. We stand on the day when the light begins to grow and the long nights are almost over. It is the time of' rebirth from the darkness, the beginnin' of the new season."

There was another bonfire built in the middle of the circle, a huge collection of logs. Aiobh walked to the stack, a wicker basket on her arm, and carefully covered with a woven plaid scarf. Declan walked in his customary place behind her and he was carrying a larger log than was on the heap. When she was a short distance away from the logs, she set the basket down and continued her walk.

"Renewal, rebirth; the Oak King comes to us again as a babe. And we represent that rebirth by riddin' ourselves of the past pain and sorrow. Only when you do that, can you move forward."

Aiobh's gaze met Toby's and he listened as if she spoke only to him.

"To release the pain of your past, you must learn from it. Only then can you turn from it and look to the future. To renew is what we all need at this time. To start a new pathway is what we come to do."

Declan stepped forward, carrying the log.

Aiobh continued. "It is our way to celebrate the end of the old by the burning of the Yule log. This was last year's Yule tree and has been in our home for whole time. We'll now burn it to put aside the past."

Declan laid the log on top of the stack and stepped back. Aiobh had retrieved a torch and touched it to the bonfire. A blaze jumped from the stack, licking at the logs and finding the taste to be fine. The aroma of the woods was comforting and invigorating, and the fire lit up the night with a gold haze.

Gwydion had told Toby and Yeshua what this night meant, and they had prepared for it. When Aiobh motioned the first of them forward to the blaze, Toby reached into a pocket he had sewn into his trousers and pulled out two items that he had carried with him since returning from the Gulf. He had been successful in hiding them until now and it was time to let them go.

He followed Siobhan, and watched the others before him, tossing items on the conflagration. They threw papers, clothing, and one even tossed a doll on the blaze for the child who had been born too early. Each person cast the item, stood for a moment, and moved back to their place. He watched Siobhan remove a scarf from her sleeve and throw it on the fire. She turned to Toby, and smiled.

"This was from someone dear to me, a love that was not meant to be. Until you came into my life, I was carrying that. To never forget him. I think 'tis time to let him be at peace. Time to let go and move on. To a new love." She didn't wait for any response; she just turned and walked around, going back to her place beside Niamh.

Toby took a deep breath and turned back to the fire. He looked down at the pictures in his hands. One was taken when he and Bion were on a recon and one of the Saudis had brought a camera. The guy had snapped the picture of the two of them, standing by the truck with their arms around each other's shoulders. The other picture was of Maeve, Brendan, and Toby at Christmas. He was so young; hell, they all were. A relative had captured Maeve's gentle smile and Brendan's loutish grin.

He stared at the pictures for a few seconds until Yeshua's gentle cough reminded him of where he was. *I will always love you. You were my friend, my parents. You gave me life, you gave me love, and you gave me memories that will never be taken away from me. But, it's time to let you go, time for me to move on. I have a real chance here, a chance to be happy...with her.*

Goodbye, Mom. Goodbye, Da. See ya, Bion.

He tore the pictures in half and chucked the pieces on the inferno. He stood a moment more, watching the paper curl up and blacken, smoke billowing from each scrap. He brushed the tears back from his eyes and moved on. He walked around the fire in clockwise fashion, returning to Siobhan's side. Her tears were flowing again and she reached up to touch his face. He rested his cheek in her palm and closed his eyes.

He let the past drain from him like the sands running from the top of the hourglass. With each grain slipping from the timepiece of his soul, he gained a tighter grip of his emotions and felt the agony that he'd carried dissipate into nothingness. In his heart, he knew that he had done the right thing and he comforted himself with that. He would always keep them in his heart but he was home now. This was where he belonged and with whom he belonged.

When he opened his eyes again, she was still there, watching him with that sweet smile of hers. He held her tightly to him and she wrapped around him like a blanket. He felt Gwydion's hand touch his shoulder. Niamh and Liam joined the little knot and gave support by touching him in some way. He felt surrounded by love and belonging.

Yeshua threw something on the pyre as well. He had chosen the locks of hair that he had cut off from his sideburns, the robe he had worn while traveling, and he consigned them to the fire. He was taking all of this seriously enough to become part of the ritual. Toby knew he'd never embrace this faith but it was a way to understand. It was enough. It was a step.

When the last person had given up the piece of his past to the bonfire, Aiobh crossed back to the basket, picked it up, and removed the covering. She came to each person standing in the circle and gave each a candle. The candles were hand dipped and the color of lemon. As she passed them along, she explained.

"Tobias and Yeshua, as our newest students, this is our gift to all. The candles represent the light of the Sun returnin', the rebirth of the Oak King. You'll burn this candle a bit on every full moon to keep the power of the Yule with you."

When the last candle had been passed out, the ceremony went on. Toby was emotionally spent by then but also energized about what was to come. He was free to make his new destiny. He also knew that destiny was with Siobhan. Somehow, he had to work up the nerve to ask her father for his permission to marry her. His new beginning would be a home and children. The confirmed bachelor was about to be no more.

When the ceremony was done, they all gathered in the barn again. The ales and whiskeys were plentiful, as was the food. But Toby was prepared for this, thanks to Gwydion. Gwydion had also explained that with the birth of the Oak King, the tradition was to give gifts to those who were closest to him. Toby not only found his way to his new future, he found Christmas.

A few of the men had gone into the forest and brought back the tallest oak they could find. The tree had been propped up in the back of the barn, and decorated with bits of ribbon, candies, cookies, and other sweets. Toby had worked hard in putting together his gifts. He offered to work the fields for Liam in exchange for some trinkets and tools. He had bartered for a new shawl for Niamh and a new axe for Liam. For Gwydion, he'd found a bone claw that Declan identified as an eagle talon. Toby had bartered a piece of rabbit hide and had cut the leather into a piece, and then braided it into a necklace with the talon hanging from it.

Yeshua had been a total mystery as to what he might get for the young man. Toby had finally found something resembling a stone or piece of quartz. It was in a trapezoidal shape, and resembled mica, but didn't flake. Gwydion had helped him with this one; it was a piece of selenite, like his ring. It was a perfect piece, about an inch and a half in diameter.

"That'll be a stone to get in touch with the Gods, Tobias," Gwydion had explained. "It'll also a stone for seeing through time, through the Veil."

So, he had bartered for a deer pelt and made a bag. He wrapped the crystal in a piece of Niamh's lace, and placed it inside.

They gave each other their gifts. Niamh squealed with delight over the shawl, and Liam and Gwydion had been equally pleased.

"'Tis grand," Gwydion said and put on the talisman immediately. "How did you know?"

"Know what," Toby asked.

"The eagle is my power animal and my guardian. When I do my spirit walkin', 'tis the eagle guides me. How did you know?"

"Well, that'll be for me to know and you to to enjoy," Toby sputtered out. He was *not* going to admit the gift had been a fluke.

"Thank you, Tobias," Gwydion replied, hugging his friend tight.

"Aye, Tobias." Liam clapped both of them with a hand on each shoulder. "And I've somethin' for you lads, too." He waited until Niamh was by his side before continuing, his arm wrapped around her waist. "With Gwydion comin' home and with you joining our family, I want to pass on a bit of my legacy. I've seen you sparkin' on Cieran's daughter and it looks serious. If you don't mind my askin', is it?"

"Aye," Toby confessed, a sheepish grin on his face. He crossed his arms, trying not to shuffle his feet.

"Good. Then, you'll need a place for your own soon, if you wish to be handfast to her." Liam sobered a bit, eyeing Toby dubiously. "Do you?"

Toby straightened, nodding. "Oh, aye, Liam. That I do."

"Well, then. Gwydion, you'll be choosin' a wife soon, too. I want you both to have a parcel of land for your own. We'll go out and mark it, come spring, and 'twill be ready when you choose to handfast and settle down. We'll use our common field to garden for all of us, but you'll have land of your own for your families."

Gwydion clasped his father's hand and kissed his mother's cheek. "Thank you, Da. Aye, 'tis time to settle down and take a wife and children. 'Tis a generous offer."

"Oh, pah, boy," Liam sputtered out. "'Tis your legacy from us."

"But, I am not of your family, Liam," Toby said. "You honor me."

Niamh took his hand in hers, so warm and maternal. "You *are* of our family, now. 'Tis *your* legacy as well."

"And Yeshua, too," Liam added, nodding to the young man. "You've not said if you'll be staying on, like Tobias has. I know you've been missing your homeland of late. But you are a son of my hearth as well. If you wish."

Toby braced himself for the coming diatribe and turned a cautioning look in the young man's direction. He was pleasantly shocked with Yeshua bowed instead to Liam, embracing the man.

"My friends, you have given me more honor than I deserve. And if my path lay here, I would be most pleased to accept this wonderful gift. But as you have said, I have been thinking of my home and my journey back." He frowned slightly, looking down at his hands. "I must lead my people, this I know. But I am coming to know that it will not be in the way I had thought originally." He looked up at Liam again. "I have more traveling to do and it will lead me home when it is time. And I will grieve to leave you all behind."

Niamh took Yeshua's hand in hers and squeezed it. "And will grieve us as well. But you'll always have a home here."

"Thank you, Mother. And I am pleased to know it." He kissed her cheek and laughed at their seriousness. "But I am not leaving yet. I still have much to learn and it is not time."

"Well, good then." Gwydion clapped the young man on the back. "And now, if you'll indulge me, I must thank my màthair and àthair."

Yeshua stepped back, watching the happy scene. Gwydion hugged his father in a hard embrace that left both of them smiling from ear to ear. He then kissed his mother and she hugged him just as fiercely.

Toby followed Gwydion's example in kissing Niamh and shaking Liam's hand. He thanked them several times with Niamh blushing furiously. He knew exactly the parcel he wanted – the one near the forest that had the small stream through one corner. It was close enough that they could walk across to her family's farm and be far enough from all of them to have their own lives, raise their children.

When he presented Yeshua with his gift, Toby was astonished to see the young man begin to tear up. "Hey, Yeshua. Is something wrong?"

The young man stroked the doeskin, pulling out the crystal and admiring it. "Oh no, Tobias. It is perfect."

"Then, why do you weep, my friend?"

When Yeshua met his gaze, it was strong look but one of gratitude and love. "You have already given me my gift, Tobias. You have done my Father's work when I did not – and it seems that you knew it better than I. You have helped me find out who I really am."

"I don't understand," Toby said, shaking his head.

"You were right, my friend. I had set myself above them and that was wrong. Tonight, I learned the true purpose of my being sent here. My Father has told me that I am to lead my people in a new way. The way is not in vanquishing Rome, but in showing my people that God's love is there. That it is within each and every heart. It is time for a new beginning for my people. A way of love and peace."

Yeshua put the bag over his head, and held out his hand to Toby. Toby took the offered hand. Yeshua closed it with his other hand, and stood for a moment, eyes closed.

"I have no present to give you, Tobias, other than my friendship and a promise. I promise you that when it is your time to pass on from this world, you will be with me in Paradise. I will prepare a place for you, at my side. You will be among my chosen."

Toby choked up, not quite able to speak. He simply nodded his head, and the two men embraced each other. When they stepped apart, Toby found his voice again.

"Thank you, Yeshua. I may call you friend, and I will."

"Yes, you will. I am sent to learn the ways of the others. To find this peace that I wish to tell others of. I have you to thank for that."

"Well, then, looks like we both have that learning. Tomorrow, we shall begin it."

Yeshua's smile was warm and friendly. "Yes, we shall. And now, I see a young lady coming for you. I'll see you back at home."

Yeshua walked away from him, clutching the bag to his side.

Toby watched him walk away, still holding the crystal.

"Well, I get you all to myself finally." she said. Siobhan linked her arm in Toby's, sidling up beside him. She buried her face in his arm for a moment before turning her beautiful face up to his.

He smiled down at her, kissing the tip of her nose. "I've been lookin' for you, lady."

"Have you, now?" she answered back with a twinkle in her eye. "Well, it so happens I've been lookin' for you as well. Here and blesséd Yule, Tobias."

He held out his hand, and she placed a necklace in it, made of her hair – she had braided and tied it at one end. He saw a small charm attached to it, a heart carved of wood. He looked into her smiling face with a question on his.

"Oh, aye, 'tis my own locks I cut for you. I made it myself. So you could always carry a piece of me with you." She turned shy, peeking up at him like a little child. She clutched his elbow and in a small voice, asked, "Do you like it? Oh, if you do not like it, I'll understand."

In answer, he placed the necklace around his neck and tucked the charm inside his shirt. He kissed her soft lips and stroked her cheek. "Aye, lady, I do, truly. Thank you."

She blushed and leaned her forehead against his chest, smiling.

"Give me your hand, lady."

She leaned back until she was upright again. She did as she was asked but she was clearly confused. Toby took one more thing from his pocket.

On the third finger of her right hand, he placed a beaten silver ring with a simple ivy pattern carved into it. She looked down at it in shock and then quickly back to his face.

"Aye, lady," he said to her in a soft voice. "I told you, I am besotted with you. I can't ask for your hand now. I must learn a trade and Liam has given me land to build a home. I must learn of your ways. But, I wish to hold you in my heart now. If you'll wear the token, I swear, that I will ask soon."

She stood totally still, her mouth dropped open and Toby was afraid for a moment that she was going to turn him down flat. His heart was pounding in his chest. If she said no, he had no idea what he'd do next. She closed her mouth and could say nothing.

Toby placed a finger on the lips he'd kissed. "I'll have no answer for now. Think about it."

He started to turn from her, but she grabbed his sleeve and stopped him.

"No," she uttered in a quivery voice. "No, you'll have your answer now. Yes, Tobias, my answer is yes. I do love you more than I ever thought I could."

Toby's heart now pounded for a different reason, and he wanted to start screaming the news. "We'll tell none yet," he said instead. "When I have our home built and we have the crops in the field, I'll go to your Da and ask for your hand, lady."

"Aye," she nodded at him.

"Will ye dance with me, beloved?"

Her answer was to take his arm and lead him out to the floor, where the others were dancing a bright jig. They danced the night away and Toby knew his beginning was good.

Chapter Twenty

"Da! Come quick! Come now!"

Gwydion's frantic shout halted them. Toby and Liam bolted from the shed and followed Gwydion back to the barn that held the horses, going to the back stall. No sooner had Toby cleared the door than he saw a mare, thrashing about on her side. Gwydion was trying to get in to do something, but the mare was too distraught to be calm.

"Gwydion, what is it?" Liam was beside Toby in an instant and the scene in front of them was enough to make him concerned.

Gwydion managed to make his way into the small stall but still having no success getting close to the mare, dodging the thrashing hooves. "Da, she's foaling, but somethin' tis wrong."

"Have ye not tried to find out?"

The mare answered the question by kicking Gwydion in the knee and knocking him out of the stall. She lay there, writhing in obvious agony and the foam of her spittle collected on her muzzle. Toby saw her eyes roll back in her head, and the thrashing became more intense. The mare began to scream, a sound that chilled Toby to the marrow. He'd never heard a sound like that from any creature, human or animal, and he didn't want to hear it again. That horse was dying.

Liam helped his son get off the floor and dust off. Gwydion had a bruise forming on his injured leg and he was limping badly. He held his arm, trying to hide a nasty bite mark where blood had coagulated. He was fine but it was obvious that he did not want to go back in there.

"She's got a breach birth," Liam announced with surety.

"What do we do?" Toby asked, his voice shaking. The sight of the animal battering itself against the walls of the stall was too much to take. He turned away from it but the sounds of the creature's torment kept bleeding into him.

"There's naught we can do," Gwydion answered. "If we can't calm her, we can't get in there to help her."

"Perhaps, I can help," a calm voice announced. Yeshua came up beside them, looking intently into the stall. He had sprouted a few more inches, standing a respectable five foot and perhaps seven inches, his head coming to Toby's shoulder. He had filled out quite a bit, as well, the boyishness in his face starting to fade. The man was starting to show in his face as Yeshua's beard was beginning to sprout and his features starting to solidify. His voice had deepened as well, becoming resonating and soothing when he spoke. "I heard the mare. Is it her time?"

"Aye," Gwydion answered. "Da said 'tis a breach."

Yeshua removed his bag from his shoulder and handed it to Toby, and continued to walk into the stall. The way the mare had fallen to give birth, her back legs were near the back of the stall. In her thrashing, she had managed to turn in an angle. To get to any part of her, Yeshua would have to navigate the sea of legs and the gnashing teeth.

"I suppose we could wait 'til she tires herself," Liam said resignedly. "She will eventually."

Gwydion stared at his father, his eyebrows rising in amazement. "Da, if we don't do something, she'll die," he challenged, snorting after he'd said it. "She was already tirin' some time ago. When I went to help her, she did this to me." He held up the bite mark to show them. It, too, was bruising and looked nasty enough to need one of Niamh's ointments.

"Gwydion, I don't know what else to do," Liam burst out. "She'll not let anyone near her. I don't want to lose the mare, I paid good money for her, but there's naught I can do. She almost killed you as 'twas."

"Wait," Toby uttered in an amazed tone, pointing to the now silent stall.

Toby's focus had been drawn back by the absence of the screaming. The mare had stopped her thrashing as Yeshua was inching slowly towards her head. He cooed to the mare, speaking to her in gentle tones. Her head came up off the floor as she watched him come closer. Yeshua knelt down to take her head in one hand, caressing her cheek with the other.

He stayed there for several minutes, just caressing the mare and murmuring to her. It was almost as if the mare was being hypnotized by the young man's voice. She stopped her frothing at the mouth and her breathing, which had been acutely labored, slowed. The mare was still in a great deal of pain, they could all see that, but she had quieted greatly.

Yeshua turned back to the men and quietly said, "Come now. You can come to her and ease her pain. Save the little one. Quickly." Yeshua turned his gaze back to the mother and continued to caress her cheek.

Liam and Gwydion came quietly but quickly to her back legs. Toby had no idea what to do and just stood by to watch. If they needed anything, he could do something then.

"Aye," Liam confirmed, "Breach, just as I feared. Tobias, fetch me a pail of water and those rags from the bin by the door. Gwydion, you'll need to help me. Hold her back legs for me."

Toby grabbed the pail, and dashed out to the pond to fill it. When he came back, he snatched a handful of rags from the bin. By the time he had arrived with what he had been sent for, he saw Gwydion and Liam pulling the baby from the mother's body. They laid it gently down on the ground next to the mare; she was so exhausted, she could no longer move. The baby was glistening with the wetness of the blood and amniotic fluid. But something was still wrong.

Gwydion reached out a hand, not looking up. "Give me the rags, Tobias."

Toby handed them to him and brought in the pail of water. Liam and Gwydion took the rags and began to wipe the goo from the baby's body. Liam paid particular attention to the fragile ribs of the newborn and kept massaging in that area. But, the baby wasn't moving. Toby also saw, the chest wasn't moving – the baby wasn't breathing.

"Oh, Da, we're too late. Oh, damn!" Gwydion's frustration was evident in his face, and he threw the rag down on the ground and sat back on a mound of hay.

Liam refused to give up, and continued to massage the body. "Come, wee one. You can do it. Breathe for me, now. Come on. Breathe...breathe!"

It became evident that the foal had been stillborn and nothing anyone could do would change that. Liam finally gave up his attempts and ducked his head, running his bloody hands through his hair. The mood quickly turned to despair and Toby leaned against the threshold.

Gwydion reached out to his father, laying his hand on the older man's shoulders. "Da, it was just not meant to be. You did what you could."

Liam nodded weakly, and turned to the bucket to begin washing his hands and arms from where he'd been inside the mare's body. "Aye, I know. I don't like to see a new life taken so brutally." He swore softly and sighed deep. "I wish I'd paid more attention to the poor mare."

Gwydion stood up and helped his father up. Liam brought the bucket out and Gwydion took up the rags, following him. They stopped outside the stall and Liam set the bucket on a hay bale. The two men were somber while they cleaned off the goo and muck from the birthing. Toby turned to watch them as they continued to discuss the hardship that losing this foal was going to cause. The foal had been promised to Toby as another compensation for his work in the fields with Liam. Horses were a rare commodity in the village and a death was a loss to them all.

Toby was the only one who heard the snort come from the stall. Again, his attention was brought back to the drama unfolding. He saw that Yeshua had moved from the mare's head to stand next to the foal. The newborn horse lifted its head and, in a disorganized ballet of knees and hooves, it wobbled to its feet in one jerk. It snorted once and quivered, shaking itself and its mane. Yeshua made the same gesture to the foal that he had to the mother, caressing its cheek with his hand, cooing softly.

Toby stood, frozen to the spot with his mouth hanging open and his chin practically touching his chest. He couldn't articulate what he was seeing; there were no words. He put out his hand, reaching out until he made contact with a shoulder and shook it hard. The shoulder belonged to Liam, who wheeled around quickly.

"Tobias, what do you – sweet Brighid, what have we here?"

Gwydion heard the shock in his father's voice and joined them to see what the fuss was. The three men now stood in amazement as the foal took its first tentative steps. It was another female, a beautiful roan foal that was all nose and knobby knees and the most beautiful thing Toby had ever seen. As Yeshua walked, it followed diligently. When the young man came to stand with them, the young one nuzzled against his side. Yeshua caressed her muzzle again and she softly nickered into his palm. The mare was still lying on her side, too weak to move, but she, too, was alive.

Toby was afraid to say anything, to utter one syllable. The

evidence of something was right before them. Or was it? Liam was just mistaken. Gwydion was wrong. The foal was just stunned from the difficult birth. It was not a miracle. *No! Miracles don't exist. I don't believe them. I don't believe he does them. I don't believe.*

But Toby's thoughts were more confident than he felt. Liam didn't seem to be convinced of what he saw either and he touched the colt to satisfy himself. Of the three, Gwydion was the only one not completely taken aback by it.

Yet he was still shaking his head in awe. "Well," he said, a bit breathless. "If I was not here to see it, I'd never believe it – even if you told me 'twas so."

Yeshua only smiled in his enigmatic way and continued to pet the animal.

Liam swallowed hard. "That colt was stillborn," he said to himself. He wasn't speaking for the benefit of the other men, that much was obvious. "I know it. I saw it."

Liam bent down to the newborn's level and ran his hands over her in an attempt to examine her. He was confused, just as Gwydion was, and the two alternated between glances at the horse and Yeshua. They were also looking at the young man with a sense of reverence.

"You were mistaken," Toby heard himself say. "The foal was alive, just in shock. That's all."

Liam stood up, crossing his arms across his chest and cocking his head to one side. He raised his eyebrows briefly and lowered them again. "Aye, well, 'tis possible. But I would swear that colt was born dead."

"She was, Da," Gwydion muttered, and then, more assuredly, "She was. I saw it."

"Aye, we saw it," Liam agreed. He touched the little one's head again, reassuring himself. When next he spoke, it was to Yeshua. "Well, perhaps I was wrong, perhaps I was not. But I think you had something to do with it, lad, and for that, I thank you. I thank you for both of their lives."

No more was said about the miracle but news of such a thing always gets out somehow. Liam told Niamh after dinner and Niamh told a friend the next day. That friend told someone else and within three days, the entire village had come by to see the miracle colt. As Toby had been, the village was divided as to the young man's role in the birth. Yeshua, however, became an apprentice to Declan because of the controversy. While Toby was playing "gentleman farmer," Yeshua was learning the arts of healing and herbs. Since he and Gwydion still took meals with the family, Toby only saw him then. The remainder of Yeshua's time was spent with Aiobh and Declan.

They also met at the instruction time when they gathered at the usual place. Toby was finding himself drawn into the classes. He liked Declan because of the man's easy way with his students but also because Declan was personable, an intelligent human. He had also been the son of a soldier before becoming an artist, working with metals and crystals. But there was so much Toby didn't know about him. Or Aiobh. He got his answers by the classes and also by talking to the other villagers.

Aiobh was the village's conscience and spiritual advisor. She was the one that was called for blessings, healing, birthing, and she conducted rituals. As the matriarch of the people, she was the busier of the two. She acted as advisor, counselor, and when necessary, mediator of issues and disputes. Hers was the first face seen at birth and the last face seen by the dying.

Declan, on the other hand, had achieved the role of village chieftain only by marrying the High Priestess. It was a role, however, that he was well suited for. Aiobh had married a man with a good head on his shoulders and a charming personality. Since the village pretty much ran itself, he tended their farm as well as taking on his role was as teacher to those who would learn of the Old Religion. He was their Archdruid, meaning that he was also the keeper of the law. When the occasion called for it, his cool thinking in a crisis also served him as War Councilor, but those situations were rare.

Declan poured the mugs of heather ale and brought a plate of warm biscuits that Aiobh had made. Toby and Yeshua were treated to butter and molasses on the bread, and they ate hearty and gave strong compliments to the cook.

"So, what do you know of your place in this life?"

Declan's question was fairly simple but Toby had to stop and think about it. He'd never pondered the question before. Life was life; you lived, you died, and you did what you needed to get through it. That was it. Sometimes life gave you hard knocks, sometimes it didn't. There were people who got off easy and the rest had to struggle every single day for a scrap of bread. The idea of questioning his existence and place in the world was a new concept. The answer just didn't come that easily.

So, again, Yeshua answered first. "The soul is born into this life to serve God. It is a hard life, true, but the reward is great. The Lord God created this earth to be Paradise. Because Adam and Eve sinned by eating from the Tree of Good and Evil, they were cast from Paradise and it was removed to Heaven. To achieve it, man must serve God."

"Hmm." Declan mused for a moment, then asked, "And the others? The animals? Trees? What of them?"

"All creatures were created for man, to serve his ends and ease his way into Heaven. Man was put here to rule and dominate the earth for God's gain."

Toby snorted into his mug, saying nothing more.

Yeshua turned his head, his brows knitted in confusion. "Tobias?"

Toby took the sip from the cup and set it back on the table. "I'm sorry, my friend, I did not mean to be rude. I just – well, do you realize what you're sayin'?"

Yeshua shook his head. "It sounds like a purpose to be here."

"It sounds like indentured servitude," Toby snapped. "You live only to serve God? That makes no sense. That's like sayin' that we were put here to serve a king and have no purpose other than that. And oh, by the way, the king will feed you, clothe you, and allow you to live in his palace but you're still here to serve his purpose. What kind of God is that?"

"The kind of God who loves you, Tobias," Yeshua explained, gently. "The kind of God who wants to care for you and cherish you, and asks only that you serve Him. He gave you this earth to rule and do with as you wish. Is that not a fair price to pay for such a kingdom?"

"Benevolent servitude is still servitude. And rulin' this planet is not fair compensation. So if God is the dominator of man, then man becomes dominator of the earth? That is not love; that's just fear and oppression."

Yeshua's face took on a look of genuine sorrow, his eyes hooded. "Perhaps I do not explain it as well as I should."

"No, you explain it quite well," Toby answered with disdain. He lifted the mug to his lips again. "That is the same teachin' I heard as child, the same stupid thinkin' that will ruin us all. If you don't have purpose of your own will, your life is wasted."

Declan drank his tea, sitting back in his chair and watching them over the top of the mug. He had not said a word; Toby surmised that the Priest had another motive in mind. He always did and it would come evident soon enough. He didn't disappoint, even now.

"Well, lad," Declan interrupted. "He does have a point. Tell me, Yeshua, do man and woman have free will?"

"Yes, Declan, they do. Man is always free to choose his path, but he would be happier with the path God has chosen for him."

"Aye and this path is to serve your God?"

"Yes, Declan, it is."

Declan lowered his mug, setting it on the table. He rested his elbows on either side of it, his chin on his fists. "And what does man gain besides conquering the earth and creatures?"

"He gains the Kingdom of God," Yeshua answered.

"And if he does not follow God's path?"

"He must be sent to the sorrows of Hell, Declan."

Toby shook his head and clapped his mug on the table with a loud thud. "And this is what he calls a benevolent God. You do as I say or you're cast into the fire and brimstone for eternity."

"No, Tobias," Yeshua raised his voice in protest to Toby's anger. "No, it is nothing of the sort. He is your Father and He cares for you, as any parent would. And any parent is to be obeyed until the child is old enough to understand right from wrong."

"It's still punishment, like sending you to bed without supper," Toby challenged, trying to keep hold of his temper. "Only it's eternity we're talking about, not a plate of neeps and beans. What father casts out his children into the nothin? What father turns his back on that child forever?"

Instead of anger, Yeshua looked confused at the questions. "A father in pain at the loss, Tobias."

"Well, your God can't be in that much pain if he can send them to hell and not bat an eye."

Declan raised his hands for them to stop. "Come, lads," Declan said, his voice soothing and quiet. He never raised it above an intimate speaking tone, forcing them to listen to hear and understand. "The question was to find out what you believed, not to spark off squabbling between you."

Toby closed his eyes for a few seconds, rubbing his face with his palms. He took a deep breath. "I'm sorry, Yeshua. I had no right to take it out on you that way. I did not mean to insult you."

"No insult taken, my friend." Yeshua relaxed as well. He was sincere but he still wore the look of confusion and sorrow.

"Good," Declan said, sounding pleased with the two for settling the discussion. "Now, let's go back to what you were saying, Yeshua. Man was put here to serve your God, aye?"

"Yes."

Declan sat back in his chair. "Well, at risk of settin' our friend off again, I must say that same thought crossed my mind. Do you really wish to impose your will over the creatures and the earth?"

"Yes, Declan, it is written in the Talmud. The Lord God created man in His own image and gave him the world to rule and all creatures in it. It was all created for man to enjoy and use as he will."

"Do you think 'tis easier to serve this God? Or that, perhaps, there is another way?" Declan crossed his arms over his chest.

"What other way could there be?" Yeshua asked, now appearing to be totally confused.

Declan turned his head to address Toby. "Tobias, you sound as if you've followed this path of Yeshua's. If you'll help me understand, why do you get so upset about his way of thinkin'?"

It was Toby's turn to sit back. He folded his hands together, resting them on the table. "I watched people I loved die in the most painful way. When I asked for an answer, all I heard was how it was God's will and God's plan, and I needed to accept it like a good boy because that's just how things are. I was told that I should never question. If you question, you go to hell. If you don't do as you're told, you go to hell. If you don't agree with what the preach—." He stopped suddenly, looking up at the intent faces watching him. "What the *rabbi* says, you go to hell." He looked back down at his hands again.

"Aye," Declan replied. "That'll be a hard answer to accept. But, let me ask you this – do you ever wonder if maybe it'll not be God's will but your own that sends you to this Hell?"

Toby glanced up sharply. "What do you mean? How so?"

"Have you never watched the spider as she spins her web? Oh, it'll be a marvel to watch for she spins her whole world in it. She finds the right place and then she weaves the fragile threads until they all connect to form the web. When her prey comes in it, she knows and come to spin the trap for it. And her children live in it, for she creates the place where they are born and grow. If you cut one thread of it, the whole falls apart."

Yeshua's face brightened. "And God is the spider, creating the web."

Declan smiled at his protégé. "You catch it aright, lad. God, Goddess, the One – She is the spider that creates the web, the world we live in. We are the children, and this earth is the web. It'll all be part of the whole. You see, we are not the creators; we do not own it. The Mother owns Herself. We are just the caretakers who make it our homes for the short time we're here."

"The web of life is so fragile, lads, that the needless takin' of one creature upsets the balance. We're all important to each other, every one of us. If one hurts, we all hurt because we are joined in the web. If you lose the grass, the cattle cannot survive, and they who eat the cattle cannot survive. Those who re-seed the grass are no longer there to pass along the seeds. One thread cut is the loss of the whole web."

"I understand," Toby said, the light dawning on him. "It'll be like the ground. If you take the nourishment for the plants, they'll not grow. If they don't grow, we cannot eat and we die. And then there's no on left to replenish the ground. All die, all are without."

"But, I don't understand something," Yeshua said. "If all creatures are connected and we all have a purpose, what is that purpose?"

"Life is the perfection of the soul, lad. And its own teacher. You come here to learn the lessons of the journey. Tobias, you spoke of hardship, but why do you think such hardship was placed in your life?"

Toby shook his head.

"You speak of hard times, of questions unanswered. If you don't have the bad times, how can you truly appreciate the good? And if in those times, you cannot find the answer, perhaps you were asking the wrong questions."

Wrong questions? he asked himself. *Have I been doing that?*

"To serve the Gods is a good vocation," Declan continued, "but 'tis not a callin' for all. To care for the land, for each other, and to learn of the mysteries of the Gods is to learn to be free and truly holy."

"You're saying that God doesn't allow the suffering, we do," Toby mused. It wasn't until Declan whispered his answer that Toby realized he'd spoken it aloud.

"That's to say we do, my friend. Some of it is just not caring about those around you, not taking care of each other. Seeing another in pain and doing naught for it. Seeing another in need and not stopping to help. That sort of suffering can be stopped and when you don't, it creates an imbalance in all."

"And the other?" Yeshua asked.

"Well that'll be the suffering that comes from the lessons we learn in our days here in this life. Tobias, you said you lost some to painful deaths."

"I did," he answered, clutching the mug tight in his grip.

"It's possible that these folks chose the death to pay a debt to another. It could be that they owed it in a past life, you see, and this was their way of paying it off."

He wanted to tell Declan that the debt had been his, not Bion's and certainly not his parents'. He looked down at the ring on his hand. Three gifts paid for with three deaths. Instead, he asked, "Do we choose this suffering?"

"Aye, we do. We choose this life we come to, lad. And when we come back to the next one, this life will be a lesson for it. You may choose to come back as man. You may choose to come back as woman. You may even choose to come back as tree or stone or bird. It'll all be the same; 'tis all learnin'."

Yeshua sat with a thoughtful expression on his face, as if running the concepts through his mind. He broke his own silence, finally. "And so, is man no better than the beasts of the field?"

Declan smiled at him. "We are the same, creatures of this world; no better and no worse than the least of us or the greatest of us. All creations have a spirit and a will, and we all have a place in the web. We find that place and care for the others, and that gives us purpose."

"But what about those who sin, Declan?" Yeshua raised his chin, the serious tone in his voice almost challenging.

"I remember you saying that sin was being separated from your God, aye?"

Yeshua nodded.

"And you said sinning would send your soul to this Hell of yours, aye?"

Again, Yeshua nodded.

This time, Declan nodded with him. "Well then, let me ask you this; is there a way out of this Hell you speak of? Or are you there forever?"

"Declan, it is not just a place for the eternally damned," Yeshua protested. "It is also where the dead go to sleep until God calls the faithful to Heaven for the final judgment."

"Ah, I see," Declan said. "No one is ever separated from the Gods; we come from them and they live in our hearts. They are part of us. And no one is damned in his own heart unless he damns himself." He patted Toby's arm. "No one goes to Annwn for asking questions about the way things are. No one is sent there because that is the way of things."

"What is it then?" Toby asked?

"It is the glorious home of the departed. Those who have done well and have learned the lessons go there to rest and rejuvenate, visit with the ancestors or loved ones that have gone on before. Those who have not learned come back to be born again, to pay for their mistakes."

Yeshua chewed on his bottom lip, frowning while he thought about this. "And, how do we do that? Learn, I mean."

"You've come to a good question, Yeshua," Declan answered. "We learn Her mysteries by performing her Rites. We'll talk about those when next we meet, but one coming soon might help you understand. We come to the feast of *Alban Eilir*. It is the beginning of spring. It is also the time when we bring the seeds out and bless them. We bless the land that they grow in. Alban Eilir is a festival of fertility when we welcome the return of the growing season, the warmth, and we ask for good harvest and growth."

"Is it just about the land?" Toby asked.

"No, Tobias, 'tis not." Declan leaned forward again, mug in hand. "You see, the seeds in a man need blessin' too. You have those seeds in you, lad. Yeshua, you have *your* seeds of growin' and beginnin'. Alban Eilir is the Festival of blessing for all of the seeds, especially the ones in your heart."

Was that what he was doing? Planting seeds of growing? Toby knew he was changing inside but growing? He began to focus on himself, look into his own heart. He saw there a man who had been crying in the darkness, searching for something to believe in. He wasn't here to debunk a myth. He'd come to find himself. He looked in his own heart and saw a field, lying fallow. He could either plant it or not.

But, what seeds did he have to grow in this field? He had lost so much, and the ground had become stony. It was too hard to try that plow. Or was it? The seeds... *The seeds in a man need growing,* Declan had said. *What seeds? What seeds do I grow here?*

He closed his eyes and immediately saw Siobhan's face, saw her standing in the field. She was smiling and throwing something to the wind. The seeds of a new life and he knew exactly what he wanted to plant in this field. He had let go of his past at Yule, had the tools of his new trade blessed at Brighid. He would now plant the field with his hopes and dreams; his hope of a new life with Siobhan and children of his own, of happiness that he'd never had before and could never find in that old life.

Toby picked at the mug in his hand, staring at it. "Declan, you said there were no damnation except in your heart. Is there also redemption in your heart, too?"

There was a kindness that washed over the High Priest's face and settled in his eyes. Toby saw it there and knew the answer.

"Aye," Declan told him, "you give yourself the redemption. If you can't forgive yourself, there is no forgiveness anywhere. It'll be in the web of life and ourselves. It is in the love you give to others and the love they give to you."

"And knowing how to speak to God." Yeshua spoke quietly, his hushed tone capturing the focus again. "The seeds also include the divine seeds within you, Tobias. I see that now. To love another as you would have him love you."

"Aye, the Threefold Law," Declan answered.

"I understand," Toby said. "I know my place. I know now that I can accept it and grow with it."

"Excellent," Declan replied. "And we'll call the lesson over for now. I've my own seeds to be workin' on as well. Yeshua, you'll be helpin', aye?"

Toby left for his cottage to take stock in what was left in the here and now. He resolved to have his purpose here, the vision of Siobhan and home. He wanted this life, and this love, and he would have friends and family. The past (future?) was gone now. His soul was at peace, a peace of his own making.

He was still reveling in this new perspective when Gwydion stopped by. Toby invited his friend to stay and they sat outside, drinking a bit of the heather ale Liam had shared with them.

"Well, sounds as if you had a bit of light come into you, lad," Gwy said.

Toby sat on the step and watched a rabbit hop across the field in front of him. Soon, that field would be full of plants. He hoped bunnies didn't eat much.

"Aye, Gwydion, I do believe it did." He raised his mug, a toast to his friend, and drank. "You know, until today, I never knew where I belonged. Talking to Declan, I know now that it's here."

Gwydion drank the toast with him, belching happily. "You finally figured it out, did you?"

"I been wondering, Gwydion, why did you leave to begin with?"

Gwydion propped one foot on the stump and leaned back against the rough bark of the tree. "Well, Tobias, if you must know, I was foolish when I was young man. I wanted to see the world and I thought there was more to it than here."

"Was there?"

Gwydion smiled, picking at a seam in his trews. "I thought there was. I wanted to seek my fortune, sure that gold and riches would please me and I was off to gain 'em. It was not what I found there in the big world."

"What did you find?"

"I found the terrible cruelty of man, Tobias. I found slavery and poverty that no man should ever know. The only gold and fortune I found was in someone else's hands and was not mine for the takin'. In the end, I found that if 'tis not here in my own home, it'll be nowhere on this earth."

Gwydion turned his gaze back to Toby, who returned his smile. Something in the story suddenly clicked and he remembered a long ago parable that Maeve used to quote quite often.

"What are ye chewing on?" Gwydion asked him.

"Oh, nothing, my friend. It was a thought, something Yeshua might be interested in knowing."

"I told him my story not too long after we come home," Gwydion said. "He asked me and I told him."

"Did he say anything about it?"

Gwydion gave a quiet laugh, and said, "Aye, he called me the prodigal son."

The seeds in a man need blessin' too.

So, Toby gathered with the others in the ring of stones. He donned his robe and necklaces, and went with his lady to stand for the ceremony. The seeds of his heart and of his field would be blessed. The seeds of his marriage with Siobhan would grow and bloom into the seeds of his children and his lineage.

They had all brought a small packet, wrapped in cloth and tied with ribbons or leather. Toby had brought one as well, provided by Liam, and he had proudly placed it with the others. The packets dressed the altar, along with the ritual broom and staff. The altar had been dressed with ribbons and brightly colored pieces of cloth. All the colors possible and the ribbons draped down over the sides of the altar, spilling like the colors of the rainbow.

"We come to bless the seeds of tomorrow's growing, the ground which will nourish them." Aiobh stood behind the altar with her arms outstretched over it, facing the circle. "This day, the light and dark are equal. This day, the blessing of tomorrow is within us all."

The High Priestess gathered the seed packages in her arms and carried them to the center of the circle. A large cauldron had been placed there and she tossed the bundles inside of it. When every bundle resided in the black metal object, Aiobh turned to walk around the circle.

"The Dagda chose as one of his symbols, the cauldron. It is the Cauldron of Plenty. All who were served by it never went home hungry. It cannot be emptied and all are welcome to take from it. It was His gift to the Children of Dana, the symbol of prosperity for all who ask it."

When she had walked the circle, Aiobh came back to the cauldron in the center. She turned her palms down over the opening and raised her face to the sky, "Mother Dana, we do call upon You to bless these seeds. We ask that they be fertile and grow strong. We do ask You to smile upon them, kiss them. Let them feed Your children with the bounty."

She drew a circle over the cauldron with her finger and continued, "Father Dagda, we do call upon You to bless these seeds. We ask that they represent Your never empty cauldron. We ask that you fertilize them and make them strong with your energy."

She drew another circle over the seeds, and held her arms outstretched.

"In celebration of the seeds that grow, come to the Dagda's Cauldron. Take with you the seeds of tomorrow's harvest. Take the road of your own beginnin'. For soon, we plant and soon, they grow."

For soon, we plant and soon, they grow. He would be ready.

Chapter Twenty-One

Aiobh's kitchen smelled full of fresh air, bread, cookies, and heather ale; Toby had never smelled anything so sweet in his life.

As soon as it had been warm enough to do so, every cottage had thrown open the doors to allow the breezes to blow through unimpeded. Spring had arrived right on time, according to Gwydion, and with it had come the first thistles, marsh violets, and meadowsweets, popping through the greening grass. The countryside was returning to the emerald glory that had given Ireland its name. The first buds peeked out from the dark browns and greys of the tree limbs, and finding it to their taste, had erupted into the fullness of coming blooms. The first robins had found suitable trees and eaves and were busy building nests for the coming season. Soon enough, the meadows would be ablaze with colors and the entire village waited with anticipation.

"It's different," Toby answered. "It's like nothing I've ever known. It just amazes me that I'm part of it."

Declan topped off their mugs, adding a plate of toasted bread to the bounty of cookies and slices of cake already on the table. "What differences are you seeing, Tobias?"

"I never thought of worshipping a Goddess, it's just not something we do where I'm from. This is a new thing for me. And worship on the phases of the moon? The special days of the seasons? The sort of thing that could get you burned at the stake." Toby looked at Declan from the corner of his eye but there was no reaction to that. Evidently that sort of thing was either unheard of or not that big a concern in this time. He went on. "You speak to tree and flower and animal like they were your friends and you worship the spirits in 'em."

Declan turned to the other person sitting at the table and asked, "And you, Yeshua?"

"As much as Tobias has said." Yeshua furrowed his brow. "It's more though. I've noticed that nature is very important to you, as a partner, as your Gods. You consult the very ground instead of taking dominion over it. I've seen how the seasons play a part in the rituals you hold. You do not have Sabbat at set times."

Declan held up one finger to interrupt. "And what is that...*Sabbat*?"

"It is the holy day of the week," Yeshua explained. "It is written that the Lord God created the heaven and earth in six days; and on the seventh, He rested. He called it a holy day."

"Aye and so you have ritual every seventh day?"

"Yes, Declan, we do."

Declan nodded his understanding. "If you do your magick every day, you do well. If you do it with the Gods' blessing, you have power. Do you not see, lads, life is magick; life is creation."

Declan held out his left hand, nestled in his palm were several small seeds. He touched the forefinger of his other hand to the seeds. "These were blessed at Alban Eilir, and 'tis come time to plant 'em."

He looked back up at his audience, and with the same forefinger, pointed to his heart. "And here are the seeds that were blessed, too. 'Tis time to grow them as well."

"How?" said Toby. "Liam showed me how to plant the seeds in the ground. But, how do you plant the seeds of your heart?"

"Same way, Tobias. First, you bless the soil and then you sow the seeds. Inch by inch, row by row, planting good seeds and seeing what crops will come from them. 'Tis Beltane and time to bless the soil of your heart, too. You'll see on the morrow at the ritual."

Toby smiled back. "Aye, I'm sure of it."

Declan nodded. "If you're of a mind, I need to speak with you, Tobias. Yeshua, would you go help Aiobh get things ready for the Beltane rite. She'll tell you what she needs gathered. She'll be grateful for the help."

The young man nodded knowingly at them and left. Toby turned his attention turned back to Declan, who waited until they were completely alone.

Declan turned in his chair until he was facing Toby. He rested on arm on the table, leaning on the elbow. "Tobias, 'tis a great favor I'll be askin' you, on behalf of Aiobh and the rest o' the village. If you've a mind to it, of course."

Toby grinned and folded his hands together on the table. He was so accustomed to Declan's gentle way of persuasion now that he found it quite amusing. "Of course, Declan, you've but to ask, you know that."

"Aye, but this will be a special favor of the High Priestess, you see. And no small feat will it be, too. If you feel the least bit uncomfortable, you've but to say so and we'll pass it on to someone else."

Toby was stunned into silence. For him to say this added a certain gravity to it and for a moment, he wasn't sure about any of it at all. Uncomfortable? What the hell could he possibly be asked to do that would make him feel uncomfortable? Well, there was only one way to find out. "Of course. Go on, then, Declan."

"See, this would normally be asked of someone who's been in the Circle longer than you have. But Aiobh feels that you're ready for such a responsibility."

"Aiobh does? Do you? I mean, if you both think I'm ready for it, of course I'll do it. You have but to ask and I'll be honored to assist in the rite."

Declan smiled at him, looking decidedly smug. "Aye, I knew it." He sobered again and straightened up in his chair. He never broke the gaze he held his listener to; he cleared his throat and went on. "Tobias, we'll be needin' someone to represent the God on the morrow at Beltane. Aiobh is of a mind you would do perfectly."

Toby's brow raised and he cocked his head to one side. *Represent the God? What does that mean?* "Oh?"

"Well, to speak true, lad, I do feel the same about your readiness. I know you can do it. You see, Aiobh will tell the legend to the gathered and then, she'll call down the God into you for the Great Rite. What you do will bless the fields before we begin to plant."

Toby sat and listened to Declan as he explained the role in the ritual. Declan was honest and held nothing back in the explanation. Toby's eyes got wider and wider with each passing moment. But when Declan finished, he had only one question.

"And who will be acting as the Goddess?"

Declan acted as if he had been expecting that question and merely shook his head. "That'll not be for you to know that, lad. As far as any are to know, it'll be the Goddess that you'll be with on the morrow. And you will be the God. Do you understand it?"

Toby inhaled sharply. *The God; I'll be the God.* He furrowed his brow trying to understand that much. With a sigh, he nodded. "I understand."

"Are you having second thoughts?" Declan asked. "If you do,

speak now. There's no shame to pass this by. 'Tis great responsibility to all to do this."

Toby opened his mouth, drawing in a breath before speaking, but Declan held up a hand to stop him. Instead, he answered his own question.

"No, lad, I need you to consider this," Declan broke in. "You're right, 'tis too big a responsibility for you to answer now. Take a bit to think on it. But I do need answer by tomorrow morn, lest you care not to do it. I'll need time to get another in your place."

Toby looked down at his hands for a moment. It wasn't that great a task. It was for the village, and they weren't asking him to commit murder. His mind briefly flashed to Siobhan and what she might say. He reached out and took Declan's arm.

"No, my High Priest, you'll get your answer now. You honor me greatly and I will do it. This village has given me so much and now it is time for me to give back to all of you. I'll do it."

Declan patted the hand on his arm. "Do it for yourself, Tobias. Do it for the crops and the village welfare, not for gratitude."

Toby lifted one shoulder and cocked his head sideways. "It'll all be the same, aye?"

Declan nodded, laughing as he answered. "Aye, Tobias. That it is."

Declan explained to him that he had to keep silent on his role and Toby agreed to do so. He couldn't talk it over with anyone, because he'd promised to keep the anonymity of the rite.

But he needed to talk it over with someone. This was...well, it was pagan, all right. But there was enough of that old Puritanical ethic in his soul to start fighting the decision he'd made. What the hell was he thinking that he could do this? And what about Siobhan? How would this affect his relationship with her? Ok, maybe no one was supposed to know, but *he* would know. He'd always know in his heart.

He sat under the small apple tree he'd planted, thinking and thinking, until he missed supper. He was so lost in his thoughts that it took two whistles for Gwydion to get through his reverie. Gwydion was standing a few paces from him with a plate in his hand and mock indignation on his face.

"I'd offer coin for your thoughts but the look on your face tells me 'tis a price I can't afford. Ma sent me with a plate for you."

Toby shook it off and reached for the proffered plate, his appetite suddenly returned. "Sorry, my friend. Aye, there's something on my mind. Thank your Ma for the plate. I am that hungry. And tell her I apologize for missing dinner."

Gwydion pointed to the extra chair. "Might I join you? I'll wait and take your empty plate back or Ma'll skin m' hide."

Toby chortled, nodding to his friend. "Rest a spell, Gwy."

Toby tore into the plate of lamb and what appeared to be hoecakes of corn flour. Either way, it settled the beast in his belly and he polished off every bite of it. Gwydion helped himself to the jug of ale and just waited until Toby had finished his food before asking his friend what he'd been so focused on.

Toby set the plate down on the floorboards and reached for his own mug. "Oh, I'm not supposed to talk of it. But, 'tis you, my friend, and if I can't tell you, who can I trust?"

"Ah, I see. It's like that, is it?"

Toby jerked his head up but said nothing.

Gwydion took another sip from the jug. "No, you can't tell. But, I've a mind of it. You're having second thoughts, are you?"

"You know?"

"I know what season it is, my friend. And I know the rite. Aye, I can make a good guess and I'm betting I'm right." Gwydion leaned back against the wall behind him, watching his friend. "So. Second thoughts?"

"I am, Gwy," Toby confessed. "I am."

"Will it help you to know that none will be watchin' you? 'Tis a sacred thing and you'll be in the field alone. Once the Great Rite begins, all of us will leave you to it. And remember, 'tis not yourself doin' this, 'tis the God."

Toby took a deep draught from the ale and replied, "That is not my problem, Gwy. Declan explained it to me. If that was the only concern, I'd have no problem with it."

"Ah, you're worrying about Siobhan."

"Aye. I truly am a different person, now. The old Tobias would've done it without question or remorse. I will not hurt her. *This* Tobias loves her with all his heart and soul."

'Even knowin' that Tobias isn't the one performing the rite?"

"Would you do it if it were you and Deirdre?"

Gwydion crossed his arms over his chest and rested his head

against the wall. He took his time watching the sun going down before he answered. "Aye, I would. It would not be me, you see." He held up the jug he'd been drinking from, and said, "It would not be me any more than this jug is the ale. And any of us would do, Tobias, for what it means to us all."

"It's an honor, I know."

Gwydion picked up the plate at Toby's side, rising out of the chair. He stopped a few paces away, not looking away from the glorious sunset in the making. "I'll tell you true, Tobias, 'tis a great thing you'd be doing. If it means anything, it's what I believe. The lady would do same, you know. But," he added with a small shrug. "It'll be your decision. Think on it and remember that."

Toby did think; he thought right up until the time he arrived at the barn. He thought about it through the discussion with Aiobh, and he was still thinking when Declan led him into the circle and to the left side of the altar. His mind raced through the calling of the Quarters, and the Goddess and God. His attention was pulled back to the rite when Aiobh crossed down to stand between the two fires.

"Fire cleanses all things, leavin' them new again," she said. "This is the day of purification and blessin', for fertility for the new season."

All day, the twin fires had raged, and every animal in the village had been passed between them. It had taken the entire day, but the fires had blessed every animal of every family, including the various household cats and dogs. Then the fires had been allowed to burn down to a reasonable blaze for there was one more rite to complete.

"Come, now," Aiobh continued, "and jump the Beltane fires. Come for the blessin'."

Toby stood quietly by the altar; the mask covering his face gave him a small amount of vision. He watched them gather at one end of the field before, one by one, they ran. Two by two, every man, woman, and able child jumped over the fire, laughing merrily. To jump the fire was to assure a season of prosperity. In some cases, they believed that a woman jumping the fire would become pregnant.

He searched every face for Siobhan's. He knew she'd helped her father lead the livestock through the fires earlier, but he wasn't able to find her now. He was going to go through with this and hoped she'd understand. Sure she would; she'd even tell him to do it.

Wouldn't she?

He was sweating under the mask and robe, but not because of the fire. He was also wearing a leather tunic that came to the middle of his thigh, and nothing else underneath that. His hood had been pulled up over his head until it touched the mask of leather. Between the nerves and the leather, he was hotter than hell, which was about where he was expecting to be damned.

As he watched the last of them jump the fires and run, laughing, around the circle, he felt that fear jump in his belly and he knew he couldn't do it. He was too much of a "one woman man" to even consider this any longer. He knew he could go through the mechanics of it all, but he also knew his heart wouldn't be in it. *And, let's just say the performance level will not be there, either.*

So, he stood there, thinking of how he was going to get a message to Declan, when Aiobh crossed to the right side of the altar and held her hand out. It was only then, that he realized there was a figure standing there as well. The figure was dressed the same as he was, with one exception; it was decidedly female. *It's my choice to do this symbolically. That's it; I'll just do it symbolically. I can do that.*

Aiobh helped the woman kneel before the altar and placed her hands on the woman's bowed head. The High Priestess raised her face to the darkened sky above her and began to speak.

"I do call Thee, Brighid, in thy guise as Maiden, to come into this daughter. For the time to bless the fields and bring forth the Mother aspect is here. I do ask Thee bless this land; bless this earth with Thy energy and seed. So mote it be."

Aiobh helped the woman up from her kneeling place and led her around the circle. The gathered muttered blessings as the duo passed until they had come back to the altar. As the Priestess started to lead her charge down to the bonfire, Toby suddenly caught a whiff of a fragrance. *No! It can't be. But, it is.*

Before he could follow the thought any further, he was led to the same place, and helped to kneel. Declan invoked the God, Lugh, to come into him, to fertilize the seeds and bless the field. As Declan walked him around the circle, each step seemed to electrify him. Every nerve ending was tingling and he couldn't help but look towards the center, between the blazes, to the woman waiting for him.

With Declan's help, he crossed down and stood before her. With her head bowed, all he could see was her mouth, the ripeness of her lips. A smile played on those lips, the ones he had tasted so many times. The smell of lavender was so strong now. Declan helped remove the robe from his body and he stood in the leather tunic and mask.

A blade was placed in his hands, and he looked down at it. A black handled, two-edged knife gleamed and he took the hilt in both hands.

Aiobh had helped her off with her robe, as well and the lady stood with a chalice in her hands. She held it out to him and in the voice that waited in his dreams each night, she spoke to him.

"As the chalice is to the female...."

He stepped forward, and plunged the knife into the liquid in the chalice, "So the athamé is to the male...."

"So that none is above the other...."

"But are equal to each other."

Toby traced the pentacle inside the contents of the glass, and then a circle around the rim, going in clockwise fashion. He held out the blade and it was removed from his hand. The cup was offered to him, the two soft hands never leaving it, and he drank from it. She placed a soft kiss on his lips, and then took her turn at the chalice. The next kiss was lingering, and deep.

Toby tasted the wine on her tongue as he melted into her arms. He never noticed the chalice being removed from her grasp nor did they notice when the villagers melted into the darkness. All he knew was that he was here, with her, with his Siobhan. Every part of his body was aching for her.

The tunic she wore was easy to remove, the lacing at her shoulders pulled away and the leather fell to the ground. He pulled her tighter to his body, and he felt her lips curve into another smile as she kissed him. He was as hard as a rock where her hand had followed down between his legs. She stroked him gently, in even rhythm, while her other hand pulled at the binding of his own tunic. It, too, fell to the ground and he lifted her in his arms. He gently laid her down on the leather blanket made from the garments.

Her hands came up to her hair where she loosed the copper strands from the braid and ran her fingers through the tresses, fanning them across the ground. His lips found hers again and he kissed her face, her lips, her cheeks, and her eyes. He followed the curve of her brow bone to the cheek beside her ear, down to the hollow of her throat. Every kiss brought a soft sigh, her fingers working restlessly in his hair.

Her breasts were like two ripe peaches and her nipples were hard in response to his kisses. He took each, in turn, into his mouth and suckled them. He kissed them, and held them, cradling them in his palms, running one thumb over a nipple while his mouth gave pleasure to the other one.

He kissed his way to her navel, taking his time as he ran his tongue in the crevices of her hips, above the leg. She spoke only once, when he had kissed down between her thighs, and that was in her confusion at what he was doing. He silenced her question by teasing at her hardness with his tongue and lips. She arched her back until it had come off the ground. He continued, tasting the sweetness that was running from her like the juices of the ripe berries. She moaned, her fingers gripping his shoulders until she had to let go to keep from hurting him in her pleasure. She buried them in the grass beneath her instead and her breathing became labored.

Toby brought her to the brink, let her relax, and then brought her a second time and a third. Before he could bring her there a fourth time, she sat up, and took his face in her hands, bringing it up to kiss his lips. He dutifully lay back and she took her place between his thighs. Again, she took him into her hand to wrap around his cock but she he lowered her head and began to lick it. She gently squeezed at the base of it while suckling the head, teasing with her tongue.

Just when he thought he could take no more, she lowered down to his hips, down over his throbbing member and guided it inside of her warmth. Together, they moved in unison, pumping in time to the heartbeat he felt inside of him. She stayed atop him for some time, before he pulled her down to him and rolled them both over. The tempo of their lovemaking pulsed faster as the heat from the dying fires raised the sweat on them both. Her fingers clutched at his back and he buried his face in her hair, whispering her name over and over.

When he finally released, he collapsed against her smooth skin. Her arms came around him, stroking his back. He could do no more than lay against her shoulder, breathing heavily into the sweet smell of her hair. He tried to move, to roll off of her, but her arms and legs came round him and she whispered, "no, stay" against his neck. He stayed inside of her, basking in the warmth of her love and the twin fires beside them. He stayed inside of her until the thought of her aroused him again.

He made love to her there between the dying blazes a second time. Where the first had mirrored the frenzied passion they'd held back for so long, the second time held the sweetness of their love. The flow of her hips and his thrusting was slower, gentler. He couldn't stop kissing and tasting her sweet lips. When his orgasm filled him this time, he felt their souls merge and mesh. The electricity of the evening flowed from his body and dissipated into the ground below them.

He fell asleep in her arms, cradled there against her breasts. Sometime, in the wee hours of the morning, he awoke to find that the fires had completely burned out and that she had gone. He lay there, for several minutes, tasting the dew on his skin, before retrieving the tunic and mask. He wrapped his robe around his waist – not that it mattered but he had to do something – and he walked back to his cottage. He threw himself on the bed and drifted back off again. He dreamed of her; the taste of her, the feel of her, the warmth of her.

The moment his eyes opened next morning, he knew he had to see her. He *needed* to see her, talk to her. *No, wait, it wasn't me last night, it was Lugh…inside of me…right.* The moment the thought popped into his head, he knew it was a load of crap. Brendan raised him better than that and Maeve would fair skin him alive. He was a gentleman, and he was going to act as a gentleman. He was going to see the lady and ask for her hand in marriage. It was time. It turned out *not* to be time. Life had other plans.

Toby's first visitor was Yeshua, who arrived with his packed bag over his shoulder. Toby invited him to sit and have a cup of cider.

Yeshua thanked him and sat down at the table. "I can't stay long, my friend, but I wanted to stop by before I left."

Toby stopped in mid-pour and gave his friend a puzzled look. "Left? What do you mean 'left'? Are you *leaving?*"

Yeshua chuckled, showing white teeth inside of the well tanned face. "Just for a few days, Tobias. I'm not leaving permanently; well, not yet. Aiobh and I discussed my traveling around Ir for a time. I told her that I wanted to see others, meet others who believed as they did. She and Declan agreed it is a good thing."

Toby set the mug in front of his guest, along with a plate of thick bread slices covered in some jam that he'd made from the apples in his root cellar. Yeshua thanked him and tucked into the food.

Toby sat down with his own breakfast but couldn't eat it. "Where will you go, my friend?"

Yeshua took a tentative sip of ale to swallow the bite. "I shall be going north. Declan has said there are several villages to the north of us and I would see them there. Declan has asked me to get news from them, and perhaps a trade between our villages of some goods."

"And to teach of the God of Israel," Toby said, smiling.

"Yes, my friend." Yeshua beamed at his friend. "It is time to learn and teach of my Father's ways to these people."

"Well, don't be too strident," Toby advised. "They have had their ways for centuries, my friend."

The young man gazed into his mug with a faint look of amusement on his lips. "You still see that child, don't you." When he raised his eyes, it was easy to see that the arrogant child was truly gone. The Savior was birthing. "I am coming to find that we are all on the same path, Tobias. We simply call it by another name."

Toby cupped his hands around his mug, watching the young man. "But it's not your path?"

"It is not. But I have learned one thing, my friend."

"What's that?"

"That the message I bring is not to force them to follow the one true God, but to offer the choice. And accept their beliefs as being holy to them." He lifted one corner of his mouth in a small smile. "Perhaps they will not come to the heaven of my Father, perhaps He will embrace them as His children anyway."

"Perhaps," Toby said. "Is that so wrong?"

Yeshua reached out and touched Toby's arm, giving a gentle squeeze. "I have given great thought to that very question, my friend. I think that the answer lies not in how you follow the path, but that you follow it. My Father has shown me that there has been too much hatred in this world. I will have none of it. I come to bring a new world, a new peace. I come to bring love for all." He squeezed again before returning to the mug in front of him. "No, it is not so wrong."

Toby returned the smile, nodding. He liked this young man, this new Yeshua ben Yusef. The child had changed, had grown to be the man that he'd always heard about. Maybe there was hope after all. "So, tell me. How long will you be gone?"

"I don't know. Perhaps a few days, perhaps a moon. But, I will return." Yeshua stood up and reached out to grasp Toby's arm. "Be well, my friend, and I shall see you again shortly. I will not leave this land without telling you. Or taking you with me."

Toby clapped the young man's shoulder, "Well, we can talk about that part later. Come and let me walk you to the village gate, at least. I can see you off on your journey. I must return these garments to Declan."

Liam met them at the gate and announced that Tobias was needed to start the plowing. The full moon was three nights hence and they needed to take advantage of the energy by seeding the field. Toby bid Yeshua safe journey, as did Liam, and the young man strode off. Any further thought of the previous night's events and seeing Siobhan were forgotten.

Liam was one of the wealthier men in the village. His lands, accumulated by himself and his family, covered at least fifteen acres from what Toby could see. Gwydion explained to him that they had several fields to make ready by tilling the earth, removing rocks and debris, and minor repairs on the fences surrounding the animal paddocks. Once the ground was ready, they could sow the seed.

Toby and Gwydion hitched up the two horses and started cultivating the soil, revealing the richness underneath the clover. For seven days, he followed behind the animal, working with an extraordinary piece of equipment. The tool he pushed was different, shaped with a curved blade. It cut through the soil, turning it over, and a raking tool behind it mixed that soil further. The finished product lay behind him in rows, and a slap of the horse's rear started another row. Any stones he found were piled up, and removed by barrow once the field had been tilled. Liam took care of removing the rocks and breaking up any large clods of earth. The three of them worked solid for the week.

Every morning, he started at first light and every evening, he came home exhausted, every muscle screaming in agony. He would take a bath of sorts and then fall asleep, wishing he'd had some sort of liniment. He slept, dreaming of her, and in his dreams, he reached for her. He would wake the next morning, resolved to see her that day, and would proceed with the same routine, exhausted sleep, and more dreams. Seven days of longing, aching, and wet dreams, and nothing resolved.

After all the fields had been tilled, Liam took him to the seed barn and they plotted out the crops. Seven more days were spent following a horse's behind, pulling the hoe, creating the furrow. Liam made sure he followed against the curvature of the land instead of with it. Where there was a mild swell, the rows were horizontal to it. This kept the soil from running down in the rain, and being lost in erosion. He guided the horse, and dug the furrows. Liam followed behind, sowing the seeds. Gwydion would follow behind him, adding mixtures of cow manure and compost, covering it all with the soil.

The last field planted, they celebrated with a good jug of heather ale, and patted themselves on the back for a job well done. It was now a matter of time and gentle rains before they would know if the planting was successful. Then, it was just a matter of more time before seeing what the crops would bring.

Gwydion took a long pull from his mug. "Well, it was a good day."

"Aye, son," Liam answered.

"Then, I suppose 'tis time to tell you."

Niamh, standing within earshot, came out of the cottage. "And 'tis time for what?"

"I'll be leaving your home, Ma."

Her face was a study in disappointment that she was trying to hide, fighting the tears. "You'll be off to the world again, aye?" she asked as stoically as she could.

Gwydion took his mother's hand and kissed the back of it. He patted it, as he spoke. "No, Màthair, I've seen enough of the world. I've asked for Deirdre's hand and her Da has given his blessin'. We'll be handfast at Litha."

Niamh's eyes grew as wide as her saucers and Liam's resounding shout of joy echoed off a nearby hill. Between the tears and the shouts, Liam brought out his best jug of whiskey to share between them. Anyone who happened to be passing by was invited up to have a drink to the family's good fortune. Before too long, it was a party and the drinking and singing was going on in earnest.

Toby shared a mug of ale and a cup of the whiskey, toasting his friend, and then begged off for the rest of the evening. He was exhausted and all he wanted was to take a good hot bath before dropping his sore body between the linens and the tick. As he made his way down the path to his home, he felt the twinge of guilt for not having gone to her. It had to be soon. *Tomorrow...tomorrow will be fine.*

The sun was now well behind the trees and there was a sunset of great proportions. The sky was ablaze with gold and red and orange. Toby got to his gate and just stood there for a few minutes, gazing at the beauty. *Had it always been that way? How had he never seen it before?* He was lost in it, drinking it in, when a hand covered his, startling him out of his reverie. He jerked his attention down before looking up into the lovely green eyes.

"I've been missin' you, Tobias," she said, simply.

The twinge turned into a sharp stab and he felt the flush on his cheeks. Maybe she couldn't see it in the gloaming but he felt it. "Oh, lady," he breathed out before finding his voice again. "I do owe you an apology. I should have been to see you long before this. I am so sorry! It was just the plowing and seeding and—"

She laid her fingers against his lips, cutting off the rest of what he had to say. "I know. The planting season was on us all. I was doing the same." She got wistful as she asked, "Did you think of me? Even just a wee bit?"

He took the hand in his and kissed the fingertips. "Only every waking moment I had. And when I slept, I dreamed of you, lady."

He walked through the gate, letting it close behind him. She wrapped her arms around his neck, pressing her lips to his. Any thought he had of bed and sleep and baths disappeared leaving only her smell of lavender in his head. She wantonly danced her fingers down his chest, his stomach, and pressed against his crotch. He moaned into her mouth.

He broke the kiss abruptly, stopping her hand before he did something he knew he'd regret. "Lady, unless you plan on a repeat performance, you'd best stop that. I'm sore in need of a bath right now."

"And how do you know I'm not wanting a repeat performance?" she teased him. "Might be that's what I came for. If you'll not come to me, I'll have to come to *you,* take you with my wiles and cunning."

He laughed and pulled her tighter to him. "Oh, lady, I'm yours."

With another kiss, he lifted her gently off the ground and swung her up into his arms. The sound of her giggles was a balm on his sore muscles and burned skin. She covered his face in kisses, and then, his lips.

"Put me down, Tobias," she admonished. "Put me down."

He did as she asked with great reluctance.

She took one hand in hers, leading him towards the cottage. "Come now, my darling," she said. "I think you need a good scrubbin' to clean the day from you. Water's drawn and in the tub, nice and hot. And I've left you a piece of some good soap to wash with. When you're done with that, I've a rabbit stew waitin' for you. Are you hungry, Tobias?"

"Aye, lady," he answered, grabbing at her dress with his free hand. "I hunger for your body."

She slapped at his hand, refusing to be turned aside from the tasks at hand. "Well, my body will come later, my love. For now, you'll go out back and scrub. I'll have the stew and bread ready for you when you're done."

She left him and went inside to get things ready for supper. He made his way to the huge oaken tub, filled to the brim with water still steaming from the kettle. He stripped his clothing, took the pitcher, and began to pour the water over his skin. The dirt and sweat rolled off every muscle, warming him to the bone. He soaped every square inch of himself and rinsed. He dried off as best he could with a woolen cloth, then laid it over the back of a chair to dry. She'd put by another shirt and pair of trousers to replace the filthy ones he'd removed. He put them on, left his other clothing to soak in the remaining hot water, and went inside.

She had set the table with a bowl of stew and several hoecakes. When he sat down, she came to him with the mug of ale and set it down before him. She sat down beside him and watched him eat. They talked of the farming and the planting, and when supper was over, the dishes had been washed and put away, they made love in his bed.

As she lay beside him, her back against his chest and his arms wrapped around her, he finally worked up his nerve.

"Lady, I need to ask you something. If you're of a mind."

A soft chuckle emanated from her throat and she turned her head slightly. "You sound like Declan. I've a mind for many things, my darlin'. What in particular strikes your fancy?"

"Lady," he whispered, serious now in the darkness. "This is important to me."

She rose up, turning to lay on her back so that she could peer into his face. Her brows were knitted and her eyes darted back and forth as she searched his face for the problem. "Oh, Tobias, I am that sorry, my love. Tell me; what is it you wish to ask me?"

He took the hand on which he'd placed the ring, and held it up, rubbing his thumb against the silver band. It shouldn't be that hard to ask this but he was suddenly afraid that the answer wouldn't be what he wanted it to be. What if she'd changed her mind? He took a deep breath, swallowed hard, and decided to throw caution to the wind.

"Lady...my dearest Siobhan – I would be that honored if you'd be my wife. Right now. I know I said I was goin' to wait but I can't. I can't go one more day without you."

She sat up in the bed, staring into the darkness for some seconds. Then, she sighed softly and turned around again to face him. "You're serious."

"I've never been more serious in my life, Siobhan. Will you? Will you be handfast to me?"

She watched his eyes for the briefest of moments before diving forward to take his face in her hands. She kissed him hard and deep, taking her time to make love to his mouth with hers. When she finally let him up for air, she said only one word.

"Aye."

As it turned out, there would be four handfastings that June. Toby formally asked for, and received, Cieran's blessing for the marriage. His announcement to the family received as boisterous a celebration as Gwydion's had been. He had few preparations to make. He had the cottage and his land; he had his own crops in the field. The brides had the lion's share of preparation and took to it with a vengeance. All that was left was the dowry to pay. Liam helped him with that. Toby gave the new colt to Siobhan's father, along with a length of Niamh's best lace.

Toby was afraid that Yeshua wouldn't make it back in time, but his fear was groundless. The day of the handfasting, his friend arrived at the cottage and helped keep the bridegrooms sane and calm. Toby had his jitters before the ceremony – did he have enough to make her happy; could he make her happy; was she questioning her choice? Gwydion was nervous that he'd forget his vows. Yeshua talked each of them through their worries, assuring them of the best possible day and happiness to come, and led them both to the stone circle to claim their brides.

All of his new friends and family were gathered, smiles and tears flowing in copious amounts. The grooms walked the circle and came to stand before the altar in the north. Aiobh's nephew was a harper and he'd been entreated to play while the bard was getting handfasted to his lady. The tune was a lively one, and the brides were escorted into the circle by their fathers.

The moment he saw her, he saw and heard little else. She came in a gown of gauze and lace that flowed from her shoulders and down her body like a cloud. She walked, barefoot, and her feet were as dainty as the rest of her. She had left her red hair unbound down her back and shoulders and her face was luminescent. The moment she saw him, their eyes locked as she walked around the circle to come to his side.

He vaguely remembered being presented to, and blessed by, the Quarters. The call for the blessings of God and Goddess never penetrated his consciousness. He was caught up in her face; the curvature of her jaw, the brilliance of her eyes the smile that painted her lips. She held his hand in her own and he marveled at the softness of her skin. The rite went on around them; for him, there was no one else.

"Tobias!"

Until someone shouted his name and he jumped so hard that he almost fell over. "What?" he shouted back.

The sound laughter around the circle brought him back to the here and now. Even Gwydion was laughing and Toby looked down at his feet with a sheepish grin.

Declan shook his head, laughing. "Come, lad," he said, trying to be serious again. "I know the dear lady's claimed you but you need to make it official. 'Tis time for your vows."

Toby turned to face his lady, and took both of her hands in his. "My beloved Siobhan, I fully, honestly, joyfully, and completely give to you my soul and all I am, have been, and shall be. You have brought me out of the dark and into the light, and there I shall stay. No matter where you are, that's where I'll be; from now until the immeasurable time has waned. I love you and I always shall."

"Siobhan?"

She squeezed his hands in hers, smiling up at him. Her voice caught just the slightest and her cheeks were wet. "My dearest Tobias, from the day you walked into this village, I knew you were for me. I give you my body and soul, and freely so. I give you all of my tomorrows and I will want no other. I wish to spend my days standing by your side and my nights comforted in your bed. I want to be a proper wife to you and give you many children. Where you go, I follow and what you want, I want too. I love you now and always shall."

Toby took her left hand and slid a new ring on the ring finger, this one adorned with ivy. She placed a simple band of beaten silver on his hand and they were handfast. There was little more to the ceremony than giving thanks for the crops and the growing in the field. Seeds of a great harvest mirrored in the seeds of four couples who would now have children of their own. The circle had no beginning and was never ending.

The party in the barn was boisterous and jubilant. The newly handfasted were late arriving, each going back to change into more comfortable and less formal clothing. Toby and Siobhan were the last to arrive as their cottage was the farthest away but they were greeted with no less enthusiasm. The musicians played a love song and Toby swept his lady into his arms and danced her out to the middle of the floor. The ale and whiskey flowed like water, and there was food and dancing. It was a proper Irish wedding.

They danced for two more songs before Toby finally led his new bride to greet his adopted family. Gwydion and Deirdre greeted their new brother and sister by marriage with hugs. Liam was having the time of his life, sharing his special cask of whiskey with all comers. Niamh was having a bit as well and she was glowing from the heat and the drink. She embraced Gwydion and Toby, kissing them soundly.

"Tobias, I am that happy for you, my son."

Toby hugged her back. "Thanks, Ma. I am that happy."

She took Siobhan by the hand and warmly kissed her cheeks. "Welcome to our family, my dear. I'm so glad you found each other."

Siobhan could only nod, smiling and crying at the same time.

"I'll tell you what I told Gwydion; you'll want to take a few days,"

Liam said a little awkwardly, tears in the corners of his eyes. "To have your time alone. Crops can wait."

"Thank you, Liam."

Toby reached out and grasped Liam's forearm in the customary handshaking, but Liam surprised him by taking Toby into his embrace. The other hand clapped against his back and Liam whispered into his ear, "You make me as proud as if you were my own, boy."

Toby hugged back before they separated quickly, both embarrassed by the contact. Siobhan tugged on his sleeve at that moment, saving his dignity by asking him to dance.

"If you'll excuse us," Toby said. He nodded to Liam and kissed Niamh's cheek, and led his bride out on the floor again. He led her through a fast jig and then another slow dance, liking the feel of her against him. He kissed her forehead and gazed into her flushed face. "Lady?"

"Aye?"

"Are you happy?"

She tossed her hair over one shoulder to cool her neck. With a sigh, she put her arms around his neck and smiled. "Aye, my love. Happier than ever I thought I could be."

Gwydion clutched at Toby's sleeve. "Tobias, 'tis a problem."

"What the hell…?" Toby stopped dancing immediately, snapping at his friend unintentionally. "I'm a little busy right now, in case you haven't noticed." He sighed. "I'm sorry, my friend. Please forgive me. What's the problem?"

Gwydion didn't take it to mind, blurting out, "We seem to have run out of whiskey and ale. Been so much celebrating of late, no one had a large supply. We've run dry. We're to go and fetch the wine stores from our cellar and Aiobh's."

"Are you daft?" Siobhan laughed. "Wine at a handfasting?"

Gwydion groaned. "Siobhan, we've nothing else. Besides, Yeshua says 'tis a tradition with his people."

Toby looked a little lost, and Siobhan explained, "Wine is for supper and silly things. You toast a handfastin' or birthin' with good Ir whiskey or ale. Not wine."

"The grain, Tobias," Gwydion further explained. "The grain comes from the Dagda. 'Tis more of a blessing with the drink from grain."

"Oh," Toby said, finally getting it. "But if we're out...."

Gwydion spread his hands in a gesture of futility. "We do what we do when we need to do it."

A shout came from the door and Yeshua and three of the other villagers walked in with large crocks. One of them carrying a crock was Siobhan's father, Cieran.

"We've more whiskey and ale," he shouted to the crowd. "Come and drink your fill, all."

Gwydion shouted, "Wait. *Wait!*"

Everything came to a halt as all turned to Gwydion. "Those are water casks," Gwydion said. "There was no ale or whiskey anywhere, I saw the empty kegs. You're servin' water, now?"

Cieran stepped out from the crowd and brandished a wooden cup. He handed it to Gwydion with a grin. "That's not water, lad. Go on and try it."

Gwydion sniffed at the cup. Whatever he smelled made him furrow his brow. He sniffed again and, with a quizzical look at Cieran, he bolted the contents back. His eyes widened and he gasped. "That's whiskey, Tobias," he wheezed. "That's good Ir whiskey." To Cieran, he blurted out, 'How?"

Toby's gulp assured him that yes, this was Irish whiskey; good, pure, and strong. He quickly caught his breath and passed the mug to Siobhan and she sipped at it. All three of them stared at Cieran.

"How, Da?" she stammered. "Gwydion is right; those are water casks."

Cieran shook his head and took back the mug from his daughter. "All I know is that your friend Yeshua said not to worry. He took us out to the water kegs. The lad stood there for a bit, mutterin' somethin', and then told us that it was whiskey and ale. I tasted 'em and sure enough, that's what we were drinkin'."

Cieran left the trio and went back to the libations, the throng gathering around Yeshua. The young man simply accepted the grateful thanks from the crowd, who continued with their celebrating. Gwydion spared a glance at Toby and after a brief shrug, rejoined his new wife and her family.

"Tobias?"

Toby took Siobhan's hand to continue the dance. "No, lady," he said, answering her unasked question. "I don't know and I don't want to think about it."

"But, Tobias – there was none."

He kissed a lock of hair away from her face, holding her close. "It's his gift, lady, his gift to us all. Let it rest at that."

His gift to us all – like the wine at the wedding of Cana. His gaze drifted back to Yeshua and the gaze was returned. Yeshua smiled at Toby and just nodded.

His gift to us all....

Chapter Twenty-Two

Five years later

Toby sat at his dining room table, a mug at his elbow and a piece of slate in front of him. He stared at it intently, trying to figure out what he could change, what he could make do without. But no matter how hard he tried, he could find no answer. Every square inch of the gardens held some plant or herb that would be necessary for all of them to survive. Liam, in his usual efficient manner, had plotted every row in minute detail.

"Darlin', eat a bit of breakfast and give your mind a rest." Siobhan put a plate in front of him, with cabbage, turnips, and a bit of the corned beef left over from the previous night's dinner. She served fresh hot hoecakes and refilled his mug of ale before sitting down to eat with him.

Toby picked at his food for a moment or two and then settled in to eat it. *There's no use wasting food.*

"Tobias, your face is dark, my love. Is it bad?"

Toby stopped in the middle of lifting the laden fork to his mouth, lowering it slowly to the plate again. He gave a moment of thought to lying about the issue but Siobhan had a way of seeing through him. Besides, she had a right to know and he had to tell her. They had promised each other that they would have no secrets and no lies.

"Aye, lady, it's bad. It's very bad.'

The previous year had brought a diminished crop because of a slight shortage of rain. They had a late harvest and had harvested enough to sustain them, but barely. The slaughter of animals had been greater than in previous years but there was no choice. It was a bigger sin to starve the animals for what the humans couldn't provide. They had raised enough for themselves. Siobhan, Deirdre, and Niamh had salted and packed away every vegetable and root that the men had raised. Every part of every animal had been saved and treated in the same way. The smokehouse had been full to bursting, but they preserved all of it.

This year was shaping up to be far worse. The spring rains had never come, leaving them in a severe drought situation. The plants that had broken through the surface were small and weak. The cattle, sheep, and horses had been put into the far fields to keep them from eating the tender shoots and the grasses they were finding were yellowed and bitter. Toby had given up on any of the milk from the cows; the calves seemed to be drinking it only because there was nothing else. The wells were drying up; the village had been placed on water rations. Declan had sent groups to the closest river, some distance away, to bring as many skins of water as could be carried. It became a daily excursion and kept the entire village going as much as possible.

Siobhan put her hand over Toby's and linked her fingers in his. She had a look of worry on her face; Toby lifted her hand to his lips to kiss it. He knew he must have the same look on his face.

"Will we lose the crops, do you think?" she asked.

Toby shrugged his shoulders and took another bite of the corned beef.

"Well," she replied, and heaved a sigh.

Toby swallowed his bite and rinsed it down. He squeezed her fingers and smiled at her. "Listen to me, lady, for as long as I draw breath, we'll not starve. Do you hear me? It is bad, aye. I'll not lie to you. But, we're far from slaughterin' all the animals."

She looked reassured, smiling back at him. She tapped the plate in front of him with a finger and impishly said, "You'll not be wastin' the food in front of you then. I'll do my part, my darling."

He went back to his meal. "I won't be wasting anything, my lady, if you keep cooking as well as this." He took a huge bite and made small humming noises, rubbing his belly.

She tossed the napkin at him, a blush on her face. "You'd eat a shoe if you could, you sod."

"Only if you cooked it," he teased. "It'll be your own fault I'm grown fat and sassy, and you've none else to blame."

"Feh! Get along with you!" She slapped his hand, and went back to eating.

Toby finished his food, and took his plate to the wash pail. She would scrub the plates off with dirt, wiping them as clean as she could. With water being so scarce, it was all they could do.

"Ma! *Ma*!"

A towheaded little boy stood in the doorway that led out of the house to the back. He had passed five summers and would be six the next March. His blond hair had a slight curl to it, his deep blue eyes were filled with his constant laughter. Toby made a loud roaring noise and scooped up his son in his arms, causing the boy to burst into giggles. He lifted the child to his face and made raspberries against the little one's tummy, causing more giggles and laughter. Siobhan joined in with her own gales from the table, around mouthfuls of the cabbage.

"Da! Put me down! I'm hungry. Ma, make him put me down."

"I think I'll eat you, my son. You're good and fat and you'll taste sweet."

The little one's eyes grew wide and round, and the look he gave Toby was almost heartbreaking, it was so serious. "*Nooo*! Da, don't eat me!"

Toby smiled at his son, knowing the boy was going to be exactly like he had been at that age. He kissed the child's chubby cheeks and set him back down on the ground, straightening the clothing that he had ruffled. "Not to worry, lad. Ma feeds me too well."

"Rohan, come sit down and I'll get your supper," Siobhan replied. "And your father won't be eatin' you, lad, for your mother will have none of it." She stood with her own plate to refill it for her son and gave Toby a stern look. "If anyone's goin' to be eaten, it'll be Da. He's nice and fat and he'll be feedin' us all for the season."

"Nooo! Don't want to eat Da!"

Toby squatted down, took his son into his arms, and kissed his face again. Rohan's chubby arms came around Toby's neck. He stood up, holding the boy tight against his chest. Tears had formed in the sweet innocent eyes and Toby wiped them away.

"No one's going to eat your Da, lad. Nor will they eat my sweet son. I'll have none of it. You hear me?"

The serious little face nodded and Rohan pressed his cheek to Toby's. Toby carried him to the table where Siobhan waiting to feed the boy. He settled Rohan on his mother's lap and kissed both on the cheek.

"I'm off to see what I can do in the fields," he announced. "Perhaps nothin' but I'll feel all the better for tryin'."

Siobhan was spooning mashed neeps and cabbage into Rohan's mouth. She stopped long enough to tell Toby, "Don't fret too much, love. We'll get by."

Toby kissed her again, this time on the mouth, and walked outside through the same door that his son entered. This was an exercise in futility and he knew it but as he had told Siobhan, he felt better just doing *something*. He took his hoe, walked into the field closest to his cottage, and attacked what few weeds were in the ground vigorously. He tried to keep his mind from wandering into areas of how to find water, where to find water...*water, water, water*. His mind wasn't co-operating one bit but he kept hoeing under a cloudless sky. He stopped to wipe the sweat from his brow and considered getting his hat from the cottage. He decided against it; it was too far to walk for the hat and he had already started. He'd get it when he went inside to get ale.

He was attacking his third row when he heard a shout and turned in that direction. He had to squint in the sunlight but it only took a moment to recognize the figure approaching him. Yeshua had returned from another of his jaunts through the countryside. He should be returning from the eastern coast and perhaps he had news of a trade or what was going on in the rest of the world.

Yeshua was now in his twenty-first year, and had reached his full growth, standing at five-foot-ten. He was a handsome young man with a dark complexion and large brown eyes. He was still thin but he had developed into a rather muscular thinness. He still wore his hair long, around the collar of his shirt and had completely abandoned any sense of the Hassidic or Essene sect from which he'd come. He was Celtic in the skins and clothing that he adopted as his dress. Yeshua still spoke the Celtic language with a marked Aramaic accent but he was understandable and that was all that mattered.

Yeshua had moved in with Declan and Aiobh, shortly after the handfasting. He always seemed hungry for knowledge and found their home the perfect place to be. Declan had taught the young man how to read and write and Yeshua read everything he could come across. He had traveled to other villages, learning law and the beliefs. When he was in the village, he would come to carry on deep conversations with Toby, discussing philosophy and faith. The change was remarkable.

Yeshua approached Toby and grasped his friend's forearm in salute. Toby returned the gesture and hugged the returning traveler. He was genuinely glad to see his friend again.

"You're home," Toby said, after releasing his friend from the embrace.

"Yes, Tobias, I have returned. I wanted to stop by here first, as I have presents for the three of you. Then, I must go home and see Declan and Aiobh. They'll want to know the news as well."

"Well, come up to the cottage," Toby replied, patting the younger man on the shoulder. " Siobhan'll get you some cider or ale."

"Can you spare it, Tobias?"

"Aye, lad," Toby answered, jovially. "You've come home, we must celebrate that. And truth be told, I'm a bit parched, myself. I could do with a good, cool drink. Come. We'll sit in the shade for a bit and you can tell us the news."

Toby whistled and Siobhan poked her head out of the back door. She saw Yeshua and waved furiously before disappearing back into the house. By the time the two men had arrived, she was standing, waiting, with two large mugs of ale. Yeshua took his with a nod of thanks and took a deep drink.

Yeshua bowed formally, smiling as he did. "Siobhan, it is good to see you. You look lovely as always."

Siobhan blushed for the second time that morning. "You're still the same smooth talkin' lad you were when you left here. Will you be wantin' a bite of something?"

Yeshua waved his hand. "Thank you but no. I am sufficient. Where's that young lad of yours? I've presents for you all."

Rohan, who had been peeking from behind his mother's skirts, stuck his head out with a shy smile. Yeshua sat down in one of the two chairs and held out his hands towards the little boy. Rohan giggled, and ran to him, climbing up into Yeshua's lap. Toby and Siobhan watched with smiles of amusement as the two carried on an in-depth discussion of Rohan's lunch.

Siobhan leaned against Toby, watching the two. "Yeshua, you've a way with the children. They do love you, so."

"Yes, they do," he answered. "And I love the children. Their innocence and joy are music to my soul. The creation of children was a gift to us all. They have such peace within them." He ruffled Rohan's hair and reached down to his pack lying beside him. "God's gift to mankind, the children, and we should be forever grateful."

"You should have children of your own, Yeshua. You should settle down and have a family. You'll make a wonderful father."

Yeshua reached into his pack, rummaging through the contents.

"Thank you, Siobhan but it is not mine to decide such things. My Father has other tasks for me and I must be to them. But not today; today I have come with gifts for my favorite family."

He pulled out a small package and handed it to Rohan, who tore the wrapping as quickly as he could to find a handful of hard tack. The little one's face lit up like the stars, and he bounced off Yeshua's lap to run to his mother to show her.

"Ma...look...*look*...sweeties."

"Aye, lad, I see. Did you tell Yeshua thank you? Mind your manners, now."

He'd already started sucking on a piece but Rohan managed a "fanoo" around it. Satisfied that his mother appreciated his good fortune, Rohan dropped down where he was and enjoyed his candy.

Yeshua reached into his pack again and pulled out another bundle. He held it out to Siobhan, a shy smile on his lips. "I do hope you like this. I saw it and it reminded me of you."

She took the bundle from his and unwrapped the most exquisite lace that Toby had ever seen in his life. It was delicate, a fragile web in its intricacy. Her eyes grew as wide as her son's had gotten. She stared openmouthed, first at the lace, then at Yeshua, then back to the lace again. She was so caught up in the gift that she couldn't speak for some moments. She held it out for Toby to see before clutching it against her breasts. When she finally could speak, she squealed in delight and rushed to hug Yeshua around the neck.

"Oh, you dear, sweet lad!"

Yeshua blushed under his tan, hugging her back. "Do you really like it, Siobhan? Really?"

She held it tight against her again. "Aye, love, I do. Where did you ever find such a treasure? Oh, Tobias! Look, did you ever see such in your life?"

Toby chortled at his wife, who was practically dancing in her glee. Especially when Rohan joined her in her dance. As they danced, Toby laughed and clapped his hands to keep a beat going. Siobhan wrapped the lace around her neck to keep Rohan's sticky fingers from smearing the hard tack liquid on it, and she and the lad jumped for joy.

Yeshua reached into his pack one more time, and brought out another bundle. "I thought you might enjoy this. You drink it in a decoction."

Toby opened the bundle and found a very aromatic blend of herbs. He held it to his nose and took a deep sniff of the aroma of the mixture. "Oh that is wonderful, Yeshua. I thank you."

Siobhan stopped her dancing, and turned back to the men. "You shouldn't have, Yeshua. These presents must've cost you dear."

Yeshua colored again but didn't look down this time. "No, Siobhan, the cost was not dear at all. It made my heart glad to get these things for you."

She clasped her hands around the lace and removed it from her neck, folding it up again. "Well, thank you, my friend. I'll be puttin' this away for a short time. I know the dress I'll be making soon and this will be just the perfect thing to make it special."

She smiled again and shifted the bundle to her left hand, taking Rohan's hand in her free one. "Come, my lad, you're hard tack from head to toe. We'll need to spare a bit of water and clean that sticky off your face."

Rohan bit his lip, and Toby knew the boy was hoping she'd change her mind if he looked pitiful. Toby could also have let his son know that Ma was not to be trifled with. A few moments of begging and a few tears soon proved that Ma was not going to be turned from the washing. Rohan abandoned his protest and trotted along dutifully.

"She is with child again."

Toby took a sharp look at his friend and then burst out laughing. "You never cease to amaze me. And I should know better than to ask how you know. Aye, she is with child again. It'll be born around Yule."

"Another son."

"You know that?"

Yeshua smiled and nodded.

"Well," Tobias said, a sense of pride growing inside his chest. "Another son." He wiped his mouth with the back of his hand, and said, "Perhaps we should be havin' a drink of whiskey to celebrate." Toby made to get up from the chair to go fetch the jug.

Yeshua raised his hand to stop him. "None for me, thank you. The ale is enough." He took a long drink from his mug and set it back down on the ground beside him. He looked out over the fields and nodded in the direction of the one that Toby had been hoeing. "Tell me, my friend, how bad is it?"

Toby sobered up immediately and settled back in the chair again. "It's worse than I thought. If we don't get some rain and soon, there'll be no harvest this year."

Yeshua's brow furrowed and clasped his hands in his lap. "None at all?"

"None. The plants are dying and there's naught we can do. We had special prayers for Litha and had another blessin' of the fields and still no rain."

"What will you do, Tobias?"

"We'll not starve, lad, not this year. But we'll have to slaughter every animal. We won't be able to feed them, and that will cause hardship to the village."

"The village cannot survive without the crops, Tobias. Nor the beasts."

Toby looked out over the dry field. He knew Yeshua was right but he couldn't give in to the doubt and despair he was feeling. He slapped a grin on his face and spoke in what he hoped was an optimistic tone. "Don't worry, now. We're due for rain any day now. I feel it." He pointed to his knee and winked at his friend. "I feel it here. I always get a twinge here when it's going to rain."

Yeshua looked up into the brilliant blue above the tree tops, answering with less enthusiasm in his voice. "Tobias, I will pray that it is so."

"Come, now," Toby said, clapping his hands together. He wanted a change of subject. "I want to know the news. What did you find in your travels?"

Unfortunately, Yeshua couldn't change it much. "The drought is hurting all of the villages round here. We'll be hard pressed to do any trading this year."

Toby sighed. "I was afraid of that. It'll come. What else is happening?"

Yeshua stood up and picked up his bag. "Come, walk with me. Aiobh and Declan would love to see you and I've other news – the sort that is probably best kept between us for now."

Toby opened the back door again and let his wife know where he was bound. She was still in the middle of Rohan's bath and only gave him a quick nod before going back to wipe the squirming child's face. Toby stood for a moment, watching them, and then joined Yeshua. The two began a leisurely pace on their journey.

"So, tell me," Toby said. "What is the big secret?"

Yeshua frowned, clutching his bag tightly. "I feel a dark cloud, Tobias. I *know* what it is, but I can't explain it."

Toby walked a few paces without speaking. A dark cloud? Yeshua wasn't given to frivolous pronouncements. If he was worried about something, there was usually merit to his unease. "Can you tell me the cause?" Toby finally asked. "What do you mean 'a dark cloud'?"

"Some of the coastal towns in the north have been raided by the Scotians. They do not seem to be looking in this direction but the southern villages are preparing. Just in case, you see."

"Do *you* think the Scots'll come down this way?"

"It is very possible, my friend," Yeshua answered. "I do not understand this. Why the anger, Tobias? Why would the Scotians want to fight the Ir?"

Toby stopped to pick up a rock and rolled it around in his hands as he walked. "Lad, there is a long rivalry between the two and no one remembers the cause anymore."

"But, why? Why fight someone just because of rivalry?"

"Why does anyone fight?" Toby answered philosophically. "Perhaps to protect what you have, hold on to what you were. Perhaps, they fight for their way of life. Perhaps, it's their Gods tellin' 'em to do it." Toby tossed the stone back to the side of the road. "Well, if the Scots do head this way, we'll get plenty of warning from *someone*."

Yeshua brightened at that. "Yes, I'm sure we shall. I am sorry to have missed Litha."

A jaunty voice behind them answered for Toby, "As well you should be, lad. You missed my best playing."

Yeshua's face lit up when he saw Gwydion, who was carrying a small carefully wrapped bundle. The bard shifted the bundle over to his left arm and grasped Yeshua's forearm in salute.

"Gwydion, my friend. How fare you? Your wife and children are well, too?"

"Aye, Deirdre is wonderful. Sean and Duncan are right smart, too. Duncan's getting his teeth in and the wee fiend bites hard, he does." Gwydion held up his forefinger, which bore a nasty little cut. "Deirdre sent me to see if Aiobh might have any licorice root for the poor babe to chew on."

"It'll be a damn sight better than your finger," Toby chuckled.

"Aye, would at that," Gwydion said, laughing as well. "I tell you true, Duncan has some fine sharp teeth."

The three men joined in the laughter and started on their way again. Yeshua repeated the news about the other villages and the possible Scotian threat. Gwydion nodded at the latter but could shed no light on the subject. No more was said of the raids and they arrived at the gate.

"Come on in, my friends," Yeshua invited. "I'm sure Aiobh will have tea and biscuits at the ready. If you have time to spare, please come and sit. Visit with us for a time before you must get to your errands and leave."

Suddenly, the young man's face relaxed and the sunny smile disappeared. His eyelids fluttered and the color bled from his face until it was pale and sweaty. When he looked about to fall over, Toby and Gwydion reached forward at the same time and steadied him. He took their shoulders in his grip and a look of horror came over his face.

"No," he whispered, a haunted look on his face. "No," he repeated, a little louder, and ran to the house.

Toby and Gwydion exchanged a glance and dashed after him, almost at his heels. They followed Yeshua to the back of the house that served as the kitchen. Yeshua was standing beside Aiobh, who was sitting at the table. Her face was puffy and swollen with tears, a cold mug of mulled cider in front of her. She sat, just staring into the mug, the tears flowing silently. Yeshua crouched down and took her chin in his hand. For a moment, she didn't register his being there, but he brought her face up to his.

"Where is he?" Yeshua asked quietly.

She swallowed hard and sniffled. She pointed back over her shoulder. "Out there. In the field."

Yeshua dashed out the back door. Gwydion tossed the package he'd been carrying to the floor and ran out behind him. Toby wasn't sure what to do, whether to follow or not. He stood, his feet frozen to the spot. Aiobh's soft voice broke through his inaction, forcing him to listen.

"He knew it was the only way, you see. He *knew*, Tobias." She gave a heart-wrenching sigh, one that shook her petite body, and buried her face in her hands. "What shall I do without him now?

What'll become of me do you suppose?"

A shout of agony from the back stopped him from asking her what she was talking about. His head jerked in the direction and her soft voice admonished him, "Go to him. He'll be needin' you, lad."

His feet came unglued from the spot and he was out the back door like a shot. Yeshua was on his knees, facing away from him and he seemed to be holding something. Gwydion stood facing the cottage, but his head was down and he had covered his eyes with one hand. Toby watched the distance suddenly stretch out before him, just like in the movies of his old life. When he finally got his feet moving again, everything was happening in slow motion.

Yeshua sobbed with his entire being, cradling Declan's body in his arms and rocking it gently. No, it was more like keening, Toby thought to himself. *Yeah, keening*. He reached out a hand to take Yeshua by the shoulder and then saw what had happened.

"Oh God," Toby cried. "No, oh God, no!"

The ground was soaked in Declan's blood, where he had slit his own throat in the field. He had done it quickly and efficiently, stabbing the blade deep into the skin and somehow had managed to pull the blade forward, tearing skin and muscle with a ragged force. The bloody knife was lying on the ground in the grizzly mud and Declan's hands were covered in the gore.

Yeshua gulped air, sobbing it out each time. He touched the face with a reverence, and gently wiped away the dirt that had collected on the dead man's forehead. He smoothed the hair from Declan's face and softly closed the eyes.

"It was too late," Yeshua said. "I was too late."

Toby knelt down beside him, laying a hand on Yeshua's shoulder. "There was nothing you could do, my friend."

Yeshua turned his head and it was obvious that he was in agony. "Why, Tobias?" he asked, tears streaming down his tanned face. "Why? What purpose did this serve? Did he not know that this was a mortal sin? Why do such a foolish thing?"

Gwydion's voice was strained as he answered, "It is what was expected of his office, lad."

That shocked Yeshua into glaring at his friend. "What are you speaking of, Gwydion? His office?'

Gwydion shook his head, refusing to explain. "Not now, lad. Help me take him back to the cottage. Aiobh'll have to prepare him for the burial and we'll need to alert the rest of the village."

Gwydion tried to help carry but Yeshua batted his hands away, insisting on doing it himself. He bore the body with all of the reverence owed a king, doing his best to make sure the head didn't tip back to reveal the slash in the skin. Toby was the most grateful for that. The sight of the wound was almost more than he could take. They brought the corpse in and Yeshua tenderly placed it on a pallet brought out from the barn. Toby and Gwydion left the two to dress and clean the body, and prepare it for burial.

The next twenty-four hours passed in a bit of a haze for Toby. For the second time since he'd arrived, the bell sounded and the village gathered. He and Gwydion passed the news and the reaction was one of stunned grief, with several of the women keening in much the same fashion that Yeshua did. Several of the men went to the village burial ground near the henge, and began to dig the cairn. Over the course of the day and night, everyone stopped by to pay their respects to Aiobh, who still seemed to be in a bit of shock.

"The poor dear," Niamh told Siobhan that evening. "She'll be doin' his Rite of Passage, poor dear."

"Aye, that won't be easy for her but she's all we have. Will she stay on, do you think?"

"When I left, she hadn't made up her mind."

"Hold on a second." Toby sat down at the table with both women. "Why would she leave?"

"Well, someone else will take on the duties of High Priest and Chieftain," Niamh answered. "And she and Declan were mated. Not that that's important to being High Priest and Priestess, you understand, but…well, it could be hurtful to the dear woman. She may think that she's no longer needed."

"*I'll* be needin' her," Siobhan insisted. "I'll be needin' a midwife when comes my time and she's the best healer we have. Oh, Niamh, we can't let her leave. We love her here. We need her."

"Well, you need not fret, my darling girl," Niamh said to her, trying to reassure her. "She'll have time to think on it; we have time to talk to her about it. We have no one else for High Priestess and she knows it. You fret not, dearie."

Siobhan was reassured easily but Toby was not. He left the two to discuss things, and went outside to sit and watch the night sky, and think. Maybe he hadn't felt all that close to Declan but he had liked the man. Declan had an easygoing way with everyone. He had been a wonderful teacher and a calming influence on the people. He had been patient with Toby's questions and frustrations. The High Priest had been everyone's friend and confessor, and Toby knew in his heart, he was going to miss the man. The tears began, his vision began to swim. He raised a hand to his eyes and left his head propped there.

"Da?"

He looked into the eyes of his son, his sweet son who was here because of Declan's choice for a Beltane blessing. The night of his coupling as the God had brought him his beautiful boy. He blinked a few times to clear the teardrops, wiping them away, and smiled at the child.

The little blond head cocked to one side and a chubby hand crept up to take Toby's. "Da? Why you cryin', Da? You sad?"

Toby sniffed, hurriedly wiping his face. "Aye, boy."

"Don't be sad, Da. I sit with you and make you happy."

Rohan crawled up his leg to take up residence in his lap and Toby helped him situate. The chubby little arms came around his neck and he held his child tight against his chest. Rohan hugged him tightly and Toby felt the pieces of his heart knit themselves together again. The smile that his child gave him was like the sunshine. They sat there for some time, watching the moon and the stars, until long after Rohan had fallen asleep.

Aiobh and Yeshua had dressed the body in Declan's robe and ritual jewelry. Toby noticed a scarf tied around Declan's throat and peeked under it. Someone had meticulously sewn the wound closed, taking special care to hide the stitches as much as possible. *It would might been Aiobh*, he thought, and replaced the bandage. Liam, Gwydion, and Toby helped carry the pallet to the burial ground, and they stood close enough to carry out the remainder of their duties as pallbearers.

The rite was simple and brief. Aiobh had, indeed, insisted on performing the ritual for her dead husband. Every man, woman, and child came to say goodbye to their friend and celebrate his life and work. They came to send him off to his next life with love and joy. Aiobh's eulogy for her husband was simple; a good man with a good heart and that was that. They lowered the body into the cairn, and Aiobh laid his book of spells and incantations, his sword, and a braid of hair from her head next to him. Those that had dug the cairn now filled it in, and covered the mound with the stones of the field. Yeshua led Aiobh away, back to her home, and the rest followed.

There's nothing like a good old fashioned Irish wake, Toby thought. Here they were, in the middle of a severe drought and it didn't matter. Everyone had brought all the ale and whiskey they could scare up, and they sat in the barn drinking it. Toby sat quietly in a corner while all about him, the stories of a life spent in love and happiness were shared with the whiskey. Toby knew from experience, it would go on all night.

After a time, Siobhan excused herself to take Rohan home and take a nap. This pregnancy was tiring her out a bit more and the tension of the day couldn't be helping. Toby kissed her and told her he'd follow. He pulled himself up from the hay bale he'd been sitting on and went to look for Aiobh to give his sympathies. He couldn't find her in the barn with the others, so he headed to the cottage to see if she had gone there. As he approached the back door, he heard her voice speaking to someone.

"No, lad, you don't understand."

Yeshua's voice was next, agitated and somewhat angry. "Then, explain it to me, Aiobh. I need to understand this. My friend has died and to make matters worse, he has committed a mortal sin against God. His soul is damned to an eternal hell for this."

Toby stood there eavesdropping; he wanted an answer, too. He stood, with his head bowed; waiting for an answer but it wasn't coming. He found he couldn't move until he knew. Just as he was about to give up, however, he looked up, and saw Aiobh watching him. Her kind eyes were brimming in her grief, but she still had a sweet smile.

"Come in, Tobias," she said to him, taking his hand to lead him to the table. Yeshua sat there with a mug of ale at his elbow. "Sit down and have some ale."

Toby felt extremely foolish, stammering. "I'm sorry, I didn't mean to...I...well, I just came to give you my condolences, see if there was anything I could do for you. Siobhan had to take Rohan home and...I didn't want to leave...."

"Thank you for what you did today, Tobias. It would make Declan happy to know it was you that put his bones in the good earth.'

Toby took the offered chair and ale, and sat silent. Aiobh sat again, and Yeshua spoke, breaking the stillness.

"Aiobh, *please*. I must know."

"Aye." Toby was a bit surprised at the sharpness of his own voice but there was nothing to do for it. "It would be a blessin' to understand, Aiobh. Gwydion said it was part of his office. What does that mean?"

Aiobh nodded and sighed. She looked so old at that moment, but she wiped her face with the palm of her hand, resigned to the duty. "Tell me, lads, do you know what the sacrifice means?"

"It is an offering to God, to ask that His grace be given or that His will be done." Yeshua had reverted to his younger self. He was struggling to keep his emotions in check but the arrogance had returned.

Aiobh was not upset with his answer, patting his hand. "Aye, you have told me of the Jews and your rites. But, do you know what the sacrifice means to the people *here*? Did it never come up in your learning?"

Yeshua answered in a shaky voice, "No. Declan never spoke of it. He was going to speak to me at Litha, he said. He wanted to tell me of his life here. He said there were so many things that I would know, to make ready for my ministry. For my path, he called it."

Aiobh nodded, taking the hand she'd been patting. "He was proud of you, Yeshua. We never had children of our own. I was too old for it and we wanted to have each other. For the work we did – well, it just didn't seem fair to have a child and never be there for it. But, you came to be with us. You became the son we couldn't have."

She released his hand, going back to her ale. "You were more than a student to him, Yeshua. You were a son and a friend. He was so proud of your learnin' and he wanted, someday, to make you the High Priest of Fireun Sidhé. He was forever tellin' me you had power in you, that you were of the Gods."

"I loved him," Yeshua said, his lip beginning to quiver.

Toby felt out of place, watching something very intimate and personal. He should leave, he knew that, but he still needed an answer. "Aiobh, are you tellin' us that this was a sacrifice? I'd heard the Druids did such in blood sacrifice, but I thought it was—"

Yeshua's head snapped up, his eyes blazing. "What are you saying?"

Aiobh laid her hand on Yeshua's arm. "Easy now, lad; there is no call for anger when it is a good question." To Toby, she answered, "Yes, that is exactly what I am saying, Tobias." She grasped her mug for security, before continuing. "You see, Declan loved this place. He was a part of it. He loved these people, and they loved him. They were his family and he'll be born again here. What he did was to sacrifice his own life for 'em, you see. That's what Gwydion meant by saying it was his office."

"To spill his blood?" Yeshua cried out.

"Aye, lad," she murmured. "There is no greater gift that can be given than to shed your blood for your people, to take their wants above your own. My husband's love was so great for this place and these folk that he gave his life to the fields, gave himself to pray for the return of the rain. He didn't want to leave this life, lad. He gave it for you."

The sentence hung in the air for some moments. So that was sacrifice, the concept of willingly giving for the good of all. The ultimate sacrifice given from love. Toby stared at his hands and wondered whether he would have the same courage of his convictions to give such a gift. He doubted that he could. He looked up at Yeshua to see what would happen next.

The young man sat, staring at the table and muttering to himself so softly that the words were inaudible at first. He shook his head, his face playing out so many emotions one after the other – anger, astonishment, love. It was hard to keep up. After a few moments, his face smoothed again and he looked up at Aiobh. "He gave his life for the people, for the Gods to bless the village with rain?"

"Aye," Aiobh answered, sadly. "He did, but it may have been for naught. The Gods seem to be upset with us for there's no rain in sight. The signs are working against it."

Another moment of silence as Yeshua processed this last bit. Toby started to feel a bit uneasy. Yeshua stiffened in the chair, sitting upright as if someone had tied him to a flat board. Something was about to happen and Toby wasn't sure if he would be able to stop the young man.

Yeshua clamped his jaw down with a determined face, and then, sparing a glance for his companions, said, "No." He stood up and walked around the table to where Aiobh sat. "No, Mother. You were right, there is no greater love for someone that to give up one's life.

To sacrifice himself, he is exalted above all others in my Father's kingdom. I shall see to it. And I will not let his sacrifice be in vain. I will not." Yeshua walked away from them and out the door. Toby shook his head and got up. Both he and Aiobh immediately followed.

The moment they stepped outside the door, Toby felt an electricity fill the air. Yeshua walked quickly and with surety toward his destination. With every step, the night air became heavier. There were a few of the men standing outside the door and they took notice, too. One ran inside, and within moments, they all were following Yeshua as he walked down the road. He was going somewhere.

It took Toby one look to realize where he was going – *to the stone circle.*

It was as if they all knew something was about to happen because they followed the Yeshua in silence. No one spoke, there were no words to say. Even those who had left early came out to follow. They followed all the way to the stone circle and then stopped. Yeshua walked inside the circle alone. Toby started to follow but Aiobh took his elbow and shook her head. She seemed to know what was about to happen and if she didn't, at least she knew he had to do it alone.

The gathered watched. And they waited.

Yeshua walked to the center of the circle and bent down to kneel in the yellowed sod. He held out his hands on either side of his body and raised his face to the sky. There was a soft light shining down. The air was so heavy now that Toby couldn't breathe. The skin on his arms prickled with electricity. And then he heard them, humming low and soft. It rumbled in the men and resonated in the women.

Still Yeshua knelt in the circle and still they hummed. Then, there was a flash in the sky and a crack of thunder. Toby felt a drop on his face. Then, another and another and another, and a gentle rain began to come down on them all. The sky darkened further and the soft light began to wane. The smell of the rain filled his senses and he, too, held his face up to the sky. The mildness of the droplets washed over his soul and through his mind.

There was a shout from outside of the circle and the shout was taken up by the gathering. In the lightning, Toby watched the villagers begin to dance in their joy. If it continued like this, the crops would be saved and they would have a good harvest after all. Toby had a feeling that they would have all the rain they needed, all over Ir. They danced, shouted, and ran in the rain like children. And when the downpour began in earnest, they went back to the barn and continued their celebrations, raising the names of Declan and Yeshua in thanks.

Toby watched Aiobh cross into the circle, after they had all left. She held her hand out to Yeshua and helped him up, leading him out of the circle. As they came to Toby, Yeshua stopped and looked into Toby's eyes. Toby didn't know what to say for some moments, but it didn't matter. Yeshua nodded and the two continued on. He stood in the rain for a while, letting it soak him. After a few minutes, he went home to celebrate with his wife.

Chapter Twenty-Three

The rain fell for two straight weeks before it slowed down to every three or four days. It was a gentle rain, the kind that soaked the ground without washing anything away. It soothed frazzled nerves, washed the dust and pollen out of the air, and made it bearable again. The river ran merrily through the valley and around the farms, back to its normal level. The wells and rain barrels were full. The rationing was over because there was simply no more need.

The crops gratefully accepted the moisture and began to blossom. It was astonishing how quickly the green returned to field and forest alike. The animals fed on the grasses in the meadows and the milkers were producing sweet cream again. Within another two weeks, the crops had doubled their growth. Within another four weeks, it was as if the drought had never happened. Corn, beans, and root crops were producing at a healthy rate. Toby harvested their first meal of fresh vegetables with alacrity, barely able to wait for Siobhan to wash and cook them. Rohan wasn't overjoyed with his first taste of parsnips but to Toby and Siobhan, they had never tasted sweeter.

The pain of Declan's sacrificial death faded and while the people were no longer reeling from the events, they were still discussing them. The people grieved for the loss of their friend but there was also a great deal of admiration for what Declan had done. The biggest part of the discussion, however, was over who had really caused the rains to fall. The town was divided in the subject of Yeshua's role – had he or hadn't he?

Toby kept his thoughts to himself about it all. He had wept his tears over the death, but the miracle of the rain was the focus of his mind. He knew, deep in his heart, which one of the men had really caused it. He had taken all this time to debunk the myth and here he was right in the center of the proof. At that moment, it didn't matter to him whether he accepted a God or a Goddess; he had been witness to an authentic miracle. *Ma would be happy, I think. I found my faith, Ma. Here with my family and with my people.*

Siobhan was finishing Rohan's feeding so that she could put him to bed. Toby had plans to sit outside with a mug of his latest brewing of ale and watch the sun go down. His was a quiet life out here among the rolling hills and forests. He had never thought it possible that he could enjoy such a simple life. He found a joy in tending to his crops and livestock, making love to his wife, and playing games with his son. The new baby on the way only intensified his satisfaction with the way things were around him. So as he was making his plans to enjoy the simplicity of the evening, he answered a polite knock at the door.

"Yeshua, my friend, please come in. Welcome. It's good to see you, lad. I was plannin' on sittin' outside to watch the setting sun. Or would you prefer to come indoors?"

"Out is fine, Tobias."

"Well, then. Have a seat on that chair, my friend, and I'll get us some ale."

He brought two mugs and served his guest before settling himself in his favorite seat. They both sipped contentedly, easing back against the rough exterior wall. There was just enough sun left to turn the world a golden orange hue. In the distance, he heard the lowing of the cattle, an occasional whinny of a horse calling a mate or a foal. The air was thick with the smell of the crops and the humidity of the day. *It ain't perfect, but it's home.*

"How's Aiobh," Toby asked. "I haven't had a chance to come by and check on her of late. Is she well?"

Yeshua nodded, swallowing the sip he'd just taken. "She is well. She, of course, misses her husband and she grieves for his absence. But, she tells me that she knows his spirit lives on and will come back soon."

Toby grunted in acknowledgment. "Is she resting?"

"Yes, Tobias, she is. I make sure of it."

"I'm sure she's grateful for your company."

Yeshua shrugged but admitted, "She said she is." He set his mug down and folded his hands on his lap. "I've agreed to act as temporary High Priest. I am not what Declan was to these people, but I would like to do that for him, for her. After they have given me so much, I would like to repay them somehow."

Toby knew that something was on the younger man's mind but decided that it would come out soon enough. He took another sip of the heather ale. "I take it Aiobh'll be stayin' on?"

"Oh, yes," Yeshua blurted. "Yes, she will stay on. She hopes to have a new High Priest and Priestess ready by Yule. She has decided that she wishes to remain as an Elder of the Grove and tend to the healing and her herbs."

"Well, that's for the best, I reckon," Toby said, simply. "The village would miss her. I know Siobhan would. I'm glad she is staying."

Again, the silence spun out between them. Inside the cottage, Rohan was crooning some sweet tune with his mother. She was obviously not succeeding in getting the lad to lie down for the night and by the sounds of her giggles, she was having far too much fun aiding and abetting her son's escape from bedtime. He wanted to be in there with them, but Yeshua seemed troubled.

Again, Toby broke the silence. "Lad, I did brew a healthy ale there, and if you're not of a mind to drink it, I'll be sore insulted, you know."

Yeshua laughed at the admonishment and picked up his mug again. He took a conciliatory sip and wiped his mouth on his sleeve. "Yes, you are right. You have given me a gift and my manners have escaped me. What do you suppose my mother would say at such a time? Forgive me, my friend."

He took several healthy gulps from the mug, and gave a hearty belch at the end. Both men burst into laughter as another memory came to them, unbidden but still a moment of their past together.

"It seems we've come full circle, lad," Toby said. "Here we are with a mug of ale and you lettin' fly with quite a belch there. I remember your first mug and you did the same then."

"Yes, I did," Yeshua replied. "I remember it well. I was very young."

"You've grown a sight since, too. You've grown tall and gotten some years on you."

The brown eyes seemed to pierce into his soul, narrowing slightly. "But you have not, my friend."

Toby gulped his own ale and stared out over the treetops. Was it that obvious? It was something he hadn't paid much attention to, and why should he? The only mirror in the house was Siobhan's and she kept it packed away to keep it safe. He had left off shaving some years ago, and the full beard prevented the need to see his face. Siobhan kept his hair trimmed to what he considered a decent length.

But, still. *No gray hair, and do I have wrinkles? And how old would I be now? Fifty? Forty-nine? How old?*

"Oh, you're wrong there, my friend," he said finally. "I have aged. I just wear it well," he added with a small smile.

They sat in the silence again until Siobhan joined them.

"I tell you true, he's your son to the root, Tobias. Tell him a story, sing him a song." She smoothed a lock of hair from her face with the back of her hand. "The wee sot is wearin' me out, Goddess bless him."

Toby reached for his lady and, taking a piece of her dress in his grasp, pulled her close to him. He leaned his head against her hip and just let it rest there as her fingers combed through his hair. For her part, she just continued her story of putting Rohan to bed and kissing him goodnight. When it was done, the sun passed behind the trees and dusk had arrived.

"Tobias, I truly did not come just to drink your ale and watch the sunset with you."

"Your company is always welcome," Siobhan said to him. "You know that, Yeshua."

"I do," he answered. "But I did have a purpose in mind. Two, in fact. One was to reassure you that Aiobh had decided to remain behind. I know you'll be happy to hear this, Siobhan."

She raised a hand to her throat and let her fingers rest there. "Oh, thank you, Yeshua. I *was* worried she would be goin' back to her family in next village. I don't want anyone else to be my midwife. There's a great comfort you bring me."

"Good," he said to her. "Then, to my other purpose; I've come to tell you both that I will be leaving soon."

Siobhan caressed Toby's exposed cheek with her other hand, his head now resting against her belly – she was just beginning to show. "Aye, you're off on another jaunt, are you? And with Lughnasadh so close? Will you be back in time, Yeshua?"

"No, Siobhan," he said gently. "Soon I will be leaving for good."

Toby sat up abruptly at this and the two began to speak over each other.

"What do you mean—"

"Leave? For good—"

"You can't leave—"

"Where'll you go, lad—"

The candlelight from the cottage spilled onto the hard packed soil and there was enough of the fading light for them to see Yeshua's hand rise. They both stopped as quickly as they started.

"My friends," Yeshua said. "And you are my friends, you know."

"Aye," Siobhan started.

"We know," Toby finished.

"Good," Yeshua continued. "My friends, this was not to be a permanent place for me to stay. Tobias, you knew that when we left my home. I came out into the world to learn of it, learn my Father's plan for me and for His people. It is time to move on."

"But...how? *When?* And where'll you go?" Siobhan blurted out, clearly flustered and trying to make sense of the news.

Toby sat back enough to take her hand in his. He pulled her around to sit in his lap and watched her face move into the shadow created by the remaining light. Toby couldn't see it but knew she was close to tears.

"I have thought of this," Yeshua answered her. "In my travels, I have heard of a place where they follow a being called the Buddha. They have marvelous animals there. The man called one an...*elephant*. Yes, that was it, an elephant. When I heard him first speak of this place, I knew it was where I was to travel next. My Father has told me this."

Toby swallowed his disappointment. "When, Yeshua?"

"Not for a bit," he answered. "I will stay till after the Lughnasadh rite. I shall leave with the next full moon and travel on."

"I promised your màthair I'd be lookin' after you, lad. And I can't leave here, you know that." Toby felt genuine regret at that statement, but he knew it was true; not with another child coming, not when his whole life was here.

"I know, Tobias. This is your home now. It's where you belong. I would no more ask you to leave this place and these people than I would ask you to cut off your arm."

"But Yeshua," Siobhan sputtered. "You don't know the way. And you'll be alone. I cannot bear that."

"Oh my dearest friend, I will be quite well. I will be very careful and I have found transportation to take me to the closest port and then I will walk." Yeshua smiled as reassuringly as he possibly could. "And I will not be alone. I will have my Father with me. My Father will provide."

Yeshua stood up, draining his mug as he did. He belched deeply and laughed at himself. He held the mug out to Siobhan, who simply handed the mug to her husband and threw her arms around Yeshua's neck. She stood in his embrace and wept into his shoulder for a time. When her tears were spent, she stepped back, wiping them from her face.

"Well," she said. "We've got time to enjoy your company, at least. I'll be takin' these mugs in then."

She took Toby's mug as well, and disappeared back through the cottage doorway. Toby walked a few paces from the cottage, Yeshua following beside him. As he walked out into the grass, he saw a waning moon above his head. They had another three weeks or so before the next full. They would have some time.

Yeshua stood beside him, gazing into the night sky. "The stars are just as bright here, are they not, my friend? The moon in the sky is the same one, I think. We'll have that."

"I'll miss your company, my friend."

"Arrogant and obnoxious as I was?"

"Feh," Toby snorted out. "I've seen worse." He turned to face the younger man. "But you've not been that person for a long time. You have become so much more. I can feel it in you."

Yeshua grasped Toby's arm. "I think we have both changed, my friend."

Toby returned the gesture. "Well, we've time for a proper goodbye. Good night, Yeshua."

As he walked away, Toby heard Yeshua call his name. There was a note of sadness in his voice and Toby couldn't help but turn to it.

"Aye?"

"Tobias, enjoy this. Cherish this." Yeshua gestured towards the house. "Love every moment and take none for granted. For you know not what is in my Father's plans for you."

Toby felt a chill on his back. He had no idea why Yeshua would say this. Was it because of Declan? He knew that the death had cause Yeshua a great deal of pain but was that what he meant? Toby waited, sure that Yeshua would say more but he didn't. "Good night, my friend," was all he said and he walked into the darkness.

Love every moment and take none for granted. It was exactly what Toby planned to do.

Although the rains had come and rescued the season, there would still be a late harvest. Toby, Liam, and Gwydion had enough hay to bale from the first mowing, but it wasn't enough to sustain the livestock for the season. They would need to bale at least two more and fortunately had time. Siobhan would begin to start her preserving of the vegetables and fruits. Her herb garden would last a bit longer before she needed to harvest the plants and bring them inside to cure and dry.

The days passed in lazy abandon, routine and comfortable. Toby awoke one day and had his usual breakfast with his family. He made his way out to the field he planned on weeding that day and set to work. He walked the rows, surveying the corn crops and plucking weeds and small bugs from the plants.

He knew they would have something for the Lughnasadh rite. Each household would provide a small corn or wheat cake to be blessed for the ceremony. The cake would be shared amongst the members of the house and then scattered to the earth in thanks to the Gods. He had a fine batch of heather ale to provide for the blessing. It was a good harvest and a good year, despite the hardships. He had a great deal to be thankful for.

"Well, well, well; will you look there. The gentleman farmer is out and about in the morn."

Toby grinned and, tossing aside a silk he had pulled from one of the ears, turned to greet the speaker. "Well, if it isn't the Mother's Bard, comin' from his quiet home. I hear tell you been quite the trained monkey for your lady these days."

Gwydion guffawed, clutching his belly. "Aye, she does keep me busy of late." His voice pitched up high, mimicking his wife's tone. "Gwy, do get Duncan's nappy; Gwy, where's the wheel you promised to make for the cart; Gwy, where's the hoein' to be done today?" His voice returned to his regular speaking tone and he shook his head, still smiling. "The woman is a blessin' most times, but she does like to make sure I'm not being idle. I've not had a lick of time for the music."

Toby laughed and elbowed Gwydion in the ribs. "But you'd have her no other way, now. Speak true."

With a wink, Gwy answered, "Aye, you're right."

Toby looked up at the clouds puffing merrily across a sapphire blue sky. "Come on," he said, inhaling the fresh air gratefully. "I need to get this section of the gardens done."

Gwydion picked up the hoe from where Toby had tossed it. "Inch by inch, row by row!"

The two went to work with a resolve, removing the weeds and quite a few rather ugly caterpillars from several dozen rows before deciding it was time to take a break to eat. Gwydion had brought a container of ale and lunch wrapped up in a length of linen, provided by his nagging wife. Toby had the same, only his drink was apple cider. The two found a shady spot under a close by tree and sat to partake of it.

Toby took a bite and chewed, enjoying the taste of the beef tongue. He wondered if something was wrong. It wasn't really like Gwy to come work a garden with him. They normally worked each section alone because the gardens were so big. He swallowed his bite and took a drink of cider to clear it. "You've heard news of Yeshua?"

Gwydion stopped chewing, looking down at the meat in his hand. It was a few moments before he finally resumed and swallowed. "Aye, he came by and told us the other night. I as wonderin' if he'd told *you*."

"Aye, he did," Toby confessed ruefully. "Siobhan was happy to hear Aiobh is stayin', but she was upset to hear that the lad leavin' us."

"Aye." Gwydion left the word hanging for the short time it took him to drink a few swallows from his ale. "I'll tell you true – when we met, I was convinced the boy was a hard lot."

Toby chuckled around a mouthful of the hoecake that Siobhan had packed for him, trying not to choke on it. "Aye, he was that."

"But, you know," Gwydion said thoughtfully. "He turned out to be right smarter lad than we gave him credit for. A good man inside, Tobias, with a kind heart; a friend to the Celts."

Toby again agreed but this time, kept eating.

"Aye, a right smart." Gwydion took a bite of his corned beef, and chewed thoughtfully on it.

Toby knew his friend was waiting for him to say something, waiting for an opening to get to the real subject. He took another sip of his cider. "I'll miss the lad, no lie. He grew up a lot, Gwy. I never realized until he came to say goodbye that I expected him to stay here forever."

"Aye."

The suspense was killing him. With no preamble, Toby blurted out, "Alright, lad, I think I've waited long enough. What's really on your mind?"

Gwydion's face flushed from something other than the heat, and he managed to sputter out, "Well...'tis only for Siobhan and your little ones that I ask, you see, but...well, I was wondering if you'll be leavin' with him." He cleared his throat as a finish to the question.

Toby stared at Gwy for a moment – did he really ask that? The peals of laughter started in his middle, he couldn't help himself. He laughed until he couldn't breathe and tears were squirting from his eyes and running down his cheeks, and still he laughed. He had to put his food down, unsure of where to grab first – his belly or his back. Both were starting to ache from the sheer force of his laughter.

Gwydion sat with his mouth hanging open, watching what had to be the most insane behavior he'd ever seen.

Toby realized that Gwy was thinking him totally unhinged and finally got control of himself. He waved away any offer of clapping his back or the mug of ale. He wiped tears from his eyes and took a deep breath before replying. "Lady help us, took you long enough to ask it."

It was Gwydion's turn to look amused and he snorted. "Well, don't be takin' on fancy airs, lad. It's for your wife and children I'm askin'."

"Oh, aye, and not for yourself at all," Toby teased.

"Aye, well," Gwydion replied gruffly.

Toby smiled, laying his hand on Gwy's shoulder. "No, my Bardic friend, I'm not goin' any place else. I chose to stay here the moment you brought me. I can't think of livin' anywhere but here. Fireun Sidhe is my home now. 'Tis where I belong. 'Tis where my wife and my son were born." Toby sniggered again and then turned serious. "No, my friend, you'll not be rid of me that easy."

Gwydion heaved a huge sigh of relief and his shoulders dropped as he relaxed.

Toby was touched by the reaction. "Were you that troubled? That I'd be leavin'?"

Gwydion sheepishly nodded. "Aye, Tobias, I was that sure of it. I don't want you to go."

"What, and leave a fine meal as this, lad? Not bloody likely!"

"Stop your teasin', brother," Gwydion said, his face suddenly even more serious. "You did more than save my life on that road, you know." Gwydion looked away, embarrassed, and tossed pieces of hoecake as he spoke. "You took me to your heart, Tobias. You took me in without knowin' me and you brought me home. You've been a good friend to me, the brother I never had. I don't want to lose such as that."

Toby felt his heart pounding in his chest; the affection was a tidal wave to wash over him. He reached over and stopped one of Gwydion's hands by taking hold of the wrist. Gwydion looked up and Toby felt moved to tears. It was unmanly, he knew, but he was that affected by the outpouring of love. He made eye contact and didn't let go, making sure that Gwy knew that this was a serious pact between them.

"I'm not goin' anywhere, Gwydion," Toby said solemnly. "And I swear to you, that it'll be *you* that leaves this place before I *ever* set foot beyond the gates."

Gwydion nodded, placing his free hand over Toby's. "Well, then, we're assured of each other's company, aye?"

"Aye, Gwydion, we are."

They both turned back to their lunches and ate with a renewed appetite. When they had finished and packed up the remains, they returned to the patch and finished the hoeing. Neither one spoke again of the fear they'd put to rest but Toby remembered it. He would always remember it, engraved on his memory and his heart.

If it was to be Yeshua's last rite with the people of Fireun Sidhe, they were determined to make it a special one. They gathered in the stone circle and stood quietly as Aiobh invoked the Quarters. Toby held his son close and his lady closer, and watched the young man before him invoke a God, knowing that the God of Israel was already among them.

"We come to the first of the harvest rites," Aiobh said. "The grains been good and first harvest has begun. The Dagda has opened his heart to His children and offered them from His never empty Cauldron."

Yeshua walked up to the altar and pulled something from behind it. It was a round tray of sorts, covered with a woolen cloth. He came to the first person in the circle, and began to collect the loaves of bread that each had brought.

"It has been a hard year," she went on, while Yeshua passed by each. Siobhan placed their loaf on the makeshift tray and Yeshua stopped long enough to give her a smile and a nod. Toby felt her soft shudder beside him and knew she had begun to cry.

"We have suffered much and we lost one that was near to our hearts. Our Declan was our conscience and my mate—" Her voice broke and she paused for a second to clear her throat. "—and he is sore missed. But his spirit lives on in Annwn, and he will return into a new birth. We come to celebrate his gift to us all."

Yeshua had gathered up the loaves and took them to the center. He placed the tray with its contents on top of the cauldron and then moved to the opposite side from Aiobh. He joined hands with her over the mound of bread. The air suddenly crackled and snapped. The hair rose on the back of Toby's neck, on his arms.

"I do ask you, Mother Dana, to bless this fruit of Your womb," she chanted." I ask You give us all strength to finish out the good harvest and see it through to the end. I ask You fill these loaves with Your light and truth that the grain may nourish our hearts and souls. So mote it be."

"I do call you, Father," Yeshua intoned and the electricity grew. "Give of Your blessings to these people and this place. I give You thanks for those who have shown kindness to me and I ask Your blessings bestow a great abundance for all time. Bless these loaves that it may nourish their bodies and free their souls. Bless the land that it may always prosper. In the name of the Father, amen."

Aiobh took the tray and carried it back to the first in the circle. She served the blessed loaves to all, no one really receiving the same loaf they'd brought but it little mattered. Each family received a loaf and Toby took theirs. He broke it up to give Rohan and Siobhan their pieces. He broke off his own and held on to the last piece while they ate.

Yeshua had turned his attention to the cauldron in the middle. The energy that he had raised still had not dissipated, holding steady around them. Toby ate silently and watched...and listened.

"My Father, you have blessed the grain and given the fruit of the vine. I ask You now to bless this ale. Let it carry Your love to those who drink. As the bread is Thy body, so is this Thy blood and all who eat and drink of it are nourished and cherished. In the name of the Father, amen."

Yeshua dipped in first one pitcher, and then another, and followed behind Aiobh to fill the drinking cups for all of the gathered. Toby had finished his portion of the bread and now crumbled the remainder as his offering. He watched Siobhan do the same, and she gave a shy smile and shrug to her husband. As Toby pulled the cup from the pocket of his robe, he leaned forward to give his wife a kiss on the cheek.

"Da, me too."

He plucked Rohan from the ground, and the little boy put an arm around his father's neck, and reached forward to do the same to his mother. Yeshua reached them at just the same time, and both parents put forth their cups. Yeshua didn't travel on, at first, just standing to watch the family.

"I shall miss you," he said, gazing at Siobhan and then, at Rohan. He nodded at them and passed on his way.

The remainder of the ale was drunk and offered in the same manner to the Gods. Yeshua lifted the cauldron from its place in the center, and there was a small stack of wood laid as a log cabin would have been. Aiobh removed the woolen covering, and Toby saw that the tray was a wheel, made of the barley, corn, and rye fronds of the first harvest. The cauldron was placed at the altar, and Yeshua brought a torch and lit the logs that had served as the base.

Aiobh stood with the wheel, as he was performing the acts, and said, "One more thing that we must give thanks for – our friend, Yeshua."

Yeshua turned towards the High Priestess and she smiled towards him as she spoke.

"He came to us so many seasons past and has been our comfort and our savior these past days. He has been as a son to Declan and I, and a pupil. On this day of the Harvest, as the last Rite I shall perform, I wish to thank him, and give thanks for him."

There was a chorus of "Bléssed Be" and "So mote it be," and the young man smiled at the gathering. Toby nodded his head in agreement and sniffed back the tears forming in his own eyes.

Aiobh held out the wheel before her, walking the circle as she spoke. "This is the wheel of the year. There is no beginning and no ending in this wheel, and each turn falls into another and another. The wheel of life is the wheel of the year. Place your blessing in the wheel that we may offer it up as thanks to the Dagda and Dana."

Aiobh turned and handed the wheel to Yeshua, who took it around the circle. Each family laid hands on it and muttered their words of thanks over it. Siobhan and Toby placed their hands on the wheel, and Toby held Rohan close, so that he could do the same. The little cherub squeaked out his thanks "for my Da and Ma, thank you, Yeshua." There was a chorus of laughter from those standing closest. It would be something to remember for always.

When the last family had blessed the wheel, Yeshua brought it to the center and tossed it on the bonfire. They watched it burn brightly before crumbling to flaming bits inside the log base. The warmth of the blaze touched Toby's face and the heat made him squint. Then the pyre died back down, the heat was gone and the electricity with it. All that was left was the release of the Gods and Quarters, and the gathering in the barn.

Toby and Siobhan danced until it was very late and Rohan had gone to sleep in a corner with the other wee ones who'd been brought. It was mostly to congratulate Aidan, who would be taking over the Chief and Priestly duties. Aidan had been born in Fireun Sidhe, had taken instruction from Declan, and was more than capable of taking the duties. Regan, from the village at the Piper's Stones, had been handfast to Aidan the summer before Toby had arrived. She had served as Aiobh's handmaiden and Aiobh felt confident that she was just as capable.

After saying their goodnights, Toby led his lady off, stopping to gather their sleeping child in the corner. Rohan sighed in his sleep and reached his chubby arms around Toby's neck, lolling his head against one arm. They waved goodbye to a few others and walked out of the barn, hand in hand. Toby and Siobhan were almost home before any conversation began between them.

"Well, darlin', would you happy for a boy?"

Toby kissed her hand. "Lady, I would be happy for good healthy children."

She tittered at his response and gently nudged him with her hip.

He laughed quietly at the gesture and nudged back. "Aye, another son would make me happy but I think I'll be lookin' for a girl, to be fair. A sweet girl that looks like her màthair with the sweet smile and copper tresses."

She moved closer to him until his arm was wrapped in both of hers and nestled against her breasts. The same lavender smell that always aroused him, the same gestures that caught him unaware and he fell in love time and again.

"Well, my handsome husband, if it's not to be with this little one in my belly, we'll just have to keep trying."

He breathed deeply of her, his eyes closed as he did it. "Aye, we'll do just that."

They took Rohan to his room and Siobhan bundled him in his bed. Toby stood, watching her smooth the hair from the child's face and kiss his sweet little cheek. When she had taken the candle from sconce, they went into their own bedroom, and Toby made love to her, slipping into her body and tasting her soul. He kissed her and reveled in her.

When the lovemaking was over, she fell asleep in his arms, her head against this shoulder. Any other night, he would have fallen asleep with her but tonight was different. His mind was racing over the day. Another child and another harvest had begun. His heart told him to take stock, and his mind ran over the elements of his life. Had he ever been more at peace? Could anything ever compare with this moment in time? His eyes closed and he slipped down into the peace of slumber.

clang...clang...clang...clang....

Bion had come back. Bion was telling him the bell was calling him for a meeting. It was his Ma telling him the school bell was ringing and he was late. It was the church bell ringing out Mass. It was the bell ringing for Declan....

It was the village bell and someone was banging the hell out of it. He reached and grabbed his trews, throwing them on as fast as he could. Siobhan was also awake and dressing in a race with time, but Toby was faster. He grabbed his shirt and darted towards the door. As he reached the threshold, he stopped briefly, and turned toward her.

"Stay here and watch Rohan. It's probably nothing but sick cow or something else of that nature."

She paused in the folds of her dress, her head peeking through the neck hole. "Tobias—"

He threw up his hand to stop her protest. "No, lady, wait here. I'll be back."

He flew down the pathway, yanking on his shirt as he ran. There was a deep fear in his heart, growing with every step. Heaviness bore down on him. He ran into the common, not the last to arrive, and joined the growing knot of people. He couldn't hear where he was standing and started to push his way through the crowd to where Yeshua stood with Aidan. They were standing beside another man, covered in blood. Not sure if it was the man's own blood, Toby stood next to his friend and immediately recognized the bloody man. It was Conor again.

Aiobh pushed her way through the crowd, carrying a bag, and Aidan and newly arrived Gwydion helped the wounded man to the ground. Toby thought he looked faint but still coherent. Aiobh began to minister to a vicious gash in Conor's shoulder, the source of the blood, and the men around him began to ask questions.

"'Tis the Scotians, for sure, a huge army," Conor managed to choke out, still gasping from the pain and from the obvious dash to the village to impart the news."Come from north, they did, burning forest and land behind 'em.'

Those closest heard the dire news and a hubbub started, growing louder until Aidan jumped to his feet to quiet the crowd.

"Folk," he yelled, "quiet! Listen to me."

The gathered calmed back down and, while the murmuring continued, at least the din was settled.

Aiden continued speaking, his hands still in the air. "Listen to me. I can't find out what's happenin' if you keep shoutin'. I know you're scared but let's find out what we're up against." He knelt back down to where Aiobh was applying a bandage to Conor's wound. "All right, Conor, tell the rest of it."

A hand reached forth with a mug of something and Conor took it. He drank deeply from the mug, nodded his thanks, and gasped to get the air into him. When he could breathe normally again, he went on. "Aye, I will. Scotians, a great horde of 'em. They poured into the village last night. Were no warning except the others that were runnin' in front."

"What others?" Yeshua asked.

"Others from other villages in the bastards' path, fleeing away from 'em. By time someone rung the bell, it was too late. Scot bastards were runnin' into the village, slicin' up any that got in their way. Women and children, it didn't mean a difference to 'em." He drained the last from the mug, spoke next to Aiobh. Nodding over his shoulder, he said, "I took that keepin' a wee one from being slaughtered by a tartan shite. Drove my dirk in his throat and he cut me deep as he fell, the miserable bastard."

Aidan stood up again and turned back to the crowd. "You heard him, the Scotians are comin'. Every man and woman who can fight, get your armor and blades, and come back here. We fight 'em." When he saw they were not moving, he shouted, "Get you goin'. Did you not hear me? Scotians are comin'. Do you want to lose it all?"

The place turned to mass pandemonium at that point. Bodies were running, here and there and beyond. Toby grasped the new High Priest by the arm and turned the man to face him.

"Are you daft, Aidan? We need a plan. We can't be fighting willy-nilly here."

Aidan shook his arm out of Toby's grasp. "Do as I say, man," he retorted. "There's no Roman army coming now. This is Celts fightin' Celts. I know what I'm doin'."

Toby started to shout the High Priest down, tried to shout anyone down to get anyone's attention, but Gwydion grabbed him and pulled him back hard. He dragged Toby back several paces, getting him to stop shouting and pay attention.

"Come, Tobias, don't be wastin' words." He pulled Toby around to face him, grasping his friend's shoulders tightly to keep him from bolting away. "Come. You need your armor if they're comin'. You can't change his mind, brother. Come along if you want to save your family."

That was enough to get Toby moving and they took off at a trot. Neither spoke until they had reached the gate at the edge of the family farm. Gwydion stopped and grabbed Toby's elbow again.

"Look, I didn't want to say this in front of the men, but I have something to ask of you."

"Aye, my brother, whatever you wish."

Gwydion's face was dark in the half light of dawn. His voice was close to breaking as he spoke. "I need your promise that if I don't make it, you'll take care of Deirdre and my children. You'll protect 'em. I need your promise."

Toby swallowed hard, the rock in his chest making it difficult to breathe. "Aye, Gwydion. I'll do it. You have to promise me the same in return. Keep Siobhan, Rohan, and the little one comin' safe."

"I'll die before I'll let 'em be harmed, Tobias."

Toby grasped Gwydion's forearm and nodded. "Tis done. Now, go."

Gwydion backed up a few paces and stopped, his lips moving.

Toby waited, also at a loss for what to say. They stared at each other before Gwydion nodded, then turned and dashed off towards his farm. Liam came running up and Toby filled him in on the news. The older man turned back around and dashed into his own cottage to suit up. Toby took several running steps before he ran smack into Siobhan.

"What is it? Tobias, tell me. You didn't come back—"

"Scotians," he answered tersely, and watched her face fill with horror and then anger.

"Aye," she exclaimed. "We'll get dressed for battle,"

"*NO!*"

She turned back to him, her brows knitted in confusion. "What you mean 'no'? You don't want to fight? Tobias, have you turned coward?"

He took her arms and pulled her to him. "No, lady, I'm no coward. But you will not be fightin'. Promise me."

She tried to pull away but his grip was too tight. "Let me go, Tobias," she sputtered angrily. "You're hurtin' me."

He pulled her into his embrace and just stood there holding her. She stopped her struggles and held him back.

"Listen to me, lady." His voice was quavering now. "I can't bear to have you in this, to know you could be hurt or dyin'. I can't bear it. Please, I beg you. Take Rohan and hide in the woods 'til this is over."

She looked up from his chest, defiant. "And you'll be needing me on your back. I'll be protectin' m' home all the same."

He released the hold on her arms, and took her face gently in his hands. "Lady, I can't live with your death on my conscience. I can't fight knowin' you could be hurt. I'll fight for both of us. Please, just do as I ask. Take Rohan and go to the woods. Please."

"All right, Tobias," she surrendered. "I'll not join the fray, but I will not leave my home. I'll stay in it with our boy. Surely, they'll not come that far."

He lowered his face to hers and kissed her, passionately and deeply. He tasted her tongue and the sweetness of her lips. *Goddess, how I love you*, he thought, and a voice came through the emotion in his heart. It was Yeshua calling his name. He released her and said, "Get my armor and blades ready. I'll fetch them as soon as I've spoken with Yeshua."

Yeshua waited until he was out the door before speaking. "Tobias, I can't do this."

Toby put his arm around the younger man's shoulders. "Aye, my friend, I know. You can't. Your Father won't want it so."

"This is not right, Tobias." Yeshua looked up at Toby, his face still so serious. "But, there is no way to stop it. I'm taking the children into the woods, to hide until it's over. I came to collect your family, if you wish it."

Toby looked over his shoulder and for a brief second, had the strongest urge to agree to the offer. In the blink of an eye, so many thoughts poured into his head of forcing Siobhan to take Rohan with her and going with Yeshua. She'd fight him but he'd make her go. No, she was defiant enough to stay and she'd just wait until he was gone to barricade herself and the boy inside. No, leave her be for now. He turned back to Yeshua, who was waiting for his answer.

"No, lad, thank you. They'll be fine where they be. Take the children and go. Look for me when this is over, aye?"

Yeshua nodded, clasping his friend's arm to seal the promise. "You will be well, my friend. I know it. I will pray for all of you."

As Yeshua ran off, Toby heard the first stirrings of the battle. Shouts and screams were carried on the morning breezes and he was torn between running to join the fighting or take his family and disappear with Yeshua and the other children. Taking a deep breath, he forced himself to run for the battle armor. Siobhan had it ready, and dressed him quickly. She placed the sword in his hands, strapped the dirk to his belt, and stepped back.

"I love you, lady wife," he said, taking one more moment to look into her eyes.

"I love you, m' céile."

He left quickly, knowing that if he didn't then, he never would. He ran towards the sounds of the screams and was joined by Gwydion, dressed in the leather armaments and brandishing his own sword.

"Did you ever think a peace lovin' bard as me would be doin' such?" Gwydion was trying to keep his voice light but it was obvious that he was frightened.

"Or me?"

"Tobias, remember your promise."

Toby spared one more glance at his friend and smiled, trying to project a confidence that he didn't really feel. And he wasn't sure why. "Watch your back, Bard o' the Goddess!"

With that, they ran full tilt into the battle. The Scots had painted their faces in mud and woad, battling with shouts and growls, and they were vicious and remorseless. Toby met one brandishing a blade that gleamed in blood, and matched blows. The clanging of the steel echoed the clanging of the bell. The Scot pounded away with his broadsword brandished in his two hands; each blow thrummed up Toby's arms. He matched the beating until his shoulder ached and he felt like it would pop from the socket. A feint to the left, a quick duck, and his enemy was dispatched with the dirk, quickly pulled him his belt.

He and Gwydion stood together, back to back, fighting the Scotians that came their way. He could feel his brother standing right behind him, the banging of his sword matching the ones from his opponent. All around them were the sounds and the smells of battle, where the villagers of Fireun Sidhe held a line against the enemy attackers. In his periphery, he saw them fighting tooth and nail. Many Scotians fell to Ir swords and the bodies lay where they dropped, the combatants merely moving to the side of them. When an Ir man or woman fell, another ran forward to take their place with the foe.

Toby was caught in battle with a painted attacker when he felt his back suddenly give way as Gwydion moved. He stepped back to compensate, but Gwydion was gone. He turned to look, and saw Gwydion running in the direction of home. His heart leaped in his chest as he saw a group that had broken through the line and were running for his farm. He took another step to dash that way himself and felt a dull thud to his temple. His vision blurred and he fell to his knees at the same time as a sword pierced a man to his right. The blood spurted and Toby felt the knife blade pierce his chest. He pitched forward in agony. His last sight was the ground flooding with his blood before darkness took him.

How long? How long have I been on the ground? I can hear her. I can hear her screaming. Dear Goddess, where's Siobhan? Gwydion, save her. Stop them. NO...no!

The djinn laughing again. "These gifts have brought you nothing but misery. Tsk, tsk. Ah well, be careful what you ask for, you may get it."

Bion tugging at his sleeve, pulling at his arm. "Wake up, man. Get your ass off that ground and wake up. C'mon, Captain."

He opened one eye, heard the silence, and knew it was over.

"Tobias? Are you awake? Are you well?"

Yeshua...I can't talk to him right now. Where is she? Siobhan! Where are you?

Toby pushed himself up, off the ground, and to his knees. He tore open the shirt, and looked at his chest. The blood flow had stopped itself and his chest looked more like an angry scar than a stab wound. It looked as if it had happened days before, not mere hours. He ran his hand over the wound and felt the pain. *Good*, he thought, *it'll keep me from fainting.*

"Tobias, you've been hurt."

Toby shook the cobwebs from his head and waved his friend off. He was shaking as he did so and fought another wave of nausea and fainting. Everywhere he looked, every square inch of ground was covered in blood and gore with bodies hacked beyond recognition. Body parts scattered like grisly litter on the freeway. His mouth was filled with bile as he fought to keep from throwing up. The trail of bodies led towards his front door.

He took one step, then another until his feet promised not to turn traitor and he ran with everything he had in him. He ran past the gate, past Liam and Niamh's cottage, past Gwydion's cottage. He ran to his own, knowing in his head that Yeshua ran behind him. Three feet and he saw the pile of bodies. Two feet and he recognized the one on top. He fell to his knees and, taking the arm, slowly and gently turned the body over. Gwydion's sightless eyes were frozen in a grimace of anger and pain.

Toby burst into tears and clutched the body to his. *No, no, no.* Another thought raced in his mind and he laid the corpse back down. *Siobhan!* The charred remains of his home were still smoldering, the blackened lumps of wood crumbling along with the ashes strewn around them. The bastards had set fire to his house, his barns, and nothing remained of his life within the walls. All he felt was the desperation to find his family.

He walked, trying to quell the fear and the dread that it was too late. He found her sprawled on the ground, her hair fanned on the grasses around her head. She lay still in her exquisite beauty, a dagger in her hand and her eyes open and watching nothing. There she was, poised beside the body of their son, a gaping slit in the child's throat and a splash of blood displayed the sword thrusts in her own.

"Tobias? Tobias – oh!"

He saw no more, felt no more, could do no more. The world around him went black again and his last conscious act was reaching out to take her hand in his.

Chapter Twenty-Four

"I don't remember a whole lot, after that. I spent so much time lost behind a curtain. But, I have spotty memories, like single tableaus in a black sea. I remember that her mother and Niamh prepared the bodies for me. I remember that they talked about rebuilding our cottage. To be honest, I was as close to dead as you can get and not be there. Or, at least, I thought I was."

John watched Toby struggle with his emotions. Toby knew he was watching, but couldn't give a damn about it. The whole thing cut through him like the blade of the knife that had taken him out of the game. So many years ago and the tears still came, hot and scorching on his cheeks. He wept silently for a few minutes, giving in to the grief that was still fresh and probably always would be. When he could finally speak again, he wiped the tears away with his palms and went on.

"Liam was cut bad. They thought he wouldn't make it, but he did. Aidan was killed, stupid ass. That's what he was, you know – a stupid ass." Toby shook his head and another sip of the coffee. "It wasn't Rome, he said. I didn't know what I was up against, he said. It was Celt fighting Celt, he said. That whole event should've been planned. It was *a slaughter*! We lost too many good people and it was all because of an untried, inexperienced, vain *ass*."

Toby had to stop and breathe. His heart started pounding, his chest felt too tight and too hard, and his blood pressure had gone through the ceiling. He could see the spots in front of his eyes. The rage had boiled up again with the memories of a defense that failed and his impotence in trying to make them listen. *Stupid, arrogant ass!* Toby buried his face in his free hand and let it drain from his body.

...the tree...I am the tree...let it run from my body like water, through the tap root, into the Mother...she takes the pain and makes it good again....

John was also affected, sniffing as well. With a quavering voice, he asked, "So, what happened? How bad were *you*?"

Toby pulled it back together. "It was bad. I lost a lot of blood, too.

But I got luckier than the rest. Immortality, it would seem, also meant self-healing. The wounds that should have killed me healed in days." He laughed, a humorless and hard sound that hurt deep in his chest. "I lost my best friend, my wife, and two children, but not my life."

The pause of silence felt bloody and Toby had to fill it. But first, he took another gulp of coffee to clear the dull copper taste from his mouth. "We buried them. The ones that were left, the ones still standing, dug the cairns and we buried them. Aiobh ended up leading the ceremony and stayed on as High Priestess. I guess Regan couldn't handle it and went a bit postal." His grin was a little more sincere this time. He'd actually liked Regan. "Well, that's what they said but, not in so many words. If I recall correctly, Donal – something, I don't remember his name – told me she'd gone off her chump, that's how he put it. I went back to visit – before I came back to my time, you know – and she'd killed herself by then."

"Sounds like you wanted to do the same thing," John observed.

"Oh, yeah, that's an affirmative, my friend. I was that damn close to checking out."

"Why didn't you?" John blurted out. Immediately, he ducked his head, embarrassed that he'd asked. "What I mean is...well, I would've...I mean...."

"I know what you mean," Toby reassured him. "You want to know what kept me from it. After all, I'm still here, right?"

Four days after the burials, Toby was at last able to stand up by himself. He was still shaky and unsure of his walking but he was standing. He'd finally stopped the copious tears and was left with the stony silence. He had been moved back with Niamh and Liam, and the poor woman had her hands full tending to both of them and grieving for her son.

Gwydion! Dear God, Gwydion, too. His brother had died trying to save his family. He should have been there. It should have been him. Siobhan and Rohan and his unborn son, it should have been him. Lost in the fog of his thoughts, playing it over and over like a tape loop in his head. The old mental VCR never stops and rewinds on its own. That technology should be shared with the world, by God. And Goddess!

He sat outside on a surviving stump and stared into nothing, never moving. The emptiness has settled in and there was no emotion, no feeling, and no reaction to anything. It should have been him.

"I wanted to. You will never know the pull that came from it. I couldn't do it, at first. I had no access to anything and I wasn't able to get up out of bed. Then, I didn't have the energy to do *anything* but sit there. And then, Yeshua came. Hell, I thought he'd gone on, but he hadn't. He was still there."

A visit from another old friend, a traveling companion; he came to see Toby. He sat down with him, Toby's eyes still staring out over the treetops, still watching the tape loop.

"Tobias," he had said, "you cannot think you are responsible. It was God's will. You cannot stop that any more than you can stop the seasons and the days."

No answer, just the stony silence.

"My friend, I am so sorry for your losses. She was a good woman. Your son was a credit to both of you. But they would want you to continue. You must do that for them."

"Yeshua is the one that talked me out of it. He said they'd want me to go on." Toby shook his head with a small smile of remembering. "I could hear her saying it, too. 'Get up off your lazy arse and get to it.' I did. I didn't want to, but I did."

"You felt guilty."

"I felt guilty and dirty and angry. The hate didn't come 'til later. It should have been me. *It should've!*"

"But, it wasn't," John said, a stern fatherly tone to his voice. "It wasn't you and it wasn't supposed to be."

"No," he acquiesced. "It wasn't. I know that now. I didn't know it then."

John stretched his legs out and started massaging his knees from where he'd been sitting for so long. Toby watched him work one knee and then the other. When John had finished with his knees, he started to massage his left ankle and foot.

"You ok, man?"

"Oh, yeah," John answered in amusement. "My foot just fell asleep."

"Sorry."

The older man chortled and shook his head. "You know, I've been sittin' here thinking. Man, there was a time when I was in a depression so black, the rest of the world looked white to me. I got fired from a recording label even though I'd outsold most of the acts on it. My dad died just when I was getting to know and understand him. My wife decided she wanted a divorce after fifteen years. I crawled in a bottle for five years and one rehab clinic."

"That had to be a bitch."

John stopped his massage, an eyebrow cocked. "*A bitch?*" He stopped and sat back, looking out over the darkness. "Yeah, I suppose compared to what you went through, it was a bitch. At the time, I wanted to take a handful of pills and check out."

"What stopped *you*?"

"This is gonna sound like the lamest Hollywood excuse in the world, but it's the truth – my work. My music and that changing sea of faces every night. I loved singin' for 'em. It kept me going when I didn't want to."

John leaned forward, as if he was going to tell this stranger in front of him the most intimate secret he had. Toby couldn't help it; he leaned forward too.

"But I'll tell you this," John said. "Every time I sang that song, I felt a knife stabbing *my* heart. I got to a point that I hated it with everything I had in me. The song that gets played at every wedding and I was dying. I got to where I sang it in every language I could, just to keep from singing the words."

Toby tossed a few more logs on the fire and the sparks flitted in the air, before burning out. "Yeah, I bet. I remember hearing you sing it in Russian."

John frowned in confusion. "How did you hear that?"

"I was in the White Mountains in New Hampshire, visiting a friend. She knew I loved your music and got two tickets. We sat on the lawn in the middle of a tornado warning."

John threw back his head, laughing as his hair flew around in a golden halo. "I remember that one. Yeah, no one was moving, everybody sat there like it was nuthin'. I couldn't believe it. I figured if those friends were gonna sit there, I was gonna play. It was a good show."

"It was," Toby agreed. "A damn good show. I sat next to this woman and her husband, she was pregnant with her second child. When you got to the encore, the song was echoing off the mountains. I remembered watching her reach down to her belly and start laughing."

"Why?"

"When the show was over, I asked her what had been so funny. She said the baby had started dancing with the music, kickin' in time with it."

John laughed heartily again. "Far out."

Toby started to laugh with him but the video in his head started to play again, and his smiles and laughter dissolved.

"God, I'm so sorry, Toby." John's guffaws dried up as well. "Thanks for the story, though."

"Sure."

Both retreated to their thoughts again and Toby watched the fire. He could smell that fire in his dreams sometimes. So many nights, he'd wake up with the smell of the birch and oak burnt to charcoal and he'd gag. After all this time, after all those lifetimes, he still smelled it; cloying, dark, and frightening.

"I always wanted to look into Druidism," John said, breaking through Toby's depressed reverie. "I used to read a lot more than I do now. I think Mom said we've got some Celt in us somewhere, some Irish relatives. I read some on the Celts."

"Try being there, you'll learn a lot more. I did."

"I'm sure you did," John said. "I just remember that the Druids were the first environmentalists. My friend, David. He's been called the Archdruid. Sometimes, I think he *was* one."

"They had inventions that were far and away better than anything else at the time," Toby said. "The jewelry that lives on is intricate and beautiful. Did you know the Druids were the lawgivers? They were the interpreters of the law. And when two villages were negotiating, a Druid went to each party as insurance. They commanded a high price for their services."

John listened, fascinated. "No. I didn't know that."

"They did," Toby confirmed. "I was amazed by them. If the thought of staying hadn't been so painful, I would have. I was at home there."

"But you couldn't."

Toby shook his head once. "Nope. So when Yeshua decided we needed to leave, it wasn't all that hard to go."

"Toby, can I be honest about something?"

Toby said nothing, only gestured with his hand, a "*come on*" gesture, and dropped it back in his lap.

"I still don't buy this. I can believe you went through a lot of pain. I can believe you lost your wife and child in some big whatever. But the whole time travel thing is stretchin' it, and...well...."

Toby drained the cup and set it down on the rock beside him. He exhaled, his cheeks puffing out while he did, and sat back against the boulder again. He cocked his head to one side. "You don't believe this? After all I've said, all the details? You don't believe me?"

John looked embarrassed enough to want to crawl in a hole and bury himself. "Truth is truth, man. I don't."

"All right."

"All right?" He stared hard at Toby, obviously expecting more than that. "That's it? 'All right'? That's all you got?"

"That's it. All right."

"Well, come on, man. If you were me, what would *you* think?"

Toby reached up, scratched the side of his head, and then pushed the shock of hair from his forehead again. "I would be asking for proof about now, I think."

John nodded his head, slowly at first, and then more definitely as if the idea had never occurred to him. "Yeah. Yeah, proof."

"All right."

Toby crossed his legs in a fakir position and took several cleansing breaths. He started relaxing every muscle, every sinew, and let his mind go blank. He closed his eyes and took several more breaths. He suddenly opened one eye and looked at John.

"If I were you, I'd make sure not to blink."

John watched him close his eyes again and then, *there was nothing in front of him. He was staring at the sand and the boulder and the scrub and the coffee cup and there was nothing – no man...no clothes...no nothing.*

His mouth flew open and his jaw dropped to his chest. His eyes grew so wide that a passerby might have thought he was having some sort of seizure or heart attack. They practically bulged from his face. His heart sped up and he was convinced his trolley had just derailed. His mind flirted with the idea that there was something in the coffee. Peyote! LSD! But he'd done LSD before and this didn't feel like a trip. He looked down at his hands. If he was tripping out, his hands would be doing something...melting, maybe. He wasn't sure.

...yeah, I'm tripping...see?...my hands are melting...shit, no they're not...I'm not tripping...there's nothing in the coffee but coffee...oh, my God...he did it....

It was true. It was all true. Every word, every action, all of it true. John was eternally glad he was sitting down because his legs went numb; he knew he'd have fainted otherwise. Just as suddenly as he had popped out of existence, Toby popped back in and John sat back in further shock. Not a man given to profanity, the next word out of his mouth really wasn't a surprise.

"Shit!"

Toby just gave an enigmatic smile, picked up his coffee cup, poured another cup, and relaxed against the boulder.

"Ooooh God," John stuttered out in a quiet, awed voice. "I believe it now, that's for damn sure."

"Sorry, man," Toby said. "I can imagine what that looked like. But I'm not lying. Not about this."

"No...uh, no. I guess not."

"John? You ok?"

John wanted to reach over and touch him, to prove that he was real. He settled for holding his cup out and letting Toby fill it for me. The heat convinced him it was all real. "Yeah, I'm fine. Ok, I'm convinced. I just have one more question – why me?"

Toby chewed on his lower lip for a second or two before making eye contact again. "It was a long time before I knew that answer. I would imagine that if you sit there and think about it, you'll know it yourself."

John simply shrugged and shook his head no.

"Good. Well, like I said, it was a long time before I knew. All I knew, at the time, was that we were off on the next leg of the journey where I would find my answers. I wish I could tell you about the traveling. I was in a haze. I just know we were headed to India so that Yeshua could see an elephant."

Chapter Twenty-Five

Toby tried very hard to swallow the gorge rising in his throat. He felt his body being forced to walk when all he wanted to do was just lie down in his misery. Step by step, he was going somewhere but the destination was still black. He couldn't even fight back because his will had been sapped away. He tried to stop once. The grip around his waist and arm tightened, causing an exquisite agony that threatened to turn the blackness into the hazy quality of reality. His feet stumbled along, unmindful of his brain's dictate about stopping.

The Tormentor forced him along this dirt pathway, often speaking softly to him only to grow silent again. *Just a little further*, the voice would croon in its cloying sweetness and his feet would obey. It spoke in Yeshua's voice, but how could that be possible? Yeshua wouldn't inflict this agony on him. Yeshua was his friend. Yeshua was his traveling companion. He was supposed to be taking care of Yeshua. *God let me lie down and just die in peace. Please, whoever you are, just let me be.*

How long had they been traveling? Toby didn't even know anymore, not that he would've cared anyway. The first thousand miles were lost in the blackness that became his friend and lover. He stared out at nothing, felt nothing. His mind refused to function as anything but that bizarre VCR, playing that tape loop endlessly.

In his thoughts and dreams, he felt the cut of the blade that pierced his chest, stabbing deep and tearing his flesh and internal organs. He watched the ground, that gruesome mud, passing underneath his feet as they dashed towards his home. He saw the body of Gwydion, one hand clutched around the throat of a Scotian warrior and the other hand wrapped around the hilt of his own blade, driven into the body of the man that killed him. He saw her eyes, her beautiful eyes, staring at the sky.

She had been running away. She'd grabbed their son, taken him out the back door, and they were running away to the forest. Somehow the enemy came around behind the cottage and saw her, ambushed her. They threatened her son, and she died trying to save them both. His mind kept running over the scenario: first, they stabbed her, then slit Rohan's throat. She died watching her son's blood drench the grasses beneath him. *Dear Goddess, let it have been quick and painless for my sweet son. Oh, Siobhan, I'm so sorry. My lovely lady, my wife, please forgive me. I should've been there. It should've been me.*

He had taken everything of value, gold and silver, and had melted it all down into something resembling coins. He didn't know why; he'd just done it. All of it except her wedding band. He had tied that on a thong and wore it around his neck, close to his heart. The necklace made of her hair was still wrapped there, too. He and Yeshua had said their good-byes to Niamh and Liam and the rest of the village, and left with morning's light. He walked without thinking, carrying the weight of the metals in the bag slung over his shoulder.

They walked until they reached the shore and a quick barter brought them back to Albion. Another barter bought their passage across the channel, back to Gaul. It was on that voyage that Toby made his first barter for the whiskey. One gold coin bought many skins of good whiskey, stuffed into his bag. It was good strong stuff. He found that he needed precious little to numb his mind and keep the images at bay, keep the pain in his heart from tearing out one more piece of it. Yeshua carried food and skins of water, but Toby ate little of it. He took his solace in the booze. Yeshua said nothing about it, even though he noticed.

After several weeks, Yeshua gave up any hope of a two-way conversation, much to Toby's delight. It didn't stop the young man from carrying on a monologue of sorts, about the traveling, where they were going, and what he hoped to see. The towns and villages they came to gave Yeshua his need for conversation and an audience for his message of his God. Through his now alcohol induced stupor, he watched Yeshua procure them food, shelter, and preach his gospel. He simply waited off in a corner, not a part of it. He was only an observer in the grand melodrama of life, a mere contestant on the great game show of the cosmos. Yeshua let him live within it, saying nothing that could be construed as an opinion or a lecture of the fine state of affairs into which his friend had entered.

Weeks turned into months, months turned into years, and every town had a bootlegger with a product. The silver he gave to Yeshua freely. It was a little more common, bought less than it could have.

The gold was far more precious and that was not shared, willingly or unwillingly. He paid for the refilling of the skins with anything that had a strong alcoholic content. He wasn't picky what it tasted like as long as it dulled the pained and stopped the visions. The problem was that he wasn't careful in what he bought either.

There was another barter and another boat, another voyage on turbulent water. They arrived in India at some point, by the looks of the people they passed. Many days and many skins later, they traveled the length of a river, the name of which he couldn't pronounce. Yeshua knew where they were going...or seemed to. More days of walking and they came to a small village of temples and shrines. He bought a home-distilled drink from a tiny old man with a thin build and a dark complexion. He looked very ancient and very willing to accept the small nugget of gold Toby offered to him. He filled the skins with the brew and they left. Toby had barely left the old man's shanty when he began to pour the contents of the first skin down his throat. He had underestimated the cloyingly sweet taste to mean the distilled liquid was little more than flavored water.

The contents hit him hard and hit him fast. His vision had blurred into blackness, and his tongue had swelled, leaving him unable to walk without assistance or communicate the danger. His skin had gone numb soon after and his sense of balance had disappeared. It was then that the Tormentor had forced a feather into his mouth and down the back of his throat. He finally gave up his battle and vomited a foul liquid from his stomach, but it was too late to stop what was happening to him. Again and again, he retched until nothing but bile and saliva came from his mouth. He retched until he thought he would turn inside out. He begged for water. He begged for death. He got only the water.

"Come, Tobias, just a little further. We'll have help from the healer. Come, you can do this. Please, my friend. Just a few more steps."

The Tormentor was unrelenting, uncompromising and forced Toby to walk, to hold on when he wanted to let it all go. Another step or two and Toby had to bend over again from the dry heaves that were pulling him apart from the inside. Two more steps, his head was pounding now. Two more steps, his throat was so parched. Then they stopped and Toby was allowed to lean against the cool surface of a wooden doorframe. He laid his cheek against the wood, unmindful of anything but the way it felt against his hot skin. A fist began to pound on a door, and Toby cringed and shrieked, covering his ears and sliding down to the ground.

"Healer! Healer, I beg of you, come to the door. Healer, we are in need of your assistance."

Toby curled up in a ball, wailing in time with the beating of the door. Only when he heard a calm voice answer, inches from where he lay, did he let the darkness overtake him. Only then, did he pass into a blissful ignorance and the pitch black of his night.

The thin elfin frame sits quietly on the stone, gazing out over the Irish landscape. It's home, where they'd been happy. He is reluctant to go to it but in his dreams, he is rarely in control. He walks – or does he float – until he is sitting beside the djinn. He expects sarcasm. He expects that teasing smile of goading. When the creature turns to face him, he gets neither.

"My friend, you have suffered so much in your quest. I am truly sorry."

"No, you're not," Toby growls back, confused but still defiant. "It's just entertainment to you, isn't it? Well, I'm entertaining you!"

The djinn shakes his head in genuine sorrow. "You promised your friend you'd take care of his family."

"I can't stay. I can't. I can't keep seeing his face in their eyes. I can't. They don't need me anyway. She has her family. They have Niamh and Liam."

"Yes, the painful memories, the agony of what you suffered. It was best that you make the clean break, to move on. But you were seeking something there."

Toby looks down at his hands and begins to wring them in his discomfort. He has no answer. He can give none.

"Have you found what you were searching for?" the djinn wonders.

"No," Toby answers, the rock in his chest getting heavier and larger. It threatens to crush what is left inside of him.

At last, the creature smiles in such sweetness and innocence that Toby is caught off guard again. The light that radiates from that smile grows brighter and brighter, filling the dream world with gold. The dream is fading, the last thing the djinn says does not.

"You will find it, and soon, I think."

Toby's eyes fluttered open and the gold that had filled his dreams now filled the room he was in. It was a room of bare walls and little furniture. There was a table in a corner, a mat on the floor, and no more. He struggled to sit up, his head pounding as he succeeded. His heartbeat pulsed in his ears; it felt like a hammer padded with cotton was beating against his forehead. He closed his eyes against the pain and massaged his temples and face until he had it under control.

Toby opened his eyes again, and took deep breaths. All he knew for sure was that he was in India and that he had been on the wrong end of the wrong bottle. And yet even knowing that, his body began to crave more. He saw his bag next to the table and decided there had to be a bootlegger close enough to replenish his supply. He should still have some gold left.

His first attempt at standing brought a quicksilver piercing through his frontal lobe and he had to lie back down again. It was either that or pass out from the agony. A groan escaped his lips as he eased his way back down onto the pillow and closed his eyes against the light. He waited a few minutes until the pain subsided before he made another attempt, far more slowly than the first. This one proved more successful and he lumbered over to the bag. Bending down to get it was his next mistake. This time, he did crumple in a heap. But he didn't pass out as he had been afraid he'd do. He held his forehead to the cool rattan floor beneath him and reached over with his free hand to the bag.

He took the strap in his hand and pulled the bag toward him, expecting the weight of the filled skins inside of it. The bag came all too willingly and with little weight to it. Toby swiveled his head around until his forehead was still touching the flooring but he could see the bag. He opened it with one hand, using the other to steady himself, and peered into an empty piece of canvas. The gold was gone, the skins were gone, and the only remaining articles were the spare clothing he carried.

He swallowed hard and pushed himself off the floor slowly, trying not to waken the sleeping monster in his head. Someone had rifled through his bag and stolen what didn't belong to them. The poison masquerading as booze was still his and no one had the right to change that. A slow anger started to build up inside of him making his head pound worse. Senseless futility followed it; his life was in shambles. Then the need pushed all the others aside and Toby dragged himself off the floor and staggered, bag in hand, to find out what had happened to his things.

When he opened the door to the outside, a stronger light than that which had filtered inside the hut assaulted his vision. His free hand came up to shield his face and again the smell of spices filtered up to his nose. He felt a brief wave of nausea and leaned in the doorframe until it subsided before he took his hand from his eyes again. There, in front of him, was a mountain range of such beauty that his breath was taken away. Toby stood, captured by the Himalayan range as it spread out in every direction along the horizon. All around him was a lush and verdant landscape, an exotic air. He wasn't in India; he was in Tibet.

He took a step out of the doorway and found himself in a courtyard behind another simple building. This building was much larger. The large yard between the smaller shack and the larger building was filled with ferns and flowering trees. One tree was set off from the others. The tree was huge, spreading over several square yards of ground, with low benches around it. Maybe he could find the time to explore it but not now. He reached back for the doorframe to steady himself when his vision blurred again. His head filled with air, making him dizzy. He closed his eyes and began to breathe deeply to clear his senses. His stomach gurgled; Toby wasn't sure if it was nausea or hunger he was feeling. He hadn't felt hunger in so long that his memory wasn't sure what it was anymore.

A sound of gibberish caught his attention and he turned away from the view to see a small man walking towards him, wearing a saffron cloth wrapped around his waist and hips.

"—said you would be awakening soon. And here you are. You still look weak from your ordeal. Please, sit in the chair and I have something for you to eat. Please, sit."

Toby did as he was told.

"Your friend has gone into the village to explore. He will be back, he said. I have promised to care for you as you recover."

The little man handed Toby a bowl, filled with aromatic rice and greens, and nodded for Toby to eat it. The very thought of food made his stomach rollover and he started to set the bowl aside, but the look of hurt on the little man's face was too much. Toby smiled his thanks and took the first mouthful. The rice was simple and bland, but his tongue accepted the morsel like a fine chocolate. His stomach growled for more, and he lit into the meal, holding the bowl to his chin and using his fingers. The watcher said nothing, only smiling as Toby ate, gesturing him to eat more of the contents of the bowl.

As he ate the simple food, Toby watched the man watching him. He was very tiny with a shaved head and large brown eyes. He seemed so eager to please him that Toby actually found himself drawn to the little man. There was an air about him, something familiar, but Toby couldn't quite place it. Maybe it was his smile that was so infectious. Maybe it was the simple gesture of wanting to please another. It was if Toby knew this little man and he didn't know why. But right this moment, he didn't care. His body was crying for food and his soul was crying for an end. He'd take care of one and worry about the other soon enough.

When he had finished, Toby gave him the bowl back. The little man took it with a nod and short bow in return.

"It is better, yes?"

Toby nodded.

"Ah, yes. Your companion tells me this. He tells me you were – how did he say it? In the grief, yes. That is what he says. He tells me you have suffered much."

Toby gave no answer, and looked down at the ground.

"It is so, that life is suffering," the little man said, enigmatically and with the same sweet smile. "So the Buddha teaches us and so we believe. Do you wish some tea to wash down the meal?"

Without waiting for a reply, the little man handed Toby a smaller bowl. It was a dark brown liquid that smelled of cinnamon and cloves. Toby stared at it for a few moments, not sure what to do with it. He looked back up to the anxious face and then drank the offered tea. It burned his sore throat on the way down, and settled in his stomach like fire. The spicy heat caused his eyes to water and he coughed until he thought everything would come back up again. The man just waited it out and then took the second bowl back again. He bowed and disappeared behind the shanty. Toby watched him and gave a momentary thought to following the little man but he didn't have to. The little man returned, carrying a hoe and a large cloth bag across his shoulder.

He nodded and bowed to Toby, and turned to walk away. Toby

was completely taken aback but curious and got up to follow him. They walked down a narrow path that ran from the front of the shanty to a small garden plot. The little man laid the bag down and proceeded to cultivate the ground around a flourishing group of green plants. Toby watched in silence and then, because he needed to do something, cleared his throat.

The little man stopped the motion of the hoe and looked back expectantly to Toby. Toby suddenly didn't know what to say. He opened his mouth a few times, but nothing would come out. The figure waited but when nothing was coming, he turned around again. Toby walked to the garden and tried again.

"Excuse me." He waited until the little man turned and this time, he was ready. "Do you have a name? I mean, you seem to know me, but I don't know who you are."

The man tittered into his hand. Toby waited but the little man's giggles didn't stop. Toby spat out "never mind," and turn around to leave but the gentle voice stopped him.

"Wait, wait."

The little man ran in front of Toby and dropped to his knees. He bowed over and staring at Toby's feet the entire time he was speaking. "I humbly beg your forgiveness, honored guest. I have insulted you. I am terrible host. I beg you, please forgive this unworthy soul."

Toby rubbed his mouth. On one hand, the little twerp had laughed at him. On the other, the little guy *had* given him food and drink. For all he knew, the little guy had been taking care of him the whole time they'd been at this place – wherever 'this place' was. He sighed and asked, "Then, what was so funny?"

"Ah, most exalted guest, your friend told me that you would not speak in your mourning. He said I would be conversing with the wind and you would not talk. I was laughing at the joy of hearing your voice for it is a beautiful voice. Please, I beg you, please forgive me."

Tired of looking at the bald head staring back at him, he gently lifted the man to a standing position. Toby saw that the distress was genuine and started to feel a bit guilty for his mild tirade. He forced the corners of his mouth to curl up. "Yes, yes, I forgive you. It is all well."

The little man put his hands together in a prayerful pose and bowed again, this time with a very relieved smile on his face. "Oh, thank you, thank you. You honor me with forgiveness." He stood up again, smiled, walked back to the garden, and began hoeing again.

Toby shook his head in amazement, but another thought came to him. *He knows where to find the booze. I bet he does. I bet he knows where I can get the good stuff. Yeah, yeah...ok.* With a quick glance around to make sure they were alone, Toby spoke again. "Excuse me. What is your name?"

Once again, the little man dropped the hoe and bowed from his waist. "I am called Ananda. It was the name I chose when I became a novice in the Sangha. I am pupil of the Venerable Naropa. He teaches of the Buddha and the enlightenment."

Toby took a breath, and bowed in return, wincing at a small, sharp twinge in his temple. When he righted himself, he said, "Ananda, I am pleased to meet you."

Ananda smiled and went back to his tending of the garden, leaving Toby free to watch him. So, Toby sat down on the ground and did just that. He still had a purpose in mind; he just didn't know how to get to it.

"Ananda?"

"Yes, Tobias."

Toby looked around at the surrounding area. "Where am I? What place is this?"

Ananda did not stop his activity this time but turned so that he could speak to Toby easily. "You are in our home."

"Yes, but, where is that? You said my companion went to explore the village. Is the village nearby?"

"You are in the Sangha."

"Ah," Toby said. "Well, that answered that question. What about you?"

Ananda looked up from his hoe. "Me? I do not understand."

"You said, you were a novice in the...san-ha. What's that?"

"Oh, no, Tobias, I have given you wrong information. I do apologize again. I am also bhikkhu." Ananda pointed back the way they had come, towards the large building. "This is the Bodhimanda-vihāra. It is where all the venerable bhikkhu live and study of the enlightenment. The village is called Uruvela. We are in the village."

Toby nodded. "Ah."

"You still do not understand."

Toby sighed and shook his head. This was almost embarrassing but nothing seemed to be sinking into his brain right now. "No, I'm sorry.

"That building houses the Buddhist monastery, the Sangha, in this holy village. This is where the Buddha received his enlightenment. We care for the sacred Bodhi tree."

Toby looked over his shoulder, but could only see the small shanty that he had spent the time in. If the monks slept in the big building, what was the smaller one for?

Ananda seemed to know what he was thinking, and answered the question that Toby hadn't asked. "The little dwelling you sleep in is my home."

"Oh. And what do you do there?"

The little man stopped again, and his face took on a thoughtful look. He took a few moments to come up with the answer before fixing a smile of sweet peace on Toby. "I am but a simple seeker of truth. As you are." Ananda went back to his hoeing. "I am the healer for the village. I sleep outside where the others cannot be disturbed."

Ah, the opening...

"So, you do go into the village sometimes, don't you?"

"Oh, yes," Ananda replied, still weeding with joy. "I must go to the village. I must make the alms round for the Venerable ones. I must attend prayers and meditations. I minister to the sick and dying, as any bhikkhu."

"You minister to every needing of the medicines?"

"Oh, yes, most honored guest." Ananda took his hoe to another part of the garden patch.

Toby followed around the perimeter until he stood side by side with Ananda. He smelled it, the familiarity thudded into his head as badly as his headache. He looked down and saw it. In the corner, next to the monk's feet, were three tall stalks of purple flowers. He must have brushed them as he walked and Toby knelt down to pluck one of the stalks. It was a terrible rudeness but he had to have it. The scent, *her* scent – it was so strong and the longing in his heart took his breath away.

Ananda was watching him with no change of the smile on his lips. Toby raised the lavender flowers to his nose and breathed in deeply, letting the tears slip down his face. He was thankful when the monk made no mention of them

"The flowers are from a traveler," Ananda answered instead. "I do not know what they are called, but there is sweetness to the scent. Does it please you, Tobias?"

"Very much," Toby said, with a dreamy quality to his voice. "They're called lavender; the color is also the name." He shook his head and sniffed back the rest of the tears, using his other hand to wipe his cheeks dry. "The flowers have pain killing properties, Ananda." He held out the cluster of tiny purple flowers to the little man, who gestured no.

"No, Tobias," Ananda replied with great tenderness. "You keep it. It gives you pleasure and there are many flowers. I will remember what you have told me. Thank you."

Toby's only answer was to breathe in the fragrance again. He saw her beautiful face in his mind but with it came the visions again, the horrible scenes that plagued his dreams and turned them into nightmares. He grimaced, unable to stop himself, and his eyes fluttered open to see his companion watching him with concern.

"Memories," he said, his voice husky and trembling.

"Yes," Ananda answered.

Toby looked back down at the sprig of lavender in his hand. "I want them to go away, the memories. To make them hurt less."

The tiny monk reached up to touch Toby's face. "No," Ananda whispered. "Never wish that. To wish the memories gone is to lose them forever. You are a seeker of truth, yes? Then seek the truth that they try to teach you, these memories. For in the truth there is the answer."

Find your faith, Toby. Find your faith.

"Please," Toby whispered back. "Help me find it." For a moment, he actually thought he meant the truth of which the little monk spoke. Then, a craving for the alcohol swept through him and his body started to shake. "Please, where are the skins? Where can I find more?"

"Tobias! You are up and about!"

The soft hand left his cheek and the sound of rushing footsteps broke the moment. Ananda went back to his hoeing and Toby turned back to face his friend. Yeshua bounded to his side and took his friend in an ardent embrace. Toby hugged his friend back but he was looking at the piece of his past that he held. When Yeshua finally released him, Toby fought to stay in the here and now.

"You are awake, my friend. I was worried for you. But I knew it was not your time." Yeshua greeted Ananda with a bow of his head. "Healer, I am in your debt. You have healed my friend. I thank you."

Ananda's return bow was enough to acknowledge the thanks and the bhikkhu turned to continue hoeing. Toby watched him for a moment, listening to traveling companion.

"You seem pale, Tobias. Have you eaten?"

"Yes, I have." Toby tried the smile again and this time, it felt genuine. "Our friend Ananda here fed me well."

"Good. You have not supped for many days." Yeshua linked his arm with Toby's and led him up the path a short way. "Are you still weary? Perhaps you would care to sit?"

"Uh, sure, I suppose so."

"Then, come. I know the perfect place to rest."

Yeshua led him back to the courtyard. It was a short walk but taking it twice, plus the standing wore him out and Yeshua seemed to know that. He led Toby to the large tree and helped his friend sit underneath it. The moment he was on the small bench, Toby began to feel a calm coming over him. Not enough to quiet the inner craving, but it was enough to push it back until it was not immediate.

Yeshua walked over to the well, and pulled a bucket up from the depths. He took the gourd that was hanging from one of the boards and dipped it into the bucket. He brought it over to Toby and waited till Toby had drunk the contents, then got another one. This one, Toby held and sipped.

"I went into the village and purchased some food for us." Yeshua pulled several packets from the bag he wore over his shoulder. "The meal you had will be the only one you will have otherwise. The sun has gone past the midpoint."

Toby raised his head and put a hand up to his brow to block the sun from his eyes. "What? I don't...I mean, they only eat once a day?"

Yeshua smiled and shook his head, "No, it's just that the monks are permitted to eat only at certain times. From dawn until midday, they are allowed to prepare and eat food. It is their way."

"How long have we been here?"

"You don't remember any of it, do you?" Yeshua answered.

"No."

Yeshua sighed and sat down next to his friend. "We have been here four days."

"Four days?"

"Yes, Tobias, four days," Yeshua repeated. "You were delirious for the first two, writhing and in great pain. The healer—"

"Ananda." Toby took another sip of the water, cool and sweet on his tongue. "His name is Ananda." His voice seemed to come from somewhere outside of himself and again, he had that feeling that he knew the little man from somewhere.

Yeshua patted Toby on the back. "Ananda, yes. Ananda stayed with you, giving you the herbs and potions. He said that if you wished it, you would heal yourself."

Toby's laugh was forced and sarcastic. "Well, that's a joke, isn't it?"

Yeshua placed his hand on Toby's arm and the simple touch reminded him of her. He jerked his arm away before he could stop himself, knowing it was rude. He couldn't help himself. She touched him that way. The lavender was still in his hand and he stared at it.

"Tobias, listen to me."

He tore his gaze away from the lavender and into his friend's face. "Yes, I'm listening."

"I cannot take your pain. I wish I could," Yeshua admonished. "I know these memories still haunt you but you cannot let them. Tobias, she would want you to fight to stay alive. To remember them always is to keep them alive." Yeshua's hand came out again, to touch Toby's arm, but stopped above it. He pulled it back and simply rest it in his own lap. "Tobias, she has gone to Heaven, with your children. They dwell with the Lord God on high and they have been given a mansion to wait for you there. Their spirits are free and happy. Can you not be happy for them?"

The tears fell down his cheeks again; he didn't seem able to stop them. "I weep for myself, my friend. I do not want to be here anymore. I don't want these gifts anymore."

Yeshua's voice was soft, worried. "You do not mean that."

"I do!" Toby threw the lavender with such a force that it bounced from the dirt to fall on his bare foot. "I do!" He took a deep breath to calm the sudden dig in his heart and continued a little more sedately. "I do. I can't help it. I keep thinking it should have been me. I should have stayed with her."

"And what good would it have done?"

"What?"

This time when Yeshua laid his hand on Toby's arm, the other man didn't shrug it away. "What good would it have done? If you *had* stayed with her?"

"I could have gotten them out," Toby asserted. "I could have—"

"You could have done nothing," Yeshua interrupted forcefully. "You have gotten most self-indulgent, my friend. The truth is, there were too many of the enemy and your loved ones and our friend would be just as dead. And you, along with them. God's will is hard, Tobias, but it is God's will. You cannot change that."

"But, I...but, Gwy...."

"But, nothing! I loved Gwydion too. And Siobhan and Rohan. You do not think that my heart is not broken? Because it is!" The tears welled in Yeshua's eyes too. "And there is no more purpose in asking 'what if' than in trying to stop the flood with a splinter of wood. Do you not hold the strength of your learning?"

Toby turned back to the courtyard, his face wet. "I have no strength anymore."

"Such a pity," Yeshua said kindly. "All the learning gone to waste. If you do not have faith in God and the promise of Heaven, then surely the promise of returning is there. If you truly believed as they taught, that there is no end and only a returning – if you truly believed it, you would have the strength that comes from knowing."

"I miss her. I miss them all."

Yeshua's hand this time rested on Toby's shoulder. "Yes, you do. And you weep for what you have lost and for missing them. I weep too, Tobias. But they have gone to a better place. And if you do not believe in Heaven, at least believe that they are happy in their Annwn. And that they love you."

He felt so defeated, so empty. "I don't know if I can, Yeshua."

"You can."

Toby retrieved the lavender sprig and wiped his face with it, the oil filling his nostrils with the scent. He could hear her again, laughing, telling him to get off it. With a deep sigh, he whispered, "I can try."

"Good." Yeshua squeezed his shoulder and took his hand away. He turned instead to study the tree that they sat beneath.

"What?" Toby asked. "It's a tree."

"No, Tobias, it's *the* tree."

Toby shook his head, the numbness returning. "It's a damn tree."

Yeshua chuckled. "No, my friend. This is the Bodhi tree, where the Buddha gained his enlightenment. It is in their scriptures that he sat here for many days, meditating. It was here that he fought the temptations of the world until he vanquished them."

"I know how to vanquish them"

The grip returned to his shoulder and the voice of the tormentor returned. "No, my friend. I stood by, thinking you would come to yourself again, to see that the drink was not good for you. It did not bury your memories, it only made them stronger. No, it is not the way."

Toby shook off the hand and grabbed Yeshua's arm. The want of his addiction was eating him up inside. "Where are the skins, Yeshua? Where is my gold?"

"The gold is in safe keeping, Tobias," Yeshua said gently. "The roshi has put it away where no one will touch it. The skins? They are gone. The contents nearly robbed you of your life, my friend. It was poison."

Toby jumped up, his fists pulled up to his chest to keep from striking out. "You had no right! You had *no right*!"

"I had every right," Yeshua cried out, his anger matching Toby's. He locked an angry gaze to his friend's. "It has been hard, these many months, to watch your torment, your agony. But it was your own free will. I did not stop you."

Yeshua broke the standoff quickly and Toby felt like he'd been untethered from a security post. The young man brushed a lock of his long curly hair back from his face and continued.

"Perhaps, I *should* have stopped you but I could not. It was your choice, as it is now," he murmured to himself. When he looked up again, this time he was addressing Toby directly. "I speak this as your friend, Tobias. I would save your life and your soul. I will not stop you, if you truly wish it, but I can make it harder for you." Yeshua gestured toward the temple. "They will not tell you how to find the poison. They will not give you the gold to purchase it."

"I'll get it somehow," Toby answered with a dogged stubbornness. "They'll have the whiskey here."

Yeshua shook his head firmly. "No. They will not. It is forbidden by their Vinaya, their code of ethics. You will not find it here and no one will help you destroy yourself."

Toby knew he was being childish and didn't care. He could be stubborn too. "I'll find it."

Yeshua closed his eyes and said nothing for a moment. A single tear escaped the lidded eyes. Yeshua finally opened them again, and said, "You will, if you wish it. But, I will pray for you to not find it. You are my friend. You are blessed by God. I will pray that, in this city of enlightenment, you will find yours."

Yeshua walked past Toby, who simply stood with his mouth hanging open. When he had gone several paces, the younger man stopped and said, "They have been preparing for Vesakha. It is the day of celebration of the birth of the Buddha and of his enlightenment. If you wish information, that will be the day to ask for it. If you wish enlightenment, it will be the day to find it. I will pray for you that you will make the right decision."

Toby ran his knuckle under his nose, sniffing as he did so. "How do you know all of this? Did you learn their language?"

Yeshua turned for a moment, his head tilted to one side. He looked puzzled, confused. "I have learned a little of their language, yes. But, I did not ask."

"How do you know then?"

A small smile played on Yeshua's lips. He shook his head slightly. "It is so familiar, this place. You said the same thing to me when we arrived in Fireun Sidhe. How it felt familiar to you."

Yeshua turned on his heels and disappeared inside the shed. Toby stood there, not knowing whether to follow or not. The craving inside of him was tearing him apart again. He needed the booze, to quiet the beast and stop the visions. He didn't just want it, he *needed* it. Was that the right decision? There was no right decision other than just letting it go.

He crossed back to the tree and sat down on the bench again. He'd never meditated in his entire life, had no idea of how to begin. He remembered all those pictures of the men with their legs crossed, so he tried to cross his. He became terribly unbalanced, almost falling on the ground, and decided to sit on the ground instead, facing the tree. It was hard on his buttocks and he lifted himself to try and wipe away the gravel underneath him. When that part of him was comfortable, he crossed his legs again, this time with better success. He let his hands rest in the fork of his crotch and just sat for a minute.

What do I do next?

He sat, completely confused as to his next step. He knew how to sit; he just didn't know what to do after he sat there. *Clear your mind. Focus on your breathing. Breathe in lightly. Focus on your breathing.* It was Yeshua inside of his head, so he listened. He closed his eyes and began to breathe. He listened to his heartbeat, felt the rise and fall of his abdomen. He felt the beginnings of the calm again, felt it all starting to drain from his soul.

Her beautiful face rises in front of him. She crosses to him and touches his arm. "Tobias," she says, "I am quite smitten with you." He takes her face in his hands and kisses her softly on the lips. The sweetness of her tongue fills his mouth again.

Toby jerked awake, the tears flowing again, and he had to gulp them down to stop the grief. It was no use; he couldn't do this. It was a waste of time.

"Siobhan, I am so sorry, my love."

He sat beneath the tree with his face buried in his hands until the darkness had come. Only then did he go inside and wait for the next day – to find his cure and his curse, to hopefully find his end.

Chapter Twenty-Six

Vesakha arrived, the day of the full moon in May. Back in Ir, they had celebrated Beltane on the first of the month. Here, they honored the Buddha's birthday. Yeshua had learned a bit about it from Ananda. In his excitement about the ceremony, he shared his new knowledge with an indifferent Toby, who listened even though it really meant nothing to him. But he listened.

The bhikkhu and bhikkhuni, along with the villagers, would walk the path of the Gautama Buddha as he made his way to the Bodhi Tree. The path would be marked with lanterns, symbols of the enlightenment. There would be service in the temple, the gathering would speak the Five Precepts and hear a sermon from the roshi. The villagers would gather food to bring to the monastery, to feed the Sangha. It was the people's gift to the venerable ones, along with those in need from the village. The wealthy would serve the poor, earning their karma in good deeds. Then, the day would finish with meditations and the teachings of the Buddha, the Prince who renounced all in his search for Nirvana.

Yeshua hadn't said much more of anything else. It seemed safer to stick to such neutral subjects as where they were and who they were with. True to his word, he wasn't going to interfere with Toby's bent for self-destruction. He didn't like it and he made no bones about letting Toby know it, but he wouldn't interfere. So, they kept to the safe subjects, the safe distance, and let each other's thoughts dictate the actions.

He tried to be interested. He asked a pertinent question here and there but it just didn't mean anything. He wanted to be home. He wanted to be working the fields with Gwy and Liam. He wanted to be showing his sons how to care for the land, how to brew the best heather ale that any in the village could ever make. He wanted to make love with his wife and maybe get her pregnant with that beautiful daughter he wanted so desperately. But most of all, he wanted to feel something more than this ache in his heart.

Toby apologized to Yeshua and left him to his own devices – he just couldn't deal with it any longer. The sun had come up over the roof of the temple and the sweet smell of flowers was everywhere. He stepped out into the courtyard and saw butterflies winging around the ferns and jasmine. The sky was a cloudless blue, the kind of blue that is pure and innocent, the color of the lake on a still day. In the distance, he heard laughter and singing. Everywhere around him was life. Inside him, there was the same stillness from the shack, the same silence. Inside, he was dying.

Toby decided to go back to sit under the Bodhi tree. He had no desire to explore the place, didn't want to meet the people. He found that he couldn't care less about the customs. There was a joke in that – Mr. Inquisitive sets out to learn of the world and finds that he doesn't give a shit. He wanted three things: to drink himself into a stupor, to be left alone, and to die. And not necessarily in that order. Someone would *have* to know where to find the booze. Maybe he would go into the village after all – but not now, maybe later. Toby took a slow walk to the base of the Bodhi tree and sat down under it.

He pulled his legs into the lotus position again, dropped his hands into the most comfortable position, and just sat. He stared at the trunk of the tree, tried to focus on it. He got nothing. He focused on the leaves that had drifted to the ground, the roots of the tree, and again, nothing. He shifted his position again, cleared the gravel and debris from underneath him and closed his eyes. But nothing was coming.

...breathe in, slowly...focus on the breathing...listen to your breath as it enters and leaves your body...feel your heart beating in rhythm of the breathing....

He heard it now, a voice from within. It sounded like Yeshua and yet, it didn't. It certainly knew what to do and sounded confident enough for Toby to listen. That voice was familiar and it was going to drive him nuts until he figured out whose it was. For now....

...breathing slowly...in and out...listen to the breathing...drive all thoughts from your mind but the breathing...do not let the distractions take you from the breathing....
...her face...her sweet face...he could reach out and touch her face....
...no...the breathing...erase the pictures from your mind...focus

only on the breathing...hear the breath...be the air that flows from your body....

...Tobias, I am quite smitten with you....

...the breathing...the air...feel your heart beating in time with the breath....

...his sweet little face turned to the sky...the blood underneath him...my son...my sweet son....

...the breathing...drive the pictures from your mind...nothing must distract you from the breathing...release the past and focus on the moment....

...Gwy...my God, Gwy....

...the breathing....

...the breathing is all....

...the breath....

And then, in one that breath, Toby's entire body relaxed. Every muscle, every fiber, every nerve ending was quiet and still. The tic that had been causing his eye to jump stopped. The muscles drawn up in the agony of his grief mask let go and his face became as serene as the morning air. His breathing became shallow, just enough to sustain the body at rest. His heartbeat slowing until it beat twice, maybe three times per minute. He slipped into the middle path of the Bodhisattva.

"Captain?"

Bion? Is that you?

"Hey, Captain, you found me. Far out."

Where are you?

"This is the place, Captain. The place in between."

In between where?

"In between the want and the need. Man, this is the place of happy."

I can't see you.

"You're not in it, man. You ain't one of us. It's ok, I can talk to you, though. How you been, man?"

I'm hanging by a thread, Bion.

"I hear that. I am one with it. Sucks to hell and gone, don't it?"

I want outa here, Bion. I can't deal with this shit anymore.

"Aw, Captain, come on; ain't your time. You gotta go with the

flow, bro. Find your faith, man. Find your faith."
   "Tobias."
  Mom?
  "Tobias."
  Da?
  "I am smitten with you, you know."
  Siobhan? Where are you? Lady, come to me. Oh God, please, come to me.
  "Tobias."
  Siobhan?

"Tobias."

Toby suddenly got the same feeling a basketball had when it's dunked into the net. He slammed back into his body with such force that his head rocked back and he could actually feel his butt slap the ground. He had been floating and then, he had been unpleasantly reintroduced to gravity and a painful reality. His mind began to reel with the possibility. Had he been floating? His practical sensible side immediately dismissed it as the fodder of too many Brandon Sanderson stories.

"Tobias?"

That voice again and he turned quickly, knowing that this time the voice wasn't coming from inside. It was coming from behind.

"Ananda – shit!" Toby reached up, wiped the sweat from his face, and forced himself to relax again. It was just the little monk.

"I have disturbed your meditation." The little monk bowed several times. "I am full of apologizing for such things. It is time for the meal, and you must come and share it with us."

Toby waved off the tiny man and shook his head. But Ananda was not accepting a negative answer.

"Tobias, you and your friend have honored our most humble temple. And I have shamefully kept you all to myself. The venerable ones have set aside part of the feast for you. Most honored guest, surely you would not turn away a feast in your honor."

The monk's face was still smiling and so earnest that Toby smiled in returned. He nodded and got up from his position. In the back of his mind, he knew that if he didn't eat now, he wouldn't for the rest of the day. The sun's position told him that it would be midday soon. He stood up and found that his left leg had gone to sleep. Walking was a new exercise in pain for the short distance to the temple door but he made it. He watched Ananda brush the dirt from his feet and followed suit. He had long since adopted the Celtic habit of no shoes except in the cold weather, so he had none to remove now. Toby looked down at the threshold and saw a pair of sandals, which meant that Yeshua was already inside.

He followed Ananda down a long hallway. As they walked, he glanced into several rooms and saw the same lack of furnishings in each. There were rows of pallets and on each pallet was a bowl. There were no pillows, no extra blankets, no pictures, no furniture of any kind. The rooms were austere and sterile. He really didn't care why but there was that part of him that was still curious. Deep inside, the old Toby was apparently still alive and kicking.

Ananda led him into a large room that Toby took for the dining area. There were at least thirty men seated on the rattan floor, bowls in their hands, and many in deep conversation. All of the men were robed in saffron yellow, the simple robes of the Buddhist bhikkhu. He was drinking this all in when he felt the tug at his elbow. He looked down to Ananda, who was gesturing to the far corner where Yeshua sat. The young man was sitting cross-legged, engaged with one of the monks at the head of the group. Ananda took his elbow in hand and led him off to that corner.

Yeshua saw Toby as he got closer and waved him forward. "Tobias, you have come. Sit with us." He gestured a place next to him, patting the mat.

Toby sat down. Ananda placed a bowl in his hands, and sat down on the mat across from him.

"Tobias," Yeshua began, gesturing towards the man across from him, "This is the Venerable Bahiya. He leads them as their roshi, their spiritual advisor." Yeshua turned back to the man. "Venerable one, this is my traveling companion and my friend, Tobias."

Toby put out his hand in the grand gesture of all men of his day and was surprised when the other man did not do the same. Instead, the old man placed his bowl on the floor and put his hands together as if in prayer. He bowed over them and sat up again with a smile on his face. Toby was momentarily confused but bowed over his own hands.

The roshi was ancient by the standards of the day. Toby wanted to put the old man's age at somewhere around seventy or so by the wrinkles of his face. He was different from the only other person he knew – Ananda. Where Ananda was tiny, Bahiya was about Yeshua's height. Both Ananda and Bahiya were bald but there was a difference in their personalities. Where Ananda was cheerful and playful, the roshi was serious and thoughtful. He didn't seem dour, by any stretch of the imagination, but he was quiet. Bahiya's eyes were always moving, studying everything and everyone.

Yeshua broke into his thoughts, "The Venerable Bahiya was explaining to me about the Law of Karma. Please, go on, venerable one."

The elderly gentleman cleared his throat. "The Buddha tells us of Karma in his teachings. It is the actions we take, those things we do to others and to ourselves. If one performs an unwholesome action of greed or hate towards another, it is an unwholesome Karma that will befall him. If one performs a wholesome act of kindness, of charity towards another, then it is a wholesome Karma that is visited upon him. To walk the middle path to Nirvana is to send only the wholesome Karma."

"Venerable one," Yeshua said, "I would ask a question."

"Yes, my son?"

"And what is the Law as it was stated by the Buddha?"

Bahiya nodded, a satisfied look upon his face, as if he were waiting for one of them to ask that question. "It is the Law of Tenfold: The Karma that one sends out will be revisited upon him tenfold."

"And, could it be said, venerable one, that we could view it as doing unto others as we would have done to us?"

The roshi nodded his approval again and answered, "It would be as such."

Yeshua nodded as well. "It is as such in my teaching, venerable one. That God, the Father, taught His children to take an eye for an eye but the new law is to treat others as we wish to be treated."

"These are wise words and wise thoughts."

"What about when you die?" All eyes turned toward Toby, and he looked up, slightly shocked. For a moment, he'd been sure he'd only thought the question but from their looks, he knew he had spoken it out loud.

"There is no death," the old man said. "There is only the leaving of this existence and preparation for the next. The Karma that a soul carries from lifetime to lifetime determines the place where you will be reborn. Wholesome Karma ensures that you will have a long and happy life, full of peace and plenty, that you may then serve others as well. Unwholesome Karma will result in a life of pain and suffering, of short duration."

"And where do we go when we leave this world?" Toby asked.

"We go to that place of rest, in between, where we prepare for the next life."

"This is the place, Captain. The place in between."
In between where?
"In between the want and the need. Man, this is the place of happy."

Toby's hand shook for a moment, making the wooden spoon clatter in the bowl, and he quickly put the bowl down to stop the noise.

"In between?"

Bahiya answered, "Yes, the middle path of which the Buddha spoke, the road that leads to Nirvana. It is the place in between the want and the need. It is the four Noble Truths that teach of this path and leading to Nirvana."

"What are the truths, venerable one," Yeshua asked.

"The first Noble Truth is that of *dukkha*, suffering: life is suffering, death is suffering, decay is suffering. Even with the wholesome karma that follows you, you are born in this world to die in it. You will suffer in hunger, in physical ailment, and in worldly pains. It cannot be escaped and that is the first Noble Truth.

"The second Noble Truth is that the origin of dukkha is craving. We are often confused by the difference between craving and needing. That which we need can be fulfilled. When we are hungry, we eat the food and the hunger is gone. It is a need. That which we want cannot be fulfilled, and it is this craving that leads us to the wrong path, away from Nirvana. It is this craving that causes the unwholesome Karma."

Yeshua nodded again, fascinated. He listened with his entire being. "Then, how does one overcome the craving?"

"It is the third Noble Truth of the extinction of dukkha: in learning what is the need and what is the want, you learn to reject those wants. You are free from the distractions that try to pull you from the path. You are free to follow the path in between to the goal of Nirvana."

"But, is that path the wholesome or unwholesome kind?" Yeshua asked.

"It is the path in the middle, my *samanera*. It is the path that leads away from the dukkha and unto Nirvana. The fourth Noble Truth teaches that if you walk the middle path, away from pleasure and pains, the path will lead you past the suffering, past the craving, into Nirvana."

"I don't understand, venerable one," Yeshua said. "Is Nirvana a place?"

"It is the world in between; where there is no death, no dukkha, no craving, no time. It is the place of perfect peace and perfect happiness. It is Nirvana."

Yeshua was quiet for a moment before speaking again. "And who attains Nirvana?"

"Nirvana is there for all who wish it. Only those who have cast aside the unwholesome karma, who have rejected the distractions and the craving, the ones who have sought enlightenment, will achieve Nirvana."

"But what if they can't?" Toby asked.

"All can reach Nirvana," Bahiya answered. "All have that capacity, but they must learn to cast off the cravings."

"But what if they can't?" he repeated.

Bahiya spoke softly, sure of his answer. "But they can. It is possible."

Toby's head jerked up, his back stiffened. "But what if they can't?"

The old man's gaze penetrated deep and Toby felt as if he was being probed, that the old man could see into his soul and know everything. He felt guilt and pain in turns and still sat underneath the scrutiny. When the old man at last spoke, it was with great sadness.

"Then he will be doomed to walk this plane forever, in torture and agony, alone."

"And when he dies?"

"It will be the same. Or he will go to the dark place, the place of no where and no thing, to wait his return to the short life of want."

There were no more words, as all of them sat quiet. Toby was still locked in the stare of the old man. The old man said it very simply with no room for interpretation or discussion. A short life, and return and return and return. And what was the alternative? Endless existence, forever feeling this agony and this pain? Was that the only option at his disposal? Here he was, an immortal man with the ability to anywhere he wanted, do anything he wanted? And he couldn't do it with the ones who mattered the most?

As the silence spun out, Toby became surer that his course left him one option only. He'd risk being in the place of no thing and no where. He'd chance that his unwholesome karma would give him the rewards that he deserved. It was going to be far easier to kick off out of this life than it would be to go on and on in a meaningless existence. He could get another chance to get it right, to do it the right way. No more djinns, no more dreams, no more being without her. The only question was how to do it.

Toby smiled, said "thank you," and got up. He left his bowl, his friend, and his indecision on the mat and the room. He could feel Yeshua's stare on his back, but he didn't turn around to see if he was right. He just walked out. He kept walking with a new stillness inside him. An absurd thought came to him, and he chuckled to himself, he'd reached his enlightenment after all. The devil he didn't know was actually going to be better than the devil he did. And, for some strange reason, it was pretty ok with him.

Toby went out into the courtyard. There was no one there; they were either gathering in the temple or off feeding the poor to earn their wholesome karmic brownie points, la dee dah! He approached the Bodhi tree with no idea of what or how to do it; at this point, he wasn't even sure he knew what he wanted to do in the first place. Maybe he could meditate on the subject and that made him laugh again. Yeah, he thought, I'm just gonna sit down under this old sacred tree and ponder the end of my existence. The djinn told me I had to do it to myself; no one else could kill me.

But as soon as the concept had been put before him, he rejected it. He wasn't going to get a bit of meditation done and he found he didn't want to. His feet took off in a direction and his mind disengaged. It would happen and it would happen soon. He knew that. Maybe if he got lucky, he'd find himself back at that river....

...*the Naranjara*....

He stopped and turned around. No one was behind him, no one

was around him.

"Who's there?"

No answer.

"Come on out and show me. Ananda? Is that you? Yeshua? Come out!"

He turned back in the direction his feet were taking him. He found a pathway through the grasses, leading him off the grounds of the monastery and ahead, a fence. If someone was following him, he'd catch the bugger on the other side of the fence and give the sod a good reason to turn back. He was being watched, he could feel it. Fine, let the bastard beware.

Walking, but to where? How would he do it?

Through the gate and Toby didn't care who was following. He was just walking and whoever was following would get sick and tired of it eventually. Another road and no one was on it. Yup, all earning their good old Karmic brownie points so they could come back as good little do-bees and have great lives and be rich and famous and all that happy horse shit. It couldn't be that damn hard to die. It suddenly occurred to him that he hadn't brought anything with him – no blades, no implements of destruction of any kind. What was he going to use?

Snake bite, his mind answered. Yeah, this place was crawling with snakes. Hell, he could keep walking and come on a king cobra. Those things were nasty, poisonous and quick. A little pain and it would be all over. And if he had walked far enough, they couldn't get to him in time to save him. Sure, snakebite was good. Maybe one of those asps he'd always heard about, like the one that bit Cleopatra; sure, snakes. He felt stupid for not having thought of it before. Now, where was he going to find a nest of cobras?

The answer came in a grassy field off the pathway. Toby stepped into the knee high vegetation with no precautions or care for what could happen. He had made a decision and now he was being guided to the destination and the way to do it. He had decided it was his karmic destiny to walk out on this decidedly nasty little play he was in. Yup, keep walking and the little buggers find you, pal. Toby kept slogging through the grasses, hoping that the next step would be right on the tail of a deadly reptile. And each step shocked him that he'd been too damn lucky.

...the eyes following him...the presence again....

He kept walking but this time, he kept looking over his shoulder in as many directions as his could. His head never stopped moving as his eyes roamed, looking for the one following him. He even walked backward for a distance, hoping that he could hear the crackle of a broken stick or see the glimpse of a bald head. There was no movement around him, save his own. Toby gave a shrug and kept going. He was getting caught up in that hoo-doo again. Screw it, there wasn't anyone there.

As his feet carried him, he was assaulted by a smell that made him stop dead in his tracks. It was the scent of an overcooked cow that had been bathed in vinegar both before and after the burning. He groaned and put a hand over his nose and mouth, trying not to breathe in that disgusting smell. It was almost nauseating but as he became more accustomed to it, he started smelling something familiar in it. It was sweet, almost cloyingly so...almost like....

He ran towards the direction of the smell, trampling the grasses in a mad rush. *He* heard the sounds of water running and followed them. He had come looking for snakes and the irony was that if he'd stopped at any moment, he would have surely been bitten, as twice he trampled on the tail of an unwitting cobra, trying to gain a little sleep in the noon day sun. His skin registered the sensation of the body but his mind was on one thing and one thing only – following that smell.

He found the rushing little stream. For a moment, he was tempted to run and have a drink from it. He was thirsty and, hey, if he was lucky, he'd get dysentery or some other nasty little bug from it. But the idea of lingering illness like that, shitting himself to death, didn't really appeal.

The smell of burned wood brought back too many memories but the sight of the campfire chased them away. Some of the sticks and twigs had not completely burned. He came closer to the small pit and bent down to examine it. He wasn't sure how long ago the fire had been lit but he knew it hadn't been that long. Mixed within the wood were pieces of something and he reached down and picked one up. It felt like a leather of sorts – a skin. He held the piece to his nose and smelled the sweet aroma. His heart sank deeper as he sat back in the sand. Yeshua had done it. He had brought the skins down here and had destroyed them all; dumped the alcohol in that stream and burned the skins, leaving no trace. *Damn it!*

He threw the piece of skin back into the blackened, stinking mess, and started to trace in the sand. He sat cross legged, shut down again, his fingers moving through the grains of dirt beneath him. They went a little deeper each time, going deeper....

What the—? What is this?

His fingers caught in something, a leather thong. The sand was packed around the thong too tightly to just pull whatever it was up from beneath, so Toby shifted to his knees and started digging in the loose sand. He didn't dig very far before he felt a bubble of something...

Oh my God!

The weight of the sand removed, Toby pulled up skin after skin until he'd brought up four of them in all. He had found them, his skins of booze. He could almost see what had happened. Yeshua had come here to burn them, but the liquid kept putting out the flame. Or maybe it made the flame burn hotter, who knew. Yeshua had gotten to dumping a skin and then burning it, but he couldn't stand the smell. So, he burned as many as he could until he started to get sick and buried the rest. He meant to come back and finish the job, and never got back here.

Toby sat back down again and the joy of finding his prized possession made him giggle like a giddy schoolgirl. He took the skin that he still held in his hand and clutched it to his chest. He'd found it again. He found it.

...no, Tobias...no, my love....

The voice was so real, so close that he stopped and turned around, wildly surveying around him.

"Siobhan?"

The only answer was the breeze that brushed his face and touched his cheek. He listened briefly but still nothing.

"Siobhan?"

...no, my love....

"Yes, my love," he whispered.

He took the skin he held against his chest and removed the cork. He stared at it for a moment, unable to bring the skin to his mouth. His breathing became heavy and his lips started to quiver. He had a moment of uncertainty and for that moment, he almost cast the skin aside, almost turned from it. But a craving hit him so hard that a spasm went through his belly and he started to salivate. He smelled the familiar sweetness and raised the skin to his mouth.

The first few swallows went through him like fire. He felt like he had swallowed a live coal, cauterizing on the way down and cooking him from the inside. He put the tip of the skin into his mouth and suckled it, a newborn suckling its mother. His head tipped back and he downed the contents before he could even draw another breath. He groaned and grimaced, and sat gasping while his stomach decided whether or not it was going to accept the poison that he'd just ladled down his own throat. There was a bit of indecision as if his body knew better than his mind or heart but the fight was over and his mind won. It was going to stay down. His stomach threw up its mythical hands in disgust and said no more.

Toby grabbed another of the skins and pulled the stopper from it. He proceeded to repeat the action with this skin and this time, it really was fire and brimstone going down. This time, it hit him like a freight train hitting a car at one hundred miles per hour and he didn't care. His lips went numb and he knew that soon, his body would be too. As long as he didn't puke, he was ok. He hated to puke worse than anything. Man, puking was the ultimate pain in the ass. He hated drunks that had too much and started puking. It was embarrassing.

The next skin empty, he tossed it aside and wiped sweat from his brow. A light sheen of perspiration broke out all over his body, making him slimy to the touch. He struggled to stand, thinking if he could get to the stream, he could cool off in it. But the liquor was having its effect on him. He couldn't move, paralyzed from the waist down. His skin was itching with the familiar tingle. Soon, his mouth would swell up. He was frying in the sun. He reached to his waist, grabbed the hem of the shirt, and pulled it off over his head. He tossed the shirt with the carcasses of the two skins, and leaned over to pick up the third.

As he leaned forward, he saw a glint of something. His focus turned away from the skin and fell on the object, standing out against his pale skin. His vision was beginning to double and he closed one eye to see it properly. It was her ring, the wedding ring he'd placed around her finger. He clumsily grabbed at it, missed it the first time, and then groped again. Holding it tightly in his fist, he unstopped the third skin with his thumb and brought the skin up to his mouth. He held the tip in the hand with her ring and lifted the bottom of the skin with the other hand. The contents slid down his throat less painfully this time. This was not a good sign, good buddies, 'cause that meant he was getting numb inside.

He drained the third skin and released a mighty belch into the air. His mouth was filling with cotton and his head was buzzing furiously with the bees filling his brain. He belched again and this time, an acidic taste filled his mouth. It was sour and full of gorge and bile, the undigested booze. His bleary eyes searched the ground for the last skin and his free hand groped the sand around him. Faced with the choice of letting go of the ring or letting go of his last bit of booze, he chose the booze. Both hands searched around and under him until he found the last skin under his left leg. He licked his lips in anticipation and couldn't feel them anymore. His tongue filled the opening of his mouth now. It wouldn't be much longer.

"Oh, my love, my dearest love...."

"She...muh...."

"Oh, my darling, what've you done?"

"She...nuh...ah taaaaaa...."

"I know, love. Come find me, then. Come on, then. I'll be waitin'."

He fought to jerk the cork out of the last skin and when it gave up the fight, his hands were coated with the sticky liquid. In the act of raising it to his mouth, he fell backwards and landed with his head against a rock. The sun was bright and blinding, and he gave up and closed his eyes. His skin was crawling with real and imagined things and his last thought was that he'd finally found that snake. As he lay there, baking in the sun, the alcohol flooding his system, a small cobra crawled over to him. It investigated the body lying in its path and rejected it as food before heading on its merry way.

Chapter Twenty Seven

...darkness...
...silence...sweet silence...
...not feeling, not being, not talking...
...falling in darkness...never reaching out, never touching bottom...just falling....
...just silence...rest...letting nothing in and nothing out...being nothing...peace...sweet peace...
...free fall....
...darkness.....

Slowly, he became aware and everything came bleeding back into being. If his eyes had been opened, it would have been like watching one scene melt into another one. Sensation crept back into his body like the fog in T. S. Eliot's poem, the yellow cat slinking round the windows. Only he was no J. Alfred Prufrock and this wasn't London. He had no idea where this was but he knew it wasn't London, England or anywhere else. He was somewhere though. And he was someone. Or he used to be. *Where am I? What is this place? Where did the world go?*

That was it, he was dead. It was the poison, his mind told him. He drank it and his body was now lying by the stream. The booze had poisoned him and it was over. The djinn told him it would have to be by his own hand and it was. He did it. He ended it. Yet he wasn't sure if it was anger he was feeling or relief. Maybe he was angry at himself for giving up so quickly, for all the missed chances. Maybe he was relieved that he wouldn't have to bear it anymore. Maybe, it was all of the above. Maybe, it was none of it.

Caught between the want and the need, wasn't that how the old wise man put it? Right now, he didn't want or need anything except the quiet and an end to the voices in his head. An end to the frustration and the hurting inside him. And still he needed her, wanted her. That wasn't so difficult. Why couldn't he have that? Why did it have to be so damn hard? Why?

His cheek registered the smooth cool surface underneath him. It felt alive and the smooth, even texture comforted him. It was solid. It felt real. The hard surface gave substance to his chest, his stomach, his groin, his thighs – all of the points between his hairline and his toes. He felt naked, lying here on this surface. That he could feel it along every inch of his skin made him think he actually was.

His eyelids fluttered open and the world around him appeared gauzy and misty as if the fog had left his mind and was now evaporating in the room. Everything was sideways to him; the blurring of his eyesight made it alien, foreign. He saw hulking shapes that made no sense, felt textures that he couldn't determine, and he could only perceive the horizontal plane beneath him to know anything for sure. He blinked several times to clear his vision. When it was clear again, he felt able to move.

Toby put his palms underneath his shoulders and pushed off until he was on his hands and knees. The floor beneath him was made of wood. It was a hard wood but it was light colored. It wasn't quite white in color, certainly not painted, but it was blond to the point of having that platinum quality. He ran his hands over it, feeling the smoothness. There was no carpeting or rugs of any kind as far as he could see. This room was bare floor— Wait, he knew this place.

Toby sat back on his heels and surveyed the room. Yes, he knew this place. There was the familiar rose colored couch, only it was white now. There was his father's favorite rocking chair, also white. The lamps on both end tables, the chintz curtains, and the ashtray next to the rocker, all of it white. His mother's piano was no longer mahogany colored but white as well. The room was white everywhere he looked. The only things that made it familiar were the smells of his mother's cologne and his father's pipe tobacco. Both were distinctive fragrances, never smelled anywhere else but in the Riordan living room.

The thought of his parents brought everything back to him. The memories came screaming back into his mind and he slumped forward until his forehead was resting on the floor again. He clutched his stomach and tried to hold off the flow of tears that were building behind his eyelids. But he saw their faces, felt them inside where he couldn't touch them again. *Damn it, it wasn't supposed to be like this. It was supposed to be love and laughter and peace. It wasn't supposed to be the pain again. The damn brochures lied!*

"You right, Captain. They did."

Toby pivoted his head and saw a child sitting on Maeve's sofa. He saw the radiant countenance of his son. But that wasn't a child's voice. When the boy spoke, it was Bion's voice.

"They lied like a son of a bitch, man. But then, you ain't in no heaven, you know. This is the place in between."

Toby's eyes widened and he gasped loudly. How could this be? What the hell was going on here?

The child on the couch smiled at him, and answered, "Well, it sure ain't hell, man. It could be, if you want, but truth is, the only hell I ever knew was livin'."

The Rohan/Bion child slid forward until his butt was tipped on the edge of the couch and then jumped off. The little boy came to Toby and held out his hand. He stood there, sweet smile affixed to his face, patiently waiting for Toby to take it.

Toby looked at the child's face and then at the offered hand, and back again.

"Come on, Da. You're ok. Get up off the floor and let's go find 'em."

"Find who?" Toby whispered, afraid to break the spell.

"The ones you're lookin' for."

"Who- who-who are you'" Toby managed to stammer out.

To Toby's utter surprise, the little head tipped back in laughter, his whole body shook with it. The offered hand rested on the cheek that Toby had so often kissed goodnight. The gales of laughter pealed out of the child's body, but the laughter was that of an adult, of Bion's. Toby remembered the man's laughter and how his friend's body shook like this, like total enjoyment had pervaded every inch, every cell.

Then the child stopped and held its little hand out again. "Come, Da, please. You need to see them. Come on."

Toby's hand went forward and with amazing strength, the little boy pulled his father up from the floor to his feet. Rohan/Bion held Toby's hand the way he always had, but gripping the two small fingers of Toby's hand. A rush of love swept through him, and without thinking, he scooped up the little boy and held him tightly. The chubby little hands wrapped around his neck and the soft cheek met his own. They stood there, father and son, just holding each other, until the boy's insistence ended the embrace.

"Come on, places to go, people to see."

"Yeah," Toby answered, his voice gravelly. "Places to go and people to see, just like the poem said."

But, he didn't put the little boy down and for his part, Rohan/Bion was content to be carried. The small hand came out and a finger pointed out the door and into the hallway.

When he stepped out into the hallway, the entire décor was white. Maeve's knickknack shelves were no longer cherry and the wallpaper, full of spring blossoms, had gone to white. The floor was the same blonde wood. The side tables, all white. Even the railing and the carpeting on the stairway to the second floor were white. He and his son were the only spots of color. For some odd reason, Toby was comforted by this.

The aromas coming from the kitchen stole his focus. He heard sounds of frying but he smelled Maeve's cologne. That sweet scent of gardenias wafted towards him, carrying the memories of hugs and chocolate cake. And then he smelled Brendan's tobacco, deep and musky. Bacon, he smelled bacon. He smelled home and family and breakfast. He looked to the cherubic face and saw a nod.

"Go ahead, Da. Whatcha waiting for?"

The spell that held his feet to the floor, released it, and he walked to the end of the hallway and into the kitchen. It was Maeve's kitchen, but it wasn't. There was the round kitchen table, the same four chairs around it. There were Maeve's plates, the Irish china that she put out for company, the crystal, and the silver service of forks and knives. There, on the table, was Brendan's pipe, still smoldering and the tendrils of smoke curled in the air. The cabinets were the same but this room was white, too. Everything was white, even the curtains in the windows and on the door.

The little boy wriggled out of his grasp and plopped to the floor. Toby's eyes didn't follow him down because he was still standing, trying to absorb all of this before him. There was a surrealist quality to all this. Ok, he accepted he was dead. He knew the place he was in; this was his parents' house. It was supposed to be, anyway. But it wasn't.

"You feel a bit strange."

"Very strange," Toby answered in a shaky voice.

A hearty chortle answered him, but when he looked down to find out why the child was laughing, he found himself staring at two genuine, US Army issued boots. His sight snapped back up to the face of his dead friend. Toby stepped back, grabbing the chair to keep from tripping. He backed up until his shoulders met the wall, his eyes practically bugged out of his head. This brought tremendous gales of laughter, and Bion's shoulders shook with the force and he clapped his hands. Toby's senses were starting to overload.

Toby rubbed a knuckle under his nose and over his upper lip. "Where am I?"

"In the place in between, man," Bion answered. "Damn, buddy, it's got so many names: Heaven, Nirvana, the Summerland, Annwn. It doesn't matter what you call it, it just is."

Toby was still plastered against the way, afraid to move away from it. "But, how can you be here? Man, you ain't even born yet?"

"Toby, it's like this, you're in between," Bion explained. "There's no time here. This is that place between all time and all places. When I passed over, I came here."

"Here?"

Bion looked around him and Toby's eyes followed the gaze. Out of the corner of his eye, he saw Bion nod.

"You got a nice place here, bro," Bion said appreciatively. "This is where you'll come when you cross over. Ain't like my place, I got me a great place. But this is a good one."

Toby shook his head. "I don't understand, Bion. I don't understand any of this."

Bion's face held a look of concern, his voice was soothing as he spoke. "I know you don't, man. It's cool. You will." He put a hand on Toby's shoulder, and gave a reassuring squeeze. "Come on, man. They're waitin'."

"Waiting?"

Bion shoved him gently, setting Toby's feet in motion. When they had reached the back door, Bion opened it and they stepped out into the meadow of his cottage in Fireun Sidhe. He looked down at his feet and saw the trampled grasses and the beaten path that led to the gardens. He took in a sharp breath and just stood there until Bion pushed him again to walk out in to the sunshine.

"Bion," he said, his voice awed and hushed, barely above a whisper. "I'm home again." He turned back to the black man standing near the back door of the cottage he'd helped build. "I'm home again," he said in a steadier louder voice.

"You are that, man," Bion agreed, grinning from ear to ear. "I bet you didn't even know you were building this place when you did it. You built it where you were, Toby."

Bion was next to him and they stood there, warming in the sunlight. Toby felt it streaming across his shoulders and raised his face to greet it, closing his eyes against the glare.

"That was why it felt like home, that place."

"Yep," Bion nodded. "This is where you come to rest, Toby. Then, when it's your turn to go back, you get ready and you go."

Toby turned back to Bion, and said, "But, how? How did I remember?"

"Circles, man. Circles."

"What are you talking about, Bion?"

"Let me show you something."

Bion motioned Toby to follow him. They crossed down the field, away from the crops and toward the trees where he had enjoyed a lunch with his adopted brother and friend. They turned left at the tree line and kept walking. Toby had never explored this part of the property when he was alive so it was alien to him. Bion knew where he was going and that was good enough for Toby. It wasn't far, though, a short twenty paces until Toby saw the destination.

It was a birdbath – no, it was a baptismal font, just like in church. No, it was bigger than that but still shaped like it. It was made of some kind of stone and as they got closer, it took on the color of white marble, dirtied from the wind and rain. It had weathered to an off white, but Toby wasn't surprised to know it was white. Hell, everything else was. The only thing that struck him as odd was that it was standing all alone with nothing around it. *No, on second thought, everything is different, this should make perfect sense.*

They walked up to the marble structure and Toby looked into the stone basin. It was deeper than it had originally appeared in the distance. Looking down in it now, in the clear water, it looked as if there was no bottom, going on forever.

"That's right," Bion said, his voice was coming from far away, in the distance. "Keep lookin' in there, man. You'll find 'em. Keep looking. Think about 'em."

He wanted to see his parents, needed to see them. The walk through the house had opened the flood of yearning to go back where he'd been safe. He thought back to when he'd seen them last. They were still so much in love, still holding hands. He still said 'thank you' when she did something special for him. She still made sure to cook his favorite, meatloaf, once a week. She still called him "Mug" and he still called her "Fae." He could see the two of them, sitting on the back porch swing, holding hands and slowly rocking back and forth.

...he could see them on the back porch swing, holding hands...he could see them....

The water had become opaque and where there had been an endless bottom, there was now a picture of Maeve and Brendan, sitting under the large apple tree. This wasn't their home; this was different. The cottage was round, not the large two story rectangle that he remembered. His family home had no apple tree that close to the house He stared at it, watched them sitting close on the wooden bench. He watched his father wince in pain and reach down to his side. But Toby watched him reach for his right side, not his left where he would have felt the heart palpitations. Wait, his father was wearing the wrong clothing. Those weren't his customary overalls. Those were—

Brendan had turned away from him and while Toby stared into the bowl, the man turned around again and it was no longer Brendan. It was Liam, clutching his side, and wincing in pain. Maeve wasn't the one who stood up, it was Niamh. She came to her husband and gingerly rubbed the spot for him. He watched the man take his lady's face in his hands and kiss her softly. She reached up and wrapped her arms around his neck, and they held each other. She was holding him around the neck to keep from hurting him. Liam didn't seem to care as he took his wife and lifted her off the ground in his arms.

He stepped back from the bowl, more confused than ever, and turned to his friend, but Bion had gone. There was no more Bion. He was standing alone. He desperately searched around but he was alone again. He turned back to the bowl and the pictures were gone. Panic was starting to rise again and he tried to beat it down, but his heart was racing and his palms were sweating. He drew in deep breaths to quiet his insides, trying desperately to hold it together. He gripped the sides of the marble font to have something solid in his hands. *What is this place?*

"Ye silly sod, what do you think it is?"

A voice, a laugh, and he turned around to find Gwydion standing, hands on hips, and a broad grin on his face. He took one step and then another until he had crossed the distance between them. He pulled Gwydion into a hard embrace, afraid to let him go in case he was the next to dissolve into thin air.

"You old codger, I've been missin' you!" He pulled back from the embrace but didn't let go of Gwy's arm.

And that was okay because Gwy held on too. "Aye, brother, I've been missin' you too. Been thinkin' of you a great deal."

The tears came, there was no stopping them as they ran free down his face. "Gwy, oh God, I am so sorry," he sobbed.

Gwydion grasped Toby's shoulder, shaking him gently. "Sorry? For what? Have ye gone daft?"

Toby dried his face with one hand, snuffling back the rest of the tears. "No, I'm not daft, my brother. I saw you run. I should've been there with you. You tried to save them and it got you killed. I should've—" Toby's voice broke in quavers and he had to swallow the rest. It wasn't going to come out.

Gwydion reached out and pulled Toby forward until his forehead rested on Gwydion's shoulder. Toby sobbed like a small child after a night terror, the grief burning his skin and soul. Gwydion held him until the tears were finally done and shook him again, this time with more conviction.

"Listen, to me," he said in a kind but stern voice. "It was what it was. You had no way of knowing and from what I've seen in the Book, you had no way of stoppin' it. I don't blame you, Tobias; why do you blame yourself?"

Toby only shook his head, and wiped the tears from his eyes. Gwydion had left his hand on the back of his neck but Toby couldn't face him.

"No, lad," Gwydion continued. "It was not for you to change it. Ye couldn't save me. It was my time and it was not for you to interfere."

"You know that?"

Gwydion smiled and nodded. "Aye, I do. It's in my Book."

Toby took a deep breath and looked into his friend's eyes and saw they were brown now. He wanted to say something, but Gwydion kept talking.

"'Tis in the Hall of Records. At the Akashic library. Your Book is there, too. You couldn't save me there but another chance is coming and you will."

There was that feeling of disorientation and Gwydion's face changed. It was like watching a watercolor print in the rain. The colors ran down, mixing and matching, and underneath was another painting entirely. He watched as the new face took shape; the jaw squared a bit more, the hair turned blonde and the lips became a bit thinner. He watched the mouth widen into a smile as the glasses appeared, perched on the nose. They were granny glasses and there was the flash of recognition in who this man was to become.

"It's you? I mean...you're him?"

"Aye." Gwydion's voice came from the new face, still grinning. "Don't you see? Circles. 'Tis all circles."

"Of course," Toby whispered. "Liam and Niamh were your parents but they'll be my parents. Rohan was my son, but he'll be my friend."

The blonde head nodded. "Aye, you have it rightly, then. You choose who you come back with, Tobias. No one ever really dies. And no one ever really dies alone. Nor does he live alone."

"But, Bion – I lost him twice. I couldn't save him either time, then."

"Wrong, bro." Bion came up and put a hand to his back. "I was there the next time to save *you*."

He turned his head, unbelieving. "Save me?"

"To put you in the right place at the right time, Captain. You was a man going nowhere. I was there for you."

"But—"

"Tobias. My love."

He heard her voice, smelled the lavender in the air, and closed his eyes to breathe it in. He felt her come to him and then, as the other two faded back, he felt her arms around him. He opened his eyes to look down into that beautiful face, that sweet smile. Her calm reassuring glance met his and a hand caressed his cheek. He brushed an errant strand of hair from her face and kissed her. He kissed her softly at first, but her tongue crept into the corner of his mouth. He tasted the sweetness there and the kiss became more ardent, more passionate, and he was lost in her again.

The kiss broke and he stood there, clinging to her. Her arms were wrapped around him and he had the sense of her as his security blanket. He felt her within his every pore and around him.

She continued to hold him, whispering softly, "What have you done, my lad? What have you done?"

"I came to find you, lady." He couldn't cry, he told himself. He *wouldn't* cry. Not this time. "I had to find you. You're all I think about and all I want."

She slapped his back with her hand, but still held him close, and he felt the teasing smile on her lips as she spoke into his shoulder.

"You silly man, it was right for me, it was my time. It is not right for you." She still held him around his waist, but she leaned back to look in his eyes. "My darlin' Tobias, I was bound to come here anyway. All you did was change how it ended. I was with you again and you gave us another life together. But it was meant to be."

"No, lady," he whispered and tried to pull her close again, but she held an arm straight to his chest to stop it.

"Aye, Toby, it was."

"What – I don't understand—"

"Toby, 'tis for me to wait here and I'll do it. But you don't belong, my love. You have so much more to do. You have these gifts now and 'tis for you to use 'em."

"I don't want to go back. I don't want the gifts anymore. I want you."

She kissed his lips again, her own tears making silver trails on her face. "I know you do. But you don't belong. You must go save Gwydion when he comes again. You must follow your path. 'Tis all for a purpose, my love. 'Tis all to be pure inside. Do you not remember?"

"Between the want and the need," he answered.

"Aye," she said, smiling through her tears. "To be pure in heart and spirit, and you need never go back again."

"Then, I have to leave you here?"

"Aye, my love," she said, and kissed his lips again. "You must leave me here. But I'll be waitin'. Our next lifetime will be together, I promise you. You and I shall be together for all the lifetimes you wish and forever here in our home. You are my soulmate, Toby."

"You'll wait for me?"

He felt the tug on his pants leg, and there was his sweet son again. He reached down, picked the lad up, and took his lady in his other arm.

"Aye, my love, I'll wait here for you. I'll keep your home bright and cheerful, and when you come, I'll be waitin'."

A hand clapped on his shoulder, and Gwydion stood there, smiling. "I'll be waiting, too, Toby. We'll all be waiting. Only, I'll be waiting for you on the other side."

Toby nodded, and answered, "I won't keep you waiting, brother."

Bion stood next to him again, his arm around Gwy's shoulder. "I'll be waiting, too, Captain. And when you *do* belong, I'll be waiting at the gate to welcome you home."

Toby nodded.

Siobhan put her hands on his chest, and kissed him softly one last time. She gently pushed him backward. "Go, Toby. You don't belong here. Go back."

She pushed him again and then, all three were pushing him. He kept stepping back from the pressure of their pushes until his hips bumped against the marble bowl. He looked behind him and grabbed the side again. It was his reflection, this time, but it, too, was changing. He watched his face as the skin and eye color darkened. He saw his face grow rounder, softer, and he heard his voice come, lilting in a sing-songy way. His eyes grew wide as he realized exactly who it was he was seeing, and then, he felt her hands against his shoulder. The last thing he saw as he tipped over into the font's bowl was that it was very deep indeed.

...falling....
...light this time...white light filling his senses...
...falling down, down, down....
...everything is a cloud, and he is falling....
...he hears the voices...they get clearer and louder as the light surrounds him...

"Heavenly Father, I ask that if it be Thy will, Tobias will be healed. Father, oh Father, please hear me. I come to You in desperation. If it is Thy will...."

Yeshua?
But the face isn't Yeshua's. The face is rounder, the hair is longer, straighter, and black as coal. He knows that face from the statues in the Buddhist Temple. He sees it clearly, sitting under the Bodhi Tree. Just like the statues.
Yeshua?

"Ah, yes, my friend, you have done it. He has turned the corner. He will pull through."

Ananda?
...falling down, down, down....
...falling into nothingness....
...falling into a deep sleep....
...the clouds turn into nothing, into darkness, and he feels the sense of floating down until he knows his body...he feels the gentle tug on his skin and feels the sheet around him...he feels the rough texture of the cloth on his forehead....

"Tobias?"

Toby felt a fierce pain in his head and stomach, and smelled the raw sourness of sweat and vomit. He struggled to open his eyes. The worried faces of Yeshua and Ananda slowly came back into focus; they'd brought him back to the shanty. He couldn't move, and he didn't want to. He was in so much pain that even breathing was a torture. The smell in the room was so bad, he didn't *want* to breathe. Damn, it smelled like something had gone rotten and rancid.

He belched hard, felt the burn in his chest, and Yeshua heaved a sigh of relief.

"My friend, you have scared a great deal of life out of me. What were you thinking to do such a thing?"

Toby's lips were parched and cracked. He tried to lick them, to relieve the arid skin, but there wasn't enough spittle in his mouth to do so. Yeshua held the cup of water to his lips while he drank, supporting the back of his head with one hand. Toby drank the entire contents of the cup and laid back again, the small movement draining his energy.

Ananda came up behind Yeshua and put a hand to the young man's shoulder. "We must let him rest. He will pull through now, thanks to you. He will be well but he is tired and must sleep. He must heal."

Yeshua nodded, and Toby watched the little priest take an armful of clothing and leave the room. As soon as he had gone, the stench was gone with him; Ananda had taken his clothing.

Yeshua took the cloth from Toby's forehead and dipped it into something that Toby couldn't see. When he placed it back, he could smell the spices again. They were sweet to his nostrils and it soothed his pain.

Toby took the last of his strength and clutched one of Yeshua's hands. He guided the hand to his chest and lay there, holding it. Yeshua made no move to take his hand away and both were silent for some moments.

"I saw them," Toby finally rasped out, with a voice dry from the fluid loss and lack of use. "I saw them."

"You saw your mansion, didn't you?" Yeshua asked.

"Yes."

"You saw your family, didn't you?"

"Yes."

"Then, you know," Yeshua said, and he brushed his fingers through Toby's hair. "Now, sleep, my friend. It is time to sleep, rest, and heal. We will talk another day."

Toby, dutifully, closed his eyes, and let the darkness take him. For the first time since it all began, he was at peace inside.

...breathing in...breathing out...
...peace inside...

His heart rate had slowed to a rate of two beats per minute; every muscle in his body had relaxed. His mind was free from the restraints of his body, and he focused on purity and finding the middle road. After six months, Toby was able to find that middle road easily. He didn't always stay on it, but he was usually able to find his way back to it. Finding his path, his faith, had been the hardest thing he had ever had to do. He realized that it was not just a one-time thing. He was going to be on this road for a while, perhaps his entire lifetime, however long that might be.

It took a long time to bounce back from this one, more than it had the first time he'd drunk the alcohol that he now referred to as "the cobra's venom." His body seemed to tell him that enough of that shit was enough, that it could bear his abuse for only so long before striking back. It had struck back with a vengeance. It had been several days before he could hold anything solid down. It was several weeks before he could walk to the Bodhi tree alone. He had needed help feeding himself, relieving his bladder or his bowels, or even sitting up. So, he had filled the time learning of the Buddha and the way of life around him.

The roshi had taught him how to meditate and he had learned willingly the art of *anapana sati*, the Mindfulness of Breathing. When he was adequate at that, he learned the *metta bhavana*, the Loving-kindness Meditation. He meditated to send out the good thoughts to collect the wholesome karma that would bring the peace. He meditated to find the inner peace and to calm his pain. He meditated to find the middle path that found the balance between the craving and the needing. But, mostly, he meditated because it was a way to slip the bonds of his flesh and be with her again, with them.

"Tobias?"

He let this voice enter his consciousness and slowly brought himself back. His breathing became deeper and his heartbeat faster and stronger. He had been with her again, walking in the field behind the house. They had made love and he had played with his son, and they had gone walking. She had told him where the daughter she had been carrying had gone, unborn but not lost to him. He would find the little one when it was time. He didn't want to leave his lady but, knowing he could be with her at any time, he left with considerably more grace and good will than the first time. He slipped back into his body easily and his eyes began to move behind the delicate lids.

When he opened his eyes, Yeshua was sitting beneath the Bodhi tree in front of him. Yeshua's pose matched his own and Toby took another moment to marvel at this friend. The young man had now passed his twenty-seventh summer and it showed in Yeshua's face. The baby face had been replaced by a lean look, but it was a kind look. The brown eyes were full of the compassion that Toby had always seen in the pictures. The months of meditation had given Yeshua an inner calm. They both had reached enlightenment.

"Tobias, I truly am sorry to interrupt your meditation, but—"

"It's time?"

The young man nodded. "Yes, it is time."

Toby looked at this Son of God before him and thought back to his original purpose. "We have come a far way, my friend,' he said.

Yeshua beamed in return. "Yes, we have. We have taught much to each other and we have learned much from each other. It was a good journey, Tobias."

"Yes, it was," Toby agreed.

"Do you know where you will go now?"

Toby uncrossed his legs and massaged his ankles as they started to tingle from sitting in the same position for so long. As he worked on them, he said, "Yes, I do. I'm going to go back to Ir for a while. I want to see Niamh and Liam again. I promised Gwydion that I would take care of his family and I want to make sure they're well. After that, I think I shall go home for a while."

"But, you will continue with your journey, yes?" Yeshua asked, an urgency in his voice.

"I will," Toby answered, smiling to himself. And for the first time, he truly meant it. "I have received so many gifts that to not continue would be to waste them."

The answer appeased Yeshua, who nodded again. "Good."

"And, what of you, my friend. What is in store for the Son of God?"

Yeshua stood up as Toby did, dusting his tunic off. He had returned to the clothing of his people. "It is time for me to be about my Father's work. In the learning, I have found what He wishes for His children. I must go to teach them and lead them to the path of purity."

Toby looked the young man up and down, taking his measure. "And you know what that road will do to you?"

"Yes, I do," he answered. "But it is God's will and though it is a hard one, it is the right one. I cannot expect God's children to walk the middle road if I do not. If I do not make the sacrifice, so many will pay the price. I would spare them that and I would show them God's love."

Toby knew that he was right and held out his hand to the young man. Yeshua looked down at it and brushed it aside, holding out his arms. He took Toby into his embrace and they held each other for a time before releasing each other to grasp each other's forearms in salute.

Yeshua looked over Toby's shoulder, seeing something. When Toby turned to follow the gaze, he saw Ananda making his way towards his little garden.

"You said to me that it was all circles," Yeshua said, lost in through. "That life moves in circles."

"Yes, I did," Toby answered.

"You have found your parents and your son. You have found your wife. But there is one that you have not found."

Toby chuckled, and said, "Oh, but I did." He laughed at Yeshua's confused look. "You know, it was amazing the first time I saw that little monk. It was like looking into a mirror. Rather interesting, meeting yourself many years earlier, don't you think?"

Yeshua's hand came to Toby's shoulder. "Have a care, my friend. I fully expect to see you in your mansion, and you *will* be at my right hand in Heaven."

"I fully count on it, Yeshua."

The hand left his shoulder and rested on his head. "God bless you, Tobias. God keep you safe."

"Thank you, my good and dear friend. Fare you well."

Toby watched the man adjust his bag over his shoulder and then begin the long journey back to Israel. It would take him a long time to get there, but he would get there in time to begin the path he had chosen for himself. He had done what he had set out to do and had found many things in his heart.

Toby looked up over the Bodhi tree and saw that the sun had just now risen over the rooftops. He bent down, picked up his own bag, and put his arm and head through the strap. He gave a last look at the Bodhi tree and the monastery, and walked towards the gate. Before he disappeared, he paused to wave goodbye to Ananda.

Epilogue

Toby sat back and sighed. He'd been talking all night, told everything he needed to tell. His body relaxed and he reached up to brush the hair from his face. The sky was just beginning to show the first, faint rose in a whisker thin line at the bottom of the violet-grey sky. Dawn was was coming. He could hear the stirrings of the birds as they greeted the new morning. It was over, finally.

The coffee was gone; the fire had burned down to the embers. He started to pack up the few things that he had brought out with him. Funny, the one thing he would miss was that vision of the breaking morning. Would it be like that when he joined her? Would they have sunrises and sunsets in the in-between? He wondered if his next incarnation would bring him the same comforts he had enjoyed her. Well, he would find out soon enough.

When everything was packed, except for the cup his companion was drinking from, Toby looked in John's direction and waited. It was now or never.

For his part, John was in the same state of indecision in which he had started this long night. He wasn't sure if he believed it, even now, but the story had touched his soul. Something resonated within and now, he *wanted* to believe. He wanted to know that there was more out there, more to see. But, there was one more question still unanswered as far as he was concerned.

"Why me?"

Toby smiled and nodded. "I suppose it can't hurt to tell you now. I mean besides the obvious answer."

"And that is?"

"Because your work wasn't – *isn't* finished here. You have so many songs to sing, my friend. Mother isn't finished with you. Her creatures still need your voice."

John's brow furrowed and he blinked a few times, trying to make sense of it. "Mine? My voice?"

"I knew it was you. I knew I had to bring this to you. You have so much more to learn about yourself and so much more healing to do.

The Dana, the Mother of all, has chosen you, my friend. And here I am to see that it's done."

John nodded in understanding. "But you said you came to save my life. I don't understand that."

"I couldn't save you the first time, my Bardic friend. But I can save you now." Toby reached behind him, and pulled out a magazine that had been folded tightly. He stopped, holding it before him. "I've noticed one thing. Having something on me physically keeps it safe from the changes made in time. I'm gonna show you this and then I'm gonna give it to you. I'm hoping the front will change once I have. You ready?"

John stared at the magazine for a few moments before he nodded his head. Toby unrolled it, spreading the edges wide open, and held it up before him. John stared in disbelief at the front cover. He saw his own face, smiling at the camera. In the background was a picture of the ocean and a boat fishing wreckage from the water. And he saw the headline. At that moment, John Denver knew the way of things.

Toby gave John a moment or two to collect himself. "Do you understand now?"

John couldn't speak from the huge lump in his throat; he could only nod his head.

"Then, I'm going to give this to you. Don't look at it until I'm gone. I don't think I'm supposed to know."

Toby rolled up the magazine again and passed it over to John, who sat with it in his hand. There were so many things running in John's mind, so many emotions along with the confusion. What to say? What to feel? What to do?

"John, I have something else to give you now."

Toby stood up, twisting the ring on his hand. He removed it and, kneeling down on one knee, he took John's right hand and lovingly placed the ring on his right forefinger. He covered the hand in both of his own and looked deeply into John's brown eyes.

"I left the keys in the Jeep. Just make a right turn and follow the highway signs back into town. I've already signed the title. Take it somewhere and donate it for me. The rest of my stuff will go where it's needed. I didn't have that much anyway."

"Where will you go?"

Toby gestured off, over John's shoulder. "Out there somewhere. It doesn't matter."

John opened his mouth to try and say something, but again, nothing would come out. He was struggling not to cry, knowing that he was going to fail at some point. Toby filled the space for him.

"Hey, it's my time. I'm ready." He smoothed down John's hair in an almost fatherly gesture. "You go on. You do what you have to do. Heal the Mother. Sing Her songs. And remember me."

"Always."

"I leave you with the same thing you always said to me at the end of your concerts. You just didn't know you were saying it to me." He kissed John's forehead. "Peace, my friend."

He decided not to fight it anymore and tears spilled down his face. He nodded back. "And you, Toby. Peace."

Toby didn't move for a moment, just stayed as he was, looking at John. Then, he smiled again and reached out to touch John's cheek.

"I love you, Gwy."

John watched Toby stand up and walk away. Toby had gotten no more than twenty paces before the night swallowed him up. But, not completely; John could still see his silhouette against the rosy glow. But in another few paces, even that was gone.

Only then did he remember the clutched magazine in his hand. He opened it. He saw what he needed to see and threw the magazine on the embers. They ignited the pages, the embers reawakening in a brief conflagration before turning back into glowing ash. He stood up, shouldered the backpack that Toby had left, and made his way to the Jeep.

"Do you have it now?"

John stood and watched the two men from a distance. No good being seen now. They were engaged in conversation. He remembered the words all too well, even after all this time had passed. (*Time? What is time?*) He watched himself and Toby as they walked away from the plane and toward Toby's Jeep. It was so good to see Toby again, after all the time that had passed. (*How long has it been? Decades? Centuries?*) He felt ancient now. But, it was time. And he had kept his promise. He had thought of Toby often over the course of his journey.

John waited about five minutes until the Jeep had been long gone and it was safe to emerge from his hiding place. He walked over to the plane. The mechanic saw him and asked him if he was sure he didn't want to fuel up before he left.

John just smiled at him and answered, "No, thanks. I'm gonna go buzz the golf course. I'm only gonna be gone an hour. But, thanks, anyway."

John climbed into the cockpit of the Long EZ he had just gotten the day before. After performing his preflight checklist and a couple of touch and go takeoffs and landings, he flew off toward his destiny.

"Do you have it now?"

Afterword

A couple of things to note about this book....

The first is that we really don't know a whole lot about the early Celts, other than what we can find in the hard archaeological evidence. The information that Toby discusses comes from the dig sites of Celtic homes and villages. But the truth is, we have no clue about their religious practices. So, I took a bit of artistic license and used a great deal of the Neo-Pagan rituals practiced today. The message remains the same.

The second is that while there was a man named John Denver, the character that you've met in this book is truly a figment of my imagination. While I have read his autobiography, *Take Me Home*, and learned a lot from people I've met who actually knew him, the truth here is that I fabricated all of the angst in the character and sprinkled in known facts about his life. How he felt about his abilities as a parent, his relationship with his children, ex-wives, or parents – all of it was created for literary purposes only and should not be construed as gospel fact. It isn't.

The final thing to note is that I want to thank you for reading. If it entertained you, that was my goal. If it gave you something to think about, that's the icing on the cake. If it compels you to buy the other two books when they come out, that just puts me over the moon. But if it touched you in some way, then I've done my job. If it moved you enough to go write a review on the bookseller's page, you'll have my undying gratitude.

Peace, my friend. And Blessed Be!

About the author

Jesse V. Coffey wrote her first books as author, J. W. Coffey –the name was chosen as homage to her mother Janice. A writer since childhood, she didn't focus on the publishing aspect until 2001, when she completed her first novel and made the decision to "put it out there for the world to love or hate." That first book was titled *The Savior* and it paved the way for more.

Ms. Coffey is a member of ASCAP, the Kentucky Independent Writers Network, the Independent Writers Network (IWN), and the Erotic Authors Association. She currently has a day job working for an online textbook seller. She lives in Lexington, KY with Whiskers, her feline queen, for whom she acts as administrative assistant and catnip fetcher.

You can find Jesse online through:

Website: http://jessevcoffey.blogspot.com/
Email: authorjessevcoffey@twc.com
Facebook: https://www.facebook.com/groups/JesseVCoffey/
Twitter: @JesseVCoffey
Goodreads:
http://www.goodreads.com/author/show/5194868.Jesse_V_Coffey
Tumblr: http://www.tumblr.com/blog/jessevcoffey